AFTER FLODDEN

ROSEMARY GORING

POLYGON

First published in paperback in Great Britain in 2014 by
Polygon, an imprint of Birlinn Ltd
West Newington House
10 Newington Road
Edinburgh
EH9 1QS
www.polygonbooks.co.uk

ISBN: 978 1 84697 283 6

British Library Cataloguing-in-Publication Data

A catalogue record for this book is available
on request from the British Library

Typeset in Great Britain by Antony Gray
Printed and bound by Grafica Veneta S.p.A.

For Alan

Characters

The Sottish court, family and followers

James IV

Margaret Tudor, his wife, and sister of Henry VIII

James, Duke of Rothesay, James's toddler son and only
  surviving legitimate child, later James V

Alexander Stewart, Archbishop of St Andrews, James's
  eldest illegitimate child (he had eight, by four mistresses)

Patrick Paniter, James's secretary and right-hand man

Goodwife Black, Paniter's housekeeper and more

Gabriel, Viscount Torrance of Blaneford and Mountjoy, a
  young courtier and advisor to Paniter

Robert Borthwick, master meltar

Nobles with James IV at Flodden

Alexander Hume, Lord Home, led disastrous plundering
  foray into England in August 1513, called the ill-raid.
  Was in charge of vanguard at Flodden, with Huntly

George Gordon, Earl of Huntly, in charge of vanguard at
  Flodden, with Home

Lieutenant General Archibald Campbell, Earl of Argyll

Patrick Lindsay, Lord Lindsay

Andrew Herries, Lord Herries of Terregles

Matthew Stewart, Earl of Lennox

William Hay, Earl of Erroll

John Lindsay, Earl of Crawford

William Graham, Earl of Montrose

John Douglas, Earl of Morton

After Flodden

THE LEITH HOUSEHOLD

Davy Turnbull, head of the house, a sea merchant and
    brigand, father of Louise Brenier
Madame Brenier, his dissatisfied French wife
Benoit Brenier, her eldest child, by her first husband
Marguerite Brenier, her elder daughter, by her first
    husband
Louise Brenier, her third child, by Davy Turnbull
Vincent, tenant, shipwright and family friend
John and Andrew Barton, Davy Turnbull's cousins, sea-
    traders and adventurers
The vixen, the family mongrel

THE CROZIERS

Adam Crozier, head of the clan, whose stronghold is in
    the Scottish Borders, near Selkirk
Tom Crozier, his younger brother
Nat Crozier, their reckless father, now dead
Old Crozier, Adam and Tom's grandfather
Martha Crozier, Adam and Tom's mother
Bella, her sister, who lives in Berwick-upon-Tweed
Oliver, her husband
Wat the Wanderer, Adam's cousin and henchman
Murdo Montgomery, Adam's cousin and henchman
Bertie Main, cousin, in charge of the clan's scouts

OTHER

Hob, an East Lothian boy, orphaned at Flodden
Ella Aylewood, a silversmith's daughter

The English court and its followers

Henry VIII

Thomas Howard, Earl of Surrey, Henry's lieutenant-general in the north of England

Thomas, Baron Dacre, Lord-Warden of the English Marches

Thomas Ruthall, Bishop of Durham, Henry's secretary and a privy councillor

Beecham, Henry's clerk of records

The Ambassadors

Monsieur De La Mothe, French ambassador from the court of Louis XII

Dr Nicholas West, English ambassador

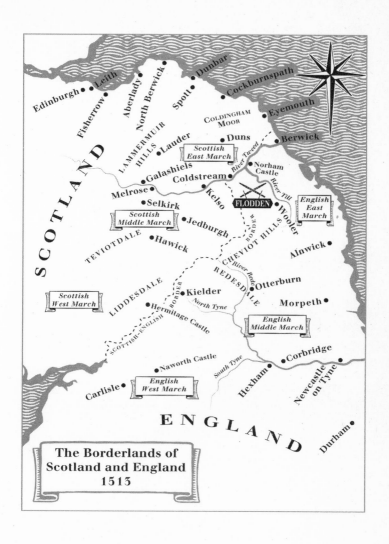

The Borderlands of
Scotland and England
1513

O coward conscience, how dost thou afflict me!
The lights burn blue; it is now dead midnight.
Cold fearful drops stand on my trembling flesh.
What do I fear? Myself? There's none else by . . .

Richard III, Act 5, Scene 3, 180–184
SHAKESPEARE

CHAPTER ONE

18 September 1513

There was a knock at the door, and then another. It was early morning and the sound of a small fist on oak would have been lost in the rumble of carts if Patrick Paniter had not been at his window. He had been standing there since daybreak, peering into the street from behind a half-closed shutter, dreading the return of his visitor the way some men fear the day of judgement.

In the years he had lived here these doors had been battered with cudgels and struck by swords, but he had not felt this kind of shiver at any previous summons. It was as if the hand was hammering straight onto his bones.

The hand was small, little larger than a child's, but it brought with it memories Paniter could not bear to revisit. The young woman at his door looked nothing like her sister, whose warm-eyed lustre carried the scent of vineyards to this cold coast. No, this woman had a boy's figure, and a boy's rude insistence. He knew what she wanted: money, more than already had been thrown at her.

He did not entirely blame her. Had Marguerite lived, had the king, there would have been a steady flow of riches

After Flodden

into her family's coffers. But the sister was dead. It was an unfortunate and untimely end, Paniter would not deny that, but for her mother to lay the blame for Marguerite's death at the king's feet was the madness of grief. The pretty little thing had done as she wanted, and with the mother's blessing. The consequences were regrettable, but not unusual.

Now the king was gone. Most of the country's soldiers too. After what he had witnessed of his sovereign's final throes, he would call Marguerite's deathbed gentle. Enviable, even. Tormented by what he had seen, it was as if Paniter's mind had been flayed. Even a whisper from happier days, a reminder of all he had lost, was like brine dripped into a wound. He could not deal with the Brenier girl, and her ill-timed greed. She came from a past that was now as lifeless and bruising as stone. The present was every bit as unforgiving. Worse, perhaps, because it promised nothing but pain.

There was a scratch at his door. Paniter kept his eyes on the street, where his unwelcome visitor's horse was tethered. The housekeeper came in, her face flushed. 'It's her again, sir, the Brenier lass, and she says she won't leave until you speak to her.' She hesitated, then ignored Paniter's hand, which was waving as if to drive off his thoughts as well as the young woman below stairs. 'She means it, master. She's taken a seat in the hall, and her dog growls like he's seen a rat whenever I try to make her go.'

A sound escaped Paniter that in a weaker man would be described as a moan. His hand covered his eyes, and he sagged against the wall, as if he had no strength to reach a chair. Goodwife Black was at his side before he could fall,

16

and with an arm around his waist helped him to a seat. He began to sob. This man who, when he stood up to speak in council rose above his peers like a mainsail mast, whose voice on a calm day could reach across the Forth into Fife, began to splutter and girn as if he were a child, clutching the housekeeper's sleeve so wildly his nails grazed her arm. His tears fell, dampening his lap, until she drew his head down onto her neck and began to rock him, to quieten his grief.

Goodwife Black closed her eyes, or else she too would have cried. Paniter had not slept since he had come home, a week past, and neither had she. The night he walked back into the house his face was so grim she had clapped a hand to her mouth. He looked like a stranger, and when he told her a little of what had befallen, and when she heard what others in the city were saying, she doubted the man she had once known so well would ever pass this way again.

Worn out by seven days of misery, of refusing all food and company, Patrick Paniter finally found comfort in his mistress's arms. He had lain there often enough before, his hands roving over her abundant form. Today, though, no whisper of lust disturbed the relief he found in her touch. For a few minutes the ceaseless roar in his head retreated. The ache behind his eyes did not fade, but its sharpness was dulled. Images he thought had been chiselled into his eye lost a little of their vividness, as did the sounds that came with them. The smells? Well, they would be with him for the rest of his life. Never again would he eat succulent roast beef or relish a plate of sheep's lungs. The butchery he had witnessed had cured him of his taste for meat.

Downstairs Mistress Brenier scuffed her feet in the hall-way. Her hound sat at her side. This house was dim as a forest, no tallow wasted for the ease of guests. Its windows were shuttered, and the grate in the entrance was unlit. The girl shivered. It was not the chill of the hall, or of the housekeeper's reception that made her tremble, but the grim business that brought her here.

Eighty miles south of Paniter's house lay the worst devastation of living memory, a blight more fearsome than plague or famine. The name 'Flodden' was already spreading like pestilence through city and country, a word so tainted with misery and anger it tasted bitter in the mouth. Some spat when they uttered it. A month before, only a handful of Borderers knew the place existed. Now, even before the last body had been stripped of coins and spurs, and flung into the village pit, it was a stain on the country's spirit as dark as the quarts of hot blood that flowed onto the hillside and seeped into the bog. Spring would bring fresh weeds and flowers, a new spurt of growth in the sturdy Borders trees, but who would be able to watch their nodding leaves and buds without thinking of the iron water they fed upon?

Paniter's young visitor had not seen the battlefield, nor could she imagine it. But like everyone in Edinburgh she knew the fate of their army. At first, like many others, she thought the rumours were part myth, the scare stories of those who have escaped with their lives and wish to be seen as heroes, survivors of terror and carnage, not the flotsam of some skirmish where skill played no part and pure luck carried the day. A week after the battle, though, and it was evident that the worst tales had yet to be told. Most of the returning soldiers would not speak; some could not.

Only one tale interested this girl. Though just nineteen,

she would not be brushed off without hearing it. Her brother had ridden out to battle, and had not been heard of since. There was little chance he was alive, she knew, but until she was told he had been killed, or died, she had to keep looking. The dead king's secretary was the only man in a position to know what had happened. As Mme Brenier had said, when Louise turned her horse towards the town, the court certainly owed their family help.

'And if he offers money as well, don't you dare turn it down,' she called after her daughter. 'We need all we can get.' Louise kicked the horse into a trot, and did not turn around.

*   *   *

There had been no thought of defeat when James and his army set out. Even the foot soldiers, eking out their month's store of salt meat and biscuit and ignoring the rumble of their stomachs, had glory in their sights; glory and – God willing – riches to repay their effort.

James rode at the head of his men, the amethyst in his bonnet flashing in the late summer sun. Its rosy glint mirrored the wood-smoke sky above the hills as they marched out of Edinburgh towards the Lammermuir hills. The old drove roads were flattened and scored, heather and bracken ground to dust beneath hooves and carts. Days earlier, four hundred oxen had plodded across this route, the castle's guns at their backs. Their yokes creaked as the cannons were hauled across earth, grass, stone and mud. Boys ran ahead of the teams, digging out the drays whenever the mud tried to swallow them whole. Cracking whips, hollering oxen, barking dogs made a fierce sort of music as the beasts and their drivers picked their way south in the melting harvest light.

For the king's army following in their wake, evidence of this violent passage littered the way: broken-boned oxen heaved off the road, throats cut to shorten their suffering; splintered drays; a gun nose-deep in glaur, so sunken it was not considered worth the effort of retrieving.

The sight of the gun grieved Paniter. It was as valuable as a score of men. They might as well have slain their own infantry before setting out as abandon these weapons. But when he edged his horse alongside the king's, and brought the gun to his attention, James shrugged. He kept his eyes on the horizon. 'The first casualty,' he said. 'There will be worse. You are too squeamish, Paddy. You must learn to steel your heart. If you are to survive this game, it should be as merciless as a blade.'

Paniter felt the first chill wind of a deadly autumn. James's teasing smile invited his secretary to raise his sights, and his spirits, but for the first time in their years of friendship, he saw a guarded admission of fear. What they were doing was audacious, and audacity takes courage. Courage is the shadow to fear's blaze, growing shorter and rarer as the fire strengthens, but never – with God's help – entirely absent. What lay ahead was daunting enough to make even the battle-seasoned James waver, and Paniter felt a new measure of respect for his king. Were blame ever to be levelled for what lay ahead, it would fall on James's head, and he was bracing himself. Their horses trotted neck to neck. The men did not talk. Behind them wound the steel river of their army, the clink of bridles, spurs and spears rattling like coins in a gambler's hand.

For years, James, Paniter and the inner circle of court had been stealthily preparing for war. They did not know who they would face, whether it would be their quarrelsome English neighbour, their French allies or some new pieces on the board. The only certainty was that conflict was on its way. And now they were heading into its mouth. This march out of the city and into England was the result of half a lifetime's preparation: diplomatic visits, parliamentary councils, and enough letters to drain a sea of ink. Not to mention the smelting of iron and hammering of weapons at the master meltar's furnaces, and the frenzy of work in James's shipyards along the Firth of Forth.

All were to vanish in a single afternoon that took with it not only James but James's son, a boy as dear to Paniter as his own child. The best part of Scotland's aristocracy fell that day, but it was the loss of James and young Alexander that brought Paniter to his knees. Which is where he rested, wrapped in his housekeeper's arms and sleeping, open-mouthed as a babe, for the first time since he fled the battlefield. Downstairs Mistress Brenier found a chair, and put an arm around her dog for warmth.

Soldiers started sneaking home days after the army left the city. Those first deserters crawled back quietly, under cover of night. Within a month, however, their numbers were swelling, and this new wave of soldiers burned not with shame but anger and resentment. Their first destination was the alehouse for beer to wash the grit of the road from their mouth. Bakeries did well out of them, oven boys staring as these filthied, hard-talking men shovelled bread into their mouths, their packs lying on the street for anyone to steal while they closed their eyes and ate, as if life could offer no greater delight than freshly baked dough. Later, though, some would be reminding themselves of even sweeter ecstasy, the flour-white attractions of the pox-house doing a trade almost as brisk as the brewer's and baker's.

'Hey, soldier,' cried one baker's boy to a Highlander, whose hand sat on his sword even as he ate. 'Hey, man, did ye get a fight?' The boy danced out onto the street, brandishing an invisible sword over an invisible enemy, running him through with a roar.

'Naw, son. Nae fight.'

'So why're you back then?'

The Highlander looked skywards, chewing. 'We'd done our 40 days,' he finally said. 'Owed the bastards nothin mair.'

He picked up his pack, and left.

The Highlander and all the others who had served their time were half-starved. Their rations had run out on the march south, and still they had seen no action. Many would call them deserters, but to their minds they had done their duty. If the king wanted them for a long campaign, he would have to pay them. Foolishly, James had made it plain that he had nothing to offer until they had trounced the English, but he called on their loyalty to their country to give him several more weeks' service. 'You will be home by the end of September,' he promised. But for those with land to hoe for winter planting, or boats that had not seen a day's catch since the summer, a call on their conscience and the promise of booty was not enough. Late in September, though, when their comrades returned from the field – and many more did not – they were not then quite so easy in their minds as they'd have liked, or let on.

The first soldiers back from the field at Flodden reached Edinburgh on horseback two days after battle, so torn in clothes and body they were more like crow bogies than men of arms. No-one could mistake them for soldiers who had slipped their leash. Even those unharmed smelled of steel and blood. As news spread of the Scottish army's rout, of the king's death and the devastation of Scotland's troops, fear licked through the city. The king is dead! The English are coming! Word spread fast. Church bells were set ringing, a heart-stopping knell that seemed to mark every one of Flodden's dead.

Mothers and daughters had heard what advancing armies were wont to do. With too few men to defend them, they hung sheets and shifts from their windows, flags of surrender that whipped at their windowsills all that night, and for many to come. At their doors they gathered their fire-irons and long-handled pots, a housewife's armoury. They set their household on watch, taking turns to sleep, but there was little rest for anyone that night.

In the dark, builders piled their carts high with lime and stones. The next morning, before full light, work began on a new wall, facing south towards the road the English would ride if they came to capture the capital – as surely now they would. Stones were slapped into place by a chain gang, sweat oiling every face despite the cold and wind. The bricklayers worked in near silence. Only when the wall had risen higher than their heads did they relax sufficiently to talk. Their conversation was so gloomy, though, it was worse than silence, and slowly they resumed their miserly habit with words, breaking it only to shout for mortar or rubble or ale.

In a small house in the port of Leith, two seagull's miles from Edinburgh Castle, the days that followed the news from Flodden were a modern sort of torture. Louise Brenier had heard of the rack and the boot, of what they did to traitors, enemies and spies in the dungeons beneath the castle, but what she and her mother suffered as they waited for Benoit's return was surely almost as cruel. She felt physical pain, listening for the foot on the stair that never came, or watching the vixen's ears prick, as if she had heard his voice on the dockside, and then lie flat when she knew it was not him.

When word of the battle reached Mme Brenier, her daughter learnt that blood drains faster from a face than wine from an overturned bottle.

'Maman!' she cried, as Mme Brenier slumped onto the settle. 'Mon fils,' her mother whispered, 'mon fils est mort. Dieu me sauve, Dieu me sauve.'

'He is not dead!' Louise shouted, 'He cannot be. He promised he'd be back.' Even to her own ears she sounded like a spoilt child. She bit her lip.

The rest of that day they cried until their eyelids were swollen, their throats rough. Mme Brenier retreated into French. This was the language of her heart, and wrapped at the centre of that heart lay Benoit.

'I thought I had lost him, once, you see,' she would explain when her preference for her son over her daughters was so blatant it could not be ignored. If her second husband, Louise's father, was not in the room, she would add: 'And he is, of course, the image of his father. I named him well, you know, for he was truly blessed when he survived near certain death.'

Louise knew the story as if it were her own. Benoit had been little more than five, Marguerite three, when smallpox, la petite vérole, spread through the family's village in Normandy. It carried away Monsieur Brenier within hours of him taking to his bed. The sight of his once fine body laid out in a shroud for the common grave would have destroyed his wife's mind had there not been Marguerite and Benoit to look after. Monsieur Brenier's sheets had been burned, and fresh herbs newly set on the hearth when Benoit too began to ail. Mme Brenier knew she would go mad if she lost her son as well. Handing Marguerite into the care of her grandmother, she hovered over the boy night and day. As he stewed and mewled, she wetted his lips with wine, and bathed his limbs with vinegar. When the pustules were at their worst, she could scarcely recognise him. He still looked beautiful to her, but she knew that if he were to survive, the disease would brand him for life.

Benoit's face was badly pocked, certainly, but the steeliness of character that brought him back to health as a child allowed him to shrug off the taunts of the urchins who mocked his complexion when he first arrived in Scotland. In time his face proved an asset. Men trusted him more for it, and liked his lack of vanity. Women were intrigued by a man with the body of a blacksmith, and the eyes of a dreamer. He was known to read books. Some said he wrote poetry. More than one longed to run her hands over his marked face and put her mouth to his wide, French lips. Now, before he had even reached his twenty-third birthday, it seemed that no-one ever would again.

Rain and wind whipped the east coast in the days after

Flodden. Mme Brenier's timbered house in Leith was set creaking, as if unseen guests were running across the roof and dancing down the stairs. As the wind moaned and whistled around the rafters, Louise retreated into misery. First her father, then her sister, and now Benoit too, it seemed, was gone. This house was emptying fast, death moving through it room by room.

It was three years since her father's death at sea – despatched by sword, not drowning, as she later discovered. Nor was it an unprovoked attack. Davy Turnbull, the kindest man in Leith, his daughter would have sworn, had been trying to board a Portuguese ship with his fellow crew. Pirates the lot of them, she learned. Her sea trader father, it transpired, was a thief, and violent too. Louise mourned twice over for him, first for his loss, and then for the man she had thought he was.

'Why didn't you tell me, any of you?' she screamed, when his body was brought home shrouded in sailcloth, and laid out on a table, a grisly, sea-stained package. No-one could meet her eye.

'He should have told me,' she cried. 'I was the only one who loved him.'

Marguerite put an arm around her sobbing sister. 'He dreaded you thinking less of him,' she said.

The truth was, of course, that none of them had fully known what Davy and his cousins did at sea. A member of the Barton clan, who had sewn up all shipping trade south of St Andrews, Davy Turnbull was that common breed of men, a merchant whose business was entirely aboveboard except when it was more profitable to bend the rules. If that meant marching off with other folks' possessions at sword-point rather than buying them at market, so be it. His wife certainly never queried the rich cloth and spices he brought home, nor the comfort of their house, even though it was plain to all that most seafarers lived cramped as herring in a barrel, with little to fall back on when storms kept their boats in harbour save a daily visit to chapel and the open ear of their patron saint Peter. While the weather raged, and fishermen grew wan, Davy Turnbull and his cousins repaired to the alehouse. The coins they tossed onto the board for food, drink, or wagers would have kept more honest men in victuals for a year.

Louise was right, though, in believing her father a kind man. If he had only a half-groat in his pocket, he would still have shared it. How he squared his knavery with his charity, she never understood. The question taunted her to the end of her life.

Indeed, it was partly sympathy that made him offer for Louise's mother, a widow with two children at her skirts as she touted roasted sweetmeats around the streets of Dieppe under the noses of foreign merchants. The hungry eyes of her children, as well as their mother's fragile beauty, fired his chivalry, and when, later, she insisted their infant daughter bear her name and not his, he reluctantly agreed.

Now, with her second husband dead, Mme Brenier was adrift. She did not particularly miss him, but she missed the security he had brought her. And she also had the grace to admit that she had used him badly. 'He was a good man,' she told Louise, 'whatever others think. He told me he only ever killed one man, when he was young, and would not do it again, if it could be avoided. He kept his word.' She crossed herself, and turned to the window.

'Good man or not, he was also an idiot, like almost every man who has ever lived. To put money ahead of his safety. To risk everything, and lose it all.'

Her hand hovered over Louise's head as she sat, staring into her lap. Louise felt its warmth, even though it did not touch a single hair. 'He thought the world of you, ma petite,' she said. It was a rare moment of tenderness from mother to daughter, and Louise later realised it was also a testament of respect, if not love, from wife to husband.

Louise felt the loss of her father like a creel of stones on her back. Anger soon gave way to sorrow, but the dragging burden of his absence proved less easy to shift.

Everyone is equal in death, the priest intoned over Davy Turnbull's grave, as he was pitched into the hole, but when Marguerite died, Louise understood that even the Church tells lies. Marguerite's death was not only a loss, but an outrage. It was as if the world had been shaken inside out and upside down: sky turned to sea, food into clay, day blackened into perpetual night. More than a year later, and the sight of her sister's velvet counterpane, and the wolf-skin on the floor by her bed, still stung Louise into tears. Yet she could not close her door, nor seal up her room. Her sister's voice rang around the house. Her laughing presence surrounded them all. It was an unexpected balm.

When she learnt that Benoit might also be dead, Louise spent the night in her sister's room, face burrowed in a pillow still scented with lavender. The touch of cold bed-clothes and a fading perfume offered her more comfort than her mother, immersed as she was in private grief for her favourite child.

Now it seemed that the only living creature Louise could

call on was the vixen. The hound slept that night by her side, her dog-breath warming her face.

Soup was simmering over the fire. Since Benoit had ridden off to war, Mme Brenier's cooking had retreated to the simplest and cheapest fare: vegetables, fish, a rare shank of lamb or knuckle of pork. Each week she took a handful of coins from the caddy where Benoit had stored his wage. The box was emptying, and she was growing uneasy.

'Écoute-moi!' she said, ladling out broth and tossing the stock bone into the vixen's bowl. 'The rain here, it is wetter than the sea. This country is barbaric, you know. In Beaubecq now it will be golden and sunny. Hark at that wind!'

The shutters rattled in the gathering storm, hammered by rain driven in off the sea. It was September, but the last fortnight had been as wet and cold as winter. The weather suited the country's mood. With the king dead and so many with him, there was a deep sense of foreboding. Sunshine would have felt like mockery.

'This surely is the most uncivilised land in the world,' said Mme Brenier, gathering her shawl close as she sucked soup from her spoon. Louise said nothing, but for once she nodded. This complaint had been her mother's refrain from the first day she stepped ashore. She seemed to have been determined to like nothing about her new home except the distance she had put between herself and her first husband's grave, between her children and hunger.

The weather was an obvious target, but she also loathed the language (impenetrable) and the people (vulgar). Everything was rough and coarse here that in Normandy was refined and elegant. Even the king was not glorious enough.

She had seen him walk around Leith docks without a courtier or bodyguard in sight. He was no more impressive than any other nobleman, and they were a penny-pinching, threadbare bunch compared with the gentilshommes of Paris. King Louis, she liked to say, would no more be seen in public without his retinue than he would go to court in his nightshift. Anyone who tried to touch his cloak would have had their hand chopped off. Yet she had seen James drop coins into a beggar's dish even though the wastrel had clutched at his boot to draw his attention, and no doubt smeared it with grease.

With a clatter, Mme Brenier cleared the dishes. Louise took a chair at one side of the fire, and her mother sat at the other, a piece of fine linen in her hands. The vixen lay across Louise's feet, warming her toes. Save for the rising wind outside, the room was quiet. Mme Brenier's needle moved quickly. The rushlight was weak, but she could sew a straight seam blindfold. She was making a shirt for her son.

In this subdued light, it was possible to guess at Mme Brenier's youthful self, well hidden now beneath her pigeon-chest and sour brow. Louise looked at her bent head. She had been lovely, once. Her eyes were large and dark, her mouth generous, her nose neat and winsome as a child's. Now that nose was sunken in flesh that spilled into rolls at her neck, cleverly concealed by a ruffle of cambric. Her black hair was now grey and brittle, but it escaped her cap in curls that recalled its once tipsy seductiveness.

By northern lights, Mme Brenier's skin was exotic, not the wintry pallor or wind-roughened rosiness of local women. Benoit had inherited that skin. In summer, when he was working outdoors in the dry dock he turned dark brown, as if someone had tipped a bottle of walnut juice over him while he slept. Louise's complexion was, in contrast, like milk that's been skimmed of all cream. That came from her father, Davy Turnbull, whose additional bequest of his ginger hair had mellowed, in Louise, to the warmth of copper. Like her father, Louise was slight. Mme Brenier bemoaned her lack of bosom, but she could not complain at the narrowness of her waist or the neatness of her hands and feet. Benoit, by contrast, had the barrel chest of his Norman father and the swaggering gait that went with it. Mme Brenier would congratulate him on inheriting his father's looks too often for Louise's liking.

Staring into the fire, she remembered the salt smell of her father's leather jerkin, as he scooped her into his arms. 'My little fish,' he'd say as she squirmed with delight. 'What's my little fish been doing while I've been away?'

He would be gone for long stretches at sea, returning with a satchel of treats for the children and their mother. At the scrape of his boots at the door, Louise would throw herself at the latch with a squeal. She was always the first into his arms, but even as a child she could tell that her father's eyes went immediately to her mother, who would approach sedately, as if he had been gone only a morning. She would kiss him, but her lips never lingered. When once he tried to pull her into an embrace, she pushed him away. Mind the children! she scolded. Sometimes at night there were sounds from their room, but it was always her father Louise heard, never her mother.

'I should never have married him,' Mme Brenier told Marguerite, shortly after Davy Turnbull's death. She did not hear Louise passing the door, and stopping at the sound of her mother's conspiratorial tone. 'I only did it to keep us from starving. When we met, I was almost ill with worry about how to look after you both. I thought he realised that. I made it plain from the beginning: this was not love. I could promise to be a faithful wife, une femme convenable, but I would never be a passionate one.'

'Maman, please,' said Marguerite, uncomfortable at such intimate detail.

'You needn't flinch like an ingénue,' her mother replied. 'Time's coming when you will be thinking about such matters yourself. And the truth is, loving or not, there is a duty on all wives to be amenable. Agréable. And so I was. Davy, he tried to fool himself I felt more for him than gratitude. Men are willing fools where bed is concerned – you'll soon learn that. A useful lesson.'

She sighed, though whether with remorse or exasperation Louise could not tell. 'He went to his death deluded, for all I tried to make him see how things really stood between us.'

'Better that, perhaps, than the cold facts,' said Marguerite. Louise caught the unease in her sister's voice, as if a door had blown open, a north wind delivering a truth about the nature and conduct of married love that she did not want to hear.

And her mother had been right. Marguerite was pitched into love and passion before the year was out, as familiar by Christmas with the urges of men as her mother could wish. Mme Brenier could not be accused of soliciting the king's attentions towards her daughter, who caught sight of her by chance, but that she then did everything she could to encourage his interest made her, in Louise's eyes, partly to blame for Marguerite's death. It must be one of the most uncomfortable feelings in the world, Louise thought, to blame your mother for your sister's death. Uncomfortable, unnatural, and unchristian. She had prayed to be able to forgive her mother, but as yet the bitterness was fresh, unassuaged by her nightly petitions to God.

There was no doubt that Mme Brenier had mourned her beautiful daughter and that she felt some guilt too. But in Mme Brenier's universe there was little room for sentiment. The death of her first husband had cured her of any tenderness or optimism, save for her beloved son. Life was hard, and the sooner one understood that, the more resolutely one would meet it. Nothing proved her point better than the news from Flodden. There would be scarcely a family in the Lowlands unscathed by this battle. Louise gripped her hands in her lap and tried not to believe that God had cursed this household. She was less afflicted than many.

The fire spat, and the vixen whined. Louise lifted her gaze from the flames to find her mother looking at her, her black eyes sparked into life by the firelight.

'I wish your father was here,' said Mme Brenier. Louise raised her eyebrows in surprise, and was rewarded by a severe stare, as if it was she who underrated Davy. 'He would know what to do in a situation like this,' said Mme Brenier. 'But in his absence, I have been thinking. There is one man who can help us. Who must help us, if he wishes to atone for his sins.'

CHAPTER TWO

June 1512

The sea was whipped into cowlicks by a breeze that purpled Patrick Paniter's cheek.

'You're blushing, my friend!' cried James, spurring his horse into a trot. 'Forget your lover, whoever she is. Let's be moving.'

They rode fast, along the coast road. Their usual visit to the yard at Newhaven had been abandoned for a longer journey that morning. Up coast, away from spying eyes and marauders, lay the king's secret shipyard. It was three hours from the city by horse, on winding, sand-spindled roads, but when they got there, James hoped to be amply rewarded.

'Barton tells me she is nearly complete,' he shouted, vying with the wind for Paniter's ear. Behind him the sea glittered in the noonday sun, and for a moment, framed against sky and sea, James looked less a king and more a boy who had escaped his dominie's eye for a day's mischief. With a schoolyard yell, Paniter whipped off his hat and flourished it in the wind, then urged his horse on to catch his lord and master whose mare kicked a taunt of sprayed earth in his wake.

The countryside grew lush as the firth narrowed, and their way was kept sweet by the plainsong of yellow-hammers. Finally, after a steep ascent between boulders and gorse, they found themselves on the brow of a hill overlooking the sea and a vista of countryside so douce and fertile it could have been used by the devil to tempt the messiah with near certainty of success.

At the foot of the hill was a miniature stage, where men the size of bees were scurrying as if their hive had just been knocked over. In the midst of them, beached on a pine cradle, lay a ship so grand in proportions it was more like a castle. James unstoppered a flask and took a draught. Paniter did the same, a drink taken for celebration's sake only, for they were already cheered by anticipation.

'The finest ship in Christendom, Your Majesty,' said John Barton, when they dismounted beside the dry dock. He was a bragger as well as a brigand, but today he was telling the truth. There was no ship so majestic anywhere in the world. Barton's servant held out a platter of wine and dried figs, but James waved it away. 'Later,' he said. 'I want to inspect her first.'

The *Michael*, the king's latest and most expensive mistress, was a four-masted, thousand-ton warship. She required a crew of three hundred to sail. She was fitted with thirty cannons, and would carry one thousand soldiers. 'For her, Your Majesty,' said Barton, chewing on a fig, 'Fife has been stripped of all its trees. There's now no shade to be had this side o' St Andrews.'

It took more timber than that. Wood from Norway, Sweden, France and Spain had been arriving for the past few years, dried, spliced, nailed and carved into place to create a vessel so magnificent it was not just the sun that made James's eyes water.

Though her sails were yet to be raised, and her wood varnished, she was glorious. She soared above them, her prow facing east, as if desperate for her first sip of water. The length of thirty Highlanders lying toe to head, nearly as tall as the Bass Rock, she blotted out the sun as the king walked round her.

The *Michael* had been his dream since he was a young king – earlier, if the idle drawings he made as a boy counted for anything. As he and Paniter walked its burnished decks, he grew thoughtful, enthusiasm replaced by a more sombre mood.

'I have done many things since I took the crown,' he said, peering through a gun loop below deck, 'and some of them will no doubt be considered far more significant than this. But none of them has made such a statement. None of them has touched my soul quite like this.' He thumped a hand on his breast. 'None, that is, apart from my children. That goes without saying.'

He smiled, leading the way out of the galley. 'I am a bleeding-heart, Paddy. Forgive me.'

On the subject of fatherhood Paniter could never understand. True, he had a brood of bastards, two by a spirited woman who lived a mere step away from his house, who had been found a sensible husband, and given a good settlement. There may also have been children he knew nothing of, but the thought neither troubled nor excited him. His offspring were pleasing enough, but he felt no pride as their father. They were the result of accident not of design, and he intended to make as little fuss of these matters as possible. When he took holy orders – and that day was imminent – there would be more awkward difficulties to sidestep than his ill-begotten family.

The king knew of his secretary's children, of course, but he was a liberal man where liaisons were concerned, his own illicit affairs being almost beyond count. Not all at court were so tolerant, however, and plans were already afoot to legitimise Paniter's heirs, and avoid future scandal.

'You have a deep affection for my boys, I know,' said the king, with the complacency of a besotted parent. But in this instance his confidence was well placed. As his former tutor, Paniter's friendship with Alexander, James's illegitimate first-born, was particularly close. It was to be one of Paniter's cruellest misfortunes, in a life that would grow increasingly afflicted, that he did not recognise in time that what he felt for the boy was love: as tender as the affection of an uncle for a nephew, perhaps even a father for a son.

By now Alexander was almost grown. It was two years since he had returned from the university in Padua where, Paniter suspected, he had neglected his studies as wilfully as he had in his homeland. He certainly forgot to write to his old tutor, for which the secretary scolded him. At that age, though, he too had lived abroad, glad to be beyond critical eyes. At the University of Paris Paniter proved himself a dutiful son – he wrote every month – and a devoted scholar but, when money allowed, he was also an avid student of the warmer arts. Those lessons still brightened his daydreams.

Now Alexander's studies were over, he had taken on his duties as Archbishop of St Andrews and Lord Chancellor of the realm. Even so, neither his tutor nor his father believed a young man should embrace the life of a monk. Already, from all accounts, the boy had drunk deep of certain pleasures. Before Alexander had left for Italy, James's greatest fear, he told Paniter, was that his son could fall prey to the pox. He had been sent off with a sachet of powders and an earful of advice about the kind of company he was to keep. And, since a man who was to give his life to God's work might still one day march to war, shortly before he left the boy had spent a month with Ernst Bastian, one of the finest soldiers in Europe, a survivor of Bosworth, whose eyes gleamed at memories of the field. By the time Alexander arrived in the narrow alleys and dark meadows of Padua he was able to give a deadly account of himself with sword and dagger. On his father's command, he went nowhere without both weapons in his belt. It was advice he continued to heed, even now he was home.

On the road back to Edinburgh, Paniter and the king scarcely spoke. The sight of the *Michael*, and discussion of her successors, already designed and ready to build, brought the future thrillingly and disturbingly close. These warships were not for show.

'Louis must be told that our fleet is under way,' said James, as they neared the city. He paused, nudging his horse forward. 'I have of course made sure Henry is aware of the fact, though by more devious means.'

Paniter nodded. Showing the world they had the means and appetite for battle was the surest way of never needing to go to war. Month by month, though, James was arming his country. He had lost his peaceable neighbour Henry VII, and now his son Henry VIII was on the throne, rapacious and ruthless as a vulture. As Europe's kings wrestled for supremacy under the eye of a calculating pope, Scotland looked very fragile and forlorn, alone on the farthest northern edge of the globe.

That night the king and Paniter dined in James's private rooms. As the flagons emptied, and all but the king's valet had been dismissed, papers gathered on the table, scribbled with calculations and daubed with spilt claret.

'We need more money,' said James.

It was too obvious, too common a statement to need a response. Paniter merely nodded.

'More than ever,' he continued, seeing his secretary fail to take his point. 'Argyll brought news last night that battle between Henry and Louis draws closer. Whatever happens in that quarter, as I hardly need tell you, will determine our future course. I fear that events will move swiftly, once they are set rolling, and we are still far, very far from ready to meet another army.'

James refilled their goblets.

'Our new consignment of meltars and foundrymen arrive tomorrow. French, most of them, barring a couple from Ghent. Borthwick has been crying out for help. They should cheer him.'

'Not the cheapest labour, though,' said the secretary, and drew a fresh sheet of paper towards him.

Beneath their room, in the depths of the castle, the fires in the foundry were being stoked afresh. Vats of iron steamed and smoked as they melted, obedient as snow, over the flames. The roiling iron was reflected on the stone ceiling in medallions of red and silver, but no-one had time to look up. Men, stripped to the waist, wearing leather aprons and arm-length gloves stirred their metal broths with poles twice their height, but even so, the heat they gave off made the skin prickle like pork crackling. There was a throat-catching smell and a hiccup of belches and slurps as the earth's metals were recast with a violence befitting their new purpose.

In a chamber where the heat was merely hellish, iron magma was tipped into moulds. Before it had begun to cool it had taken the shape of swords, spears, arrows; of lancets, pikes, knives, axes, halberds, shot and balls. In a smaller room, cannons were fashioned, narrow guns as slender as virgins, with a reach to outrun any arrow.

In the heart of the foundry was the man who oversaw this industry. Robert Borthwick, master meltar, ran between smelters and smiths, shouting orders that they must guess at under the tolling of hammers and irons. He almost danced with excitement.

Above ground, Edinburgh slept. Its people had no inkling of the foundry's business. Their most blissful dreams were of peace and prosperity; their worst, the outbreak of war. For Borthwick, the nightmare was that his new-cast weapons would languish cold and clean, never to sit in a soldier's hand, or harrow the guts of the enemy. These were times when steel was almost as necessary to man as bread. Borthwick would not allow his country to be unready. Under his direction the castle thrummed, a sweltering crucible for war.

*   *   *

Benoit was planing a spar for a ship's hull. The rhythm lulled his senses, and while he continued to work with care, the squalling of the shipyard gulls and the clatter of workmen slowly faded into the distance. Wood shavings fell at his feet, curls perfumed with resin. Transported by the scent, Benoit found himself in a forest, trees whispering like petticoats above his head. Underfoot was moss and loam, a bed crying out for company.

His plane brushed the spar over and over. The jawbone arc of the plank grew smooth beneath his hand as every roughness was tamed. Benoit loved handling wood and under his touch it responded almost like a live thing. But he knew a limb far sweeter even than this. Suddenly, he was no longer alone in his forest.

The king and his men rode into the yard, quiet as commoners. Scarcely a week went past without James inspecting the boats and the shipwrights' sheds. Some seasons he was upon them every day. Paniter, that Scots pine of a man, was with him again this morning. Also the chiel with yellow hair, known in the yard as the Angel. Gabriel Torrance was his name. He wore a look of per-petual good humour, as though the world pleased him, whatever face it showed.

The party handed their horses to the stable boy and went in search of Barton. Benoit put his head down and carried on with his work. He was out of their sight in the shed, not required to doff his cap or bend his knee. Barton's son Andrew was in the yard today, and he'd scrape low enough for all of them.

The shipyard was on the Firth of Forth, within a couple of miles of Edinburgh Castle. On quiet days Benoit could hear the chatter of rigging in Leith docks, half a mile to the south. Close behind the yard lay the broad streets and slow river of this Dutch-gabled town, and the quayside where

41

Davy Turnbull's high-roofed house stood, so close to the water that a badly piloted boat would send spray over its door.

Benoit had liked his stepfather, a man who never was silent if he could find a reason for laughing, whose left hand would dig coins out of his pocket for urchins and beggars while his right found a way of distracting his companions from the actions of his soft heart. His stepson still mourned him, but it was a sad truth that Marguerite's death had dislodged this lesser grief from its proper place.

At the sound of the king's laughter, Benoit lifted his head. His fists closed on the spar. For one long, never-ending year that laugh had rung throughout their house, morning, afternoon or night, whenever the king chose to visit. Closeted alone with Marguerite in her chamber, his bark would be echoed by her merry voice. And then by a silence so full of meaning that Benoit could not stay in the house, but would slam his way out of the door, off to the docks, or the dunes.

Around this time he and his mother began to argue, Benoit accusing her of prostituting her child, and she deflecting him with bemusement. 'Are we so hard up ye need sell her body?' he roared. 'Ye are aware, aren't ye, that she is only one a many? That when he has tired of her, she will be kent as his cast-off?'

'You don't understand, mon cher, they are in love,' his mother cried, as if the louder the words, the truer they would be. 'In love! James told me that, lui-même. And Marguerite – ' she smiled up at her son as if begging him to share her joy: 'I have never seen her so happy, so jolie. How can you begrudge her that?'

'Begrudge her?' Benoit sank onto the settle, his head in his hands. 'Maman, maman.' He drew breath, to steady himself. 'D'ye ken how dangerous a game you're playing? The sorts of things folk are saying about Marguerite?'

But the mother who all his life had indulged him, cosseted him, and protected him from even the hint of a cross word from others, seemed suddenly deaf to his meaning. She was determined, it seemed to him, to set Marguerite on the road to high-class ruin.

Benoit softened his tone. 'Imagine the day when he has finished wi' her – when the Church or maybe the queen herself begs him no to stray from hame – what kind of reputation do you think she'll have left? Whit man will marry her then? She will be like one of the king's poor nags, driven so hard its only fate is the knackers' yard.'

'The king, he is a generous man,' said Mme Brenier, her bosom swelling at the prospect of wealth. 'So say everyone. If ever he and Marguerite part – and many kings keep their amours for as long as their wives, you know – then he'll likely thank her well. Look what he did for Janet Kennedy! They say she has a castle of her own. A new robe every season. He has been gracious to other lady loves too, I'm told. None of them is cast off. None of their enfants, their love children is abandoned.'

She glared at Benoit, roused to fury by his look of horror at the idea of a king's bastard born in their home. 'You are far too severe, mon fils. Don't you see what a good turn this is for our family? When Davy died, I was in despair, absolument désolée. I thought we'd lose this house; be paupered. Now my prayers have been answered.' She crossed herself, and bobbed towards an imaginary altar.

Benoit's face blackened. 'Ye think it God's will that Marguerite earns a living by servicing the king? That velvet skirts and ear-rings can repay her for the loss of her virtue? She is far, far too decent for him, as we both ken; but she's no jist sweet and gentle. She's completely innocent. Nothing more than a wean. And you shouldae protected her.' He ran a hand over his face. 'Mairlikes I shouldae protected her.' His voice dropped. 'It's as much my fault as yours, maman. And now she's no much better than the half-naked lasses you sneer at on the street. We ken she loves James; and we ken she's no in it for money. But we also ken that everyone else will be calling her a hoor.'

'You are crude, Benoit,' said a quiet voice. It was Marguerite, drawn downstairs by his shouting. 'And wrong. James is a great man, but he's also a good one. He has a conscience. He has a heart. He has given it to me, and I have promised to keep it safe. It is my precious nightingale, and it flutters here' – she put a hand to her bodice – 'every hour of the day.'

Benoit scarcely recognised the girl in front of him as the sister who used to throw crab apples at winching couples in the woods, scrambling off sniggering while they pulled their clothes together and looked around to find their assailant.

Gone was the unruly smile of those days, replaced by something more like a simper. 'Nobody forced me into this, Ben,' said Marguerite, her refusal to be angered making his rage burn more furiously. 'I know it will not last forever. But it's enough to have it, even for a little while. It's more than I could ever have imagined, so fine a love it is beyond words. I don't need to be his wife. I believe our union will be looked upon kindly in heaven for the pure thing it is. And I hope one day you too find such joy. Such unmatchable joy.' She laid a hand on her stomach, and glanced at Mme Brenier, who covered her mouth to stifle a cry of delight.

Benoit looked up. He caught the gesture, and after a frozen moment while its significance sank in, flung himself out of the room. He crossed the quayside at a run, shaking his head as if clearing his sight. He did not come home that night, or the next.

In the weeks that followed, while Marguerite's child was swelling in her belly, and she and her mother spent their days stitching laying-in chemises and small clothes, Benoit was often absent from home. He had begun to travel far from Leith, searching for new suppliers of wood to feed the king's insatiable hunger for ships. Riding borderwards for days on end, he would return looking weary and sullen. His conversation dried to nothing, as if he had been tapped and drained of words.

'Where 'ave you been?' Mme Brenier would ask, as he took his place at the table for dinner, the mud of his journey still on his cloak and bonnet.

'Down south,' he would reply, avoiding her eyes.

'You're a changed boy,' she complained. 'Never a kind word any more. No cadeau for your mother from your travels. This might as well be lodgings as your own home, the way you treat me and your sisters.'

'I can leave, if ye like,' he responded, gathering himself for a fight. But Mme Brenier was wise to that, and would shrug. 'Makes no difference to me, mon fils. Your bed's your bed, for as much or little as you want it. So long as you pay your board, I'm happy.'

At which Benoit would lower his head to his food, and retreat into silence for the rest of the night.

Neither Marguerite nor Louise could lift the black mood that descended on him whenever he entered the house. From the foot of the table, Louise watched her brother with astonishment. He was the best-natured man she had ever met, yet he seemed now as rough as the other men at the yard. When his eyes fell on his mother, they narrowed into an expression she could not read. If the king's name was mentioned – and in Marguerite's company it often was – he would turn his face aside, as if about to spit. One day, taunted beyond patience, Marguerite begged him to grow up. He stared back at her, emotionless, holding her gaze until, with a shriek of fury, she burst into tears and left the room.

Later that evening, the king paid her a visit. From their stools by the kitchen fire, Benoit and Louise heard his boots on the stair overhead. He did not stay long, and shortly after Mme Brenier had seen him out, Marguerite's tears could be heard again, louder than ever. The king, it appeared, found his loved one less interesting while she was in this condition. The nightingale was flapping its wings. Instead of staying to talk and soothe her nerves, he had come only to deliver the name and address of a midwife in Queensferry, and of her sister, a wet nurse, who between them had birthed and suckled other of his infants. Not his heirs, but those by his lovers. He could recommend them highly.

The kiss he dropped on Marguerite's forehead before he left – he had not even stripped off his riding gloves – was as unmistakeable a farewell as a slap. So too the pouch he let fall on her bed to pay for the sisters of mercy. Sisters who took the money and hid it under their skirts, even before the scarlet sheets from Marguerite's delivery had been burned, and her body wrapped in a shroud.

From his hut near the dry dock, Benoit could follow the progress of James and his men around the yard without taking his eyes off his work. They spent half an hour fondling the new fittings on the *Margaret*, whose name he hoped turned a skewer in the monarch's bowels. From there they were shown to the master mariner's boathouse, to examine the models for the *Edward* and *Mary*, elegant warships both, though smaller than the *Margaret*. Benoit's plane did not slacken. If wine and ale were offered as they pored over the models, they might, with luck, feel no need to inspect the shipwrights' sheds.

Luck was elsewhere that morning. Benoit heard boots approaching his shed, led by Andrew Barton, prattling every step of the way. Patrick Paniter and Gabriel Torrance entered ahead of the king. Paniter saw Benoit, alone in the workshop, and made to turn back, but James anticipated the move and stepped around him. For the first time since Marguerite's death, he faced her brother. From the set of his mouth, it seemed he had sought out this encounter.

He approached the bench. Benoit lowered his eyes, his only concession to the royal presence. Andrew Barton was too excited by his own eloquence to notice Benoit's in-subordination. No-one else missed it; the story of Marguerite and James was widely known. Gabriel's face held a glimmer of sympathy, Paniter's not a morsel. Barton had plainly forgotten the scandal, and the significance of this meeting escaped him. He looked bemused when James raised his hand and Paniter ushered the party out of the shed, leaving the king and Benoit alone.

Benoit put down his plane. His heart was thumping. He could not have spoken even had he wanted to.

James too was quiet. He picked his way around the shed, skirting pyres of planks, prodding the earthen floor with his cane while he summoned the words he needed. Benoit did not turn his head. He stared at the bench, so that when the king began to speak, he was addressing the young ship-wright's back.

'I have asked God's forgiveness,' he said. 'Now I ask yours.' Benoit's back was unmoving.

After a pause, he continued. 'It was easier to face God.' He gave a dry laugh. 'He and I are old acquaintances. I have had much to beg forgiveness for over the years.'

There was a clink of metal as James tugged the belt around his waist from beneath his cloak. 'Look,' he said.

Benoit turned, as if at sword point.

'See this?' said the king, an iron chain looped over his hand. 'See? Two more links, each engraved with Marguerite's name. She will forever be a weight on my soul.'

'Your soul be damned!' cried Benoit, suddenly finding his voice. 'God can forgive ye. So would I, if it would help. But nothing, nothing ye say or do can bring her back, and that is all that matters.'

'You must believe I cared for her,' said the king. 'She was – '

Benoit raised his hand to silence him, his mouth twisted as if he were about to vomit. 'Ye barely knew her. She was just another trophy. She suited ye fine till she was with child, and then ye found ye cared less. A lot less.'

'That night,' said James, approaching the bench. 'That night, when the message came, I tried to get away.'

'And what? Afraid of confessing to your wife, were you? Or just afraid of the mess ye had made.'

'Yes,' said the king, 'I was afraid. I admit it. I have seen too much death in my time. And I was ashamed. Mortally ashamed, God forgive me.'

'I don't give a wheen about your feelings,' said Benoit. 'There is nothing ye can say to make this better. Ye treated her cheap.'

Tears ran down his face and into his mouth. The salt taste brought back the smell of pumping blood that the midwife could not stem, as Marguerite's life seeped away and all he could do was hold her hand, and wash it with his weeping.

Benoit closed his eyes as he gripped the bench. 'Yer Majesty, ye treated her life as wantonly as ye treated her. It's as if ye dinnae realise how precious folks are, each of us. Everything ye do is about buying and owning, winning and boasting. Ye wear a flash chain of penitence. How easily ye add another link. How easily ye ask to be shriven. It's all a show. Ye are as selfish and ignorant in your desires as any common man.'

He was sobbing now.

James was white. He laid his cane against the wall, as if about to set upon Benoit with his hands. 'No man has ever spoken to me thus,' he said. 'You forget your station, young man. I could have you sent to the gibbet for any one sentence you have just uttered.'

Benoit raised his head to look him in the face. His heartbeat was steady.

The king's eyes were troubled. They flickered over Benoit, then sank to his ruby ring, whose stone seemed to mesmerise him as he turned it, round and round and round. He was silent for a long minute. Finally, as if in answer to a question Benoit had not heard, he said, 'No, I cannot. I cannot. I am not the beast you take me for. And there is enough truth in what you have said to shame me from taking a petty revenge that would lie on my soul for eternity.'

An arrowhead of geese flew low over the yard, wings beating a low note. It was a melancholy sound, a reminder of the emptiness of sea the birds were about to cross, of the fleeting nature of company. The king removed his cap, and for the first time, whether as prince or king, he abased himself before one of his subjects. He swept a wide bow, one knee to the ground, his long greased hair falling over his shoulders. 'Once more,' he said, 'I crave your forgiveness. Yours, your family's, and all heaven's.'

'Get up,' said Benoit hoarsely. 'What d'ye care if I forgive you or not?'

The king stood, pale as if dizzied. 'One day I hope you will judge me less harshly,' he murmured, fitting his cap back on his head. Its feather was dusted with earth. He picked up his cane.

Benoit looked at him. 'As my king you will always have my loyalty,' he said. He had regained composure enough not to risk adding that his respect was lost for ever.

CHAPTER THREE

16 September 1513

'There is one man who can help us,' said Mme Brenier, her eyes showing their first flicker of life since the news from Flodden. 'A man who owes us, you could say.'

'Who?' asked Louise, as her mother pulled her chair closer to explain. 'The king is dead. He can't help us.'

'No, and very sad that is,' said Mme Brenier, crossing herself, 'especially for his poor young wife, who I believe is expecting another child. Pray God the shock does not bring it on too early like the last one.'

'No, of course,' agreed Louise, bemused at such piety from a mouth that only a year before had been calling the king and all his court the devil's accomplices. Her mother's religion was a peculiar substance, she was learning, more weapon than solace.

'But do you not recall the man King James was with the first day he came to visit Marguerite?' asked her mother. 'When they all came into the house and I had not enough wine for them all, and I sent Marguerite upstairs to put on her boudiche à la rose and powder her cheeks?'

Louise reddened. One man had indeed caught her eye,

as the king's party dismounted by their door in a swirl of capes and laughter. A lean-faced man, with hair the colour of butter, and smiling green eyes. She later learned his name was Gabriel Torrance. He was a minor nobleman, but often at the king's side.

'You mean the fair man, on the black stallion?' she asked, spirits lifting at the suggestion. 'The one who asked for beer, not wine?'

'No, no, he's nothing. A scribe, at best. No, I mean the older fellow, the tall, lanky one, dressed in black. With the chapeau à plume, who 'ave those chains around his neck.'

Louise remembered now. He had stared down his nose at her as if observing a dull-witted child.

'Well, that man may 'ave looked like a schoolmaster who's never got dirt under his nails, but I have been told that he was in charge of guns at Flodden, and came home in one piece. Vincent says so.'

Louise understood now. She sprang to her feet. 'He must have seen Benoit!'

'Calme-toi, calme-toi!' cried Mme Brenier. 'You can do nothing about it tonight. I will ask Vincent where he can be found. We will have an answer by morning, be sure of it.'

It was Vincent's rent that stood between the family being poor and poverty-stricken. A master wright, with his own team of apprentices, he had worked at the Leith yard with Benoit before Barton promoted him to his works at New-haven. With added duties now, he left the house at sunrise, and returned after dark. His shift was ten hours, but every spare minute God allowed he spent with his lips clinging to a tankard. When he sweated, diluted ale gave a sheen to his forehead. When he spoke, his breath was barley.

His walk home from Newhaven at night took twice as long as the outward trip, each step doubled in a lurching gait that from a distance bore some resemblance to a hornpipe. On those nights when the alehouse proved more seductive than ever Mme Brenier would leave his dinner under wrap on the cooling gridle. The house was often in bed when he returned, but Madame preferred to wait up for him and serve him herself. She rose early each morning to lay out his bannocks and cheese, and pour the day's first draught of ale. 'The man's rent should buy him more than just a room, n'est-ce pas?' she would protest, when quizzed.

Her children were baffled by her affection for Vincent. Benoit knew him to be kind, tolerant and even generous, when drinksilver allowed. But on first acquaintance there was no denying that his accent was impenetrable, his habits uncouth, and his bald head lumpy as a neep. When Benoit had brought him home as a prospective lodger, he expected to be met by Maman's famous disdain. They were not in a position to sneer at anyone's money, but as he had learned over many years, Mme Brenier could bury commonsense and dance on its grave when her dislike or disgust was kindled.

Mme Brenier never explained her fondness, nor did Vincent trade on it. He was a single man and happy with that state. When fire destroyed his lodgings in the centre of Leith some two years previously, he was concerned only to find another berth for his head and his tools. Home comforts barely featured on his list of requirements. The room need only be pest free and close to the shipyard. Gradually, though, the family warmth of the tall house on the quay percolated, and the domesticity he had avoided since he had left Prestonpans as a boy slowly posed less of a mortal threat to his peace of mind. While to the Breniers' sober eyes he was an incurable ale-fly, had a man of science taken note of his habits, he would have observed that month by month, Vincent was spending longer in his lodgings with Madame and her offspring and less time supping from the brewer's tap. Between them, had they known it, the Breniers had achieved something close to a miracle. Family, for Vincent, was no longer another word for misery. That he continued to feel this even after Marguerite's love affair and death, when Madame and her son and daughter could barely talk to each other, was either proof of the harshness of his earlier life or of his affection for each of the Breniers.

As the wind roused itself to a fiercer assault on the house, Louise and her mother waited for Vincent's return. 'I wish he had a horse,' said Mme Brenier. 'It is a miserable cold journey on foot at this time of night.'

'He says he can't bear seeing good barley go to waste in a nosebag,' said Louise. 'He would rather feed the nags mutton than rob the oasthouse.'

'The man talks nonsense,' said Madame Brenier, her needle flashing in the firelight, an implement modelled on her tongue. 'He's not the fool he would have us believe.'

When he was heard at last on the doorstep, Mme Brenier launched herself down the passageway, with Louise close behind.

'Whoa!' cried Vincent, as they crowded in on him. 'Gie's a minute, and let me get ma jaikit aff! Whit're ye like, yous pair! I'm drookit.'

As he hung up his jerkin and cowl, and tipped off

his boots, water ran onto the flagstones. 'Crabbit, crabbit weather,' he muttered. 'Aye, bad times all roon.'

Mme Brenier took his elbow and hurried him into the kitchen. The smell of soup and the sight of a warming loaf quickened his step.

'Ye're a good ol' soul, Madame B. Come on, then, tell us whit's up.'

While he ate, Mme Brenier explained.

'Patrick Paniter, aye?' said Vincent. 'He's some chiel. No blate, ye could say. The king's right-hand man. He disnae – didnae – make a move withoot his say-so.'

Years of alehouse talk made Vincent a vat of information, much of it gossip, and some of it true.

'He was manning the guns, like I telt ye. He wis the brains, Borthwick the brawn. God alane kens how they scarpered oot o' there alive.'

'Do you know where he lives, Vincent?' Mme Brenier asked. 'We pray he might know something about Benoit.'

'Aye,' said Vincent, 'ye're mibbe right.' He stared into his soup, avoiding the naked desperation in his landlady's eyes.

'He bides up the Cowgate, ken, nae far frae the castle. Gie's a while tae speir and I'll get ye a better idea. Yous pair git tae your beds now, and I'll see ye the morn.'

He drained his bowl, crammed bread into his pocket, and was back out the door into the storm before the women could stop him.

The fire was banked down for the night, and mother and daughter were hunched as close to it as their chairs allowed when he returned. They shivered as the main door let in a chill that had no trouble finding its way to the kitchen.

'Right, then,' said Vincent, who was even more sodden than when he first came home. 'Andra in the Nag's Heid kens the secretary's hoose fine. It's aboon the castle, he says, on the Grassmarket side. Ye cannae miss it, like. Twa muckle oaken doors it has. It's an imposing beast, built frae black wid. And he's at hame, all right. Folk say he's gone mad, like. Aye hovering at the windae, fingers in his mooth.'

He looked at Louise, and cocked his head. 'So ye're gaunae pay him a visit?' Louise nodded. 'Wid ye be needin company?'

'Bonne idée,' said Mme Brenier, warmly.

Louise shook her head. She had seen the way Paniter had looked at her. Vincent might have the soul of a gentleman, but he disguised himself as a vagabond. She might have little chance of speaking to the secretary as it was, but with Vincent at her side she would be refused admittance before he had his cap off.

'As ye like,' said Vincent, with ill-hidden relief, and climbed the stairs to his room above the kitchen. His stockinged feet padded over the boards, and they settled under his weight. A little later, from the box-bed by the hearth where Louise lay awake, his snores rattled like the windows. Lying at Louise's feet, the vixen whuffled in her dreams, as if in duet.

*   *   *

The secretary's doors were dark with rain. At this hour of the morning the shutters were drawn, but at an upstairs window Louise saw a chink, where they had not been fully closed. What she did not see was the figure that stood by the gap. He had watched her ride up the street and tether her horse, and he heard her knocking. When the house-keeper came to tell him there was a girl asking to see him, he yelled so loud, Louise heard every word from the doorstep.

'I won't see anyone, I tell you. Send her away!' And the doors were closed in her face.

She came back later. 'Please,' she begged. 'It's about my brother, I only need to ask him about my brother.'

'What about him?' said Goodwife Black, although she could guess.

'He's never come home from the battle,' said Louise, holding her voice steady by pressing her hands together like a nun. 'The secretary knew him. He might be able to help me.'

'The name?'

'Benoit Brenier.'

'Wait here.'

Goodwife Black climbed upstairs to her master's room and once again Paniter roared.

The following morning, Louise returned. Like Paniter, she had not slept, and like Paniter she was angry. Good-wife Black opened the doors no more than a crack. When, as expected, she saw Louise, she would have closed them at once, except that something shot past her legs into the hallway, and she shrieked, letting go the bolt. Seeing her chance, Louise pushed her way past the door. She whistled and the vixen skittered to her side across bees-waxed boards.

'Get that filthy dog out of here, and you with him!' shrieked the housekeeper, outraged at this breach of her domain.

'I'm not leaving until I have spoken to Patrick Paniter,' said Louise, surprising herself at how firm she sounded. 'If I have to stay all day and night, I will.'

'Is that right?' said Goodwife Black, advancing on her. She'd dealt with tradesfolk dunning for bills, and knew how to twist their arm to make them glad to escape back into the street. It would not take much to encourage this thin lass to leave sharpish, once she'd got her hands on her.

There was a growl, a streak of gold, and the vixen crouched before the housekeeper, hackles raised and teeth bared, ready to spring.

'Jesus and Mary!' gasped Goodwife Black, retreating to the far side of the hall. 'This is outrageous. You force your way into this house, and now you set your dog on me.' She began to back up the stairs, moving very slowly for fear of the vixen launching itself at her. 'I promise you, you little slut,' she said, reverting to her fisher-row roots, 'if he dares so much as touch me, he'll be strung up and hanged. He won't be the first hound I've put a noose on and watched scrabble as the rope tightened.'

Louise caught the vixen by the scruff. The dog continued to growl, her eyes never leaving Goodwife Black. Louise dragged her back to a bench, where she sat, keeping a hand on her. 'I won't let her bite you,' she said, 'but I refuse to leave until I can see your master. I'm in no rush.'

The housekeeper gave her a look that would turn fresh herring rancid, and ran up the stairs. Louise heard her disappear into the room overhead. The house went quiet. The vixen stopped growling, and sank onto her belly, head on paws, eyes on the stairs. Beyond the oak doors, the day's work was gathering pace, oxen drivers cracking their whips above the beasts' heads as they lugged drays of stone toward the infant Flodden wall. But in Paniter's hall, nothing stirred. Nothing, but Louise's skipping heart.

*   *   *

He plunged his face into the bowl, and held his breath. The water was cold as stone, but for the first time in a week he felt a flicker of life catch in his veins. In that deep wooden dish he found something of his old self, as if he'd carelessly dropped it there before he rode off to battle and only now closed his fingers around it again.

Shuddering at the medicinal cold, he raised his head, sending a spray of droplets across the room. Water ran down his neck and arms. He gripped the cloth and scrubbed, rubbing at his skin until the water's chill was banished in a red glow. Arms, chest, belly, groin, legs and feet were lathered and rinsed. With each swipe of the cloth, the smell of the field grew fainter.

Goodwife Black held out fresh clothes, and Paniter dressed with care: shirt, hose, stockings, shoes and waistcoat. He slipped on his ring and chain, and smiled. 'I will see her now, thank you,' he said, and took a seat by the window, whose shutters his housekeeper latched open, letting in the late morning light.

Louise bowed as she entered the room. The air was stale, very different from the polished hallway. Before she left Paniter's room, Goodwife Black had placed an ashet of pot pourri on the dresser, but its sweet rot could not disguise the smell of metallic dirt and sweat that her master had brought home with him.

The man himself was immaculate. Louise had been

waiting all morning, unaware of the torment going on above her, certain only of her own growing impatience and unease. By the time she was shown into Paniter's room, Goodwife Black's face as expressionless as a chapel carving, she was rigid with anxiety. If Paniter could not help, she did not know what she would do.

The distance between the door and the window where Paniter sat was a gangplank, and Louise's steps were unsteady. As she approached he looked at the vixen and raised an eyebrow.

'Your housekeeper threatened to kill her,' said Louise. 'I couldn't leave her outside the room.'

'She does not care for animals,' he said mildly. But to Louise, he looked far from mild. Dressed in black, with a great silver cross on his chest, and a topaz ring that winked in his lap, he was a man from a world so different from her own it was a wonder they spoke the same language.

Louise had heard how Paniter could hold the council spellbound. It was a rabble of opinionated men who were not easily silenced, yet Paniter was second only to the king in the awe he inspired. Some, fearful of his power, wondered if he might be the son of a witch. Others said one need look no further than his agile brain to explain his rise from tutor to the king's boys to secretary to the state.

It was said that he had written all the king's letters, as a secretary would, but most without the need for dictation, and many on his own whim. While his official position was as clerk, not policy-maker, the secretary was regarded as the most influential man at court. He had been the king's right hand. What did that make him now his master was dead? Was every word he spoke guided from beyond the grave? Louise shivered.

'Come over here and take a seat,' said Paniter. Louise joined him by the window. 'I hear you are searching for your brother.'

Louise explained that Benoit had ridden out of town to join Lord Home's men, and never been seen again. 'I am told Home's troops were first into battle and first out,' she said, 'and many survived, yet we have not heard a word from him.'

She clasped her hands to hold back her tears, but it was no good. One, then another, fell onto her hands. She dashed them away, but could not speak.

Paniter's face offered no comfort. One man among such mayhem would have gone unnoticed, whether he fell or fled.

Louise was too blinded to see the secretary's harsh look, and his words were gentler than his expression. 'I know your brother. Marguerite's brother. A dark, squat lad. He looks like a solid worker. A steady man, no doubt.'

Louise nodded, though this description did no justice to him. Benoit's serious demeanour and shyness among strangers hid the kindest heart Louise could ever hope to find. In a moment's distraction, she saw her brother's face in front of her, his quiet half-smile as he took her hand and hauled her onto the back of his horse for a day's tramping over the hills.

She shook her head to be rid of the image, and found Paniter talking about Lord Home, Benoit's commander.

' . . . and has returned safe, as you know. I could write to him, and see what he can remember of your brother, whether he has any information about his welfare, or . . . '

Paniter coughed, brushed the air with his ringed hand to cover the obvious conclusion of the unfinished sentence. 'His lands are in the East March, his castle near Coldstream, so one of my men can take a message tomorrow. I will stress its urgency.'

What he did not tell her was that it took an effort to say the name 'Home'. Even in his private thoughts, Paniter could scarcely bring himself to utter the word. It was a more contemptible name indeed than that of Henry or Surrey. Home and his fellow commander Huntly had charged into battle with their cavalry and acquitted themselves with courage and honour, cutting down the first wave of the English, stamping them beneath their hooves into the mud and sodden grass of that treacherous bogland.

For a short while it had seemed that the Scots army had fortune and skill on their side. There was a cruel moment of hope, on Paniter's iron hill, as he and Borthwick and their men charged the guns and volleyed shot over the army's head, scarcely able to see the cannons' mouths for smoke, but fuelled by excitement, and a furious wish to wipe out the ranks of Englishmen on the facing slope.

But the guns were almost useless. Their range was poor, the cannons unbalanced, badly positioned and out of kilter. There had been panic as they were dragged into place, and they paid for their loss of good sense. Balls were rammed home, and fuses lit, and at first it seemed the English were cowed. A mile distant, Paniter and Borthwick watched English footsoldiers throwing themselves to the ground as the shot whined overhead. Some legged it off the field almost as fast as the cannonballs' flight. It was some minutes before the secretary realised that nothing was hitting its target, most balls soaring so high and long they seemed headed for the border. His heart clenched, and for a moment his head swam. He thought he would faint.

When Home and Huntly returned from their glorious charge, they looked less blooded or toiled than if they'd been on a day's hunt. Even before Huntly had wheeled around and found a vantage point close by the Scottish guns and beyond reach of the English artillery, Home was mentally stripping off his gloves, adamant he would not be going back into battle. By this time, the Scottish foot-soldiers had begun their advance, and were already sinking to their knees in mire. Home refused to go to their aid. 'Our work here is done. He does well that does for himself. We have fought our vanguard already and won the same. Let others do their part as well as we.'

For Paniter, the rest of that afternoon passed in a confusion of smoke, sweat, fear and fury, the guns belching hot clouds, the ground beneath them a porridge of glaur. The noise was enemy enough, the teeth-jarring scrape and clash of steel, the roar and scream of attacker and slain killing rational thought stillborn, and inspiring terror and despair, where courage and cunning were required.

While the fight was on, Paniter had not one second in which to dwell on Home's treachery. But on his slinking journey back across the border that night, and every hour since, Paniter had thought of him, and of the ways in which he would be made to pay for his cowardice.

'Come back in two weeks' time,' Paniter told Louise, 'and I shall, I hope, have information for you.' He hesitated, twisting his ring: 'Young lady, I must warn you to prepare yourself for bad news. It would be little short of a miracle if your brother had gone back into the fight, and come out alive.' He stood. 'I am sorry to be blunt. I don't mean to be cruel.' He pressed his lips tight, refusing to relive the sight of the dead that crowded behind a door in his mind, fingers always on the latch, boots ready to kick it down even when he'd thrown the bolt.

He led her to the door. 'But you never know. With God's mercy, miracles are not unknown. Now, go and look after your mother. With one daughter lost already, she will be distraught.' It was the only reference to Marguerite's death, though it had hovered unspoken over their conversation, and Louise was grateful for his tact.

With a bow, she left. Before she had even untied her horse from the ring at his door, the secretary had drawn a paper from his cupboard and begun writing to his lordship. At the first reconvening of council, with or without a regent at its head, Home's behaviour would be judged. Before that longed-for revenge, it might prove convenient to lull him into the belief that his reputation was intact and that he had no need to flee the country. This simple enquiry would do that.

Paniter's pen scratched across the paper. The letter was dusted with sand, sealed with hot wax, and his servant, Kerr, dispatched to the Borders, to place it in Home's hand.

CHAPTER FOUR

February 1511

Thomas Howard, Earl of Surrey, looked out across a landscape of washed fields slowly appearing in a dawn that was in no hurry to show its hand. There was more sky than land, more reeds than trees. He smiled. After five days of rain, the clouds at last were empty. Dressed only in nightcap and gown, he opened his window and leant out, breathing in the sodden Yorkshire air.

He had barely slept. The cause lay on the sheepskin that covered his bed. It looked quiet and unthreatening, unlikely to disturb the rest of an old soldier like Surrey, who could sleep like a newborn on bare ground, wrapped only in a cape, with a storm flying overhead, and the prospect of hand-to-hand fighting the next day. And yet last night he had watched every hour pass, turning so often his bed-clothes were wrung out of shape as if they had been stirred by a mischievous spoon.

The thief of his slumber was a letter. Sealed with black wax, it was crossed and re-crossed with information, details and speculation. King James of Scotland, it said, was preparing for war. Ships were being built that could sail round the world, or bring the end of the world to any their cannons were trained upon. The monarch, wrote his informant, was hiring foreigners to show the Scots how to fashion vessels. More worryingly: how to fight. Edinburgh was filling up with Flemish wrights and French archers.

It was two years and more before Flodden, but Surrey could already smell the battlefield. Behind woodsmoke and wet earth he caught the scent of trouble ahead. His smile faded.

Scotland was a running sore on England's flanks, but alone she was little threat to England. Her alliances, though, were powerful. It was said, and Surrey believed it, that James and the French king Louis were thick as twins. It was one thing to have a rowdy neighbour on the border, whose behaviour was that of a resentful, ill-behaved child. However irksome he could be, James did not have the money, the forces or the will to launch a full-scale attack across the border. But in the company of France, he could be dangerous. That was an alliance made with the devil's blessing, and Surrey had no intention of allowing England to become the next roast on Louis's spit.

He ripped off his cap, and called for his man. 'Saddle my mare,' he said, as his valet de chambre appeared at the door, his lordship's fresh shirt and hose over his arm. 'And pack my gear for two weeks on the road,' he added, stripping off his nightshirt, and reaching for the clean linen. His valet picked up the discarded clothes, and hovered, waiting to help him on with his boots. 'Raise William,' said Surrey, leaning on his servant's shoulder as he forced his way into his boots, 'and give him something to eat. There's a long ride ahead. And bring me bread and meats for the journey.'

Surrey and his man were on the road to London before any, except Pontefract's bakers, were out of their beds. They did not speak, but gripped their mounts between their knees and spurred them on into the brightening day.

Morning had not long broken, some days later, when finally they reached the Thames and the king's city residence. Richmond Palace was as large as a village. At its heart lay the old castle, its moat glassy green in the early light. The expanse of modern turrets, roofs and gardens that rose around it inspired awe. It was the work of Henry's late father, but the exuberance and scale of the fresh palace grounds were a fitting home for the brash new monarch.

Rising from a sea of furs, Henry greeted Surrey with a kiss on each cheek. The king's secretary, Thomas Ruthall, Bishop of Durham, stood at his side, but merely inclined his head in acknowledgement. He and Surrey knew each other, but had no desire to deepen the acquaintance. Neither trusted the other, Surrey believing Ruthall held too much influence over the king, the bishop disliking soldiers, whatever their rank, their company not to his taste.

The earl was saddlesore. He and his servant had spent five nights on the road, and had set out again that morning before light. When the towers and walls of London came into view they quickened their pace. The sight of the city sent a shiver through Surrey, but by averting his gaze from the Tower, he banished unwelcome memories.

By the time he reached Richmond, he was more dust than man, and his tongue was a kipper. Henry recognised the signs. He raised a hand, and a page appeared at his side. Minutes later, a full board was spread for the earl in Henry's rooms, and a commoner's version of the same laid out in the kitchens below for his servant.

Surrey reached first for ale, then for the ham. While he ate, Henry picked up a knife and whittled a leg of heron for his amusement. The bishop neither ate nor drank, though his majestic belly, and rings embedded in fat, suggested this was a rare abstinence.

There followed a long silence, broken only by slurping. Henry sucked a string of meat into his mouth with a slither of grease. He ate until his beard glistened with oil. 'You have vital news for me?' he enquired at last, rubbing his chin with a cloth, and casting it to the floor where it was retrieved by a page who hovered by the table.

'Aye, I believe so, Your Majesty,' said Surrey, too mindful of his manners to talk through a mumble of food, and pushing aside his plate with regret.

'My agent in the north sends word that James is fitting out ships for war.'

'He always was keen on boats,' said Henry, running his tongue over his lips. 'He has haunted the shipyards since he was a boy.' He reached for a pork pie, jewelled fingers dandling over the dish while he chose the plumpest.

'Aye, very likely,' said Surrey. 'But the ships he has been building of late are not mere vanities. James, as you know, prefers looking at boats to sailing them. These new craft are built for soldiers; they are handsome, but they are not works of art. They're too cumbersome for that. They're perhaps not beautiful, but they are fitted with gunloops, lance-hooks and embrasures for cannon. It is hinted that they are for France's use, not merely his own.'

Surrey held the king's eye: 'He is also making weapons,

Your Highness. Far more than he needs for a country at peace. And last week I learned that a party of French gunners has been invited to Edinburgh Castle, to help make weapons. There seems little doubt where his loyalty lies.'

Henry was quiet.

'Tell me about your agent,' he said, finally.

'He is a quiet man, sire, and unostentatious. His credentials are watertight.' Surrey shook his head: 'Unlike the last,' he added.

Henry raised a hand in irritation.

'Quite,' said Surrey, before the king could voice his anger. 'I'd rather not think of Walser myself. A fool. A damnable, dangerous fool.'

'He was exiled, was he not?' asked the bishop.

'Sent to Sweden,' said Surrey. 'He protested, but he was owed nothing more than that. He came within a whisker of being found out. Just to impress a woman, would you believe, a jezebel who would have much preferred a couple more coins than state secrets whispered on her pillow.'

He warmed a hazelnut in his palm and rolled it across the table, as if it had been the dice that decided the agent's fate. 'He was lucky to survive the crossing. I was sore tempted to give orders for him to be pitched overboard.

'The new man, on the other hand, is far shrewder. He behaves the part, too: anyone less like a spy would be hard to imagine. He appears utterly open, and a little naive.'

'His name?'

'Even I do not know his real name. His public name, I am sworn not to reveal. For safety's sake, I refer to him only as the Eye.'

'And has he access to James's court?'

'Indeed he has. And his contacts are good. I trust him as I have not trusted any informer from that side of the border for many years. Some of what he has told me has later been corroborated from our own marches.' Surrey frowned. 'I believe he is motivated by some strong private passion, but I see no need to know what that is. His commitment seems absolute, and he's brave. That's enough for me.'

Henry nodded. He rose from the table, and sank onto a settle by the fire. He stretched out his legs and unhooked the crimson mantle at his neck, shrugging it off to lie at his side, a puddle of velvet gore. The bishop bent to retrieve it, but the king waved him away. 'You are not a maidservant, Ruthall. Be seated.' The bishop took his place, and picked at his cuticles like a sulky child.

Surrey stood with his back to the fire, the blaze easing his joints. 'I think this is serious, Your Highness. I think it is possible that all James's promises to you are lies.'

'Or that he does not know his own mind.'

'What d'you mean?' asked Surrey, with a hint of the sharpness his lieutenants were familiar with.

Henry stared into the fire, the flames reflected in his eyes bestowing a rare impression of warmth. 'He is a devout man, Thomas, more interested in his soul than in war. Every year he makes the pilgrimage across the moors to Whithorn. On foot. There's no shrine in Scotland that he has not honoured with a visit. Or so they say. He prays morning and night, and speaks the language of the cloister. For a man of the world, he is uncommon pious.'

He picked up an iron and poked at the logs in the grate. They sparked and hissed, sending a welcome surge of heat into the room. 'Margaret herself was taken aback at his habits. Early in her days as wife she wrote me that he wears a chain of iron around his waist, and every year adds one more link to it. This is his notion of paying penance for his role in his father's death. His murder, that is. The girdle will get heavier with every anniversary. By the time he is an old man it will weigh a ton and no horse will be able to carry him.'

The flames sizzled as the king spat on them. 'Such behaviour turns my stomach. It is the act of a coward. He fears his own conscience more than the eye of God.'

The bishop nodded. 'No-one and nothing should have dominion over us but the will of God, and our Lord Jesus,' he said, in a preacher's whine.

Henry continued as if there had been no interruption. He laid the iron in the hearth and looked up at his lieutenant. 'But,' he said, 'his piety is also of a piece with a man who dreams of going on a crusade.'

Surrey stared. 'A crusade?'

'He, and Margaret, and his envoys all speak of it. Jesus and Mary! He has his heart set on Rome at the very least, and Jerusalem if he can.'

'A laudable enterprise,' said the bishop, 'if it did not presage trouble for our realm.'

Surrey swore under his breath.

His king's voice found an edge. 'So that ambition lies rather at odds with a desire to turn upon us, does it not? Would a true Christian raise his sword against his brother-in-law? It's hard to picture a man of such pure heart making a pact with our oldest enemy, planning to creep up behind us and cut our throats in the night.'

'To be sure,' said Surrey, 'but – '

'I agree,' said Henry, silencing him with a sigh. 'But. James is all buts. I cannot fathom him. Nor do I trust him. He is weak enough to be swayed by any option that is to his best advantage, whoever offers it. When his own needs are at stake, he is as ruthless as . . . ' Henry snorted. 'By Jove, when I think of it he's as steely a bastard as you are, Thomas, and that's saying something!'

Surrey did not laugh, but not because he resented his portrait, unfair though it was. Wisdom had it the best soldiers were made more of flint than flesh, and he had always wished he'd been of their kind. The images he had gathered over the years from battle fields, from pillaged towns, from his own sentence in the Tower, might not then still visit him as regularly as unwanted relatives. Peace from reminders of his past would be worth a calloused soul; or so he imagined.

But he was perturbed by Henry's picture of the Scottish king. This was a very different image from the one his agent painted. Was it possible they were doing James a grave injustice? Was his accumulation of weapons and ships no more than the act of a cautious ruler? Were his invisible enemies not his neighbour but his own people? There had, he knew, been trouble enough from the lords of the isles to make any king nervous.

'What we need to find out,' Henry continued, 'is whether James is truly the religious sap we take him for, or whether he's playing a fiendish deep game. A man capable of leading a rebellion against his father and colluding in his murder cannot, surely, change colour overnight.'

'He was but a boy back then, Your Majesty, a pawn in

the hands of his father's rebels. He never wanted his father dead.'

'Maybe so,' said Henry, 'but he well knew what he was involved in. And where's the difference between wishing your father removed from power, and him being slain? No, James is no fool. I doubt these isles have seen a wilier prince.'

Surrey was silent, and Henry too looked grim.

'He may look like a willow, but he is made of steel. He might well be stricken with guilt, as rightly he should, and his sleep may be dogged by bad dreams, but it is almost inconceivable that he would be more at home in a monastery than at the head of his troops.' Henry gave a sour little laugh – 'and I don't refer to his taste for quim.'

Surrey raised an eyebrow.

'You must have heard,' said Henry.

Surrey shook his head.

'Little James, whose beard was so fine he had to cut it off before he married my sister in case it came out in her hand, and now has not the vigour to regrow it, will tumble any woman whose muff he catches whiff of.'

The glimmer of a smile eased Surrey's expression. 'So not all saint,' he said. He relaxed, profoundly relieved that the king had come round to his own view without a word of coercion. The Scot might have the Bible engraved on his tongue, but he was, thank God, as fallible as any man. And while that made him more of a threat, it also made him familiar. After decades of military campaigning, and too many hours spent at court, Surrey was of the opinion that knowing the enemy was only a step away from having him under his boot.

The king shifted on his settle, stifling a belch. He had the look of a knight of old: broad and tall, solid with muscle, and eyes hard as a hawk's. He stretched his legs, and laid a hand on a stomach still firm for all his eating. He and the bishop exchanged a glance, whose meaning was hidden.

Surrey was as yet unsure of the monarch. He was said to have a temper of a cast never before seen at the palace. Rumour had it he had once kicked a hound across the room so hard he broke its back, and had cuffed the ears of a simpleton page with a ferocity that threw the boy into a fit. So far the earl had not witnessed this side of him, but he trod with care.

There was little of Henry VII in the young king's demeanour – no delicacy of dress or manner, no caution or compassion – but in his intellect and acuity, they were a match. Indeed, from Surrey's observations Henry VIII more than equalled his dead father's capabilities, and brought to them an impatience and assurance that augured well for his ambitions.

Surrey perched on a stool on the far side of the fire, his scabbard scraping the floor. Henry did not bother to suggest he remove it in his presence. Surrey was a soldier to the backbone, never happier than in the saddle with orders in his knapsack. If he preferred to have steel under his hand at all times, Henry would not complain. Those who kept their swords sharp were men of his own kind. Few prizes were won in this world by words, and much by aggression. Where months of letters and confabulation achieved nothing but bellyache and gripe, the mere sight of an army, before even a sword was unsheathed, could bring a city to heel. Some of Henry's happiest memories were of subduing his enemies using nothing more than menace.

'Your instincts echo my own, Thomas,' said Henry. 'You may not be aware, but I have not yet paid my sister her dowry. She writes – she writes often – complaining and wheedling. You know women. But she won't have any of it, not even her seed pearls, until I see Scotland and ourselves bonded and James's back turned on his French fancies.

'Your agent must now turn his talents to finding out what goes on between James and Louis. Do you think he can do that?'

'It'll be testing,' said Surrey. 'It'll be risky, but I will inform him of your wishes.'

Henry nodded.

'And on our side, we must send Doctor West north, to remind James of our claim on his loyalty. He must be made to see that any alliance with France that hurts our interests is tantamount to a declaration of war against us.' Henry's face grew still, as if the mould had set. His eyes were bright as steel: 'He must be made to appreciate how grave a matter it would be to anger us. Because when we are angered, we give no quarter. Sister or no sister, I would treat him, and her, as rebels. The consequences of crossing us would be dire.'

Henry smiled without mirth.

'It would be good for him to be aware of that fact before he goes any further down the road to bed with Louis.'

The king rose to his feet, and shrugged on his crimson cape. 'We will ask Master Beecham where we stand.'

They left his chamber, Surrey's spurs rasping against the

flagstones, while Henry's leather slippers were so soft with linseed he might have been barefoot. The bishop followed behind, breathing heavily.

The palace was a cheerless place, for all its pomp. Surrey thought of his Yorkshire home, where narrow passages and small windows were sealed tight against the weather, and the smallest hearth swallowed some of the chill. But at Richmond the corridors were broad, the ceilings high, and even those rooms swagged in drapes, tapestries and rugs were hostile to rheumatic bones the moment they moved a yard beyond the fire.

Beecham's room had no hearth. It was little larger than the bole of an ancient oak, and as dark, with only a single lancet window, set high in the wall, giving sight of the sky. From floor to ceiling it was lined with leather-bound documents and vellum scrolls, tied with ribbon. The smell of old parchment and dust infused the room, a scholar's pomander. Surrey, used to the rain-washed outdoors, sensed that the atmosphere had scarcely been sullied by fresh air for years. Older still was its occupant.

At the centre of the room, from where he could touch each wall without leaving his chair, Beecham sat behind his desk. A rug was pulled around his shoulders as he bent over a parchment, a pale finger following its faded account. A rabbitskin hat was pulled low over his face, and a shadow beneath its rim was all that Surrey could see of his eyes. Vapour escaped from beneath the fur as he breathed.

At the sight of his king, Beecham struggled to get to his feet. Henry laughed, and waved at him to keep his seat. 'Stay as you are,' he barked. 'No need to grovel. This is not a formal visit, good sir. I merely need to borrow your brains.'

Henry introduced the earl, and the pair bowed to each other. There was barely room in the library for four of them, and Surrey dared not move from the doorway in case he dislodged a book. If one of these tomes fell, it could break a foot.

The king prowled around the edge of the room, and his scribe had to twist his head left and right to follow him, like an owl watching from its perch. 'Master Beecham,' Henry told Surrey, 'is clerk of the royal records. He knows more than any of us about the details of state – yes, Lord Bishop, more even than you, though you burrow like a mole through the books.'

Ruthall gave a dutiful smile. 'Would that my burden of work allowed me time to read, Your Majesty. If it were not a sin, I would admit to envy of our good clerk here, who can spend his days cloistered with documents and ignore the ugly world beyond these walls.' With a sniff, he gathered his cloak over his chest.

Henry turned to the clerk. 'There is not a statute or act of parliament or treaty of war from the past hundred years that Master Beecham does not know. You can even recite pages from the blessed Domesday book, can't you, brother?'

'Only those relating to the southern shires, Your Highness,' Beecham mumbled, with the lilt of a west country accent, never lost despite fifty years' service to the court. Henry laughed again, looking at Surrey, 'Mirabile dictu! The dullest book on God's earth and he has it by heart. This man is more valuable to me than a company of archers.' He put a hand on Beecham's shoulder.

'So tell us, good sir, where we stand with Scotland. As I

recall, my father brokered a long and peaceful deal with young James.'

'That is correct,' said Beecham, retracting his hands into his sleeves, and licking his lips, which were so cracked they might not have spoken a word in days. His voice was as high-pitched as the wind that moaned at the window. 'Your esteemed father negotiated the Treaty of Perpetual Peace when James married your sister. That was eight years ago. Of late, however, James has tinkered with the finer detail of that treaty, claiming that we have not followed its edicts to the letter, and thus taking the liberty of bending its rules to his own ends.'

'Where stand we now?' said Henry.

'In law, the two countries are still amiable towards each other. Any act of aggression on land by one would of course annul that agreement.'

'And what does it say about Scotland's Auld Alliance with France?' Henry no longer sounded warm.

'It says nothing on that score,' said Beecham, staring at the shelves in front of him as he retrieved the words from memory. 'But it is implicit that for the purposes of continued peace between the two countries, no nation at odds with England can become an active ally of Scotland; and vice versa. Your father was alert to the dangers of that liaison, and of many others – I speak of Norway, and the Netherlands, to name only two.'

A gruel of a smile crossed the clerk's face. 'Am I to understand that Your Majesty would like to compose a new deal, and oblige Scotland to eschew its French association? To make plain the limits of what you will and will not tolerate?'

'You are,' said the king. 'It needs to be explicit, so simple a suckling babe could not mistake its meaning. Norway, Denmark, and the like, are small beer. James can whistle them up for all I care; between them they couldn't knock a single stone out of the Wall of London. But France is less easy to dismiss, and I grow mistrustful of brother James. I need him brought to heel before he smuggles our enemy over the border like a Trojan horse.'

Beecham drew a sheet of paper towards him, and picked up a knife. His tongue darted out with anticipation as he began to sharpen a pen. 'Then I shall prepare a draft,' he said. 'It will be with you by and by.'

Henry nodded and left, the bishop hurrying in his wake. Surrey and Beecham bowed again to each other, at which the rabbitskin hat slipped further down the clerk's nose. Peering from under its brim, he started to scratch words on the page. Surrey left him, clouded in frozen breath as if generating a steam of diplomatic heat.

*   *   *

Overnight, Surrey's horse had been watered, fed and rested. He was eager to be off, stamping at the frosted earth as his master approached. The earl climbed into the saddle, and gathered the reins from the groom. Henry stood looking up into his soldier's face, his crimson cape a roar of colour against the bleached blues of morning.

'I will have Dr West spend the night with you on his way to Linlithgow Palace,' he said. 'He will explain the detail of the proposed agreement we'll be putting before James. You can tell him whatever news you have for me. Thereafter, I expect to receive regular bulletins from your Edinburgh man. I do not expect you to disappoint me.'

Surrey raised his hat. 'Trust me, Your Highness. We will get under James's skin as if we were ringworm.'

The king laughed, a bark that set rooks flying from the battlements, and slapped the horse's rump. With a kick of earth Surrey and his servant cantered off.

England was still in the clutches of winter, but in the king's heartland, spring was not far away. The undulating fields and woods of Essex and Hertfordshire passed effortlessly under Surrey's hooves, buds already quickening on the trees, aconites threshing in the wind as if they wanted to snap off their own heads.

As a younger man the earl would have felt a pang leaving these shires behind. They were his home, and he knew their smell and taste so intimately they still crowded his dreams. But since those years in the Tower, when he had feared he would never set foot outside again, the south had lost its hold on him. When Henry made him Lieutenant General of the North, he had not doubted for a second that this was the post for him. The north was a challenge for any soldier, and it promised more hardship than comfort, but a seasoned campaigner like Surrey did not want ease. Comfort meant old age, age brought feebleness, and feebleness signalled the end.

On the ride back to Pontefract, the earl let his horse find its own pace. He spent ten nights on the road, and indulged himself, and his man, with beef and wine, to put heart into their chilled blood. Out of the dripping mists of February the north crept up on them slowly, trees thinning, oyster-catchers piping. At the first scent of peat-smoke, Surrey smiled. Yorkshire was close.

The king and his kind might call it north, but Surrey

knew where true north began. The Borderlands were the limit of civilisation on these islands. Their fierce terrain and cold-blooded people were a race apart, so heartless and unpredictable that Surrey at times found himself bereft of speech at the treachery he and his march wardens encountered there. Sons would turn in their fathers, mothers kill their babes, sisters betray their brothers. If they had a code of honour, it was unfathomable to those unversed in its edicts.

A man who found solace in a God who had interfered little with his life beyond setting down the rule-book, Surrey often wondered if He had given up on the Borders. There was something abandoned about this place, as if a sickness of spirit bubbled up from its springs. Abundant troubles would be found here, for king, earl and commoner. There was no tougher bailiwick in England. Henry turned his attention across the English channel, listening for word from Spain, France, and the Holy Roman Empire. Surrey kept his eye on the border where, to his mind, the more desperate threat lay. It might look like a rabble of ignorant peasantry, but in their anarchic savagery they made the serried ranks of Pope Innocent or Ferdinand look like wet nurses. Quite apart from the rumblings of war coming from James's court, the border promised an unquiet future. Surrey felt the familiar stir of tension and anticipation in his gut. It was time he inspected the marches.

CHAPTER FIVE

16 August 1513

'There are five schiltron, formed from the army's sturdiest men, each equipped with a twelve-foot pike. Forty French pikemen work tirelessly to show them how to wield them; seventy companies of archers; seventeen cannon; various culverin, large and small; twelve carts carrying gunpowder and two score gunners. Of infantry it is hard to be sure – twenty thousand, perhaps more, and reinforcements to be met on the march south; cavalry: at least a dozen mounted divisions. More to be met en route.'

The pen scratched on. 'Fewer Highland divisions than anticipated; the king will not await them. None is come from the isles, but there is a full recruitment from the Lothians, Fife and Perthshire. Word has it the army is thirty thousand strong. I believe likely more. French troops expected to land from France on the west coast in the next few weeks.'

At this hour silence closed in around the letter-writer like high tide. Enveloped in a wash of solitude and quiet, his activities by rush-light were almost as secret as his thoughts. So faint was the glow cast on his desk from the miserable taper on the wall that its glimmer did not escape as far as the crack beneath his door. He was not fooled, though. The city might have been quiet, his household at sleep, but if he were discovered, it would be the end of him. Writing privately in the eye of the night, in these times, would raise suspicions, shortly followed by the palace guards. There were distractions and deceits in daytime, sleights of hand, diversions and camouflages that made it possible to ply his business under the noses of those he deceived. In daylight audacity was his finest tool. By night, his only security was invisibility.

As he wrote, his hand grew firmer. His letter was urgent, and he had little time. Dawn approached, and with it, his messenger. In neat cramped lines he itemised King James's forces gathering now for the march to the muster at Ellem, near the border. He advised of the French pikemen who were training Highlanders and peasants how to wield their lances, and how to make their fearsome hedgehog formation work on the field, when soldiers of flesh and blood were transformed into a ball of bristling pikestaff steel. He relayed the king's intention to have a bit of fun disguised as revenge by harrying the English border before taking the battle to Henry. That he aimed to swell his ranks with French support, and to have his business over and done within a month of leaving Edinburgh. That he planned to return with his role as a serious player in continental affairs affirmed, and – best of all – with England squeezed into submission between its most hated enemies, caught in a vice that could be tightened whenever they pleased.

'James has no notion of defeat,' the letter writer continued. 'He truly believes God is with him. And whether or not he has harnessed God to his cause, the number of his men, and the quality of their arms are terrifying. As already advised, the French ambassadors make the Scottish court their second home. There is no mistaking the gravity of what is about to follow.'

The letter was signed with a flourishing initial, dusted and folded small as his thumb. From a niche in the wall, he took out a grey sliver of sheep gut, filched from the kitchen, which he wrapped around the letter before stuffing it into a hunk of bread, whose centre had been hollowed out. This went into his pocket.

Now his pulse quickened. He opened his door, and listened. The wheezing of the dog snoring by the kitchen hearth was the only disturbance. It slumbered on as he slipped past, down the passage and out by the scullery door.

Already the sky was lightening. The soft blackness of a summer night had been diluted as if a pitcher of water had been thrown over it, but there was an hour or more before it would be scrubbed clean, and as yet no-one was about. Not even a gull disturbed the peace, although the smell of woodsmoke from newly laid hearths signalled the start of the day, a reminder that others in the city were also awake. He stood in a passageway at the corner of his street, felt hat low over his face. From under its brim his eyes burned. In his belt, a small sword offered a measure of comfort. Used well, it would give him time to make his escape. But tonight he was in luck, and his hand did not go to its hilt.

The first gull of morning had awakened and begun to harass its slumbering mates, when the muffled thud of hooves reached him. Round the corner came a black pony, ungroomed, saddle-less, its rider in little more than rags.

Its hooves were wrapped in sacking, and it approached him so softly, appeared so barely detectable in the dark, that it seemed more like a dream than a creature of flesh and blood.

The pony put its nose into his hand, and its breath was the first comfort he had felt in days. He gave the bread to the rider, who pocketed it without a word, though he searched the face under the hat for further instructions; at the very least for a coin.

'Frae this evening, I'll be wi' the king's troops,' whispered the letter writer. 'I'll hae to make other provisions to get word to his lordship, so ye may rest easy for a while. You've done good work, these past months, and I thank ye.'

He handed over a coin, and then another, both speedily hidden by a grimy hand under the rags. The rider nodded, and his neck sank back into the wreath of his plaid. He kicked his heels and pony and rider continued up the street. Soon they had slipped back into the dark, as if a door in the night had briefly opened to allow them access to this world, and now had closed behind them.

The traitor hurried back to his house. He would catch a few hours' sleep before saddling up and joining the king's troops. Wrapped in his cloak, he stretched on his bed, sighed, and slept. With a hand tucked under his cheek, his breath even and sweet, he looked as untroubled and harmless as a child.

Two days later he was riding with the army out of the city. His steel hat was heavy, and his quilted leather jerkin soaked up the sunlight, roasting his ribs as if they were a dish for dinner in camp that night. His scabbard grazed his boot as his horse trotted over the cobbles.

He had slipped away from his company, and rode beside the outfit of French lancemen, whose spears bobbed down the street, a coppice of knives. In the rush to set off, and the buoyant humour of the army's ride out of Edinburgh, no-one was troubled by disorder, and his disappearance from his comrades was scarcely noticed. As the pageant of the day caught up soldiers and citizens alike, the rules of military discipline were relaxed. Flying banners, glinting arrows, the rattle of sword on spur made this a festive scene, the brilliance of the procession as cheering as a volley of trumpets. And there were trumpets too, and fyfes, and bodhrans, making for a joyful cacophony as the country's finest fighters rolled their way south, their king at their head.

The letter-writer scarcely noticed the cheers of the crowd and the speedwell and forget-me-nots flung under their hooves by young women and red-eyed mothers. He edged closer to the Frenchmen. They were saying little now, but as the army passed through the city gates and the noise died down, they might start to talk. He needed to be there when they did. He jogged by their side, pretending to smile at the crowd, his breaking of ranks intended to look like nothing more sinister than inept, innocent enthusiasm. In the knap-sack strapped to his horse's rump was a bottle of ink, and parchment: unusual weapons for a soldier, but in his case deadly.

The French paid him no attention as his horse blundered close to theirs. Such seasoned fighters knew that the time for strict formation would come later, when to ignore an order would be a treasonable act. By then, the spy intended to be long gone.

*   *   *

30 August 1513

When next the spy picked up his pen, the army was camped out, deep in Border country, with one victory already to its name. Its boozy breath rose into the night air, as did its snores. The spy's bivouac was under a canopy of beeches and oaks where the cavalry were stationed. By using his cape as a tent, he was able to shield the meagre light of his lantern from his sleeping companions, who, until dawn, would be woken by nothing less serious than tempest or earthquake. Was it his fate forever to write under darkness, scratching more furtively than a field mouse? His mouth twisted with displeasure. This skulking life must soon come to an end. He could not bear sidling and eavesdropping and dissembling, as if he were a player in some cheap, gaudy mummery, his character smiling at the crowd when behind his mask he was sneering. Their blindness deepened his contempt.

Writing on his knees, his hand was cramped but clear:

'Beloved mother, star of my soul,

'I write not to alarm you but, in the event of my not returning, to offer some consolation. We are stationed, for the time, on the outskirts of Norham a few miles across the English border, once a well-favoured township, now smouldering. The cries of the dying and their kin have faded, but it is a desolate scene and I fear we are about to wreak further and far worse devastation as we move south to meet the English king's army.

'That conflict may come before this letter reaches you. The Scots army is likely far to exceed that of Henry's in men and skill, but it remains possible that I shall perish one way or another.

'Should I fall, I need you to know that I have all my life held you in my heart as the most dear and cherished mother a son could wish for. The trouble and torments you have endured since my ill-fated birth have pained me almost as if they were my own sufferings. If I die, rest assured I go to the grave with your name upon my lips.

'If the worst befalls me, I must also warn you that I stand the risk of being publicly denounced for acts of treason. A wiser man would not commit these words to the light of day, but where you are concerned I am governed not by caution but by love. And I further tell you that I have been guided in all my deeds by the desire only for justice, for the restitution of our family's name and fortunes, for your happiness and future.

'I am a man of unwavering fealty, but those to whom I give my allegiance are not always those with whom I appear to associate. If my affiliations should be discovered, and I am punished, have no doubt that I shall meet my maker with a dignity and courage that would make you proud, and safe in the knowledge that the Almighty, who sees into my heart, will mete out the justice I deserve on the day when the trumpets call, not as the unholy foot soldiers of the Scottish army see fit.

'When this letter reaches your hand, fear not. I am as certain as one can be that I will be close behind. I embrace you, and I salute you, and I will soon do so in person,

'Your only and most loving son.'

The spy rolled up the paper, and bound it with twine. Before reveille had been called, it was in the hand of a camp follower, as was a fistful of coins, and the same again promised from the recipient when the missive reached her.

By the time the bugles sounded, the young messenger was already out of the valley and heading north, wondering how much bread and sausage the coins would bring if he had first bought himself a mule.

*   *   *

7 September 1513

The camp lay quiet under darkness. Rain fell, steady and unrelenting. Overhead, leaves dripped. Underfoot, the ground was damp, sizzling as drops from high above rolled branch to branch onto the forest floor. Horses stood, dozing in the fug of their woodland stable, their breath creating a midnight mist. Under tents and makeshift awnings strung between trees, the soldiers slept. Only a bugle would wake them now.

In the dark, troops covered the forest floor like a land-slide, a tumble of black shapes. No matter where the army was pitched, when reveille was called it was like the day of resurrection, slow, aching, earthy figures dragging them-selves out of their plaids and bedrolls and rising, rubbing their eyes, as if they had been long underground, and the living world only a memory.

The letter-writer slithered out of his bedroll and fastened his small sword onto his hip. He crept onto his horse, his head low upon its neck. Were it noticed, the horse would appear to be straying riderless from the camp.

He allowed it to amble towards the edge of the forest, picking along a path only it could see, between slumbering soldiers. When at last the trees thinned and the horse stepped out into the rain, its rider sat up, slipped his feet into his stirrups, and spurred the beast on into the dark.

The English camp was not far away, but the night was black, and the hillsides rough. It would be a demanding ride.

By the time he smelled campfires, his horse was in a sweat, its sides heaving at the speed he had forced on it. The spy patted its neck and bent to whisper in its ear. It was as much owl as horse, keeping its footing in the dark as surely if he were holding a torch over its head, but it was tiring work, and both rider and mount were glad of a rest.

Surrey's messenger had told him to meet beneath the bridge outside the village whose pastureland the army had commandeered. After crossing hills and valleys, guided only by a river and a shy, pale moon, it was simple to find the bridge, and a relief to take shelter beneath it.

He waited, listening to a month of rain racing by. It was the first moment of inaction the spy had enjoyed in weeks. Under the bridge's vault, he felt as if he had escaped the world, and himself. He had hidden as a boy in bolt holes like this, able to watch his pursuers while they could not see him. He remembered that prickling sensation, part hysteria, part power as their steps grew closer, and he must decide whether to bolt, or give himself up. Always, he preferred to run, no matter how close the pursuit. He could outrun anyone.

His heartbeat slowed, and the tremor in his eyelid eased. For a few minutes he was almost at peace. The sodden land soaked up the sounds of the night, and they reached him as if muffled. A fox barked, deep in the wood nearby, and there was a scurry from the bank near his horse as a vole or water-rat slipped into the current. The river had just swallowed it when he heard a hoof upon the bridge, followed by the scrape of spurred boots, and the commotion of grass as a large figure made its way down the verge to the riverbank.

Thomas Howard, Earl of Surrey appeared under the bridge, a formless shape in grey. His size was shocking in this confined space, and the spy took a step backward as the soldier scraped a flint and made a flame, sending his shadow bounding out across the vault. There was barely room for two men and a horse under the narrow stone arch, and their intimacy gave the meeting an air of friendliness that was soon to fade.

'I huvnae much time,' said the spy, glancing over Surrey's shoulder as if expecting to see King James follow him into the rendezvous.

'Well, what news then?' asked the earl. 'Any sign that James will negotiate?'

The spy shook his head. 'None whitsoever. He's hell-bent on battle. He believes himsel' the aggrieved party, and nothing will temper his fury, or self-righteousness. He looks forrit tae meeting yer troops.'

Surrey's voice was harsh. 'We are in a damnable position. Almost a day's march from Branxton, and already the men are exhausted. James is so well dug in, he might as well be in the Tower of London. His position is like a fortress.'

'No' all's well on the Scottish side either, my lord. They've lost hunners through desertion in the past week, and a thousand or mair since the campaign began. Many are sick, and a good number's deid. Some say it's the plague. Those who are healthy are hungry, an' angry, an' wabbit. James is under pressure. He argues wi' his advisors. He threatened one wi' exile for daring to question his judgement. He's losing his calm. He talks of being trapped in his position, because his guns are too mighty to be moved fast, like.'

The earl relaxed a little.

'Ye should ken also,' continued the spy, 'that when it comes tae battle, James will very likely be at the heid o' his troops, in the very thick of the advance.'

'Really?' said Surrey, sharply. 'I thought he would be commanding his men himself. Why so?'

'Because he's an arrogant fool, and a dreamer, who loves nothing better than his image of himsel' as one ae God's warriors. Action, not caution, is what excites him. That could be to your advantage. If he were tae fall early in the fight, ye would not need to overwhelm his army to claim victory.'

'And even if he does not die, who will marshall the troops as the fight gathers pace? Without the king in charge, there will be confusion. You greatly cheer me, young man. Greatly.' The earl's voice lost some of its edge. He put a hand on the mare, stroking her nose as he considered this information.

The spy stood rigid. The flame revealed a face chiselled from basalt. 'I'm glad I cheer ye, sir. I terrify mysel'. Every day since leaving Edinburgh I hae risked discovery and death – a most horrible death – and the money you've promised would scarcely pay for ma shroud. I wonder why I do it, for so poxy a reward.' He stared at Surrey.

The earl straightened his back. 'You exaggerate, sir. The sum we agreed, and monies you have already received are scarcely mean. They would pay for a requiem at least.'

'I dinnae deserve yer mockery,' said the spy, turning away from him to stare at the water, invisible but loud at his feet. 'I've been a faithful agent nigh on three years. Ye've never had cause tae doubt my allegiance, or my courage. On two occasions I've come close to discovery. I cannae survive a third. Even James will grow suspicious.'

The earl nodded in apology. 'It was not my intention to mock. You have done fine work for us, some of the most fruitful I've known. But you must see that this is a most inconvenient time to state terms.' He raised a hand to silence the spy, who had begun to interrupt. 'As I say, your work has been invaluable. Henry rates your intelligence very highly. There is every chance he will give you whatever you request, if we are successful. But it is not in my keep to promise you anything more than we first agreed.'

'I dinnae believe that,' said the spy, his voice tight as if holding back his bile. 'Wi' Henry out of the country, ye're his earthly representative in England. Ye can gie me whitever sum ye think I am due.'

'But for God's sake, man, why have this conversation now? Can it not wait? In a day's time we go into battle. Money should be the last thing on anyone's mind. Say your prayers, and hope to live this week out. If you do – if any of us does – we will talk again.'

Something close to contempt was detectable in the spy's tone. 'If the Scots win this battle, as it seems likely they will, ye will need me even mair than you do now. I can continue tae report back until ye've gleaned enough tae overcome them. At which point I want a promise of land, somewhere far frae the border, and a new name, to ensure my safety.'

'My boy,' said the earl, all friendliness gone, 'are you really in a position to bargain?'

The spy shrugged. Even by flickering light the earl could not miss the coldness of his stare. 'So be it,' said the spy, as if resigned. 'I hae an idea of James's battle plan, and very interesting it is too, but,' he gathered the horse's reins, 'if ye cannae afford that information, that's yer choice.'

'Blackmail?' The earl was startled.

'Jist a business proposition.'

A pragmatic man, Surrey knew he was beaten. He needed facts more than he needed to win this encounter.

'Very well,' he said, with the sigh of the outwitted. 'I'm not sure I can even blame you for your tactics. God knows we are all dispensable in this world. The Almighty may come to our aid, but each man must also look out for himself. And in your case, you are worth a good price.'

A blackbird flew through the arch with a chattering cry. Morning was on its way. As the riverbank slowly awoke, and the rain clouds grew pale in the leaden dawn, the spy passed on what he knew of James's deployment of his troops. It was an urgent exchange, Surrey repeating each fact so as not to forget, and the spy speaking fast because he must be far away from here before first light.

CHAPTER SIX

1 October 1513

The letter from Coldstream arrived as Paniter had expected. He broke the seal and spread open the sheet. Lord Home's hand was a sprawl, wasting paper as only a man with money and no sense could afford. Its message was bleak. Benoit Brenier, he wrote, was a decent soldier, who made up in enthusiasm what he lacked in military finesse. Home recalled him in training exercises in the days before battle, but after that had no memory of him. His position was on the flank, beyond Home's sight.

His script grew wilder as he relived events: 'The smoke, the confusion of moving our position, the sheer ill-fortune of the day meant I noticed nothing but what was essential to carry our men to victory. By the time I could draw breath, mayhem had overwhelmed the field. Most likely Brenier, bull-headed, courageous, foolish man that he was, returned to the fray against my express orders. I would wager that his body now lies limed in Branxton's pit. My condolences to his family. His was another needless death.'

Paniter's vision narrowed and his temples began to throb. His palms grew damp. Home's suspicions about Brenier's fate were hardly unexpected, but his disrespect for his fallen companions, his refusal to acknowledge that he as a commander had played a craven part and might even be held responsible for the turning of the army's hopes, was sickening. The secretary crunched the letter in his hand as if it were a rag. Damn the man. He would pay for his treachery that day. He would pay, with his neck on the executioner's block.

Paniter's lips worked like a toothless crone's as he invoked every curse he could find in his heart. For a man about to take holy orders, there was an abundance to draw on, and it was some time before his muttered incantation came to an end. When he raised his head, he started to discover Gabriel Torrance in the room, watching the street from his window, studiedly not looking his way. The arrival of the letter had driven his guest out of Paniter's mind.

He ran a handkerchief over his brow. 'Forgive me, Torrance,' he said. 'I am not myself still.'

'Bad news, I gather?' Gabriel looked concerned.

The secretary nodded.

'Would you like me to leave?' Gabriel waited to be dismissed, but Paniter stared at the wall behind him without answering. He held Home's letter out in a trembling hand as if he were beseeching an invisible authority for help with its contents. At last he dropped his hand, and the letter fell to the floor. He turned to the courtier. 'War sounds a noble venture, does it not, Torrance? An honourable pastime for kings and their braves. The only fair guide to who wins good fortune, and who loses it.' He retrieved the letter, his face flushing with anger. 'But you know, my son, it is only when you see its scarlet teeth, when you smell its stinking cannibal breath that you realise that war is the devil's own work. It is very hell. Whoever wins.'

Gabriel sat down on the edge of a chair. Unease urged him to leave at once; compassion insisted he do his duty. A well brought up young man, his sense of duty won. He pressed a hand to his arm, where he was bandaged, and indicated that the secretary should continue. While his liege talked, Gabriel fingered the rough cotton that held his wound together. He felt a little queasy.

'D'you recall the king's late mistress, that comely girl in Leith?' Paniter asked. Gabriel nodded. 'Well, her brother has died at Flodden, it would appear, and his younger sister needs to be told. She's only one of thousands like, but it tears my heart to pieces' – he made a wrenching gesture over his shirt – 'to destroy another with such news the way I have been destroyed. Like me she will be ruined, her spirit cast away as if it were as light and useless as dust on the wind. I pity her.'

Paniter was panting as if he had run up the stairs. His hands were clenched. 'The Brenier lass is due to come here tomorrow for the news, but I cannot keep her waiting.' He heaved himself out of his seat, gripping the settle while his dizziness cleared. After a pause, he spoke, his voice again firm and familiar. 'I must ride to Leith now and break it to her, and her grasping doxy of a mother.' An apology of a smile crossed his face: 'I will not sleep if I do not, you see.'

'Let me go,' said Gabriel, rising. 'You are still weak.'

Paniter gave a bark more like a yelp of pain than a laugh. 'And you, lad, with your arm wrapped in a sling, are in the very best of health?'

Gabriel smiled. 'It is nothing, sir, trust me. Merely a

flesh wound, already well on the way to healing. I was graced with great good favour on the field. More than my skill with a sword deserved.'

Paniter looked grave once more. 'I forget, you were in the thick of it all, Torrance. I cannot imagine how that must have felt. From our hill, Borthwick and I felt we were watching a charnel house. If it was desperate at that remove, God alone knows what it was like where you were.'

'I confess I'd rather not discuss it,' said Gabriel. 'It was unspeakable. Best for everyone it remain that way.'

'Quite,' said Paniter, reaching for his cloak. 'I understand. But let us go to Leith together. I cannot commission you to do this for me. It is my obligation and mine alone to bear the news, but your company will give me comfort in what I know will be a most miserable task. Also,' he added, as they left the room, 'Mme Brenier will no doubt try to sue the court for guiltsilver for her daughter's death. I need make it plain for once and forever that she has no cause, and no claim, for a groat more than she has already won.'

They began to make their way down the stairs. 'I regret the day our king set eyes on that girl,' Paniter continued. 'A dreadful error of judgement, even had neither she nor the king perished. Yet who could have known this liaison would haunt the court after James was gone?' Unable to answer, Gabriel remained quiet, the wisest course with Paniter, as he had learned.

For his part, Paniter appreciated the courtier's talent for silence. Too many ambitious young men thought to ingratiate themselves with a demonstration of wit and knowledge so incessant, it was like a slow but steady drip, capable, over time, of wearing down the hardiest of men. King James was more tolerant than his secretary, with the result that the court had too many chatterers and dreamers who talked more than they would ever act. The king said their fancies amused him. That they irritated Paniter sorely was an additional source of pleasure.

In recent times, with his former pupil Alexander so often absent, Paniter found himself glad of Torrance's company. Indeed, he was fast growing into an indispensable companion. There were few similarities between him and James's eldest-born. Alexander had a lightness of heart that mirrored his father's blitheness. The fact he was a bastard and could never be king was, for the boy, a source of relief rather than regret, and as he frittered away his time on the continent, and made heavy weather of learning the serious business expected of him as the precociously young and marvellously unsuited Archbishop of St Andrews, he exasperated Paniter to such a degree he had once caught himself tearing at his hair, a parody of the demented teacher. He was obliged to pause and smile at himself, but as a scholar who was never happier than with a book or pen in hand, Paniter could not fathom such a lack of gravity.

Torrance was a more sober man. He could not raise Paniter's spirits as Alexander did, nor coax a laugh out of him whatever his mood. What the secretary felt for this handsome lord was fondness only, and nothing like love. Yet affection was a rare enough event in his life for it to be remarkable. In the young man's Roman nose and elegant limbs, in his air of natural authority, and languorous entitlement, he caught a glimpse of the high-born Alexander.

Over time, Torrance's provenance became clear,

though he never spoke about his background without being prompted. That too Paniter respected.

'I am the only son of a man who did not want me,' he once confessed, with such a broad smile Paniter could not guess how sorely the fact pained him. 'He died when I was young, but by that time he had gambled and drunk away almost everything, and he left me little but his title, and a house with a leaking roof and empty stables. My mother lives for the present with relatives in Glasgow, who are in the wine trade, but I hope one day to bring her to Edinburgh, where she can set up her own house. She is quite an accomplished musician.'

'I don't like to be impertinent, but where is your father's estate?' Paniter asked.

'Ireland,' he replied. 'My full title is the Viscount Torrance of Blaneford and Mountjoy. A mouthful for everyday conversation!'

'Yet useful,' said Paniter, 'however impoverished you may be. And the Irish connection explains everything. I had at first put you down as from the Ayrshire coast, or possibly the Isles.'

'Many find me hard to place,' said Torrance. 'In fact, I wish I had less of a brogue. I am endeavouring to sharpen it while at court among these more . . . shall I say robust accents?'

'Rough, you mean?' said Paniter, raising his eyebrows.

'Maybe I do. I am told the English court is less rural, and yet . . . ' He paused, examining his neatly filed nails, 'I find I prefer people who do not disguise their origins. Maybe that's the Irish coming out in me. No honest man need be ashamed of his background.'

'So you will soon be speaking as if brought up in a woodcutter's hovel,' said Paniter, smiling.

But there were no smiles this unhappy day. Both were stony faced as they mounted their horses and set off abreast down the high street. The road to Leith was empty, their only companions the herring gulls diving for gutter scraps, and an occasional dog truffling by the roadside. It was as if merchants and workers feared to be abroad, as if they would be too exposed to the eye, if not of God, then of the enemy. Paniter could not recall such stillness since the last outbreak of plague. It made him uneasy and, sensing this, his horse danced and skittered, refusing to settle.

As they left the city, heading east towards a sea so still it might have been carved from wax, the chime of hammers and trowels from the Flodden wall grew faint. There was some comfort in knowing that this barricade was now almost in place, but as they neared the port of Leith, the road narrowing, and the dwellings growing more crooked and ramshackle as its knitted streets drew together, Paniter thought of the tumbling coastline north of the English border. Though much of it was sheer cliff, pounded by waves whatever the tide, there were enough beaches and unpatrolled harbours between Berwick and Edinburgh that if Henry wanted to seek retribution, no bricks or gates could hold him back. They could not fool themselves that with the wall in place they were safe.

But all thoughts of invasion fled as the Breniers' house came into sight. As they approached, the king's men sat taller in their saddles. They rode the final few yards along the quayside in silence.

Louise and her mother met them at the door before they had dismounted, warned of their approach by the vixen's bark. The courtiers' faces told their news, but with the calmness of disbelief, Louise led them into the house and offered them ale, hoping to delay what was to come.

'No beverage, thank you,' said Paniter, removing his cap. He looked at his hands, and lowered his voice, as if speaking in chapel. 'We have had an answer from Benoit's commander, Lord Home. I am afraid – ' He swallowed under the stare of the girl and her mother. 'I'm afraid he believes he must have been killed in the fight.'

'He's not sure?' asked Louise, in a pitch above her usual.

Paniter shook his head. 'He cannot be. He does not recall seeing him in the battle, and certainly not after it. It is the obvious and most likely conclusion. Failing that, he may have been taken prisoner to Berwick.' He avoided her eyes. 'But few survive capture, not even those fit enough to make it as far as the gaol. Those places are little short of open coffins. Forgive my bluntness, but I do not want you to be under any further illusion that your brother still walks this earth. If you had seen what we have seen, you would understand what I am telling you.'

Mme Brenier put an arm around her daughter. This was not news to her. She had said farewell to her son days ago. She'd had no hope to lose. But Louise had believed her brother lost, not dead, and this report would, surely, destroy her faith in miracles.

Louise stood rigid, so brittle it felt as if she could snap. She looked at Paniter as if this crag of a man was as insubstantial as haar and she was seeing through his foggy shape to a scene played out behind his back. But what she saw there made no sense and she stared, wide-eyed, willing the picture to become clear.

Gabriel glanced at the secretary. The young woman opened her mouth to speak, but no words came. Her eyes closed, and she seemed to sway. Gabriel stepped forward as she began to slip from her mother's hold, but before he reached her, she dropped to her hands and knees on the flagstones, lowering her head to fight off the faintness that swept over her.

Gabriel crouched and put a hand on her back, but she shrugged it off, heedless of his or anyone else's concern. While her mother's shoes clipped out of the room to bring cold water, Louise was aware of nothing but darkness and a surging heat that threatened to melt her. She gave a moan, raised a hand, and slumped unconscious, sprawling amid a tumble of skirts like a guttered candle wreathed in wax.

Gabriel looked around for a cushion. 'Voici,' said Mme Brenier, who was at his side with a bowl and cloth. The courtier took these while she pulled off her shawl and bundled it into a pillow under her daughter's head. The vixen was licking Louise's face, but Mme was too distracted to chase her away. 'N'aie pas peur, ma p'tite,' she whispered, chafing her hands, 'n'aie pas douleur.' Her tears fell onto her daughter's bodice as she tried to revive her, stroking as if she could rub life, and spirit, back into her. 'Benoit is at peace, little one. He cannot be harmed any more. He is safe, at last, and happy.'

Gabriel knelt and pressed the damp cloth to Louise's forehead. A trickle of water ran down her neck, and with a shudder she opened her eyes. As she regained her senses, the hollow expression that had unnerved Paniter faded.

She gripped her mother's hand, but her eyes were on Gabriel. Seeing her conscious, he brushed her hair back from her face, his gentle smile more that of a nurse than a man of the court whose sword was scraping the floor. A blush of colour crept back into her cheeks. She frowned, turned away, and was sick.

Gabriel left Mme Brenier to attend her daughter. Paniter, who had played no part in the crisis, was trembling. 'An accursed business,' he said, addressing no-one but himself. 'This is what I mean by war's stinking breath. It reaches everywhere. It is not only the dead who die on the field.' He twisted and dubbed his hands as if they were dough.

Gabriel touched Paniter's sleeve. In ordinary times this would be a gross liberty, but it seemed to the courtier that the secretary was almost as close to collapse as the Brenier girl. 'Come, good sir,' he said, 'we should leave them alone.'

It took time for his words to reach Paniter.

'We should go, sir,' Gabriel repeated.

Recalled to himself, Paniter nodded. He smoothed out his cap, which he had been throttling. 'Of course. Of course. They will want to grieve by themselves. We above all people are a cruel reminder of far better times.'

By now Louise was seated on the settle, the vixen at her feet. Mme Brenier faced the king's men with a dignity her daughter would always remember.

'We thank you,' she said, 'for your kindness in seeking information about Benoit, and coming down here with it. We are eternally in your debt.'

She opened the door. Paniter and Gabriel bowed to Madame, and again to Louise. The secretary swept out of the room without a word. 'My deepest commiserations to you both,' said Gabriel, and looked at Louise as if he would like to say more. Then he too was gone.

The day was still light, but Mme Brenier had nailed a mourning cross to the door and closed the shutters on all floors before the king's men had even reached the Edinburgh road.

CHAPTER SEVEN

3 October 1513

'Sshhh!' Louise put a hand over the vixen's muzzle. 'Not the smallest yap till we're out of here. Otherwise I'll have to leave you behind.' The vixen understood, her mistress's whisper as stern as she had ever heard. She thumped her tail meekly, and followed her down the passage with only the faintest scratch of claws on stone.

It was black as a winter night, and the wind had set the shutters rattling. When Louise slipped out of her bed in the kitchen, fully dressed save for stockinged feet, she was glad of the wind as her tiptoes set the boards creaking. Stealthy as a thief she wrapped bannocks and dried fish in a cloth, and put them into her pack. From Benoit's caddy she took a fistful of coins and stuffed them into her boots. Her belt was slung over the back of the settle, weighed down with a simple small sword. This was a piece of burgling she felt no shame about at all. Overhead, Vincent had slept on unaware, ale fumes hovering around his head. Harrumphing and kicking as he always did in the first hours of oblivion, he had not heard her creeping into his bedchamber, nor the fumble as she removed his blade from his scabbard. With nimble fingers she fitted it into her own belt, a hand-me-down from Benoit, taken without his permission but, she believed, with his blessing.

Packed for her journey, Louise untied her bodice. She took a shawl filched from her mother's press and wrapped it, with one of her own, around her shoulders and midriff, securing them with Benoit's belt. She patted her new girth, and gave a grim smile. She could scarcely fit her bodice over her bulk, and she left the ribbons dangling, too short to meet over her matronly bosom and waist. Next she wetted her hands in the butt, knelt by the fire, and clawed together a pile of cool ashes. She rubbed a handful into her hair, stifling a sneeze as soot flew around her head. The vixen cocked her head and sniffed, but made no noise.

It was a grey-haired, fat little woman who crept out of the back door, a docile hound at her heels. Only when she reached the outbuildings, well beyond sight of her mother's window, did Louise dare stop to light a wick. Sheltering the flame from the wind, she hurried over the courtyard. In his stable, Hans whinnied and shuffled at her approach. It took an age to quieten him. He had once been a fearless creature, a good-natured adventurous bay, whose temper matched his master's. When her father died, Louise took him as her own, despite Madame's complaints at the cost of feeding him. Benoit reminded their mother that in these times, a family horse was essential. His own little mare was a working beast, used every day in the yard, or on his travels, and rarely available for anyone but himself.

Reluctantly, Madame agreed, persuaded that between them her daughters would put the animal to good use. Marguerite, however, would not go near Hans, complaining that he was too edgy. She preferred Benoit's docile grey, and somehow managed to wheedle him into lending the mare out whenever she wished. Marguerite liked the picture she made with her skirts spread over the mare's flanks, and her riding hat perched aslant over her eyes, as she rode to rendezvous with her king. Hans would not have tolerated those slow afternoons, where Marguerite wandered through woodland with her lover, never giving him a chance to burn off his nerves. He would have killed romance with his prancing and pawing. Once placid, Hans these days had grown fretful, as if still waiting for his owner's firm hand and voice. Louise understood. She felt much the same herself.

While the old horse lipped at her sooty fingers, nosing out the apple she had tucked up her sleeve, she stroked his neck, not daring to think about the time she was wasting, or imagine her mother coming downstairs, sleepless, and finding the ill-written and ink-spattered letter on the kitchen table. Vincent would read it to her, because while Madame claimed her eyesight was poor, everyone knew she could not read; she had never needed to. That her daughter could not only read but write was entirely to Benoit's credit, who believed a woman should be able to run a business like any man.

Louise murmured to Hans, to keep him calm and quiet. But as the horse crunched up the apple, exhaling a grassy scent with every mouthful, Louise's own fears began to ebb. This was a strangely soothing sound, familiar since childhood, and its domestic sweetness steadied her. 'Good boy,' she whispered, kissing his nose. When she began to saddle him up he stood, calm as in daylight, and her own heartbeat was almost regular as she snuffed her light and led him out of the stable.

When his hooves struck the cobbles she hesitated, certain a window would be thrown open and her mother's bonnet appear behind a candle. But nothing stirred except the wind, and she urged him on, round the side of the house and out onto the quayside. There she got into the saddle – an ungainly manoeuvre with her added weight – and set off at the quiet, plodding pace of a wake. On one side the vixen trotted at her heels; on the other the Water of Leith slurped at its banks, an oily wash and slap that had been the sound of home since the hour she was born.

When they reached the street, Louise nudged Hans into a brisk walk. She wanted to be clear of the city walls and well on her way before her mother found her gone. Slowly, her eyes adjusted to the dark. There were no lights to be seen, but behind their shutters a window or two gleamed like a narrowed eye as a fire within was stoked for that morning's work.

The road to the south wound along the coast, a crooked seam stitched in mud. Louise knew it well. Benoit had often ridden out with her to the fishing villages beyond Leith – Fisherrow, Prestonpans, Port Seton. They had eaten hot mackerel on the sands at Aberlady, squinting into the sun as the oil ran down their chins and they eyed the milky blue trees that fringed the Lothian coast, knowing that it would be long after dark before they were home, with their mother's fierce tongue to face for their day's escape.

Louise could, if she wished, follow the coast road all the way to the prison at Berwick, but that was not her plan. Paniter's words rang in her head, dolorous as a church bell:

'If you had seen what we have seen. If you had seen what we have seen . . . ' She could not banish them, because as soon as he had spoken, she knew she must go to Flodden. It was dread at that prospect, not the news of Benoit's likely death – which she did not fully believe – that had made her faint. Flodden had swiftly become the most fearful name in the Scots language, and to visit the scene of such slaughter would take a degree of steeliness and resolve she did not believe she possessed.

Yet, if Benoit had died there, she must see the hillside where he had fallen. She might never find his body, but she would have the painful comfort of knowing in what sort of place he had spent his final hours. If she found no proof of his death, however, then she would ride on to Berwick, and its fortress of a prison. Paniter said few survived capture, but few had survived smallpox either, which was surely more lethal. As her father had taught her, jiggling the dicing cup in his hand, the braver the gamble, the better the odds of winning. He brought home so much money from the alehouse tables, he must have been right. She would try to live by that rule.

She rode on. Hans's breath, and the clink of his bridle were a comfort in the dark. Yet even as dawn crept over the sea, coaxing the night to dissolve, the shadowy land she crossed felt alien, no more familiar or safe in gathering light than it had by night. Keeping her eyes on the path, she pressed on.

The sea had been her close companion for hours when at last she dropped the reins and allowed Hans to rest. The vixen panted at his side, and sat, as if to take in the view. While the horse grazed, Louise looked out across the red earthen fields that ran between the road and the clifftop trees. Some distance behind her, Dunbar castle crouched on its outcrop, guarding the harbour like a miser stooped over his hoard. Under a pall of cloud, fishing boats moved slowly homewards across the horizon, their day's catch already on deck. Ahead of her lay grey sea, woodland, and a rutted road running between the two, so narrow it looked too puny to fight its way through the trees.

Louise had never ridden this far from home. Benoit had once told her about the herring-wives' track that ran south-west from Dunbar, the route he used on his trips to the Border foresters. That was her road. She remembered him saying that when he reached a village called Cockburnspath, a huddle of houses clinging like barnacles above the sea's edge, he would turn south-west, climbing into the Lammermuir hills, where the ancient path wound its way over some of the loneliest moorland in the country.

So this was where the Borders began. The name rang like a bell, a frightening toll as if it described the home of giants and not ordinary, workaday folk like herself. Benoit had spoken of these people often, and rarely with warmth. The Borderers, he had told her, were a tribe apart. They could be kind, but they were more often treacherous. They were suspicious of outsiders, and were fractious among themselves. So far as Benoit could tell, the list of those of whom they were wary covered all kinds, from march wardens and merchants, to the king himself. Even for their monarch they would not lift a finger unless it was to their advantage. It was said that only a handful had joined the king's side at Flodden. The rest had melted into the trees, to watch and wait.

And yet this past year or two, Benoit had seemed almost eager to leave the bustle and cheer of Leith for these unwelcoming parts. Louise tried to take heart from that. She surely had no need to be afraid. Crumbling a bannock, she gave a corner to the vixen, ate the rest, and took a long draught of ale from her flask. It was already noon, the sun as bright as it would get this day, yet even now shadows were fingering their way across her path. It had been a relief to ride out of Dunbar a little earlier, leaving behind a main street turned to stew with mud and slops. A posse of weans dressed in sail-cloth rags had splashed alongside her, catching at her boots and begging for a coin. Their whining turned to curses as she spurred Hans on out of their reach, but as she faced the empty road ahead, she was sorry to have left even such bad company behind.

Hans trotted at an easy pace. The vixen jogged a yard ahead, turning now and then to check the horse stayed close. With the hovels of Cockburnspath at her back, Louise began to look for the turn in the road. Waves rolled onto a rumbling beach far below the path, and the wind began to strengthen, blowing her ashen hair into her eyes. A speck of rain prickled on her cheek, followed by another. Soon she was squinting into a downpour, fighting to keep her hood in place while also holding Hans steady. The horse picked his way between the ruts and stones as the road plunged downwards, out of the wind, and away from the sea. The growl of milled pebbles receded, replaced by the melancholy drumming of rain, and the slush of hooves on a sticky path that was designed for nothing wider than a waif and her horse.

Louise sniffed, wiping rain from her nose. The sky was

purple, and the path so confined by rock face on either side, she could not see much beyond Hans's ears. Relief at being out of the worst of the squall soon turned to worry. After what felt like hours, their passage grew even narrower, and Louise's skirts were turning green from the moss brushing her on either side. Unsettled, Hans snorted and tossed his mane. The vixen had slowed to a walk, and Louise was beginning to fear she had taken the wrong road. She was wondering how they would turn back in such a confined space when without warning the rocks dropped away and they emerged into the open, spat out from their funnel onto a hillocky plain where the rain and wind could come at them in full venom.

There was nothing to do but keep going. Putting her head down, she kicked Hans into a canter. There was still some time before dusk, and before then they must find shelter. She tried not to imagine what a night outdoors in this weather would be like.

They had been riding doggedly for some miles, the ground underfoot growing steadily rougher, when Hans stumbled, and Louise was thrown onto his neck as his knees buckled. He quickly regained his balance, but Louise reined him in at once. 'Easy, there, boy,' she said, dismounting, her boots sinking into the sodden trail. No wonder the horse had lost his footing. They were ploughing through a marsh.

Cursing her heedlessness, Louise ran a hand over his fetlocks. Hans nuzzled her shoulder as she crouched, looking for a sprain or tear. She found nothing swollen, nothing that made him flinch. In relief, she laid her head on his neck. Whatever the weather, they would have to ride with caution. A cold, wet night stretched ahead.

Some considerable time later, when she looked up to see where the vixen had gone, she blinked. Absorbed in her hurry, she had not noticed the country changing character under her feet. It was as if someone had wiped it clean. Woodland and fields had melted behind them, as if they had never existed. This was a new land, like nothing Louise had ever met before. Without realising it, she must have moved inland faster than she expected. This was the moor that Benoit had warned her about, a desert of wild, inhospitable terrain that would, eventually, bring her to Duns, and the road for Flodden.

In the thin afternoon light, heath and bog stretched on every side. Wind-whipped oaks crouched by the roadside, bent as beggars. They were sinister not for their human shape but for whatever might lurk behind them.

Hans sniffed and pawed, catching a scent he did not like, and the vixen gave a yap, darting around the horse's feet, her ears pricked. Louise patted Hans's neck, more to reassure herself than him. She walked him on slowly. The rain had turned to drizzle, thickening into a haar that cloaked the moor in a drenched gauze. 'Watch your step,' Louise warned, holding the horse in check, in case he trip again. Now she began to understand what their old servant had felt like, as she descended by degrees into blindness. She remembered Sally haunting the window seat, holding her stitching up to the light and squinting at it like a jeweller with a gem; when the milky cloud finally claimed both eyes, she would stroke Louise's cheek as she spoke to her, as if to remind herself that though the girl was invisible, she was just as she'd always been.

Now, like Sally, Louise could not see a horse's length

ahead. Peering into the mist until her eyes ached, she could make out nothing until it was upon her. An alder loomed over them, shaped in a pounce, and she shrieked as its arms reached for her out of the pall.

Though it was still day, they might as well have been in the dark. The moor and its sodden silence closed in around them, a cold cloying prison as secret as the bottom of the sea. Out here they were alone. If anything happened, they would be lost forever. Benoit had told her of the body he once found by the wayside out here, a herring carter who had lost her footing, and broken her leg. By the time he came upon her, she was pickings for the crows. Louise put the other details of the story out of her mind. Overhead, hidden, an oystercatcher flew by with a piercing cry, and she bit her lip. She tried to believe there was nothing out here to be afraid of, that there were worse things to cope with than a bit of bad weather. And then she saw something moving towards her.

Her heart keeled over. Just out of sight a dark shape darted, keeping to the corner of her eye. She pushed her hood back, and the emptiness of the moors washed over her with its muffled wet breath. She strained to see into the haar, but it eddied and swirled as if in a dance, and gave nothing away. The shape appeared again, the height of a bush, but moving. Too big for a fox, too narrow for a deer. There it was again. Two legs. The vixen dropped into a crouch, and began to growl.

With a trembling hand, Louise pulled the dagger from her belt. 'Who goes there?' she cried. 'Show yourself. I am armed.'

Hans came to a stop. Louise kept her eyes on the heath.

There was nothing there, but now she could hear steps, the hush of feet on grass, the suck of air as if whoever was out there had been running, and was breathless.

Suddenly, a face appeared at her knee, hair plastered over its eyes with rain. Louise screamed. The vixen sprang through the mist at the man and fixed her teeth on his arm. With a bellowing neigh, Hans reared. As Louise fought to control him, a bony hand gripped the bridle, and pulled him down, seemingly unmoved by the dog clamped to his other arm. 'Steady. Steady.' The voice was soft. Hans shied from the stranger's touch, but after a moment's scuffle, when Louise thought both she and the horse must fall, Hans allowed himself to be calmed. As the horse regained his balance, the vixen let go her prey, and began to bark and snarl, darting in every few seconds to nip his heels as he held the horse's head.

Shaking so hard she could barely keep her grip, Louise brandished the dagger at arm's length. The stranger dropped the bridle and stepped back.

'Wh . . . wh . . . who are you?' Louise asked. 'Wh . . . what do you want?'

'Please,' he said, 'I didnae mean to frighten ye. I need help.'

The voice sounded more alarmed than she was, but Louise had heard of tricks like this. The Borderers were cunning. This could be a ruse, to lure her off her horse, away from her saddle pack. She stared at the stranger, and saw he was a boy. He would be perfect bait for a trap. Yet he was scarcely more than a child. His eyes were rimmed with crimson, and rain coursed down his cheeks. Except she now saw it was not rain but tears. His hand reached out

for the vixen, whose snarling ceased. To Louise's astonishment, the dog's tail had begun to wag.

'What help?' she began to ask, when the lad dropped to
his knees. 'My faither,' he sobbed. He covered his face with
his hands. His fingers were smeared with blood, as was his
jerkin, bearing an assortment of stains old and fresh that
told her he'd been on the road for weeks.

All thought of thieves and murderers fled. If the vixen
trusted him, so could she. Louise jumped down beside him.
She touched his arm. 'Get up, boy. Come on, now. Please.
Tell me what's the matter.' But he could not speak. Instead
he ground his palms into his eyes as if to blot out the
memory of everything he had seen.

'Show me, then,' she said, pulling him to his feet.
Hiccuping with tears, the boy stumbled off down the road,
the vixen at his side. Leading Hans, Louise hurried to keep
him in sight. After a short distance he stepped off onto
the moor, and the road evaporated behind them. Louise
tensed, but she said nothing. Hans followed willingly.

The ground moved under their weight. Black water
welled at their feet with each step and she saw the boy was
barefoot. It would be worth his while killing her just for
her boots. Who couldn't conjure tears and a pitiful story if
they could not afford to buy shoes? Her heart began to
thump. Where and to whom was he taking her?

The boy turned and spoke to her over his shoulder.
'Close,' he said, in a whisper, 'Very close now.'

As he spoke, a huddle of figures began to emerge from
the mist. An hour on the moor had taught Louise a little
wisdom, and she did not falter. They were too still and
angular for men. As the boy led her nearer, they revealed

themselves as a thicket of oaks, a rustling, sweet-scented haven on this desolate heath.

The trees grew out of a bowl of grass and moss, as if with their roots sunken deep out of sight they could summon the courage to face down the moor and its weather. Boy, dog, woman and horse picked their way through the dripping oaks to the heart of the hollow. Their steps sounded rough and loud in this sheltered space. The boy came to a halt. Louise reached his side, and caught her breath. At their feet, on a bank of moss, sprawled a man in ragged uniform. His back was braced against a boulder. His padded jerkin was black with blood, and his helmet, which hung from his neck on a strap, was smeared with red. At his side was a studded shield, and a pike as long as a fishing rod whose blade gleamed in the grass.

The soldier's chin had dropped upon his chest, as if he was about to sup from his helmet. His arms lay loose at his sides. He was dead, but newly, and the violence of his end was written so fiercely on his face, and in his bitten fists it was hard not to believe his tormented spirit was still at large in the grove. Around him lay a litter of bandages, wet and scarlet. Louise's stomach shifted. When she saw a blood-stained dirk at his side, her legs turned weak. She looped Hans's reins over a branch. The boy was already crouched at his father's side, clutching his fist to his breast. He rocked back and forward on his heels, eyes closed, as if begging him to come back.

Louise approached slowly. 'How did this happen?' she asked. She had to repeat the question before the boy answered.

'He's a soldier,' said the boy. 'He got hurt.'

'Flodden?'

He nodded, without opening his eyes.

'That's a long way off. How did you get this far?'

'I carried him.'

Louise looked at the figure rocking by his father's body. He could be no more than twelve or thirteen: slight as a girl, thin as an urchin. His face had the pallor of a lifetime's poor food, and too little of it. Though his father was slimly built, he was twice the size of his son. How they got this far was unimaginable.

'And when . . . ' Louise put a hand on his shoulder. 'When did your father die?'

'Yestreen. Before dark. After he'd used the knife to cut out the badness. He said it was the only way. He said it would save his life. Told me not to watch, but I could hear.' His voice dropped to a whisper. 'I heard everything.' He stopped rocking, frozen in that memory.

Louise's eye travelled the length of the soldier's body, and saw a molten mess at the end of his leg where his boot had been removed. The foot had been almost, but not entirely, severed. A maul of flesh, bone and blood melted into the moss and grasses like wax from a candle. Hot liquid rushed into her mouth, and she turned away to be sick.

It was some minutes before she could compose herself enough to speak.

She put a hand on his shoulder. 'What's your name, boy?'

'Hob.' He ran a hand over his face. 'Same as faither.'

'Well, Hob, we have to bury him,' she said. 'We can't leave him here. And then we have to get away, find somewhere for the night.' She picked at the torn sleeve of his jerkin, where the vixen had bitten him. 'This is a good jacket. Without it, she'd have hurt you.'

'Found it in the camp,' he said. 'Faither told me to take it, said I needed it as much as anyone.'

Louise gave a grim smile. 'He was right.'

The boy nodded, but did not move. He would not let go of his father's hand.

Louise took out her sword, and carved a narrow grave in the grass. She began to dig with sword and hands, clawing her way as deep as the meagre earth allowed. After a while, as if recovering his wits, Hob joined her, scrabbling at the roots and soil with broken nails until between them they had made a hollow deep enough for the wretched remains of his father. Together they dragged and rolled him into his grave, taking as much care not to disturb the corpse as if it could still feel pain. When they had crossed his hands over his breast, they scraped earth and sods over him until the clotted rags had disappeared under dust. They piled stones onto the earth to weigh it down and keep foxes and crows at bay. Then they looked at the mound, and fell silent.

'You can come back some day and put up a cross,' Louise said finally. The boy took her hand. His father's helmet, his only inheritance, hung from its strap down his back, like a steel hood. 'Do we say a prayer?' he asked.

Louise nodded, and they knelt, bowing their heads under the dripping oaks. The haar was beginning to lift, and the moor's emptiness pressed in at their backs as the words of the 'Miserere' rose over the trees and out across the heath. It was as if the sadness of the chant and the bleakness of the scene had been created specially for each other:

'Miserere mei, deus: secundum magnam misericordiam

tuam.' Louise spoke gently. The psalm had been sung at her father's and sister's funerals, and she knew it too well. 'Et secundum multitudinem miserationum tuarum, dele iniquitatem meam.' Have mercy on me, Oh God, according to thy steadfast love; according to thy abundant mercy blot out my transgressions . . . The boy did not understand the words but he had no trouble divining the bitterness of the message, the lack of hope, and the promise of nothing more to come but judgement. He held her hand tighter.

As they rode from the graveside, Louise tied the soldier's helmet onto her saddlebag, and wrapped her cloak around the child. The words of the lament swaddled them both in misery, yet she found she was praying not for the dead soldier's soul, which was beyond her help, but for the boy. She knew nothing about him, but it was all too clear that with his father gone, he had nothing left in this world to call his own.

CHAPTER EIGHT

4 *October* 1513

Crumbling with neglect, Crozier's Keep stood in the forested heart of the Borderlands. Built on the lip of a gorge, its back was protected from marauders by a vertiginous fall, where buzzards glided beneath the keep's arrow-slit windows. Seen from the valley floor, the tower rose from the forest straight as a Scots pine. Its turrets peeked from the canopy of autumn leaves like eyebrows above a mirthless face. Only birds were familiar with these heights. They and the keep's men, that is, who walked the ramparts every hour, casting an eye over their land and out to the horizon, where the Cheviot hills were painted in blue.

This day, under steady rain, there was no view except of cloud. The trees shivered, and the keep's walls ran with water. In the torch-lit hall, a posse of armed men gathered around a table by the fire. They took it in turn to kick at the logs to coax out more heat, but nothing they did could turn the feeble tongues of flame into a roaring blaze, and the dank chill of the hall lapped at their heels.

'There's more warmth in the devil's prick than in this

place,' said one, pulling his cowl over his head. 'Is it any wonder my bones ay ache up here?' He stamped, sending a wolfhound skittering across the flagstones from his boots and the only congenial spot before the hearth.

'Quit your whingeing,' said another. 'Too many years in the saddle, that's your trouble. Hard riding, and hard living have done for you. There's none of the clan who's done his due that doesn't feel his joints in this weather.'

'Aye, you could be right,' was the reply. 'But it wouldn't hurt to build a fire that reached ayont the grate, would it?'

'Gentlemen,' said the only man seated, whose white hair proclaimed his vintage, 'kindly remember why we're gathered. Our comfort is not important.'

There was a ripple of coarse laughter. 'Gentlemen, eh?' said the first speaker, taking a swig from his flask. 'You'd think we was already in court afore the judge.'

As if they'd been waiting for their cue, the men started upon a litany of stories from the dock and the dungeon, many of the tales recalled first-hand. Ancient grudges and unfulfilled promises against march wardens and neighbours were revived with such practised swagger it was clear this was a familiar and bottomless pit of entertainment. When it looked as if the anecdotes would last all morning, a lean man peeled himself off the wall, and made his way to the centre of the group. He rubbed his hands before the fire, his back to the men.

'We all know why we're here, right?' His voice was quiet, but it cut across the hubbub, and the noise subsided. Young as he was, he was leader of this pack. He turned to face them. He was more heavily armed than the rest, a sword on one hip, a cudgel on the other, and a dagger tucked into his boots. His hair was cut unfashionably close to his head, and his beard even neater, framing a gaunt, high-cheeked face flushed with years of riding against wind and rain. He was not tall, but there was a horseman's power in his shoulders and legs, and a fighter's heft in his arms. His eyes were cold and hard as he surveyed his men. He looked at each of them in turn.

His eyes swept the group. 'So what do we do?' No-one spoke. He waited for an answer even though he knew they were waiting for his. He raised his voice, as if addressing an army, not a huddle of underfed, half-sottish relatives. 'We do what we're best at. We use our brains. We plan one jump ahead. We outwit the enemy. That way we might live to see another winter, and maybe the one after that, if we're lucky.'

'You're the clever one, Crozier,' said the hooded complainer, known as Wat the Wanderer for his nocturnal habits. 'Just tell me what to do. I can handle an axe, but I never was much of a thinker.'

A laugh ran round the hall, but the old man hushed them with a raised hand. 'Let Adam speak. We don't have much time.'

'Gather round,' said Crozier, and they scraped their stools up to the table. 'The rumours are bad,' he said, 'and getting worse. Dacre is busy, acting as go-between between Henry's man Surrey and the Scots court. We know Henry's planning something. Whatever it is, you can be sure it won't be pleasant. After what happened at Flodden, no-one on the border is safe.'

A youth whose face was livid with an unhealed scar thumped the table. 'Bastard sons of whores!' he shouted.

'Armstrongs, Elliots, all the scum of the Borders.' Seeing the eyes around the table on him, he continued, quieter now he had their attention. 'Stole from the camps at Flodden, while they were on the field. Didn't care if it was Scots or English they were robbing. Drove off their horses and oxen. And cut the throats of any who got in their way. Children and wives among them. Not a groat of mercy.'

The old man, Crozier's grandfather, nodded in sorrow. 'I heard tell they robbed the dying on the battlefield, and ran them through, in case they lived to bleat. Sliced off hands and fingers to get their rings. Pulled off boots and jackets, didn't care if the bodies were quick or dead.'

There was a moment's silence as the men contemplated the scene. Several shook their heads, as if even in these lawless parts, some vestigial code of honour had been broken, and shame been brought on them all.

'We're all under suspicion,' said Crozier. 'As far as Surrey or the widow queen knows, it could have been any of us did that. What we can be sure of is that they won't let this go unpunished. They won't care if the innocent are hurt along with the guilty, they only want revenge.'

'Revenge,' said Murdo Montgomery, from the far end of the table, 'and an excuse to corner and kill us like rats. They won't be happy till the border is vermin free. Far as they're concerned, we're all fair game.' He stroked his beard. The look in his eye suggested the feeling was reciprocated.

'So what do we do?' asked the boy with the scar.

'You do what our father would have done, Tom,' said Crozier. 'You make the first move.'

Tom's eyes brightened. 'Aye? How, like?'

Crozier lowered his voice, as if he feared eavesdroppers in the rafters: 'We ambush Dacre.'

'Pah!' said Wat the Wanderer, who as Crozier's cousin had no fear of offending him. 'That's child's talk. How are we going to get close to him, do you suggest? Just stroll past the guards and into his castle?'

'No, you fool,' said Crozier. 'We get him when he's out on the road. There's as many of us as he will have body-guards. More, perhaps. And we'll choose our position well. They won't stand a chance.'

Wat was unconvinced. 'And what if he won't talk?'

Crozier looked at him, and the hall's chill deepened. 'Oh, he'll talk.'

A smile spread across Wat's face. This was the kind of action he liked. There was a shift in mood in the hall, a rising of spirits. The men nodded with approval, and shuffled their stools closer to the table.

'Tonight, then,' said Crozier. Lowering his voice, he began to explain his plan.

*   *   *

There was no name the Crozier clan hated more than that of Lord Thomas Dacre, warden general of the English marches. From the day of the old soldier's posting in the north, Adam Crozier's father had toyed with him as a cat plays with a sparrow. There was no malice in this; Nathaniel Crozier had been flouting the law and riling its officers since he was old enough to spoon broth. Many wardens before Dacre had found his image swimming before their eyes as they tried to sleep. Nathaniel Crozier and his ilk – the Procters, the Fords, the Thomsons, the Scotts – were a daily irritation to those charged with keeping order on the marches, a human itch that kept the wardens' skin perpetually aflame. They were gleeful in their thieving, unrepentant in their venality. Wardens on both sides of the border read their names so often in court and on writs they were more familiar to them than those of their own families.

But wild as they were, few Borderers were reckless enough to taunt the wardens. Most saved their energy for their true enemies. Nathaniel Crozier, however, seemed oblivious of the danger his actions held for himself, and his kin. It was almost, his son later thought, as if he needed to prove that he was king of the middle march. And for a few sweet years, it seemed as if he were.

When Nat Crozier was dragged before the assizes for fighting with his English neighbours and stealing their sheep, he used the occasion as a stage. Standing in the dock, hand on his hip, he ignored the warden's questions and replied instead with a salvo of contempt against the Saxon king and his lickspittle servants. A year later, he languished six months in Carlisle Castle for rustling English piebalds, one of which he rode off upon when he had served his sentence. A year after that, he broke free from Corbridge gaol, with the help of his men, leaving behind a letter expressing his thanks for such lavish board and lodging, to which was attached a silver coin to cover his keep, and a salutation to Dacre's fragrant spouse.

This last insult to Dacre's pride turned contempt for one more Scots ruffian into such personal enmity the warden would idle away his waking hours dreaming of retaliation. That his wife had chanced to speak to the lout as he lay in captivity and found him amusing only added gall to his mood. Before his time in this barbarian fastness was done, he swore that Nat Crozier would be dealt with.

His wish was answered. One midsummer night, when Crozier's Keep and its men lay stupefied in liquored sleep, their fate crept up on them in the shape of two hooded intruders. Nat was warm in his bed, his wife tucked into his arm, when a tap on the forehead made him open his eyes. In the dark he smelled the sword before he saw it, three feet of bitter steel, pressed between his eyes. But while he lay transfixed by the blade, it was a keelie's gutting knife that did the deed. It came at him out of the night and sliced his throat so fast and deep he had time to do nothing but gurgle before his head lolled back on the straw, windpipe gaping. His wife was drenched in his blood as she cowered, hands over her ears. Her screams scared the crows from their trees and they whirled around the ramparts, a cawing wake for the departed spirit below. By the time Martha Crozier was silent and the birds had settled, the intruders were long gone, and so was her husband.

Fifteen at the time, Adam Crozier remembered only the smells and sounds of that night. He wanted never to think of them again, but as he rubbed linseed into his saddle, ahead of the evening's ambush, they refused to be banished. It was the stench that clung to him still: the slaughterhouse stink of blood, and his mother, daubed in it, holding out her hands to her boys who had rushed into the room. Tom's wails, as he stared at his father's body and the bloodied stranger who was his mother, were at the heart of that picture. Even now the memory made Crozier's eyes smart. The child had retreated to Crozier's side, reaching for a hand, and his brother had swung him up, hiding his head in his shoulder. Crozier had no recollection of what happened next. His mother had told him he pulled her out of the bed, as if rescuing her from a blaze, and the three stood, shivering in each other's arms while Nat's brothers and retainers stumbled into the room in their nightshirts, and saw what was left of their kingdom.

It was over ten years since Nat Crozier was murdered. No-one had yet been put on trial, though there was no doubt that the men who'd done it were Elliots from over the river, a clan as inspired in their thievery as Nat ever was, and – it now was clear – considerably more vicious. The week after he was buried beneath the beeches at Crozier's Keep, the enemy's messenger arrived at the door. He brought an offer from Ethan Elliot for the keep and its lands. The message boy's blackened eye was answer enough when he rode back over the river.

News of the killing reached Dacre before the body was stiff. That evening, he and his wife and brood ate well, a belated solstice thanksgiving that carried on till midnight. As the fire sank to ash, and his children fell asleep alongside the dogs, Dacre bundled his wife upstairs for further celebration. Later he fell into a sleep sounder than he had enjoyed since Nat Crozier slipped out of his clutches.

Within days, all the border knew who the murderer was. Ethan Elliot, they said, was holed up in his farmhouse in Liddesdale, emptying his cellar keg by keg and plotting further revenge. He was not denying what he had done, but defied anyone to take action. The Keeper of Liddesdale and the Scottish warden of the middle marches were both informed, but they valued their own skins too dearly to challenge the wolves of the march, and left well alone. When the news reached Lord Dacre, he not only did nothing but from that day remembered the Elliots fondly in his evening prayers. A petition from Martha Crozier lay on the English warden's window ledge, fading in the damp. A year passed, and no charge was brought. And in that year, Adam Crozier was to learn just how rough was the justice in these lands.

Man of the house at fifteen, Crozier turned to his uncles for help. Like their brother, they were fighters, but unlike Nat, they were not bright. Where Nat went to work with his wits as well as a sword, they blundered straight for their target, without guile or strategy. Their enemies not only saw them coming, but could hear them, a mile off. Within months of Nat's death, the Crozier lands had been pillaged, burned, and much of their livestock stolen. New cattle disappeared overnight, as if swallowed up by the fields. Higher hedges, better gates did nothing to protect their animals, and in time the Crozier inheritance shrank to a swathe of thistly wasteland, a few good fields on the valley floor, and a meadow for livestock within a brisk drive of the keep's barnyard. A watch was posted on the meadow, night and day, and slowly order was restored.

Pride was less easy to recover. To look at the Crozier clan as it stood today was to know that the Elliots and their allies had won. A once thriving, powerful family had been brought close to poverty. As she picked at her thinning dresses, or bound her boots together with twine, Martha railed at Crozier for his feebleness. 'Yer father would have torched the curs who stole our sheep,' she'd say, on the occasions now when neighbours rampaged over their land. 'You, you can do nothing but mend gates and traipse all o'er the place trying to find your blessed lambs. And when you track them down, all you do is bring them home. What sort of message does that send? And you call yourself a Crozier. Your father would be sick at you.'

Crozier did not remind her that it was his father who had squandered their best land at cards, lost his health in gaol, and made the enemies who took his life. Unlike Nat, Adam did not seek trouble, though he'd meet it head-on when it came. He was defter with the sword than Nat had ever been, and a keener horseman. His blade had scarred men the length of the border, but it was never done with relish. The few he had killed would visit him at night, their youngsters at their heels, and he longed for a time when the border was quiet, and he could ride out to his fields unarmed.

The long years of aggravation, of skirmishes, theft and squabbles had left Crozier's Keep a near ruin, pitted from battering rams, arrows and grappling irons. Martha appeared to have forgotten the end her husband had provoked. Along with the horror of that deathbed, she had chosen to erase from her memory what kind of man he was. Over the years, she and Adam spoke little of the past; nor was there much about the present that either wished to discuss.

The land and its livestock kept Crozier away from the keep from early light until dark. 'He's jist a farmer,' Martha would tell Tom, when he came home, muddied and wet. 'The Croziers used to be a proud people, and folk respected us. Now, we're nothing more than peasants.'

It was Tom who carried his father's mantle. By twelve, he was getting in rough fights with boys from the village; a year later, he had spent a night in custody. He had never seen his brother so angry. For a week after paying for his release, Adam Crozier could not look at him. Tom was chastened, but that feeling soon fled. As he grew into a young man, it took only a thoughtless comment, or a sideways glance to fire his wrath. Without a word, he would be off on his pony, sword at his side, and not back until he had avenged the insult or righted the wrong he felt his family had suffered.

Crozier despaired. No punishment or hard talking made any difference. Sweetly, Tom went his own way, bit by bit unpicking the work of a decade in settling old feuds, and restoring peace. Tonight, though, his temper would be put to good use. The Borderer gave a grim smile.

After saddling his nag, who gleamed from his brush, he led her out into the yard. His grandfather would not join them tonight, but the others – cousins Wat and Murdo, and the best riders among the retainers still loyal to the family – would make up the party. Revenge was not on Crozier's mind, but if Dacre did fall into his hands, he wondered what the outcome would be. In the moment of capture, it would be easy to persuade himself that the warden was to blame for the family's misfortunes. Given the nervous state of the border after Flodden, and given Crozier's mood, he hoped for Dacre's wife's sake that he was not out on the road tonight.

CHAPTER NINE

3 October 1513

There was, Louise estimated, an hour's daylight left. The haar had fled, chased off by a wind intent on drying every stitch the mist had soaked. Shivering, the boy and Louise eyed the road ahead. It stretched empty before them, and they rode on without a word. Hans plodded dutifully, though he was flagging. At their heels the vixen trotted, unwearying.

After a couple of miles Hob fell asleep, his head bobbing over the horse's neck. Louise did not waken him, though his weight hung heavy on her arm. Rising anxiety kept her alert. Surely there must be an inn somewhere on this road? Her brother had never spoken of passing a night outdoors.

When the boy finally stirred, Louise tried to cheer him. 'We'll find a hostel soon, don't you worry,' she said.

'Alang this road?' Hob's voice was weary. 'There's gey few.'

'Did you come this way with your father?'

'Naw, though we should've. We wis heading west, by mistake. When we got to the moor, faither seemed to liven up. Knew we wis on the right gait, mair or less. He started talking about the priory, heading there for help if we could.'

Louise pulled the horse to a halt. 'What priory?' Her voice was sharp.

'Coldingham.'

'This is Coldingham Moor?'

'Aye. Did you no ken that?'

Sweet Mary. She dropped her head in her hand. She had taken the wrong road. Instead of heading inland into border country, she had clung limpet-like to the coast. She was miles from where she needed to be and, worse, there was nowhere out here for shelter until they reached Coldingham itself. She kicked Hans into a brisk walk, though it was herself she wanted to kick.

As if reassured by the fact that the night was likely to be as miserable as his day Hob curled into Louise's arm, buried his fingers in Hans's mane for warmth, and went back to sleep.

Dark had fallen long since by the time Coldingham Priory loomed into view. A dour, imposing building, with a perimeter wall that would need ladders to scale, it did not look welcoming. Ignoring its glower, Louise found a side gate, where travellers looking for a bed could ring. The bell was still humming when a nun peered through the wicket. She looked at Louise and the boy, and nodded, opening the gate to let them in. Louise dropped a coin into her outstretched hand. The woman turned, without a word, and led them into a courtyard cushioned in moss. She pointed towards the stables, and left Louise to settle her horse.

Roused from sleep, Hob was shaky and close to tears, remembering in an instant everything he preferred to forget.

But when he saw Louise unsaddling Hans, he gathered himself and picked up a handful of straw to help rub him down. A stable lad hurried out of the stalls with a torch, bringing hot mash for the horse and a bone for the vixen. Only when Hans and the dog were fed and at rest did Louise and Hob cross the cobblestone yard in search of their own dinner.

The priory kitchen was more inviting than the night, but not much. A handful of sticks flickered in a grate wide enough to hold a tree, and a table fit for a banquet was set with two pewter dishes and a couple of bent spoons. Overhead, a cavernous vault cast shadows thick as smoke into the corners of the room, and while Louise and Hob appeared to be the only travellers staying the night, they could not be sure that no-one else was sitting in this vat of gloom, watching them.

The nun pointed them to the bench, and poured a slurp of mutton stew into their bowls. Her apron was spattered with grease, and her fingernails were grimed, but when she smiled there was a weary friendliness to her face that chased away the eeriness of the kitchen and the brooding presence of the priory at its back.

'Best dry your clothes,' she said, indicating a rail near the fire, though its flame was so meagre Louise doubted it could warm a flea. 'Your beds are down the passage. I'll get you shirts for the night.'

The robes were so scratchy they might have been made from straw intended for their mattresses, which in turn had been filled with rubble. And yet Louise and Hob slept more soundly that night than they had for weeks, a sleep without dreams or night sweats or tears.

It was late morning before the nun shook them awake. 'Looked like you needed the rest,' she said. 'Young lad in particular,' she added, to excuse her soft-heartedness. A breakfast of watery soup was set before them, but when the nun waved them off in dry clothes, with bread and ale for their journey, they felt as grateful to her as if she had offered them a feast and feather beds.

A grey, sunless afternoon awaited them. 'We need to talk,' said Louise, as they followed the priory's winding walls out onto the road to Eyemouth. Hob pulled his leather jerkin closer round his neck. In his experience, talking never led to anything good. It was village talk that had brought his father to Flodden. If he had not been fired up by his friends' blustering blether about fighting for king and country, he would not have left his forge and Hob might still be stoking ovens and sweeping up sawdust. He said nothing, and hoped Louise would follow suit.

'I can't take you with me,' she said, ignoring his silence. 'I'm going to Flodden, to find my brother. You need to be taken back to your family, or to someone who can look after you.'

'I can look after myself,' Hob growled.

'I know,' said Louise, 'but you still need a home – somewhere to stay, at least. I'll be out on the road for God knows how many weeks.' She suppressed a shiver. 'I have no idea what I'm heading into. I can't expect you to come with me.'

'Seems like you need company,' said the boy. 'And I dinnae have anybody to go back tae.'

'No-one at all?'

'Naw. Ma died when I wis a bairn, and my faither brought me up alane. There was naebody else to dae it.

That's why he took me alang wi' him tae Flodden. I walked at the rear of the army, wi' him and the infantry. I slept next to him at night, and never saw him during the day.'

'What did you do when the battle broke out?'

'Hid in camp, under a kitchen cart. Went out after dark to find him. Didnae come on him till it was light.' His body tightened at the memory.

'You're a brave lad,' said Louise. 'He must have been proud of you.' She did not know if she would have had the courage to pick over the mounds of dead and dying to find Benoit.

They rode without speaking for another mile, putting off the decision that had to be made.

'Ye're no far frae Eyemouth now,' said Hob as a sullen sea came into view. 'The road goes south on to Berwick, or west to Chirnside. That's the one you're wanting, surely.'

'How do you know all this?' Louise asked. 'Where is it you're from?'

'A village near Dunbar, up in the hills. It's called Spott. But my faither and his friends joined the army over at Duns, and he used to take me wi' him on trips to Berwick, so I ken all these roads.'

Louise sighed, and reined in Hans. The horse stood, snorting and stamping, tossing his head. Hob patted his neck while Louise chose her words. 'Look,' she finally said, 'it's your decision. Do you want me to find you a hostel, till I can return for you? You could go back to the priory, I have enough to pay them for that. Or do you want to come with me? It'll be a hard journey, where I'm going. It'll bring back bad memories for you.'

'I'll come wi' you,' said Hob, as lightly as if he was

choosing between a parsnip and a neep for his dinner. 'You might need me.' He whistled for the vixen, and she wheeled back to their side. He reached down to rub her nose, the picture of a boy out for nothing more serious than a holy day spree.

They rode on, one with lighter spirits, the other more troubled than ever. Shortly after, they turned west and left the girning sea behind.

Already the sky was growing dull, the shadows lengthening. The nun had told them of a farmhouse ten miles or so along this road where they could spend the night. Flodden, she said, was half a day's ride beyond that.

As they reached the brow of a hill, Louise and Hob dismounted, allowing Hans to rest. Louise looked out at the coast road, snaking towards the border. In the distance, Eyemouth was visible in the fading light, boats huddling in the harbour as if the open sea had yelled at them. A few miles out of sight beyond the cliff tops lay Berwick. She prayed that Benoit was not lying in prison there, trapped in the enemy's hands. Better by far to be on the run than caught in a snare.

She was helping Hob back into the saddle when a movement far below caught her eye. A horse was cantering along the Coldingham road, kicking up turf and earth in its haste. The rider was bent over the horse's neck, urging him on with spurs and whip, as if he was the bearer of terrible news. Louise narrowed her eyes. When the horseman pulled up hard, raising a spindle of dust under the horse's hooves, she held her breath. He had reached the turn-off they had taken. For a moment the rider hesitated, holding his steed in check while it pawed the ground. He looked down the broad road to Eyemouth, and then he stared up at the track Louise and Hob had taken. Louise's heart began to skip. The rider's urgency suggested a man in search of prey, and she clenched her hands as she waited for him to make his decision. 'Keep still,' she said quietly to Hob, who was watching in fascination. 'Don't say a word.'

Finally, the rider turned and his horse cantered on, down the road to Eyemouth.

Louise swung up into the saddle, and kicked Hans into a gallop. For no good reason she felt uneasy. The vixen ran close at her heels, and they hurried on. As dusk descended, and the road grew rougher, Hans slowed to a trot. Louise began to wish they had not set out so late in the day. The farmhouse was not far off, but even a mile or two was further than she liked, when such a man was out on the road.

They were making good time when she heard the sound she had feared. She looked over her shoulder. 'Can you hear something?'

Hob listened, then nodded. 'Another horse,' he said, 'coming fast behind us.' With a kick, Louise plunged Hans off the track and over the heather towards a straggle of pines some distance from the road. They had barely reached the trees and crouched for cover, when a horse came cantering into sight. Hob put a hand over Hans's nose, to keep him quiet. The vixen panted, her ears pricked.

In the grainy twilight, the figure on horseback appeared more wraith than human, a figment of mist. Louise tried to steady her heartbeat. Without looking to either side, the rider passed their hiding place and rode on, a faceless swirl of cloak, hat and sword. They listened as the jangle of bridle and spurs faded down the road, until the road was once again quiet. A lapwing called, and its mate answered. Nothing else stirred. Dusk was overtaken by dark, and the first stars came out. None of them moved. Time passed, and still they remained, frozen in place as if rooted. It was no surprise to any of them when they heard the hooves returning. This time they came at walking pace.

The rider stopped and got off his horse. There was a spark from a flint box, held low to the ground, where Hans's tracks disappeared onto the heath. Snuffing the light, the rider began to lead his mount across the heather, towards the trees. His shape was a blacker patch of night, but all too solid, moving towards them like the worst of dreams. Louise pulled her short sword from her belt. Hob, she saw, was clutching a gutting knife. It looked comfortable in his hand – a hand steadier, she noticed, than her own.

The rider reached the edge of the trees and came to a halt. He was a horse's length from them now, though he could not yet see them. They could hear his horse's breath. The blood in Louise's veins was hot as boiling water. The man came a step closer and ducked under the fronds of the first pine. 'Louise,' he called softly. 'I know you're in there. Come out now. You're quite safe.'

Louise's heart contracted, as if it had been squeezed. The vixen launched herself from her hiding place with a snarl. Her jaws closed on the rider's arm and he yelled, stumbling backwards and falling. 'Louise!' he shouted. 'Call the dog off! Call it off! It's me, Gabriel!'

'Praise the saints!' gasped Louise. She was out of the trees and at Gabriel's side as she spoke, dragging the vixen off by her scruff, and using both hands to hold the growling, bristling animal back.

'Mother of Christ!' Gabriel got to his feet with an un-steady laugh. 'That's some beast you've got there. She could have snapped my arm in two.'

'What are you doing here?' asked Louise, her voice shrill with fear. 'You nearly scared us to death.'

'Your mother sent me. I've been riding since dawn.' He picked up his hat, where it had fallen, and slapped it against his leg. 'She was deeply alarmed at your disappearance. She does not want to lose the only child she has left. I admit, I did not like the thought of you travelling these roads alone myself, especially in these times. You are very young, you know, Louise. Very vulnerable.'

In the dark it was impossible to see his expression but his voice softened. 'You are also courageous. I know of no other woman who would have set out like this on her own.' He took a step towards her, his tall, lean figure as reassuring a presence now as it had been terrifying a moment before. After the events of the last two days, Louise found herself longing for the comfort of this man's arms. She had wished for them since the day he tended her when she had fainted, the gentleness of his touch a warm memory to set against so much misery.

She moved towards him, and saw that he was clutching his arm.

'Oh, you're hurt!' The vixen, panting, watched Gabriel, her hackles raised. 'I can't believe she did that,' said Louise with remorse, like a doting mother startled at her child's bad behaviour. Gabriel said nothing, but it was as well that the night hid his face.

'Hob!' cried Louise, 'Bring the flint from my pack.'

Gabriel started. 'You are not alone?'

'Oh no,' said Louise, examining the rip in the courtier's fine shirt. 'Can you sit against this tree, and let me look more closely?'

'It's nothing,' he said, though he did as she asked.

Hob appeared at her side, and struck a light. He stared at Gabriel, who smiled up at him. 'Good evening, young squire.' The boy did not reply.

'Who's your silent companion?' Gabriel asked, as Louise slipped his cloak off his shoulder, and untied his shirt sleeve.

'This is Hob,' she said. 'His father was at Flodden. He was mortally wounded.' She looked up. 'Hob, this is Gabriel Torrance. One of the king's men, and a good friend to my family. We can trust him.'

'Right ye are,' said Hob. He held the light steady as Louise rolled back the sleeve and uncovered the bite. Thanks to the cloak, it was little more than a scratch, but the force of the vixen's attack had opened the wound on Gabriel's arm, and blood was beginning to seep into that morning's fresh bandage.

'An old wound,' said Gabriel, seeing Louise's shock. 'Taken at Flodden field. Your hound is not to blame. She's a fine guard dog, and you're lucky to have her. I was a damnable fool not to declare myself earlier. I must have scared the wits out of all of you, creeping up like a cut-throat.'

'I wisnae feart,' said Hob.

'Good man,' said Gabriel. 'But still I owe you an apology.'

Louise frowned. 'Do you have another dressing, or bandage? This one will be soaked through in no time. Or should we bind you up tight till we can wash and dress this properly?'

'There are linen strips in my saddlebag, but if you can help me put another wad of lint under the bandage, that will staunch it. That's all it needs.' Louise looked at him anxiously, and he smiled down at her. 'Believe me, this is nothing. What's more pressing is that we find a place for the night.'

'There's a farm close by, where we were heading.'

'I know. I called in there a while ago, and when they had seen nothing of you, I came back.'

'How did you know we were on this road?' Louise pressed clean lint onto the wound, and pocketed the bloodied wad.

'I didn't. Not with any certainty, anyhow. At first I thought you'd have gone due south, straight to Berwick gaol. But then I reckoned you might start the search at Flodden. I did not think you could have gone far this way. Hence why I came back.'

'Well,' said Louise, tying the bandage back in place, 'we are glad you found us.' Her voice dropped to a whisper as she fastened his shirt and jerkin, but she did not meet his eyes. 'I've never been so glad as when you called out my name.'

Gabriel put a hand on her shoulder, and its heat burned through to her skin. He was about to say something when Hob bent closer with the light. The farmyard smell of tallow caught their throats, and they rose to their feet. Gabriel seemed to sway for a moment.

'Come, both of you,' he said, mounting his horse with obvious pain. 'We don't have far to go.' The vixen ran close to Louise's heels, with the courtier in her sights at every step.

CHAPTER TEN

3 October 1513

The evening after he had taken the bad news about her son to Mme Brenier and her daughter in Leith, Patrick Paniter retreated to his bed. Goodwife Black could do nothing to stir him. He turned his back to her, his nightshirt yellowing with sweat. That he would occasionally drink a bowl of broth gave her hope that he would recover, but in the meantime he was sunk in a sea of guilt, toiling to get out of its clutches but driven back onto his pillows by wave upon wave of regret.

As he lay sleepless, staring at the canopy above the bed, the past paraded before his eyes. He found himself reliving decisions he had taken on his own as secretary, letters he had composed, in James's name. Often the king barely read them before scrawling his signature, trusting his servant to conduct affairs with delicacy, and acumen. And until the day of battle, Paniter believed he had done just that.

But as autumn began to chase leaves down the streets of Edinburgh, and shutters were closed against the rising winds, he was haunted by each order he had delivered as the king's counsellor, every document sanded and sent out.

As he saw it now, he and James had been steering Scotland straight onto the rocks. In the dead of night, the only hand he saw on the tiller was his own.

One man loomed larger than most in these waking nightmares. Doctor West was Henry VIII's ambassador, and a frequent visitor to the Scottish king's palaces. He was a welcome guest, much liked by the court, to which he always brought a crate of Alicante wine, and a stream of irreverent anecdotes that set the dinner table alight with laughter. Of scrawny build, when dressed in the puffed and padded style the English preferred he looked like a child's drawing, his legs thin as a pipe and his head as small as a button above his bulbous jerkin. He would arrive with gifts for the queen and her infants, treating them as fondly as if he were an English uncle, and it seemed he genuinely grieved at the toll of nursery deaths that dogged this marriage. For that reason, perhaps, on his most recent visit he had been particularly affectionate with Jamie, the queen's only living child, a beefy infant whose crawling antics at his mother's feet he would watch for hours at a time.

Mind you, thought Paniter, we gave him many hours to fill. On his last mission, as the secretary now acknowledged, the ambassador had been badly dealt with. Though the business he came to conduct was often irksome to James and Paniter, in previous years he had been given their full attention. This past spring, however, he had been treated no better than a troublesome commoner, kept waiting for meetings, and cold-shouldered in council. Paniter winced at the memory of their last encounter. With hindsight, he believed their complacency heralded the start of the disaster that was soon to unfold.

It had been a brisk spring morning, trees coming into bud on the road from Linlithgow Palace to Edinburgh, where James had summoned the ambassador with the promise, or so the Englishman thought, of finally giving him the signed papers he had so long requested.

'At last, he appears to have come to his senses,' said West to Paniter, as they waited in the antechamber to James's rooms at Holyrood Palace. The ambassador rubbed his hands before the fire.

'Mmm?' said Paniter, laying aside his book. 'What do you mean?'

'I mean that after keeping me kicking my heels here since Candlemas near enough, and doing everything possible to avoid my company, it would seem that the king has finally had the wit to realise he must sign his old accord with Henry. He knows he cannot ally himself with the French king, and take war to England on his behalf. And that if he did, Henry would consider the Treaty of Perpetual Peace to have been broken.

'Should that happen, all hell would be unleashed on Scotland's head. For believe me, Henry is a man with some knowledge of hell. He has it at his command, or so many of his servants and mistresses have told me.' He stroked his beard. 'I wouldn't fancy risking it, myself.'

Paniter flicked dust from his britches. 'Is that so?' West's frown should have warned him to be cautious.

'Sir,' the ambassador replied, with unusual asperity, 'for your sake, and all of ours, I truly hope it is so. No monarch can be trusted who will break a deal signed with his neighbour, purely on a whim. I know there have been faults on both sides, and resentments, but there are no serious barriers to a full alliance between our kingdoms. Yet James has been as skittish as a maid. Louis appears to promise him everything his heart desires, but will he produce it? Has there been any sign yet of the largesse, the soldiers, the ships for his crusade that Louis assures him are his, yet for some reason never quite delivers?'

The doctor turned his back to the fire, but kept within its reach as he looked down on the secretary where he sat, unperturbed.

'So far as I can see, Master Paniter, all the gifts flow from the Scottish court into Louis's hands. Forgive me for being blunt, but your king is more like a swain suffering unrequited love than a ruler who knows his own worth. Even his wife thinks he is mad not to affirm the Peace with England for all to see.'

Paniter began a sharp reply, but West held up his hand. 'It's true, I assure you. She told me so herself, just yesterday, when James's invitation arrived to summon me here today. She was hopeful it meant he had rethought his position, she said, because in the public eye, and in her own, Henry is in the right, and her husband wholly in the wrong. It grieves her that he should be so sly.'

Unwilling to acknowledge the awkwardness of this revelation, Paniter would not meet his eye. Instead, he stared at the portrait of James that hung over the fireplace. He disliked this painting. The Dutch artist had imbued the king with a melancholy that infected even the hound at his feet. He did not recognise the mischievous, spirited man he knew in this sour-lipped, sanctimonious figure. After James's death, however, when just such a mournful monarch paid him nightly visits, he began to wonder how a mere artisan, in the space of a few sittings, had seen deeper into the king than his closest companion. Thereafter, he would avoid this chamber and the sorrowful James.

The doctor had clicked his tongue in irritation at Paniter's silence. 'His excuses and prevarications make him look slippery, sir, a man no-one can do business with for fear of being cheated. I warn you, in some quarters Scotland is being spoken of as an outlaw country, a nation of bandits, whose worst criminals are to be found at the court – the royal court, that is, not the courts of justice.'

Paniter did not like his tone, and it took an effort to remain calm. He reminded himself that as he and his king had discussed the night before, the cards were all in their hands. James need not put his name in writing to any affirmation of amity with England. By giving a verbal agreement only, he could maintain good relations with both Henry and Louis, for as long as was useful. That way, his plans for a great crusade would be aided by the pious Louis, while the threat of Scottish action from the north on Louis's behalf would keep Henry unsure.

Unacknowledged by either party, though it was the bone over which each side snarled, was the possibility that one day James might claim the English throne for himself, and with French support. That fact hung tantalisingly in the air, like smoke after gunfire or, in this case, before it.

But had the secretary known then what he discovered after West had finally taken the road for England, he would have summoned the guard to throw him into the cells. As he later learned, to his fury, in the Englishman's pigskin purse, hanging from his belt before his eyes, was a copy of a letter from the pope. All the time West was decrying James's manoeuvring, he was being even more duplicitous.

The letter spelled out very clearly how wide the gulf between Henry and James was growing, and what forces were allying themselves on each side. The pope's missive, couched in platitudes and scripture, welcomed Henry VIII into the Holy League – whose greatest enemy was France – and promised to excommunicate James should he break his pact with England.

Had James or Paniter even suspected he was in possession of such a treacherous document, West would have been pitched into prison, and the chill between England and Scotland hardened to ice.

If only, the secretary now thought, that had been the next page of this story. Instead, West had maintained his air of injured propriety. A few days later he was handed a sheaf of letters from James which were virtually meaningless in their vagueness, their masterly wording a feat of supreme ingenuity by Paniter's pen.

As the ambassador made his disgruntled departure, Paniter and James congratulated themselves on a diplomatic coup. But now, lying wide-eyed in the dark, Paniter wondered if they had not that day lit the fuse on a powder-box that would in a few short months ignite beneath them.

CHAPTER ELEVEN

4 October 1513

The farmhouse hid itself well. In the dark, Hans plodded along the road, his nose to the tail of Gabriel's horse. An hour into their journey, and they were all, riders and ridden, dizzy with fatigue. As they entered a wood, and were enveloped in the nutty scent of beech-masts, Louise found herself yearning for the warmth of a kitchen fire and a place to lay her head. 'It can't be far now,' Gabriel called over his shoulder, as if his thoughts were hers. 'Whit does he ken?' muttered Hob, but his words were lost in the rustling leaves.

Gabriel's hand was pressed to his arm, holding back blood and pain, when the night erupted around him. His horse reared, the reins slipped through his fingers, and he was thrown onto the path as figures rushed in upon him. His cheek was pressed hard against the earth by a boot stamped on the back of his neck, and his arms were bound behind his back by hands that did not care how roughly or tightly they worked. Louise's scream was stifled before it escaped, a greasy glove smothering her face while its partner pulled her from her horse. Hob was already being carried off the road, legs kicking like a frog heading for the pot. He bit the hand that gripped him, and there was a strangled oath, followed by a child's squeal, as the vice-like arm tightened unkindly around the boy. Louise's breath stopped with shock, but at the sound of the vixen being kicked into the air, she began to struggle.

'Don't,' said a voice in her ear. 'If you make another move, I'll have to knock you out. And sometimes I dinnae ken my own strength, know what I'm saying?'

She felt sick, grateful almost for the hand pressed against her lips and holding back the bile. In the darkness, the wood was alive with men, formless and fearsome as ghouls. 'So, what we got?' whispered one. 'A fat wee wifie and her boy,' replied the man whose hand was over Louise's mouth.

'A lang streak o' misery over here,' hissed another.

'A scrawny dug, but he's no trouble now,' said a third.

A low voice spoke, close to the tree where Louise and Hob huddled. 'Now listen, my friends. Make one sound, and you're as good as dead. Your hands are tied, but we can silence you if you start to shout. It's your choice.'

After a moment's silence, when none of the three captives moved, the hands were lifted. Louise licked her lips and tasted blood.

To her horror, Gabriel's voice rang out: 'You are a pack of cowards.' He had barely spoken when there was a dull crack of wood on bone, and the sound of a body slumping onto leaves.

What followed was worse. After the fierceness of their assault and capture, nothing happened. It was as if time had stopped. The ambushers stood mute around their captives, still as the trees themselves. Even their horses were quiet. Louise felt as if they had been plucked off the face of the land and submerged in a netherworld of brooding shadows, waiting for who knew what.

Then it came, and she began to understand. Down the road from the south she heard a reedy note breaching the night, faint as a curlew out at sea. Gradually it grew into a song, and in time she could make out the tune. Richer and louder it approached, swelling until it was so close, Louise could follow the words. The singer was bellowing, defying the dark:

'Merry was the hour she came, Bright as Mayday's morn. I took one look, and I was hers, Lost in love newborn.'

A jingling bridle kept the rhythm, and there was a squeak, as of a flask being stoppered. The singer paused, drawing breath for a new verse, but as the song started up again, the men surged out of the wood. The messenger was thrown from his horse in an uproar of shouting, a bristling of drawn swords. The powerful voice from the wood cut through them all. 'Keep still, sir,' said Crozier to the felled singer, 'or I'll run you through.' There was a whimper from the roadside.

'Get his satchel,' Crozier ordered. With a yell the men crowded in upon the messenger, and cut his bag from his side.

'I've nowt of value,' the man cried. 'No money. Nothing. I have ne'er a groat for you, believe me.'

'Well, then, I'll just take yer bevvy,' came Wat's thick voice, as he rummaged in the man's cloak.

A voice like the north wind halted the thief as he lifted the flask. 'Take anything from this man without my permission and you will never ride with me again. We are not criminals.'

The group hushed, as if they had all been chastened and not Wat alone. 'Now then, sir,' said Crozier, 'we mean you no harm.' He opened the satchel. There was the scrape, scrape, scrape of flint against steel, a spark in the blackness, and finally a glimmer of orange light as a lantern was lit and held low over the paper. From under her tree, Louise saw the crouching shapes of the men caught in the circle of light. At their heart were the singer's upturned boots, motionless as if they belonged to a dead man. A sword was pressed to his breastbone, holding him in place as if he was on a spit.

Crozier broke the seal on a small square of letter, and all sound ceased while he read. 'Damn this flame,' he muttered at one point, squinting to read the words half lost in the dark. Then he went quiet once more. A tide of wind passing through the tree-tops filled the silence, the comforting scent of loam it raised mocking the terror of the night. When finally Crozier spoke, Louise recognised anger as pure as she had ever encountered. His was a voice to be feared, and everyone present knew it.

'I wonder that you dare ride through the marches carrying this,' he said softly, folding the paper and pocketing it. 'If you knew what was in this letter, you'd not be singing your head off like a soused old fool. If you had any brains, you'd have caught a boat out of the country.' He lifted the lantern over the messenger's head, so that they could see each other's eyes: 'This letter is a death sentence, for you as much as me.'

There was a sob from where the messenger lay.

'Be grateful we have saved you a long ride,' said Crozier, handing the lantern to one of his men. He dragged the songsmith to his feet, where he swayed, nerveless with shock. 'Get back to Berwick, and take this message with you.' His voice hardened. 'Tell your Master Dacre that the Croziers have business with him. That if he does not begin to deal out justice, justice will be done to him. And remind him that our idea of justice is not his. We do not consort with murderers, and nor do we protect them. Unlike him – and thanks to him – we have nothing more to lose. We don't want vengeance. We simply want our father's killer put behind bars. But if the price of that request turns out to be Dacre's own head, then that will be his choice, not ours.'

He whipped a cord around the messenger's wrists, and hoisted him back into the saddle. Tying the trembling hands to the reins, Crozier turned the horse to face the way it had come. 'You got all that?'

'Mmmmm,' came the mumbled reply. 'Then be gone with you!' cried Crozier, slapping the animal's rump. With a bound, it sprang off, the messenger bent over his horse's neck like a monk at prayer.

Crozier's men were subdued as the hooves faded. They gathered around their leader, who spoke too low for their hostages to hear. When they stepped back under the trees, Louise tried to still her pounding heart.

There was a groan from the tree where Gabriel had been flung. 'What'll we do wi' him?' asked Murdo Montgomery, kicking the near-senseless courtier's feet as if he was as worthless and expendable as the other dog he'd just dealt with. 'Ask me, we should dispatch him now. He looks like evil trouble.'

Crozier's lantern passed over Gabriel's face, taking in the silver-clasped cloak and filigreed scabbard. 'Who's this?' he asked. 'One of the king's men,' said Louise through clenched teeth. 'Kill him, and you'll all swing.' Crozier approached and crouched beside her. She smelled the leather of his jerkin, and bitter sweat on his brow. 'Jesus and Mary. What a night's work.' He rubbed a hand over his face. 'And are you and the boy also from the court?' The light moved over her ashen hair, and the matronly chest under its homespun cloak. 'You don't have the look. Servant, are you?'

Louise did not reply. He untied her wrists and ankles, and as Louise rubbed her hands and the blood rushed back, her fingers tingled and buzzed. 'If you had got in our way,' said Crozier, in what she later realised was a Borderer's apology, 'that would have been ugly.'

'And this is not?' Louise's voice choked at the thought of Gabriel half-dead and the vixen in Lord knows what condition. Only Hob seemed unharmed, close at her side, and watchful through all the proceedings.

As she spoke, there was a slither of leaves, and a warm snout found her hands. She gave a cry of delight, but as her fingers sank into the vixen's pelt, there was a yelp. Holding the dog steady, Louise ran her hands over her. A feeble tail swished the undergrowth at her side. 'Petite mignonne,' she murmured, 'pauvre petite.' The vixen whimpered.

Pressing the dog to her side, Louise turned to Crozier, whose expression was harsh in the dim wick's flame. 'Look what you have done,' she hissed. 'Her rib is broken. She is in agony.'

'She will survive,' he said, and the curtness of his tone was more chilling than the gale gathering overhead.

He stood. 'And now we must leave. There's a long ride ahead.'

Louise's panic began to rise once more. 'We?'

'You have no choice, ma'am. We cannot abandon you and your child out here. Nor the king's man, not in his condition.'

He was already untying the horses. 'Trust me. You are safer with us than wandering out here this night.'

'And if I do not trust you?' Louise asked, a tremor in her voice.

'You will have to,' said Crozier, and strode off. A moment later, the lantern was snuffed, and the trees swarmed around them blacker than ever.

It was an ill-tempered party that set out from the wood. Gabriel was thrown, unconscious, across his horse's back, and led off by cousin Wat, who had designated himself nurse and keeper as if hoping to atone for his bad behaviour earlier. Hob leapt onto Hans, and Louise lifted the vixen into his lap, before climbing up behind him.

'We will ride fast,' came Crozier's voice from the front of his men. 'Whatever happens, you must keep up.' With a cry, he wheeled off into the smothering dark.

*   *   *

The first thin light of morning was creeping over the hills when the party reached Crozier's valley. So tired she could scarcely keep in the saddle, Louise was aware at first only of a slackening pace as the horses slowed to file along a track by the river. Even in the dank mist of an autumn dawn, there was a beauty about this valley, its larch and pines a haven after the barren, bitten hills they had crossed that night.

The horses slowed, whickering as they drew close to

home, and Louise touched Hob's shoulder. 'We're nearly there.' There was no answer. The child was asleep, as untroubled by the fierceness of their flight as if he was on a blanket by the hearth. At the sound of her voice, however, the vixen's tail thumped. Even in sleep, Hob had held her fast. Until now, she had curled unmoving in his lap, making a sound only when the horse had stumbled or leapt. In the course of the night's ride, Louise had not dared to think what condition she might be in after a journey that had ground her own bones nearly to dust. In the lantern's dim light she had seen the matting of bloodied hair, but there was no way to know how badly the dog had been injured. The wagging tail raised her hopes as nothing else this past week.

Picking their way up the valley side, the party reached Crozier's Keep. The ambushers dismounted beneath a sheer wall, cloaked with ivy, and led their horses, and the corpse-like figure of Gabriel, through the gate. A young man clanking with sword and knives lifted the vixen from Hob. 'Thank you,' said Louise, slipping to the ground, and taking the dog into her arms. She felt bruised from the ride, so stiff she wondered her legs had not buckled. Spritely as a silverfish, Hob gathered Hans's reins, and followed the young man into the keep.

With a whine, the vixen struggled to be free. Louise's eyes filled with tears of relief as, once on the ground, the bloodied animal limped around her mistress's legs. She bent to pat her, and the vixen licked her face.

She stared up at the grey battlements, rising out of the smirr. The night's gale had dropped to a gentle breeze, but the morning's birds were not yet in song, and there was a quietness about this place that she found ominous. Up here, at the head of this narrow, wild valley, it was as if the world she knew had been muffled, or gagged, all security and comfort now far out of her reach.

Catching her skirts up out of the mud, Louise followed the vixen through the gate. In the dark, narrow courtyard there was no sign of the horses or of Gabriel. Louise touched the arm of one of the ambushers as he crossed the yard. 'Where is he? What have you done with him?'

'The king's man, you mean?'

She nodded. Wat used his thumb to point out a low studded door that led into the heart of the keep. 'I reckon he's already abed. In poor shape, but still breathin.'

'It's been a bad night's work,' said Louise, her voice shaking. 'Have you no idea what the king's men will do when they learn how you've dealt with a courtier?'

'Aye, dreadful things I hear,' said the Borderer, screwing his eyes up as if even the glimmer from a dawn sky was too bright for a man of the night. 'Yer man woke up long eneuch tae tell me hissel.'

'He woke?'

'Till I shushed him. A bletherin sort, ain't he? It wid wear you doon, right enough.' Wat shouldered his pack, and made for the keep. 'No the kind of chiel we much like round these parts. All bluster and nae spleen, is what we say.'

'He's a man of noble birth . . . ' Louise began, but Wat was gone. She hurried after him, through the studded door and down a narrow set of stone steps that led into the keep's main hall. Here she came to a halt, adjusting to the dimness.

By the light of tallow flares the vaulted cavern appeared to be peopled by shadows, shapes flickering around the walls and running over the blackened stone arches high above, as if it were the haunt of wraiths and not men. It was the scene of a fairytale, a goblin hall or the lair of some reclusive magician.

Light seeped in through windows thin as pikestaffs, but the unwelcoming gloom was tempered by a sullen pine-wood fire, which perfumed the smoky air. Beside a hearth large enough to roast a bull, the head of the gang stood, alone. The English messenger's letter was open in his hand, and he was staring into the flames. For all the expression Louise could detect on his face, he could as easily have been contemplating what to eat for dinner as the troubling information that missive held.

By now, Crozier's men had passed through the hall to chambers deep in the keep's warren. The great room was empty, the only company Crozier's pair of wolfhounds, stretched beside the hearth. Their eyes glittered as they observed Louise and the vixen, who kept close to her skirts, but they did not move. A growl rolled like dice in the little dog's throat. The hounds yawned, and closed their eyes.

Louise approached the gang leader, her heart thumping. Her boots scuffed the flagstones, but for all the notice the brigand took of her, she might have got close enough to bury a knife in his back before he realised she was there. She and her companions had been captured, and carried off as if they were stolen sheep, and yet her ropes had been cut, and she was under no guard. Had she wished, she could have walked out of the keep into the woods, and never been seen again. The Borderer's preoccupation was oddly reassuring. Those with rape or murder on their minds were not usually so easily distracted.

'You,' she said, as if summoning a serving boy. The man looked up, and Louise held his gaze. She had never seen such ungiving eyes, the pitiless pewter of a winter sea. It was as if they merely reflected the world, offering no window on the emotions behind them.

She raised her voice. 'Who are you? Why have you brought us here? Where are we? I demand you release us at once.'

Crozier put the letter back in his leather pouch, and drew the strings tight, as if throttling the thoughts it had raised. He stared for a moment. As he took in this plump wifie, a sooty-haired pigeon of a woman, who screeched like a harrier, his expression eased.

'Ma'am, I apologise for our rough handling. Believe me, it was necessary. We have done you a good turn, as you will one day appreciate.' He prodded the flames with a poker, and provoked a crackle and flare of pine-cones. 'You are in Teviotdale, a short morning's ride from the border. This,' he said, gesturing at the hall, 'is Crozier's Keep, and I am Adam Crozier, head of the family. The men you encountered last night are all my kin. We are honourable folk, whatever you might think.'

He took a step towards her. 'But you must be weary. My mother is preparing a bed for you. It's been a heavy ride, a long night.' Seeing her scowl, he added, 'I assure you, it is not our intention to hurt you, or your boy. When you have slept a little, we can talk.'

Louise's hands clenched. 'I don't need rest, I need to see Gabriel Torrance, the man you so cruelly used. He must be half dead, or worse after that beating. You and your filthy, foul men are cowards, to attack him as you did.'

'You are not the first woman to call the Croziers cowards, ma'am,' said Crozier. 'Nor filthy.'

Louise lifted her chin. 'Take me to him at once. When I have seen he is alive and fit, maybe I too will be able to jest. As it is, I have seen nothing tonight to amuse me.'

Crozier straightened. 'As you wish.' With a country-man's stride, he led her across the hall and down a window-less corridor, faintly lit. At its end, they came to a door criss-crossed with so many bolts and locks it was more iron than wood. Inside, on a pallet, lay the courtier, turned on his side, his bound hands clutched to his chest. A none-too-clean cloth had been wound around his head, and the worst of the bleeding and bruising was covered. Cousin Wat was surveying his handiwork with satisfaction. 'Wis no easy winding yon thing on a head like that, wi' a' they girls' curls. No tae mention him wriggling like an eel, and chittering like a wren. Are they a' of his ilk, where you pair come frae?'

But Louise was not listening. She was on her knees at Gabriel's side, pressing his hand to her cheek. He was the colour of sour milk, and his face was damp with sweat. With the edge of her cuff, she dried his brow.

His eyes opened, and seeing her, he smiled. She found herself smiling back, the first time in weeks she had felt a moment's release from the stranglehold of misery and fear. 'Sweet girl,' he said in a whisper.

The smell of the woods was on Gabriel, a pleasant leafy earthiness, but beneath that there was a bitter scent, and in this confined and airless space it was growing stronger.

Louise ran her hands over his cape, and found the leather jerkin beneath. With unsteady fingers, she unhooked the fastenings and revealed a shirt blooming with blood. She looked up in alarm. Wat was standing apart, at the doorway.

'We need fresh bindings,' she said sharply. 'His arm is bleeding badly.' Wat turned, saw the blood, and was at her side at once.

'We didnae do that, surely?' He looked appalled.

Louise shook her head. 'He took this at Flodden. It refuses to knit, but our desperate long journey here has not helped.'

With a frown, Wat took charge, as if care of the injured was his trade. Louise watched as he untied Gabriel's hands, stripped off his clothes and swabbed his arm. The well-meaning touch of the Borderer, as he wound lint tight over the weeping flesh, brought the courtier close to a swoon. By the time Wat had finished, Gabriel was weak as a suckling wean and the floor was strewn with blood-crusted old wrappings.

Wat left to find a fresh shirt, and Louise hurried to his side. It took an effort for Gabriel to speak, but he clasped her hand again and fleetingly brought his lips to it. 'Fret not, sweetness. I only need sleep, and my wound will quickly heal. My headache too, no doubt. Once I am on my feet, we can leave here. We will find Benoit, never you fear.'

'These men are brigands and thieves,' Louise whispered. 'What do they want with us?'

'God alone knows,' said Gabriel, and closed his eyes, as if the question was the cause of all his pain.

Before he could say another word, he was asleep, as if once more hit by a cosh. Wat arrived in the doorway, a clean chemise in his hand. He stared down at his patient, an almost maternal expression sitting oddly on a face composed of hard deeds. 'A good sleep, and he'll be back to his troublesome self, don't you worry, hen.'

Louise got to her feet and swayed as a wave of exhaustion hit her. 'What have you done with the boy?' she asked.

'He's with the horses in the stables. Couldnae keep him away. The bridle-boys will no doubt find him a berth, and some fodder.' Louise nodded. There was a hand at her elbow, which she recognised as the grip of a woman, though she was too weary to turn and find out who. She gave a last glance at Gabriel, sleeping softly as if in his own bed, and then found herself being guided up the corridor and into a small chamber where a bed piled with furs lay ready. Not unkindly, the woman told her to sleep, and the door creaked shut, but not before the vixen had slipped in.

As the woman's footsteps faded, Louise lifted the vixen onto the furs beside her, and got under the covers. Her last thought, as she tipped into darkness, was that even the wolfskins in this place smelled of pine. The sharp scent of resin was soothing, and despite the terrors of the past few hours, she fell not into nightmares but to untroubled dreams.

*   *   *

There was no sleep for Crozier and his men. Their only comfort was a jug of strong ale, and new-baked bread from the oven. Huddled over a table in the warmth of the low, vaulted kitchen, they spoke quietly. The presence of strangers in the keep was a reminder that there were enemies close at hand.

'It's as bad as we feared,' said Crozier, tossing the messenger's letter on the table. 'Dacre is acting on the orders of Surrey, Henry's lieutenant. This is a death warrant, sent from the weasel warden to King James's widow in Holyrood. It offers certain terms. It tries – ' here he averted his head as if to spit, but composed himself by taking a deep breath. He turned back to his comrades: 'it tries, would you believe, to forge an alliance between the English king and his sister against all our people. God rot him.'

'Whit in the name of God is a wee clan like us supposed to have done?' asked Wat.

'No jist us you fool,' said Murdo, 'he's referring to the entire Borders folk.'

'Aye,' said Crozier. 'All of us. Elliots, Armstrongs, Kerrs, Scotts, every good man, and every evil bastard this side of the border. And not just them, but their women and children, their cattle and sheep.'

'But they're no oor people . . . ' began Wat in outrage. A look from Crozier silenced him, and he bowed his head.

'What he says is this.' Crozier picked up the letter: ' "If it please Your Majesty, grieving relict of James IV, erstwhile King of the Scottish isles, to take matters into her own hands, His Highness Henry VIII, your loving kin, would be agreeable. You may find it to your advantage, indeed, in the matter of claiming the dowry for which you have for so long and importunately petitioned your most patient and generous brother to deliver.

' "All I ask is that your men find and annihilate the culprits for the dastardly and unchristian deeds committed at Flodden upon the bodies, quick and dead, of our gallant English warriors. Atrocities, we are told, that were committed upon the Queen's own noble troops as well as our own.

' "For these acts of barbary, we demand swift justice. We feel certain your views will concur with ours in this matter. The Borderers are carrion. We want them snared, and their necks wrung. Produce the severed heads of the ringleaders for me to inspect, at the next assize at Berwick Castle, and we shall consider the matter dealt with. Failure to do so will mean that as His Royal Highness's senior envoy of the marches, I shall have no option but to ride into your borderlands and mete out retribution. During any such reprisals it would be unfortunate but also un-avoidable if many innocents – babes, women and ancients – were also to lose their lives." '

Crozier laid down the paper, and drained his tankard. His hand was steady, but his heart was not.

'She'll never agree!' said young Tom Crozier, eyes alight as the prospect of mortal danger drew closer. 'He writes to her as if she is chattel.'

'That is his plan,' said Crozier. 'He hopes to belittle her into agreeing to act with him, to scare her with a reminder of how little power and comradeship she can muster. With James gone, and most of the court with him, she has few advisors to turn to, and barely a man at arms to protect her and her child. Surrey's men could walk into Edinburgh today and take the country as if it were a plum ripe for plucking. Who could stop them?'

'They do say Patrick Paniter got out alive from behind the thunderin culverins,' said Magnus. 'He's a sharp mind, if ever there was.'

'Gone mad, is what I hear,' said Bertie Main from the

end of the table, a seasoned skirmisher in charge of the scouts Crozier had sent out across the shire. 'Lost his mind. No use to woman or beast.'

'Dacre's a two-faced cur,' said Murdo, taking the letter out of Crozier's hand and squinting at the imperious hand racing across its page for all the world as if he were able to read. 'One day he's all matey wi' Jamie, taking his hospitality, playing wi' the queen's wean. Then, as soon as she is alone and friendless, he's taunting her. Whit a gentleman.' As he toyed with the vellum, he smiled, a faraway look in his eyes.

'What's amusing you?' asked Crozier.

'Ach,' he replied, 'I jist recalled how easy it once wis to rile the English court. Remember the Bartons' trick wi' yon English pirates? Sent their heads to Henry Lard-Arse buried in kegs of salt. They say the king didnae eat for a week after the sight o' them.'

'The smell mair like,' began Tom. 'Imagine the jellied eyes . . .'

'Enough!' barked his brother. 'This is a deadly business. It's no time for stories. We need a plan.' He turned to his cousin, a man broad and solid as a church bell. 'Magnus, when's the next assize?'

'The final Thursday of the quarter, sir. Last day of this month, in fact.'

Crozier calculated. 'If the queen misses Dacre's deadline, or refuses the deal, as we can only pray she will, the warden and his crony Surrey will set in motion their own plans. It might be fair to assume, then, that we have until All Hallows' Eve before all hell descends.'

Tom raised his hand, unusually meek after his reprimand. Crozier nodded.

'But this letter isn't going to reach the queen, is it?' he said, looking around the table. 'Not if we've got it. Do we pass it on to her? What'll she do when she knows we've intercepted it? Isn't that a treasonable offence?'

'Surrey will have sent it three different ways, or more,' said Crozier. 'One of these will reach her – it may indeed already be in her hands.'

Bertie Main nodded. 'That's why we sent scouts out on the bridle paths, and tae the coast an all, as well as the main road frae England. These divils are like ferrets; they can get through any net.'

'But it would be as well, and not just for us, to find out what action she decides to take, would it not?' said Old Crozier, who had been silent till now, crumbling a piece of breadcrust into a fine dust in which he stirred a crooked finger.

'Happens you're right,' said Crozier, whose hawkish features he had inherited from his grandfather as well as his shrewd mind. 'If she agreed to hunt the ringleaders – let's just call them scapegoats and have done with it, we know the real culprits will evade the rope – it would be a better result for the border. In the short term, at least. It might mean she'd lost her wits, but there is no queen on God's earth who would torch the lands of her subjects and kill wantonly without reason.' He paused, before adding, 'Is there?'

Tiredness tricked Crozier into a rare moment of doubt, but in that lonely hour not one of the men gathered under the hissing crusie lamps had any confidence in their over-lords, especially not when, as in this instance, their liege was the husbandless sister of the country's most implacable foe. Once a regent had taken charge the situation might feel less precarious, though the Croziers put no faith in any authority, least of all the crown. For the moment it was troubling enough that Margaret, a grieving, vulnerable young widow, held the reins of the kingdom. There was silence, as the clan considered what was coming their way. The thick walls and sheer battlements of this hilltop tower felt flimsy as mud and straw in the face of the forces that might descend upon them. Fearless as they were, each felt a flicker of unease.

Crozier scraped back his chair and rubbed his cropped head as if to sharpen his wits. 'This is what we'll do,' he said. 'Bertie will send another scout to Edinburgh, and get him close to the palace quarters. He can report back when or if he hears news of the widow's response.'

'I have jist the lad for it,' said Bertie. 'He's winching wi' a servant in the Canongate, close by the palace, though not much good'll come of that pairing, I rue.'

Crozier continued. 'Our other scouts are to be recalled, to report here by noon two days hence. They must spread the news across the Borders of what is being planned. We need to inform the heads of the clans.'

'Even the Elliots?' asked Tom. 'They're in the king's protection, or so you've always told me. They can't be in danger, not like the rest of us.'

'Even the Elliots,' said Crozier, 'though it pains me. They may have fought at Flodden, but when vengeance comes to the Borders, the vermin and the valiant are as one. We owe it to them.'

'Are ye aff yer heid?' Wat was on his feet, toppling his empty tankard as he slammed the table with his fist. 'They are our mortal enemies. They murdered yer faither, destroyed our land, and stole our beasts. If it werenae for them, Crozier's Keep would still be the pride of Teviotdale, and we lot wid be chiefs o' the march.'

Crozier shook his head, a gesture so sorrowful that Wat fell silent. Breathing hard, he looked down at the young man in disbelief. After a long silence, he picked up his overturned chair. 'I dinnae ken, I jist dinnae ken,' he muttered, taking his place at the table. Crozier pushed the jug of ale towards him.

'We have our own codes in these parts, we all know that,' the Borderer continued. 'My father always said he'd rather be a galley slave than be in the king's pay. But some of the clans fought at Flodden, and that was their choice. If they can sleep at night, that's their affair.

'All I know is that honour comes higher than revenge. The good and noble name of the Croziers depends on us warning our neighbours. I have no more love for the Elliots than any of you – or the Beatties or Humes or Douglases for that matter.'

He passed a hand over his beard, and in the hush of the vault the rasp sounded like a whetted knife. 'But let's not forget that our family has helped make its own misfortune. The Elliot knaves are no worse than many others. It's my certain belief that Dacre paid Ethan Elliot to kill my father, and destroy the rest of us. One day I intend to find out the truth of that. One way or another, whoever is to blame will pay. That day will be sweet.'

He sighed. 'But that is for the future. Right now, we face the greatest threat of our lives.' He looked around the group, at these wild riders of the valleys and moors. Threadbare and underfed, in the feeble lamplight their eyes were dark and mysterious, their shameful raggedness hidden. Crozier felt a tug of respect for his men, an affection no exasperation could quench. He had been brought up on tales of their courage, and that of their forebears, but it was only since his father's death that their mettle had been truly tested. Those fallen on hard times, with no money, and no influence, needed stout hearts to survive. His kinsmen, gossips and braggers and woolly-witted as they were, had nerves to match their steel helmets and ideals that needed only a little stoking to glow as bright.

Crozier cleared his throat. 'Too many folks in these parts live by treachery and lies. God knows we're not innocent ourselves. But this I say to you: I would rather my worst enemy in the marches evaded the royal sword than that I did nothing to warn those who have never done us any harm, or have given us friendship.' He splashed ale into his mug, threw it back in a gulp, and surveyed his men with a bitter eye.

'The Borders are our kingdom, not the crown's. Here we're masters of our own affairs, not the serfs of any lord or monarch. I, for one, would rather die than submit to their rule, or put their needs ahead of the life of a single Borderer.'

The table came alive to the thumping of tankards on the polished pine, and the kitchen maid was summoned to pull another jug of ale, and set some broth on the fire. By the time a lazy sun had crawled above the treetops, the men of Crozier's Keep had forgotten their fatigue, and were back at business, sharpening knives, polishing scabbards, and preparing their horses' tack.

CHAPTER TWELVE

7 October 1513

Goodwife Black was weary of answering the door to the secretary's house. It thudded so often these days, it might have been an archer's target. Better she flung it wide open at the start of day and pinned an arrow to the wall pointing to her master's chambers, for all to follow. That way she could get on with her work.

There seemed no end to the visitors, most of them from the court, or lords of the shires, all seeking guidance in these rudderless times. Yet at least she no longer need turn them away. Patrick Paniter appeared to be recovering his wits. By morning, he spoke with his guests, by afternoon wrote letters, as if paper cost as little as ale. At night he ate well, and in bed he dreamed more peacefully, holding her less like a drowning soul clinging to a buoy, and more as a man with his love. Even so, her ribs were a perpetual ache, as was her heart. There was a blankness still in Paniter's eyes that made her wonder what fresh trouble awaited. Almost a month since his return, and he had yet to say a word about what he had witnessed on the battlefield. There was a quality to his silence on this subject which made her wonder if he ever would.

That morning, however, all seemed well. He dressed himself with more than usual care. Other than a plain linen shirt, his garb was black. It was an outfit that made him look more like a priest than a counsellor of the court, but by this he wished to signal to the world that he, and the country, had suffered a great and smothering loss. Only the glinting of his rings suggested a spark of returning life. Slapping his housewife's backside and planting a kiss on her cheek, he left. His shoes clipped the stairs as he hurried out, a leather purse under his arm in which he carried the papers he had been writing late into the night. A velvet chapeau sat on his untied hair, like a cat crouching on a chimney pot.

He was headed for the palace of Holyroodhouse, where the widow's counsellors were waiting. The day was fresh, an easterly wind bringing a taste of winter from the north sea, its icy touch chapping his bloodless face. His steps beat on down the high street, and for a moment, as he looked across the city to the sea beyond, his spirits lifted. It was impossible on such a morning not to acknowledge the joy of being alive, to feel one's strength returning, and with it the self-confidence he had once taken for granted. Even the news that the *Michael* had run aground in a storm, and neither she nor the rest of the fleet had reached France in time to join the fight, did not dent his mood. Grief, like defeat, was a sore that would eventually heal. He was not so foolish as to expect it would fade fast, but today he had the first glimmering of hope that the weight of despondency he had been carrying was lightening, just a little.

It was he who had called this meeting. The newly crowned James V was barely out of swaddling, taking his first steps in the safety of Stirling Castle. The coronation had been dismal, more like a wake than a day of anointing, and the memory of it was raw. The little boy had been dressed in brilliant velvets and silks, but the rest of the party wore black, soaking up the light and casting shadows deep as gloom. As the solemn words of kingship were intoned over the child's head, his mother burst out weeping. Distressed, the boy set up a wail. Not even the sight of new toys brought for his amusement could console him, because he had been told he could not touch them until the proceedings, the speeches, the never-ending fuss, was over.

There was none present that day who did not feel as miserable as young James. For his part, Paniter spoke barely a word, his throat aching with tears he dare not spill. He and the queen conferred that evening, but he could recall nothing of what was said, remembering only his throbbing head and the overwhelming desire to get back home and bolt his door.

In the days that followed, Margaret dispatched a sheaf of letters to her family and advisors, but she had not sent a single word to her brother, whom she blamed for her husband's death. Wan and thin, she was queasy with a bairn so newly conceived it must have come into port in the days or hours before James had left for the campaign. God willing this one would thrive, as her short-lived last had not.

In his weeks of self-imposed isolation, Paniter had responded to no-one from the court except the queen. Her letters, smudged with tears and ink, had gathered on his table, a deepening drift of questions, fears and orders, each more anxious and confused than the last. Even in his misery, he could not neglect her, and he found himself replying in a tone of consolation and encouragement, very unlike the formal, cold diplomat of earlier times.

Margaret had been appointed regent in her husband's will, but she knew that scarcely before James's last testament had been opened and read, half the privy council, and most of Scotland's remaining lords, deplored this decision. It was enough, they said, that she was the child's mother. What did she know of running a country? Worse still, as Henry VIII's sister, could she be trusted? With these and other questions, nobles were jostling to claim this most powerful role. No wonder the queen felt alarm.

It was Paniter's duty, he felt, to bring the privy council to a firm, irrevocable endorsement of Margaret's regency, and quash all thoughts of challenge. He sighed. It would be a long meeting, and no doubt unruly, as the dead king's will was queried, and his widow's rights debated. Such talks could turn violent, with fists raised as well as voices, but Paniter, who was bred to the debating chamber like a pit pony that's known nothing but the mine shaft, was not daunted.

At the palace, guards were posted like candlesticks on the walls and stood at every gate. He took the narrow staircase up to the inner chamber, where the council was to meet. The way was narrow so no sword could ever be drawn. His shoulders brushed the walls, and the stairs creaked beneath his weight, but the sound was lost beneath the voices that reached him, as the queen's advisors took their seats ahead of the meeting.

Paniter's steps slowed, and came to a halt. The door of

the council chamber was ajar, and he could see the silk sleeve of one lord, the boots and spurs of another. Their voices were low, but urgent. His breath came roughly, and his head began to spin. He put a hand on the wall, waiting for the weakness to pass. Instead, the dizziness started to roar around his head, and he was back on Flodden Hill, the conversation around him not that of the court's council but of James's advisors, the night before battle. And of those who spoke, he had been loudest.

'You fool!' he roared. 'You must think we are knaves, to ask us to pick them off like flies as they cross the plain. You insult your king by even suggesting it. There will be no battle, let me tell you, until we face them, eye to eye.'

James put out a hand to quieten him. 'Enough, Paddy. Let the man speak.'

Robert Borthwick, the master meltar, passed his helmet from hand to hand as he faced the king's lordly retinue. It was early evening. Flodden Hill was already dusky with driving rain and a clinging mist out of which the sounds of the English army passing almost beneath their noses chimed and jingled and sighed so loud it might have been a hand's reach away. No-one spoke as, from their high vantage point, they watched the smoky shadow of Surrey's troops move steadily across the fields below.

'It would appear they are headed for the Merse,' said James, almost absently. 'I do believe the old war wolf has lost his taste for battle.' The relief in his voice was heard by all.

'But Your Majesty,' said Borthwick who, with Paniter was in command of the artillery, 'this is our time. If we fire on them now, the victory is ours. They wouldnae be able to withstand it.' He pointed to the ridge of the hill where his ironmongery stood, barrels trained on the enemy as if they were the fingers of a vengeful god. The guns had been dragged into position some days past by cattle who would never walk easily again. Now they were embedded, wheels sunk deep in the soil, like the rocks around them. 'See yon,' continued Borthwick, 'the cannon are primed and ready. They'd make mince of them. We've enough ammunition for twice the army they've got.'

Paniter could not restrain himself. He stepped forward and knocked the helmet from Borthwick's hand. 'Coward!' he hissed. As Borthwick stooped to retrieve his helmet, the secretary raised his boot, but before he could kick him into the grass, he was dragged off by a stronger hand than his own. 'By God, you may be right, but you cannot treat him like a serf.' It was Alexander, James's son. 'He may deserve a beating, but that is not for us to decide.' Paniter was panting with fury. He swept his pupil's hand off his arm, but before he could speak, another voice was raised.

'I agree with the gunner. His proposition is entirely sensible, en effet très intélligente, et juste.' It was De La Mothe, the French ambassador, and he caught the king's attention. 'Your Majesty,' he said, with a bow, 'what this man says is commonsense. It is not unchivalrous. Our army has been positioned on this hill for days. Surrey knows you wish to meet him. That he walks his men past us in this manner is not only insolence but provocation. Does he really expect we will not fire a shot? In my country we are sticklers for manners, for obeying the rules of good behaviour, but in this instance, to do as the gunner says is entirely within the laws of war. I endorse the idea. Vraiment, I applaud it.'

There was a murmur of agreement around him. The lords of the council pressed in on each other, their cloaks and helmets black with water, their eyes bright with the thought of battle.

'I am with De La Mothe and Borthwick,' came the soft voice of Argyll, whose whisper hid a constitution and soul of steel. 'Let's make a beginning, the sooner to make an end of this.'

'Aye,' said Huntly. 'We've got them in our sights. Give the order, Your Highness. Our men can be ready to charge at a moment's notice, and they are chafing to fight.'

'Added to which,' said Patrick Lindsay, 'the gunners' contract ends tomorrow. We have them only for one more day.'

Huntly nodded. 'They'll start leaving, soon as the money runs out.'

James turned from them, and stared out across the plain. Below, the English snaked their way north. It was too tempting to turn the guns on them. At this hour, in this light, they were an easy target: defenceless, tired and unprepared. Not for the first time on this campaign he brooded on his mother's caution: 'Nothing achieved by violence, be certain, can endure.' He had grasped her hand as she spoke. She was dying, and the advice was urgent. In that moment, haunted by the foretaste of her loss, he had promised to cherish her words. He did not believe that battle counted as violence, not of the sort she had meant. But he suspected that picking off Surrey and his men when their backs were turned most certainly would.

He faced his men. 'No,' he said, very quietly. 'Paddy is right. It is an act of cowardice. Whether Surrey is abandoning the fight, as I suspect, or whether he is merely taking up a new position, I will not have this army's good name ruined by outlaw tactics.' He looked at De La Mothe. 'I mean no offence, monseigneur, but Scottish rules are my only guide. I have much reason to be grateful to you for your help already on this march, and I would not wish to lose your friendship and counsel, but in this instance, we must disagree.' De La Mothe raised a hand in gracious defeat, and with a lace handkerchief wiped a drop from his nose.

The Scottish lords swayed in the rain and mist, dejected and cold. 'But take heart, good fellows,' said their king. 'Now we eat. In the morning, we will make fresh plans.' He clapped his hands, and with heavy steps they dispersed to their ranks and the best meal the army's cooks could offer from their dwindling stores of dried meat and biscuit.

That night James, his son and Paniter dined together. Little was said, but in the press of the king's hand on his shoulder as he left the pavilion, Paniter was assured of his sovereign's trust. On almost every matter of importance, they agreed. And where not, Paniter's advice was often accepted. Now, in hindsight, he cursed his wicked, persuasive tongue. Had he been known for a fool, it would have been far better for his country, and his king. Instead, both in that evening's work, and the next day, he had, he believed, tied the noose around the army's neck. But not his own. Not his own. And that was hardest of all to live with.

That council had gathered again the next day, and soon the previous night's disagreement was to seem like childish prattle. On the morning of 9 September, under ceaseless rain and mist, day broke late and without conviction. When the air cleared, a brief opening of shutters that would part and close throughout the day as if worked by a mischievous maid, the king and his men gathered on the hillside to look out on a field that might have been designed by the devil himself.

'Saints and sinners,' swore Argyll, putting a hand to his sword. As they took in the scene, the others were quiet. They shifted uneasily, sheep scenting a fox's musk in the wind.

'So he has decided to fight after all,' said Lindsay. There was a muttering of oaths. James's face was grim. 'That is a damnable position. He has cut us off from Scotland.' He ground a gloved fist into his hand. 'How could I have ever thought they were in retreat? That man was raised on the smell of blood.'

Before them, the English army was stationed on the valley side across the River Till. In the dark, the night before, they had somehow navigated their way across the swamps, and were now ranged on a low ridge on the edge of Branxton village. By day, their numbers looked daunting. This was not the ragged and underfed army their scouts had led them to expect. Red and white flags whipped in the rain, the crimson presaging the carnage to come. Horses and guns stood at the rear, and the sturdy bills of the tightly packed infantry were tall and proud as a field of black wheat. There could be no doubt. Surrey was waiting for James and his men. The challenge could not be more clear, or immediate.

James's face was ashen, but though there was fear in his eyes, there was also exhilaration. At last, the day of reckoning was upon them. This man who had spent years preparing for showdown, for putting Henry in his place and trapping the English bully between himself and the French king's forces, was ready. He brightened as he led his men back into his tent.

Under the sodden canvas their breath created a sour fug, testimony to a month on the road with little fresh food, and too much salt meat and wine. James removed his helmet, and faced them. 'My lords, our position here is secure. Impregnable. Surrey must bring the battle to us, if he wishes to engage. He has known this past week where we are encamped, and if he feels obliged to enter the engagement as agreed, he knows what he must do.'

'But, Your Highness,' said a voice from the back of the group – it was Lord Herries – 'Surrey need do nothing, and still he might win. The date means nothing to him. His position is clever. His army is small, but far fresher than ours, and as of today it cuts us off from the border. We have no line of retreat. And should you decide to play a waiting game, our supplies are likewise strangled. There is a limit to what we can pillage from this region, while waiting to go to war.'

'Aye, and a limit to what our men will tolerate too,' murmured Argyll. 'By next week, I warrant many foot soldiers will have turned tail. And as we said last night, the gunners are paid only until tomorrow. Thereafter, we will be relying on goodwill and . . .'

'And that has all but evaporated,' growled Paniter. 'They are hungry, and tired, and many are ailing. Most thought the sack of Norham was sufficient prize. Now, they have had enough. Your Majesty, I urge you to change tactics. We must engage at once.'

James ran a hand through his hair. It fell in girlish waves around his shoulders, but there was nothing soft about his expression. He turned to Borthwick. 'Can we relocate two miles immediately, and still get the guns ready for action today?'

Borthwick hesitated, and it was Paniter who spoke. As he recalled that moment his stomach griped, and in the palace's cramped, airless staircase, he feared his bowels would open and flood onto the steps, visible evidence of his putrid conscience.

'Your Highness,' he said, coaxingly, the voice he had used when urging the king's son to remember his Latin conjugations, 'trust me. We have the finest weaponry in Europe. Borthwick's furnace has created an armoury that would be the envy of any king or general. With their deadly range – begad, they could almost reach the Roman wall, if they were turned that way! – and with the training of our French compatriots in how to wield their weapons, we gunmasters, and the entire army, are nigh on invincible.'

'That much I already know, sir,' said James. He turned a cold eye on his closest councillor, his dearest friend. 'What I must be told, and truthfully, is if it is possible to reposition these huge guns, at this late hour.'

Paniter raised his voice, sensing the decision was in his hands. 'We had some problems in getting the sakers and serpentines into place when we arrived, in finding their range. That we acknowledge.' He looked to Borthwick, who refused to meet his eye, but nodded. 'It's a question of simple mathematical calculation, and we have now mastered this. We have learned their reach, and their tricks.'

Why he had sounded so certain, he would never be able

to explain. Had he simply grown too used to his own voice? Had he turned into an arrogant, boasting windbag, over-sure of his opinions and his privileged position at the king's side, where his every word was listened to? In the bleak stretches of the many sleepless nights that lay ahead between that miserable hour and the day he died, Patrick Paniter would never be able to answer himself, let alone anyone else.

'And can we get them shifted alongside the troops?' The king sounded brisk.

There was an awkward pause. Rain drummed on the canvas. 'I think not, Your Majesty,' replied Borthwick at length. He rubbed his hands together, knuckles cracking. 'Given their weight, it's best they set off first. They will need a good head start.'

Young Alexander stepped forward. He had his father's gallant air, his courtly figure. 'Your Highness, Patrick is most likely correct. He knows what he talks about. And the rest of us, we are all wanting to engage. Waiting even a day longer will do a great deal more harm than moving our lines.'

James touched his hand to his son's golden head, but his expression did not change.

Lennox was next: 'The guns will be the first frightener, nae doubt about it, but it's the soldiers who will win or lose the day, and it makes not one whit ae difference if they descend from this hill, or that at Branxton. I say let's get on wi' it, and make the charge today.'

A heated discussion followed, more so each could have his say than to decry the growing consensus that moving hills was the only sensible option.

Still the king seemed unpersuaded. He raised the tent flap, and looked out on the sodden morning. 'It is most vexatious. We are trapped, and by our own good fortune. Damned if we do, and in worse peril if we don't.'

No-one said a word. The king seemed to address the elements, rather than the group. 'Branxton Hill will give us a good vantage point, but we will be late on the field, and our tactical advantage will have been utterly lost. Who would have thought that dotard would have been so wily?'

The blast of cold air raised goosebumps on the soldiers' arms. So too the king's iron voice when he turned to them: 'Well, we must make the best of our situation. And you, Paddy: I have put my faith in your wisdom more times than I care to remember, and you have never failed me. If you assure me the guns will be ready, I believe you.'

He put a hand on Borthwick's and Paniter's arms, as if about to join them in marriage. The injunction on them to mend their quarrel was clear. 'Your guns must be moved at once.'

Now he looked at the lords, each in turn: Huntly, Home, Argyll, Erroll, Crawford, Montrose, Lennox, Morton . . . the nation's finest fighters. 'When the bugle sounds, the priests will make their mass among the columns. Thereafter our men will follow close behind the guns: by rank and file as trained. We must be in position, fed and watered, by three hours after noon.'

He gave a thin smile. 'Our troops are the bravest a king could ever dream of calling his own. Each is worth ten of Surrey's scurvy pack. And with the backing of Master Borthwick's guns, we can, and will carry the day. This change of plan is an annoyance, but nothing more than a fleabite. We will look back on this parlay and smile, in years to come, at our fractious tempers and childish fears.'

There was a jangle of spurs as Patrick Lindsay parted the group and stood before the king. His timing was bad. James was charging his council up for war, and his interruption had broken the drumbeat as it rose to a crescendo.

'Your Highness, forgive me.' Lindsay bent his knee. 'In your orders you do not tell us what position you will take.'

James looked annoyed. 'I shall lead the charge from the central flank, of course.'

'You will lead?' Lindsay could not hide his horror.

'What else?' The king's words were scalding. 'You expect me to sit at the rear and polish my sword while all others risk their necks?'

'No. Well, perhaps . . . '

De La Mothe came to Lindsay's help. 'Prie dieu, votre majesté, I believe your servant asks that you do not place yourself in such grave danger.'

'Yes,' stammered Lindsay. 'That is precisely it. You most certainly cannot be in the vanguard. Who will otherwise command the troops? Who will have the oversight? Who can give orders?'

Several of the lords nodded in agreement – those, that is, who were positioned behind the king.

'Ye can be very sure the English general will be at the rear, that's a dirty fact,' growled Huntly.

'And rightly so,' said Lindsay quickly. 'There must be a commander at the helm, not in the fight. And,' – he crossed himself – 'Your Highness, were you to be slain, God forbid the very thought, what will befall Scotland? You owe it to your people to take care, to return unscathed. To lead the country in years to come.'

James looked at him, an odd twist to his mouth. 'Speak on,' he said, with ominous mildness.

'As I see it, Your Highness, the stakes today are too high to risk your life. Were you to go onto the battlefield, it would be like playing dice with a common gambler. You would fling your coin against his. The loss you risk is immeasurable, compared with what he stands to lose. And it might be his is a bad penny, yet he has been cunning enough to coax you to put all that's dear in jeopardy for the sake of one single, short game.'

'You speak in riddles, my man,' said James. 'Am I to understand you think I should not take the field? Set not even a boot upon it?' He smiled, like a hunter who has cornered his beast.

Lindsay, an unobservant man, as his wife would confirm, nodded eagerly: 'I do, Your Highness. I – and most others here I hazard – think it best if you were to watch the battle from another hill, where you will be safe. For if we lose you, we lose the whole realm of Scotland, and all its nobles and gentlemen. The . . . the commoner sort having fled in recent days from . . . from hunger . . . ' His words petered out as he saw, too late, his mistake.

The roar the king gave was heard across the valley. Soldiers paused in the act of strapping on their swords. Horses stamped, and birds rose from their trees.

'I will flay you for such insolence,' cried the king, drawing his sword. 'Who are you to tell me what to do? Am I a milksop, to watch my valiant men head into battle, but raise not even a finger? To sit a mile away, and know myself secure?' He advanced on Lindsay, who began to back away. 'As soon as we are home in Scotland, I will have you hanged above your own gate for this act of treason.' His lips glistened with rage.

'Father,' began Alexander, 'for God's sake calm yourself . . . ', but he went unheeded.

James descended on the unfortunate lord, whose back was now pressed to the canvas. 'You are unworthy of this army. I will have your lands confiscated and your title removed.' Before Lindsay could make his escape, the king had grasped him by the collar. Under his clutch, the lord's face began to purple. 'Fight from the rear, eh? What Stewart has ever done that? Lindsays perhaps. Oh yes, maybe that is the Lindsay creed. That may explain why you and your lickspittle kin have done so well for yourselves over the years. But me?'

Sheathing his sword, to everyone's relief, he took off his glove, and slapped it across the lord's face. The council gasped. He slapped one cheek, then the other, again, and again, and again. Lindsay looked close to fainting. It appeared as if only the king's stranglehold was keeping him upright.

Paniter was appalled. Never had he seen the king so angry. Never had he been afraid to intervene, but to do so would be to risk his own neck. Yet Lindsay's question was legitimate. It was not one Paniter would have dared raise alone: he knew too well James's love of the fight, his pride in his fearlessness, but never before had he, and his country, faced a challenge such as this.

In the past few months, the contempt with which James had treated any of his advisors who had cautioned against war had acted as a warning to all who might otherwise have raised doubts. On the subject of the English threat, and of his role among his troops, the ordinarily sweet-tempered king was terrifyingly sure and ferocious. Even so, Paniter had not once shirked challenging him, if his arguments were well prepared. Now, far, far too late, he cursed himself, and the council, for not discussing this privately between themselves weeks before now, when they might have come to a united front that even in this mood James would have been obliged to heed.

As it was, Lindsay was the scapegoat. The council looked on, embarrassed and afraid, until the king's fury spent itself. With a deep sigh, he released the lord, who could be heard choking as if he'd swallowed a bone, before falling to his knees. It was Paniter who helped him to his feet. 'Come, you need some air,' he said, ushering him out of the tent, and the king's sight. Once on the hillside Lindsay bent over, and was sick. Paniter left him to it.

Back in the pavilion, James was laughing, but there was no mirth in it. His colour was hectic, his eyes glittered, and for the first time since they had set out on this campaign, Paniter felt a flicker of doubt. Was James in his right mind? Were they all mad? What could they hope to win by this battle? The months of fighting talk, and the king's invincible sense of a destiny blessed by good fortune were nothing more than hope and superstition. What if they failed?

James approached him, and the secretary knew he had seen the uncertainty in his eyes. 'There is no place for the weak in this army,' said the king, loud enough to reach Lindsay beyond the tent, but the words cut Paniter to the quick. 'After today I will make it my duty to root out any such from our ranks. But right now, we have a battle to face. And face it we will, with the lions' hearts that can only be found in Scotland.' He summoned his vassal, standing sentry outside the pavilion, who entered with servants bearing trays of wine and goblets.

The circle around James stood straight, as he surveyed them. 'Lords, gentlemen, and trusted friends, we go out today in the name and under the cross of our Lord, whose will we are doing. Whatever the outcome, God will preserve our souls, now and forever more.'

He gave a great smile, and raised his cup. 'And now, a toast. To Courage. To Victory. To Scotland!'

The council echoed his cry. At the memory of the chinking silver, the peppery red wine and the brotherly back-slapping, Patrick Paniter staggered down the palace stairs and out into the courtyard. Tears drenched his shift, but he did not feel them. Nor did he observe the perplexed faces pressed to the privy council chamber's windows as he lurched his way out of the grounds, a black-sailed galleon caught in a rip-tide no-one else could see.

CHAPTER THIRTEEN

5 *October 1513*

A green light was playing on the walls when Louise woke. It was mid-morning, but the brightness of the day was filtered through the ivy that framed the window, entering the room in spangles of colour that shimmered and danced as if inviting her to join them. She sat up, jolted back to her senses. She was in a stranger's fortress, in a part of the country so unknown and wild, it might have been a foreign land.

The name Teviotdale came with the ring of swords and war cries. This fertile, gentle shire, twinned with its bleak and fearsome neighbour Liddesdale, was well known as the crucible of the Borders, a place where trouble bubbled and brewed as if on a bed of coals. After their initial assault, the clansmen had been, she admitted, unexpectedly civil and even kindly, but as Benoit had often told her, subterfuge and deception were a Borderer's prime arts. For all she knew, she and her companions were being held prisoner. No-one would ever know where they had gone. She recalled the story of a madwoman found wandering the streets of Leith, claiming that day to have found her way back, after an abduction twenty years before, by an apothecary who had needed a living creature on whom to experiment. People had scoffed, and the poor woman was despatched to the city hospice. Louise wished the memory had not swum back at this time.

Throwing off the wolfskin, she peered on tiptoe out of a window set in a wall so deep she could not reach the shutters. She saw a sea of early autumn leaves, and beyond it a sky the colour of tin. The smell of baking bread reached her, a reminder of ordinary matters that did much to improve her spirits. She and the boy had not eaten for almost a day, and the need for food overcame fear.

A warm, damp snout felt its way into her hand, and she crouched to pull the vixen close. The dog whimpered. Hair was matted to her ribs with blood, and she looked more bone than body, but her eyes were bright, and her tail thrashed like a landed trout. Louise looked around. There was a pitcher of water beside the bed, with linens for her face and hands. Gently she began to swab the blood off the mongrel. It was a slow task, as she avoided the cuts and bruises, but she suffered no more than a cautionary nip as she got close to the broken rib. By the time she had finished, the vixen looked almost presentable once more. Louise dropped a kiss on her nose.

Her thoughts turned to Gabriel, and she lifted a hand to her hair, still gritty with ash from her mother's fireside. In dismay, she felt the wadded shawls around her waist, forgotten in the previous day's events. With a tug she began to unwind the layers of fat from beneath her bodice, turning back the years, from middle-age to youth. With a fresh rag she washed her face, and, dipping her head into the pitcher, as best she could soaked the ash from her hair.

When Louise opened her door, the night guard was whistling his way down the stairs, like any retainer caught going about his business. She paid him no attention, so did not catch sight of the knife and sword attached to his belt, nor a nose reshaped by a hundred brawls. She had the impression only of a lumbering woodsman, burly under his wrap and leather bonnet. Heedless, she stepped over the castings of mud and leaf his boots had shed outside her door, the spoor of a sleepless minder.

The vixen limped behind her down the narrow stairs, too hungry to nose out the tantalising smells at every twist. A low rounded door at the end of a passage led to the main hall, as bright at this hour as it would ever be, and still little more than a smudge of shadow and lingering wood-smoke. Louise crossed the cavernous room beneath a pair of tapestries draped on the walls. They must once have been magnificent, but now their loom work was so dulled by age and dirt it was impossible to guess what their pictures conveyed, let alone their original colours.

By the fireside hung a collection of hunting horns, their polished shine a rebuke to the stains and neglect of the rest of the hall. They were within easy reach, and were clearly often in use.

She looked down into the kitchen. In the flame-lit dimness she saw a woman in a crimson wimple and guessed it was she who had seen her to bed the previous night. Her back was turned as she stirred the fire, and Louise hurried past, up the stairs and into the courtyard.

By day, the keep looked more forlorn and forbidding

than in the half light of dawn. Rain-sodden walls rose to a fearsome height, the dark stone pockmarked by shot and cruder missiles. The damage in parts was so severe it seemed as if ivy alone were holding it together. To new eyes, the tower and its crow-gabled turrets looked like a beggar's face, gap-toothed with decay. Rooks patrolling the battlements did nothing to soften its expression.

The hill-top air was cool, and Louise walked fast towards the stables, at the rear of the keep. Hob saw her approaching, and darted out. He said nothing about her overnight change in appearance, as if it was his experience that women's looks were as changeable as their moods, but put a hand in hers and led her towards the stalls. Hans had been fed his morning mash and was dozing, one foreleg bent. The smell of his newly-brushed coat was the scent of home, and Louise breathed deep, pressing her face to his mane. His night-long ride was evident in the way he stood, and she hoped sleep would be cure enough for that punishing race.

'Did you sleep?' she asked the boy, once they were outside.

'Nae trouble,' he replied. 'Ye're never snugger than in straw. They telt me you wis given a bed wi' a mattress, but I didnae believe them. No in a place like this – they'd have mair sense than that.'

'And have you eaten?'

'Aye,' he said, but with a wistful air suggesting a lack of plenty.

Louise put a hand on his shoulder and led him back to the keep, in search of food. They were crossing the yard when Crozier appeared, saddle over his arm, and scabbard scraping his boots.

He halted, puzzled. Louise stared back, but as she realised the source of his confusion, she reddened. She put a hand to her hair, to explain. 'My cap is drying. It was covered in soot. And I have washed the ashes out of my hair too,' she said. 'I couldn't bear it any longer.'

Crozier's eyes travelled over her, head to boot, and as understanding dawned he nodded. The sight of this slender young woman, copper hair falling around her shoulders unbound even by a ribbon, was hard to reconcile with the fierce matron who had barked at him the night before. Her appearance, in this grim setting, had taken him aback. With the exception of his mother and her shoddy servants, the keep rarely saw women, and never one such as this.

Crozier was not a man for romance. He had been catapulted into manhood early, but while he had taken on his father's obligations, and proved himself precocious as a leader, he was a mere beginner, and a slow one at that, in the subtler arts required of a grown man. Too shy and severe to engage the heart of any woman of his family's standing, he had for some time enjoyed a liaison with a lissom young seamstress in the village, whom he imagined he might one day, should time and events allow, make his wife.

In the meantime, she asked nothing, and gave herself willingly, whenever he rapped at her door. She was so undemanding, indeed, that he had of late suspected he was not her only guest, a rare flash of perception in a man unversed in such matters. That she lived alone, and unwed, was the least of the clues she dropped, but he was grateful for her company and the comfort she offered on his increasingly rare visits. The coins he left by her bed were a gift, not a toll, or so he told himself.

Louise watched, as Crozier's mind raced. She was unnerved by the blank look in his eyes. 'I needed a d . . . d . . . disguise,' she said, 'riding out alone as I was. I thought a fat old woman wouldn't be of any interest to anyone . . .'

How true, Crozier reflected. 'But now you feel safe to drop your guard,' he asked, 'in this nest of thieves and abductors?'

Louise's flush deepened. She could not admit to herself, let alone him, that she had not wanted Gabriel Torrance to see her in such a guise. At the thought of the injured man, she found her tongue.

'The boy and I must eat, and after that, we must do what we can for Gabriel, before making our departure.'

'You're not travelling with him?' Crozier sounded surprised. 'I thought you were a party. You seem to know him well.'

'Not well,' admitted Louise, aware she had been forward in showing her attachment to a man who was little more than a stranger. 'He came searching for me, at my mother's request. He is what you might call a family friend; certainly he has been kind to us. But no, we are not travelling with him. I must get on, whatever his plans.' Her eyes widened as a thought occurred: 'Perhaps we could leave him here to recover, and return for him when our journey's done?'

Crozier returned her look with a glance that was at best unfriendly, but felt more like contempt. 'You cannot leave, ma'am. Have some sense. You are in the Borderlands, in a time of ferocious danger. Even the woods around us might be thick with the enemy. I cannot let you set foot outside the keep on your own. And no . . . ' he raised a hand as the girl raised her chin, 'that does not mean I am holding you against your will. Your father, were he aware, would approve my sentiments, I am sure.'

Louise flinched.

'Deid, like mine,' said Hob, looking at his feet as his own memories returned.

'Forgive me,' said Crozier curtly, 'I did not know.'

The woman's pallor disturbed him. With an ungentle hand he took her elbow and guided her towards the keep. The resistance he met from that joint, a piece of bone and gristle one might have thought incapable of such self-expression, made him drop his hold at once.

'Perhaps I should have guessed you are fatherless,' he said, 'since you are reckless enough to be out on the road. In times like this, though, I need to know why you are abroad, and prepared to take such risks.'

Louise said nothing, and he softened his tone, replacing granite with gravel. 'But first, you must eat. The boy too. And,' looking down at the small dog padding at his spurs, 'no doubt this tyke needs a few scraps.'

As if she understood, the vixen gave a yelp. 'Looks as if she is recovering from her kicking,' said Crozier, in a voice warmer than Louise had yet heard. He bent to rub the mongrel's ears and in that moment made a friend, the first in many years, who did not care about his ramshackle manners or the uncouth company he kept.

Over barley bread and cheese, laid before them in silence by Crozier's darkling mother, Louise and Hob told their story. Louise began like a child reciting a lesson for a tutor dandling a tawse in his hand. Forced to reveal her family's business to a man like this, with as little choice as if he was holding a sword to her throat, she would offer him no more than the bare facts.

But in the telling, she found her resentment fading, determined only to make it clear why he must allow her to leave the keep. Caught up in her tale, her cheeks glowed. Glancing across the table, she caught, unguarded, a look of sympathy on the Borderer's face. She paused for a moment, and as she continued, her suspicion of him began to recede. It was a retreating tide that, after so violent a first encounter, would take time fully to ebb, but in that wordless exchange, chill grey eyes meeting summer green, they began to understand each other.

Hob had wolfed down his platter, and despatched a second serving by the time Louise reached the part of their story where she had found him on the moors. Like a fairground mummer, his mouth floury from Mother Crozier's bread, the boy started to prance around the kitchen, enacting the scene. His impression of the horse was particularly lively, but the orphan's ordeal was pitiful to hear. His refusal to be child-like in his misery, despite his extreme youth, touched the older man. Hob was far younger than Crozier had been when his father was killed, and there was a spirit about the boy that impressed him. Already, he seemed to be taking on the position of protector to this hot-headed young woman, who had no idea of the danger she might encounter in these parts – or any other, for that matter. She could have met with trouble in the backstreets of Edinburgh, let alone on the country's frontier. Such eldritch looks would bring her attention wherever she went.

'Now you understand,' Louise was saying, 'why I must

get to Flodden or Berwick. Every day counts. I can't . . . ' – she broke off, and swallowed – 'I can't bear to think of my brother in distress. Better, almost, that he is dead and beyond care than that he needs help and I sit here doing nothing.'

'I understand that, ma'am,' said Crozier, 'and I can imagine only too well what you and your family are suffering. But explain to me, if you can, how you come to be in tow with one of the dead king's men? That part eludes me. How do I know you are not part of some trick to inveigle the court's reporters into our ranks? They've long wanted our heads, and never more than now.'

Louise's reluctance to talk about her sister was evident, but Crozier was not a man to accept a half-truth or evasion. Hesitantly, under his hawk-like eyes, she spelled out Marguerite's relationship with James, and its mortal outcome. There had been a time when she would have bitten her lip till it bled rather than give a stranger the idea that the women in her family were open to free offers of love. Now, such prudery seemed ridiculous. Who cared what the world thought? What did it matter?

In the past few days, as she had brooded on her sister's plight, and found herself thinking too often, perhaps, of the king's courtier, she had had the first stirring of under-standing. Maybe love was more important than convention, and happiness to be grabbed, wherever it was found. As she had seen, joy could be fleeting, as was life itself. Even at nineteen, when Marguerite had caught James's eye, and the age Louise had reached now, the future could slip from one's fingers faster than an oily spoon.

As she spoke of her sister, Louise did not need to voice

her fury at the king, or his people. Crozier heard the anger in every word. As she described her meeting with the king's secretary, Patrick Paniter, it would have astonished that figurehead of the realm to know with what little respect this young woman regarded him and his kind. It was all the more telling, therefore, that her tone changed when she discussed the courtier, and his affiliation with Paniter.

'He is his companion, and advisor, I believe,' she said, scraping bread around her bowl, and avoiding Crozier's eye. 'A nobleman of small but good Irish family, living in the west of the country. He much prefers fields to the city.'

If she hoped to make Crozier recognise a kindred spirit in his prisoner, she failed. Innate mistrust of the crown coloured his view of any from that quarter, and the golden-haired Torrance, with his fine rings and diamond ear-stud, fell foul of that prejudice. He might be the most true and gallant soldier this side of York minster, but he would have a hard time persuading the Borderer of his credentials.

'He will not be fit for a time yet, anyway, to accompany you, even if you wished,' he said. 'Wat tells me he slept well, and has eaten this morning, but he needs more rest before he fully gets over his cracked head.'

'It looked bad, last night,' said Louise. 'His arm too. Will he recover?'

'Sure to,' said Crozier. 'He's strong, and his wound is not serious. I am willing for him to stay here while he recovers, but not' – he looked at her, unable to disguise the strength of his distaste – 'not a day longer. I am no friend of the court and its hangers-on.'

Louise nodded, aware that, even by this meagre dole of hospitality, he had stretched a principle as far as it would go. 'I am grateful to you,' she said, conscious as she spoke that the words would have been unthinkable a few hours earlier.

'As for your brother,' Crozier continued, 'perhaps I can help. Once I've spoken with a pair of young lads, who are just arrived from the coast and awaiting orders, I am going to Berwick, on my own business. While there, I will find out what I can about who lies in the cells.'

Louise cast him a warm look. He nodded, as if offering no more than a simple courtesy, but both knew that Berwick was hazardous, a nest of English soldiers and local informers, and nowhere more perilous than the castle and its gaol. It was not a place to linger, and adding the hunt for Benoit to his own search for information doubled the danger.

'First,' said Crozier, 'you must tell me everything about your brother that would help me find him. Remember, the place will be teeming, and in filth and rags everyone looks alike. Is there anything remarkable about him?'

Louise took her time, choosing her words carefully as she described Benoit's appearance, and his accent, his favourite words and his habits, as if in drawing a close and vivid portrait she was keeping him alive, and not just in her own mind.

Before leaving for Berwick, Crozier sliced the ropes from the courtier's wrists, and posted a permanent guard on his door. He reminded Wat that he was in charge of their high-born patient, and his well-being. 'No roughing up,' he said, 'unless he asks for it. I want him fit, and out of here, as soon as can be arranged.'

'And the other pair, the wifie and her boy?'

'They are house guests, and to be treated as such. But keep an eye on them, nonetheless.'

'It'll no be hard keeping track of yon laddie,' replied Wat. 'If there's a horse or cow in sight, he'll be at its side. He's already milked half the byre, wi'out a kick even from Bonnie, and ye ken whit wey she is wi' strangers.'

Crozier nodded, but already his thoughts were far from the keep. A few hours later, as dusk was falling, he caught up with them, his mare slowing to a walk as she reached the muddied tracks that led from the woods down to the river and sea where Berwick sat, a barnacle on the very border between England and Scotland.

*   *   *

Cupped between sea and river, with rich fields at her back, hers was so desirable a location that, like the Old Testament infant, Berwick was tugged this way and that between Scots and English, claimed by one and then the other over the years. Without King Solomon to make a final decision, the citizens scarcely knew who or where they were. To save unnecessary confusion they had long since retreated into a brooding taciturnity that took no sides, showed no favours, and made for a dour and fractious population.

The tussle had ended some time back with English victory, and for the past few decades the town had been paying its tithes and taxes into the House of Tudor's treasury. But the coins flowed both ways. This outpost was precious to the English crown, and so much money was poured into its ramparts and fortifications that by now it was as well defended as Jericho, a town encircled by its very own Hadrian's Wall, and even more fiercely policed.

In late afternoon, the sea was a darkening scowl behind the chimney smoke of the narrow, rugged streets. A sandstone fortress dominated the skyline, seeming to cast a shadow the length of the town. There was no missing the castle, crouching as if ready to attack, nor the bristling pikes of its sentries as they walked its walls in full fighting gear.

Crozier got off his horse and led her along the riverbank until he reached a common where she could graze. He preferred not to enter the city gates until it was dark, when he could pass himself off as an English farmer, arrived for the morning's market. He sipped aqua vitae from his flask, pulled his leather hood over his eyes, and waited for the sun to set.

The portcullis was raised, but the thickness of the town's walls reflected the depth of its guards' suspicions. Crozier produced a smeared and creased old document, stamped with the English march warden's seal, the only object he had stolen from Dacre's messenger's knapsack, beyond the letter he carried. In a spidery hand it testified to his name and profession – Dick Hawley, cattle-breeder on a small-holding near Wooler.

'Your business tonight?' asked the soldier, squinting to read the pass by a flickering torch. 'A stud bull,' said Crozier, in a voice none of his family would have recognised, not just for its cringing meekness, but for its southern lilt. 'I had hopes of finding one the mornin to drive hamewards, ahead of winter. The dams need a good sire, since the last yin died of the bloody flux. I'm keen on a Galloway, but I'd settle for a longhorn, or mibbe even a Swiss Brown.' Crozier drew his sleeve across his nose, and gave a mucous sniff.

Bored, the sentry waved him into the town. The mare's

hooves sounded thunderous in the low cave of the gateway, and her shoes struck a spark as she skittered, uneasy in such confinement. Crozier was relieved when they were out once more in the open street, away from the evilly curved blades on the soldier's billhook.

The town was noisy and jostling as tradesfolk touted for final scraps of business before curfew, and citizens scurried between booths and stalls, anxious at the approaching hour. In the wake of Flodden, the streets were to be cleared by eight. Only those with legitimate reason to be abroad were allowed to pass after that time, so that a garrison, apprehensive at its catch of felons from the late battle, and plain scared at the thought of retribution from the north, would not fear being taken by surprise.

Before the church bells tolled the hour, Crozier needed to find a bed. First, though, he made for a booth by the town cross where chestnuts were roasting on a bed of hot irons beneath a canvas canopy.

The owner nodded at his customer, and appeared to ignore him, beyond placing a twist of chestnuts in his hand, and receiving a grubby coin in return. Only the keenest eyes would have seen words exchanged, the Borderer's hood hiding his face, and the stall holder so practised in discretion he could speak with barely a twitch of his lips.

'Surprised to see you here at this time. Then again, maybe not, given the rumours flying around since yesterday. Are you needing a room for the night?' he asked.

'Aye.'

'Tap thrice and thrice and thrice again at the back door, and Bella will know it's you. You can sleep in the hayloft above the stable. Keep your voice down, and make no trouble, d'you hear? They'll put our heads on spikes if they find you.'

He dropped the coin in a hessian pouch around his belt, to which he continued to address himself. 'And thank the lord you are alone. Your little brother is too much even for me to handle.'

'God bless you, Oliver. I will repay you when things are better, and we're free to be family again.'

'And when will that be? Terrible times, these are. And worse coming, they say. You're risking your life out here, ye ken. Especially if you had aught to do with the warden's recent trouble.'

'Needs must,' said the Borderer, leading the mare on down the street, beyond the packmen and stalls, and the shouts of pie cooks and whelkers. As the chestnuts cooled, he fed them to his mare, holding tight to her halter to steady her as the town sloped sharply away towards the river mouth.

The hot-griddler and his wife lived in a stone cottage by the shore, where tide met freshwater. By day, oystercatchers picked their way over the mudflats, piping as they went, but in the dark only the cry of a solitary tern broke over the shush of deepening water, creeping in from the north sea.

Their house stood apart, lonely as its location. Its neighbours were little more than shacks and, set back as they were on the high shore road, seemed to shrink from this sturdy intruder who had no fear of tides and spray. Those needing a louse-free bed and hearty dinner, however, welcomed its wind-tight walls and wide fireplaces, its oak settles and fresh sawdust.

The mare was familiar with the path and tossed her

head, knowing the stable was near. As they approached the inn, lights warmed the night. The mare whinnied, and Crozier heard a fiddler scraping a reel as he led her to the stable yard and the inn's back door.

The smugglers' nine-beat knock was an all-but silent summons, but Bella was sharp of ear – of face and voice too. Wrapped in a shawl against the night, she slipped out of the door, and latched it quietly behind her. She hurried Crozier across the yard to the stable, and pointed him up the ladders to the loft. They were a good distance from the cottage, but she did not speak above a whisper.

'Rub your horse down and let her feed, and by then I'll be back with something for you to eat.' She handed him a blackened lamp, its light so weak it seemed bashful. She noted his look. 'An old watchman's crusie,' she said, 'the kind used to signal boats making a drop from the clifftops.'

She looked up into his yellow-lit face, her own a charcoal etching, so angled and lined it might have been a lesson in geometry. She was his mother's sister, but there was nothing in their looks that suggested they were kin. Martha was tall and handsome with generous features whose message was misleading. With her thin mouth and shrewish eyes, Bella was the kind one. Even as a child Crozier had recognised that.

He took her hard-worked hand in his. She looked anxious. 'We didn't think to see you this while, things being as they are. Sickening, the sights we've seen from Flodden field, wounded, wailing soldiers carted through the streets to the gaol, a pit dug for the dead they throw out each morning, and that not big enough. I've never known times so bad.' Her eyes narrowed as she attempted to read her nephew's expression. 'And it's trouble that's brought you, no doubt.'

Crozier nodded.

'Whole place is set about the ears,' said Bella, pulling her shawl closer, 'after the warden's man was flummoxed out on the moors. The soldiers are all feart there's a brigade of painted men from the north, just biding their time to slit their throats in the night. The townsfolk think their houses will be set alight while they sleep. Everyone's on watch.'

'Bella, it was me and my men who ambushed Dacre's messenger.'

She drew in her breath as if she'd been scalded.

'Dacre's threatened to raze the entire border,' he went on, 'but I know what kind of a man he is. We've humiliated him, and he'll want to make a special example of us. I need to find out what he's planning for us, and when.'

Bella stared. After a long silence she nodded. 'Mibbe I can help. You know the sort we get here. There's always one with a foot in the warden's door. I cannae abide them, but they're how we make our living. I'll see what I can do.'

Shaking her head she left, returning shortly with fish soup and a basket of barley cakes.

'Mind and stay quiet,' she said. 'We're right busy the night, and there's soldiers in there who'd love nothing better than to take you back to the gaol with a knife in your ribs. Your mother would never forgive me if I let that happen.'

'I'm here for only a couple of nights,' said Crozier. 'You're a fine, brave woman, helping like this. I won't forget it. Mother always said you were as stout as your brothers.'

'She's a blether,' she said, patting Crozier's cheek as if

he was still a boy, and she on a visit to her sister in her god-forsaken castle. 'The spit of your handsome father, you are,' she added, 'but a bit quieter and more sensible, thank God. I pray you last longer in this world.' With a sigh she was gone, back to her thirsty customers.

Crozier ate in the stall where his mare was tied, at the farthest end of the stable. The horses stamped and snorted as they settled. A long night lay ahead, but he was glad of the rest, the time to think. Climbing into the loft, he removed his spurs and sword, and stretched out on the straw. His dagger remained in his belt. Since his father's murder, he had never slept unarmed.

He had fallen into a doze when footsteps crossing the yard woke him. Voices approached the stable, and he raised his head. They had a ring of arrogance that denoted military training or a lordly background. When he caught the buttery vowels of the Borderlands, he knew they were soldiers.

'Naked, he were, and tied to his horse. They say he had frozen to his saddle, it were that cold a night, and they had to peel him off. Lost a lot of skin on his nether parts, as you might imagine.' The voice was a whine, gossipy and obsequious.

'He always was a fool, old Warrender,' said his companion, speaking like one accustomed to giving orders in the barrack room. 'He'd had a jar too many, is what I was told, and had been careering around the countryside, looking for an ale-house rather than doing his duty. It didn't need much cunning to find him.'

'But the men that did it, they must be fiendish sharp all the same,' replied the other. 'I hear it was the work of the Hermitage and its diabolical lords . . . '

'You hear altogether too much, if you ask me. You cling to the innkeeper's bar when you should be at your post. The Hermitage and its men are on the king's side, and never forget it. Elliot is one of King James's retinue, insomuch as any from that benighted part of the country can be said to be on anyone's side but their own, or the devil's. He is too wily to have anything to do with an act of lunacy such as that.'

'So who then?' asked the whine, as if hoping for a bedtime story, the sort to make shivers run down his spine.

'There's many that hates Dacre's guts, that's for sure. Whoever it was, Warrender knows full well because he carried a message direct from them. We will find out soon enough, when Dacre takes his revenge.'

'Oh yes,' said the whiner. 'Oh my goodness, yes. If there's anyone does revenge, it's his lordship. We all remember what he did with the Redpaths, when he imagined they'd crossed him, don't we?' Crozier could not tell if he heard or only imagined the man licking his lips.

The pair stopped at the stable door. 'We part company here,' said the superior. 'Make haste back to the garrison. The night air might sober you. I am headed in the other direction.' There was a rustling of hooves as the men entered and moved down the stalls. They untied their mounts, and led them into the yard. With a grunt and a belch the whiner, full-bellied with beer, heaved himself into the saddle. Wordless, the other rode off. Crozier marked the slow retreat of the barley-head by a series of diminishing hiccups.

*　　*　　*

It was not yet daybreak when he left the stable and made his way on foot into town. The inn's chimneys had not begun to smoke, and his aunt and her husband were still abed, their windows ajar, for the first sound of approaching trouble.

Wakening gulls cried high above him on their way out to sea as he took the beach road into town. The tide was coming in, and as the waves washed up to the path, his face grew clammy with brine. He pulled his hood lower, and was glad of it when he heard the rattle of a cart heading his way. He kept his head bowed, but in the gathering light he could make out a wide, swaying tumbril, pulled by an ox. In the box sat a hunched figure, so still he might have fallen asleep over the reins.

As the cart drew closer, so did an unearthly stench. It was a nightsoil man, carrying human slops away from the town to a cesspit far from the public nose. As the cart passed, Crozier saw the mounds of filth piled high, and was thankful, not for the first time, that he lived in the hills. The keep had its midden, but it was fragrant by comparison.

A short distance farther and another cart passed, with the same stinking load, and another after that. Behind them the castle loomed ghostly in the fading night, and he guessed that was where they had come from. One more cart appeared on the road, and made its wavering way to the shore, the ox straining at its task. A figure not much bigger than a child held the reins. As it drew close, Crozier stepped in its path. 'Stop there, I beg you,' he said, raising his hand. The driver stared, stupid, the reins still slack in his hand, and the cart rolled on. Crozier reached for the ox's bridle, and pulled it to a halt. The beast snorted, glad for respite.

Crozier felt in his pocket and produced a couple of coins. At the sound of them, the driver put away the stick he had picked up, and grew alert. He glared at the stranger. 'What's you wanting?'

'Information,' said Crozier. 'Are you come from the castle?'

'Why should ah tell yous that, man?'

'I am not your enemy, lad,' said Crozier, trying to hide his urgency. 'I mean you no harm.'

The driver chewed, as if at the cud.

'So do you deal with the gaol?' Crozier asked.

The driver shifted his wad to his other cheek, and paused before replying. Time in his world was infinite. 'Ah dae, reet enough. Putrid, it is.'

Crozier moved closer, and regretted it. The young man smelled as bad as he looked.

'I'm looking for a prisoner who might be lying there.'

'Haud on there, man. It's nae ma joab tae gang looking fir folks, ah've eneuch on ma haunds as it is, wi' the mucking oot.'

'Of course, I know that. And I'm not asking you to do anything, but get me into the castle.' He chinked the coins, and the young man's eyes fixed on his face.

'How much?'

'Five groats.'

The nightsoil man stretched out a hand, so black and grimed it was like a badge for his trade. Crozier dropped a couple of coins into it. 'The rest,' he said, 'when you've got me in there.'

'Ah've nae mair trips the morn. That's me finished.'

'What time do you start out again tonight?'

'When the bells ring three.'

A deal was struck, and to mark it, the driver shot a triumphant squirt of grass juice over his ox's head. It was not an assignation Crozier looked forward to. He hoped the day ahead would give him the facts he needed without recourse to the gaol's drain mucker.

Skulking around the town, like the shiftless farmer he pretended to be, he was drawn wherever there was a group, hoping to hear what was known of Dacre's plans. There was plenty of talk, but the Croziers' name was never raised. People were keener on adding colour to the story of the messenger's humiliation than on finding out who did it. From what he heard, Crozier realised that to these sheltered people, the Borderers were all as bad as each other, and it mattered not a whit who had done the deed. They could all be exterminated, and the Berwick folk would not lift a finger in protest.

More worryingly, it also seemed that Dacre was keeping his counsel, certainly from any who would bleat to commoners. Yet there could be no doubt that trouble was brewing. The streets were crowded with soldiers, and the castle gates and walls thrummed with life, carts wheeling in and out of the portcullis, and columns of soldiers marching back and forth at the gates, as if an air of frantic activity alone could ward off danger.

Crozier dared not get close to the castle for fear of raising suspicions, and had he even attempted to ask questions about the prisoners, the guard would have been summoned. Already his loitering, presumptuous ways had earned him suspicious looks, which only a slurring display of bon-homie to all mankind, and serving maids in particular, deflected. Aware of the growing risks he ran with each hour he lingered, he felt his pulse quicken. He took great pleasure in walking beneath the nose of the enemy. The thought that he might outwit them was almost worth the danger. His eyes gleamed. He was more like his father than his mother knew.

As he hung over the rails of the market, watching cattle and sheep whipped and sold under the eyes of red-cheeked farmers; as he supped in a tavern, and made a quart of ale last a lifetime; as he wandered the streets and tried to look purposeful, it seemed the day would never end. Finally, in what felt like a new month, the curfew tolled, and he slunk back to the stable. There he found his aunt, with a plate of mutton and herbs. As he slurped it down, she spoke, keeping her eye on the door.

'Oliver knows a man who works for Dacre. He's a bit of a sniveller, but he's got good reason for loathing him. Added to which he'd do anything for a week's free drink. Ollie had a quiet word with him this morning.' She wrung her hands. 'It's not good, Adam, they're coming for you.'

'When?' he asked, tipping the bowl up and draining the juice.

'All Hallows' Eve.'

'You're sure about that?'

'That's what the man said. He seemed very certain of the date, said Oliver. First you lot, then the rest, is what he told him. The widowed queen will have nothing to do with him, and he's taking matters into his own hands – as you said he would.'

'You're a good soul,' said Crozier, and gave her a hug. 'I'll be gone by the morning,' he added as she left. She raised a hand in goodbye, but did not turn.

In the chill early hours he made his way to the shore road, hiding himself behind the castle's buttresses. The young driver was the first out that morning. He slowed as Crozier stepped out, and without a word from either, the Borderer climbed into the foulest-smelling cart in Christendom.

Gates high as a church tower closed over them as the cart rolled into the belly of the castle. It was a steep decline, and the ox slithered on cobbles wet with slime. After the sentry's harsh salute, there was at first no sound beyond that of the wheels and hooves. But slowly, as they descended deeper, stone gave way to beaten earth. Crozier became aware of a thickening in the atmosphere, the sense of a denser presence than air alone. It took a moment to appreciate what was around him: the sound of a thousand men, breathing, gasping, and moaning in their sleep. The hairs on Crozier's neck prickled. It was as if they were in the gurgling stomach of a huge beast, like Jonah in the whale.

The cart drew to a halt. 'Git oot,' whispered the driver. Crozier scrambled over the side. The driver grabbed his shoulder, a hand reached down, and Crozier's coin was snapped shut in the young man's fist before his passenger could get his bearings. 'If ye need a ride oot, be here when the castle bells next ring. Otherwise, ye're on yer ain, and guid fortune tae ye.'

The cart rolled off, and by the time its creaking had faded, Crozier could make out shapes in the murk. A brazier high in the wall cast a rusty beam, but its reach was short. It illuminated enough, however, to reveal cells on every side, as far as the light reached, and no doubt much farther. As he approached the first grilled door, the prisoners' breathing grew louder. He paused. A pale hand gripped the bars, and deep-socketed eyes stared out.

'Bread,' said the inmate, reaching out talons.

'I have none,' said Crozier. 'I am sorry.'

The eyes closed, and Crozier drew closer. Behind the grille lay a stone vault, the floor a tangled skein of bodies. Some were sitting, knees drawn up, others lay their length. A few were asleep, and more were unconscious, but some were awake, staring dull-eyed into space. As he peered he felt their gaze lock onto him. The nightsoil cart had cloyed his senses, but he became aware of a different smell, bittering the air. It was the iron salt of blood and sweat, of filthy clothes, and mouths so parched they had swollen beyond speech.

He touched the fingers at the bars. 'I have nothing for you, God forgive me. But I need your help.' The eyes opened. 'I am looking for a soldier, from the Scottish army. Name of Benoit Brenier. French, but speaks like a Scotsman. A short, square man, with a face that is pitted from an old pox. His sister is desperate for news.'

The eyes flickered, and after what felt like an age the prisoner turned and spoke to the men behind him. A current of interest ran through the room, before ebbing. The man turned back.

'No,' he said in a rasping whisper. 'No-one of that name here.' He closed his eyes, and Crozier heard him swallow. The sound was close to a rattle, and they both knew his time was short.

Down the tunnel he went, from grille to grille, and

always the same reply. No Brenier known to any. At one door, the request startled a man awake so violently, he began screaming, a panic that set the wounded in all the cells groaning and girning. Crozier's jaw clenched. He was in the very bowels of hell, and could do nothing for these wretches. Some needed no more than a good meal and fresh air; others might recover if a surgeon with a clean knife could be found to pare away rotten flesh or saw off splintered bone. But for too many, life was seeping away by the hour. There was likely a cold logic to it: the longer the prison held onto them, the fewer the authorities had to deal with in the courts, and on the gallows.

Crozier felt sick. And as he proceeded down the passage, where the air grew warmer and riper, his head began to swim. The men he had spoken to were from all parts of Scotland and a few prisoners were French, no doubt deeply regretting their part in coaching the Scottish troops. Some had been here only since the battle, but a few had been locked up following Lord Hume's ill-judged raid across the border in August, when the English had surprised his cocksure, greedy men, who had been intent only on grabbing what they could for themselves. In what proved to be an omen for the following month's encounter, the English roundly routed them.

The figure at the next grille was more sinew than flesh, his rags as holed as lace, but his eyes were unclouded and his voice, though weak, was clear.

'Been in here over a year,' he told Crozier. 'A small personal matter between me and Lord Dacre that I doubt will end well. I don't expect to last another year. Not that I'd want to.'

Crozier repeated his description of Benoit, and the man shrugged.

'We might have the man you want,' he said and beckoned into the gloom.

Slowly the limbs on the floor parted as a figure stepped over them.

'Man here asking questions you might be able to answer, Ben,' said the grille-keeper.

Crozier strained to see who was approaching from the press of bodies. The form was as Louise had suggested – squat, sturdy, youthful – but when the face presented itself at the bars, he recoiled. The man had only one eye, the other hidden by a head-dress black with blood.

'Benoit?' asked Crozier, reaching a hand towards the maimed man. 'Are you Louise's brother?'

'What good'll it do me if I say yes?' asked the man, in a faint French accent.

Crozier blinked. 'Nothing. Nothing tonight, at least. Your sister needs to know you are alive. She is worried to death. And she has powerful friends who may be able to help you.'

The man spat, the spittle clearing the grille and landing at Crozier's feet. 'Fat use that is. There's no help for any of us in here. We either die in these pits, or they hang us. Or if they are feeling merciful, they might send us as slaves across the seas. What use can a woman be in these circumstances?'

Crozier hesitated before speaking. 'Have you any message for her I can take back? Any private signal that only she will know, to prove you are her brother?'

The man cleared his throat. 'You can piss off. You want secret passwords, like a child, and I want liberty and the sight back in my eye. I'm not playing your games. Tell my sister that the day she rides in here and blows the lock off this door, then I'll have something to say to her. Until then, wish her adieu, and kiss her pretty little cheek for me, and anything else that takes your fancy.'

He turned, and hobbled back across the cell. Crozier put a hand against the wall, to steady his thoughts. Was this Benoit?

The grille-keeper sidled back to his post. 'There's naught more kept down here,' he said. 'You've seen them all. There's the oubliette, but nobody gets to see those poor souls. Anyway, only the worst criminals are dropped in there.' He lowered his voice. 'Ben the lad, he's not right in the head now. None of us is. He's been a hireling soldier since he were a boy, and he'd hoped to be a free man by now. He has not taken kindly to his fate. He meant no harm by what he said.'

Crozier dug out his last coin, and pressed it into his hand. 'Get the warder to bring fresh food and drink for you and him and your companions,' he said. 'I thank you. And I pray for you.'

The prisoner's nails scratched his palm as he took the coin. He pressed his face against the bars, and his breath warmed Crozier's cheek: 'Tell folks up in the living world about us. It's like being buried alive down here. The worst is thinking you've been forgotten. We could die at peace if it weren't for that.'

'I will, my friend,' said the Borderer, keeping his voice steady with an effort. 'That at least I can do for you.'

CHAPTER FOURTEEN

8 October 1513

When Crozier reached the keep, day was fading. Smoke rose from the kitchen fires, deepening the dusk. He dismounted on the path that led to the gate, and filled his lungs with the scent of woodland. He walked briskly. He had ridden through relentless rain, but beneath his sodden cloak his hose and tunic dripped from the dousing he had taken in the river Tweed, as he scrubbed away the nightsoil cart's stench. No amount of water, though, could clear the gaol from his mind. He shivered, and rubbed his hands.

In the keep's yard he found his mother, arms folded. The bosses on her wimple quivered like the horns of an angered cow. 'A fine thing to do, laddie,' she said, 'leaving me these past days with two turtle doves from the city, and a boy with a stomach as deep as a well. If he is here much longer, I will need to bring out the salted beef.'

'It was necessary, mother,' he said. 'They'll be gone soon, believe me.' He led the mare to the water trough. 'Has the king's man got to his feet yet?'

'Yes, although the way he looks at that girl, he'd maybe prefer to be on his back a while longer.'

An expression of distaste crossed her son's face, but he said nothing as he made for the stables.

Hob emerged, a bristle brush in one hand, a half-eaten apple in the other. Since coming to the keep he had changed from a white-faced child to a ruddy, bright-eyed stable-boy. 'Evening, sir,' he said, looking at the horse and not the man. Crozier hesitated, then handed over the reins. 'Do you know how to rub her down?' he asked. 'She needs a good drubbing. It's been a long ride.'

Hob nodded, as he led her to her stall. 'I looked after my faither's cuddies and horses. I know one end frae the other.'

'I'll be back shortly,' said Crozier. 'See she gets a good feed too.'

'Aye, aye.'

In the great hall, Louise sat on the fireside's lip, the vixen at her feet. When she saw Crozier, she rose. The hounds raced to greet their master, but with a curt command he sent them back to their places. His face tightened at the scene. From a winged seat in front of the fire, the courtier eyed him. His arm dangled over the chair, his emerald ring brighter in the tallow-light than the narrowed eyes above them. A less prosaic man might have read a threat in the ease with which the stranger occupied his hearth. Crozier saw only insolence, the braggadocio of a royal fop whose tricks, in this place, were useless.

He addressed Louise, who had guessed the message from his weary step: 'Ma'am, I have no success to report. No-one matching your brother's description lies in the gaol. No-one, indeed, had heard of him, or knew him.'

Louise made a sound, and sat down again by the fire. She washed her hands in her lap. 'Nothing?' she said, 'No-one?'

Crozier moved towards her, but the courtier was faster. He was out of the chair and crouching beside the girl, a hand on her shoulder. 'This may be good news, dear heart,' he said. 'He may be well, and free.'

Crozier cut across him. 'Or he may be in Durham. That is where I'm told the fitter prisoners were taken. And I heard word, in the town, that the column Benoit fought with under Lord Home was the first to be despatched there, few of them though there were.'

Louise nodded, but her head was loud with racing thoughts. Durham was bad news. Healthy prisoners were for the scaffold, an example to the world. Her hands tumbled faster, until Gabriel covered them with his own. 'Be still,' he said, 'and keep faith. We will find him.'

He had said as much the day before, words of comfort now carved into her heart. That morning Wat had packed the courtier's head-dress tight with moss, and freshly bandaged his arm. After two days' rest and Mother Crozier's chicken broth, he was almost recovered. 'Reckon you can take a turn round the yard,' said his nurse. 'I'll be watching youse, mind.'

With a hand on Louise's shoulder to steady him, Gabriel stepped into the courtyard. He straightened his back, turned his face to the sky, and closed his eyes. Louise felt a sigh, almost a shudder, run through him. He was still for so long, she grew alarmed, and put a hand on his back.

'Sir, are you feeling quite well?'

'Hmm?' The courtier opened his eyes and looked down at her.

'Are you giddy?'

'By no means,' he said. 'A little light-headed, perhaps,

but strong, my sweet. I feel very strong, thanks to your care and kindness.'

'I have done nothing,' she said, her colour rising.

'You have helped me, and may yet help me, more than you will ever know.'

His smile wiped the harsh lines from his face, leaving a glimpse of the boy he had been not so many years before. Louise felt her pulse quicken. There was a gentleness about this man, despite his superior and self-important air, that made her want to know him better. Unlike most of the men she had met, he appeared to notice what other people were feeling. That he had ridden to the Borders in search of her, solely at her mother's request, suggested he was kind as well as sensitive. She could think of no other acquaintance who would have done as much.

'Come,' he said, 'let us walk. I have almost lost the use of my legs trapped as I've been in that wretched little cell. And I don't imagine you have been having a great time of it either, in this cold, benighted place.'

'They have been more hospitable than I expected . . . ' Louise began.

Gabriel laughed. 'Ah yes. The famous Border charm has been busy at work, I see. No, no, ' – he raised a hand, as if to ward off protestations. 'I like your open heart. You see the good in people. You draw it out, too. Me,' – he gave a rueful grimace – 'I trust no-one until they have earned it. They sense that, the way an animal smells fear. Our good host Crozier, for instance. His nose wrinkles like a hound on a fox's trail each time he sees me. He knows I understand what he and his men are up to. How they plot, and steal, and deceive.'

He squeezed her shoulder, to concede a point. 'They are not wholly bad, I grant you that, not entirely rotten. But their kindnesses would cease the minute it compromised their own plans, you can be very sure of that. And they are not honourable men in the sense we understand it. They have no allegiance to the king, or their country. They watch out only for themselves. To such people, we are as much the enemy as the English.'

Louise looked troubled. No-one could deny the Borderers had manhandled them cruelly when they were ambushed, and their behaviour had been outrageous. And yet, she did not see them as he did. Perhaps she was too trusting. Benoit often used to say she needed to learn that people were not always what they appeared to be.

Gabriel guided her towards the keep's gatehouse. 'Sit here for a while,' he said. The absent guard's seat was narrow and cold, with barely room for them both. The courtier's padded jerkin, with its puffed-up shoulders, the jut of his elbow in its sling, made for a tight squeeze. The closeness of this man, the rich linen scent of him, made her nervous. She could not meet his eyes, and stared at her filthy toecaps. Was this how Marguerite had felt when she was first alone with the king? She had spoken of the fluttering heart and lightness of head, of how, when James had first kissed her –

Her thoughts were broken as Gabriel drew breath with a hiss. She looked up. 'It's nothing,' he said, pressing a hand to his forehead, his eyes screwed tight. 'The merest twinge.' The pain subsided, and he relaxed. 'For all his many faults, that man Wat is a good physician. A few days more, and I will be fit. Then we can be away from here.'

There was silence as Louise weighed up her response. Sparrows twittered from their ivy redoubt by the gate. As children, she and Benoit had lain under hedgerows, still as sticks, watching these birds going about their domestic chores a hand's reach away, oblivious or unconcerned at their presence. Nesting time was best, when the chittering and fluttering were busiest. But even on quiet autumn days they were good company, their ceaseless chatter preferable by far to the roaring, reeling talk of Leith's boatmen that breached their shutters day and night, and made them long for the country.

The memory made Louise's eyes sting. When she replied, her voice was firmer than she felt.

'My lord, you have been an excellent friend to me, and my mother, but I must leave here long before that. Unless Crozier finds Benoit in the Berwick gaol, I have to go back to Flodden and pick up whatever news I can of him.'

Gabriel turned towards her, but she kept her gaze on the flagstones. A warm look would destroy her resolve.

'My child,' he said, taking her hand and pressing it between his, 'don't you think you stand a better chance of tracing your brother with my help? Two minds are better than one. As are two horses. And it's not safe in these parts for a military man, as we've already seen, let alone a defenceless young woman. Let's wait for Master Crozier's return. When we have his news, we will know better how to proceed. But be assured of this.' His voice grew grave, and he put a finger under her chin, turning her face towards him. At last she met his eyes. She searched their depths for something she could not name, nor find.

'Be assured,' he repeated, 'that finding your brother is,

from this moment, as important to me as it is to you. I will do everything in my power to help trace him, and give you the heart's ease you seek.'

Louise felt tears gathering, but before they could spill, the courtier bent, and pressed his mouth to hers. The sense of a protector was so longed for that thankful tears broke free. She raised her hand to touch his cheek, but by then he had released her, leaving his salt taste on her lips, and a memory that would keep her awake that night, and many more. He stood abruptly, and walked out of the gateway, beyond the walls.

'Forgive me,' he said, his back to her. 'I lost myself for a moment.' His words were terse.

Seen from behind, his soldierly figure was daunting. It was as if a stranger had stepped into his clothes. Louise reached his side, unsure what to say. She touched his arm.

'I am full to the brim with Master Wat's possets and potions,' he said. 'I am not in my right mind. What I did was . . . '

'You did not want to kiss me? It was only the work of drugs?'

She tugged at his sleeve. 'Look at me,' she said. 'Please.'

He turned and grasped her by the shoulders, as if he were about to shake her. 'Of course I wanted to. You are a beautiful girl, and uncommonly brave too. I have never met a woman like you. But this is no time for such a business. And you and I, we are from different worlds. We cannot . . . '

'I know my family is not grand,' she said, bridling at the reminder, 'but . . . '

'No!' He almost barked the word. 'That is not what

I mean. My family is nothing to boast about. Titles are meaningless. There's as many scoundrels who can claim an escutcheon as you'll find among a galley's hands.' His voice quietened, and he let her go. 'I meant only that we come from very different circumstances, and our aims and hopes in life are leagues apart. I could not ask you to . . . '

'To . . . ?'

He shook his head, dismissing his thoughts as if they were buzzing around his ears. 'No, Louise. I am gentleman enough, despite what's just happened, not to commit you, or me, to anything at a time like this. Your mind cannot be clear while you are searching for Benoit; and I must not, and will not, take advantage of that.'

He looked up to the treetops, his mouth settling into a grim line. 'Shameful though it is to admit, I am still plagued by the battlefield. It dogs my dreams, it makes me liverish, it clouds my thoughts. It would not be fair to make a contract now, when neither of us is steady. When Benoit has been found, and brought home safe; when this nightmarish year is past, perhaps then we can pick up these feelings once more.'

No words could have won Louise over more completely. In putting her brother before their desire, in postponing whatever hopeful future lay ahead for them together, he had captured her affections in a way no fulsome declaration ever could. She walked into his arms and laid her head on his chest, holding him close, as if she would never let him go. As they stood like that, each found a comfort beyond words.

*   *   *

The intimacy of that moment was in the air as Crozier looked down on the pair at his fireside. At once he guessed how things stood. So tired his bones ached, he felt as if his last reserves had been drained. His vision narrowed, and as Louise began to speak, he had trouble concentrating. She faltered at his vacant expression, and he raised a hand to quieten her.

'We can talk more over dinner. Things may be more hopeful than you fear. Surrey would never order the mortally ill to be carted all the way to Durham. Whatever the English have planned for these prisoners – and it won't be good, I must warn you – if Benoit is one of them, it gives us some time. There's a great deal to discuss. But first I must see to other, more pressing matters.'

He left, without casting as much as a glance towards the courtier, who had been watching the Borderer as if hoping his face would reveal secrets he would not commit to words. Murdo Montgomery, who had been sitting in a corner, whittling a pipe while watching the couple, emerged from the gloom. He followed his master through the door that led to Crozier's rooms, and that of his men.

'I dinnae trust yon fella,' he said, as the latch dropped behind them. 'Reckon he'd whip the food from under yer nose, and take yer place as lord of the keep if he saw a mousehole's chance.'

'What else would you expect from one of the king's hired men?' said Crozier. 'Fortunately, I do not intend for him to be here long enough to get his feet under the table.'

In the deepest chamber of the keep, Crozier gathered his men. This was the Croziers' armoury, its doors as thick as the keep's walls. As the men pressed around him, he reported the gossip from Berwick, and his certainty that Dacre was planning a most serious revenge. In turn, he heard Murdo's reports from their scouts. Messages warning of the All Hallows' Eve threat had been sent out across the eastern, middle and western marches, not excluding Liddesdale and the Elliots, though, as Old Crozier chipped in, the scout had been so reluctant to discharge his duty towards them, the watchmen on Hermitage Castle's gate had been obliged to prise the paper from his glove. Since returning to the village, he had drunk himself into a stupor. 'We'll hae no use of him for anither day or two,' said Murdo.

'Wretched fool,' said Crozier in a voice barbed as gorse. He stared around the room, at each of his men in turn. None could hold his wintry gaze. Haggard, red-veined, lined and scarred, their faces emerged as from an oil canvas against a backdrop of strife. Arranged around the walls was an array of pikes, swords and knives plentiful enough for a small army. There were halberds, gloves and helmets, all cast in steel, and from hooks in the ceiling hung chain mail headgear and breastplates for their horses.

A crate of lead shot was at Crozier's side, and as he spoke he juggled a ball from one hand to the other, as if to prepare the missile for the feel of flesh. He spoke so quietly he might have been addressing none but himself, but each word was a command that no-one dare ignore. Crozier was a fair man, but everyone in that room had seen how he could behave when angered. His slowness to wrath made him more to be feared than a firebrand. So too his punishments. He was no bully; he never lashed out with his fists or knife, though his words could wound. The cold shoulder was his finest weapon. Duties were removed from offenders, as were privileges. If the sin was severe, the culprit could find himself banished, as when Murdo had been posted to the coastlands for a year and set to work on a fishing skiff, for blabbing the Crozier family secrets in the village; Swire, the pig hand, was exiled indefinitely to the care of distant kin in the outer isles, after slicing off the ear of a stable-hand in a fight over a servant girl. And even his own brother, Tom, had felt the force of Crozier's fury, when he had been forbidden to leave the keep's grounds for a six-month after one too many raids of his neighbours' prize sheep – sequestered, that is, only after he had returned his booty and suffered the beating from his astonished victims that Crozier later said he roundly deserved.

Remembering this, and more, the men listened well as Crozier spoke. 'None of us is to touch a drop of spirits until this matter has come to a head,' he said. 'There will be no drunkenness. There will be no shirking. We are about to come under attack. God willing, not before the end of the month, but whatever Dacre and Surrey have planned for the Borders, it is likely a separate, and worse fate is being prepared for us. I doubt they will mete that out before that date – why waste good men on an unnecessary expedition, when they can deal with both affairs in one? Even so, we cannot be sure when they will descend. So as of tonight, we stand a twenty-four-hour guard on the walls, and a dawn-to-dusk vigil in the watchtower at the valley pass. We get our gear in order. Clean the culverins and get them into position on the battlements. Sharpen the blades. Fill the vats with oil.'

He spoke without pause for an hour. Supplies were to

be laid down in case of siege. Hay and water stored in the great hall, should the stables be destroyed. The village warned of what might be heading its way, and given help to plan a refuge. Cattle, goats and sheep moved to the pastures nearest the walls. The trees encircling the keep felled, but not cleared, where they would act like spillikins and wrong-step advancing horses and men alike.

On and on the orders continued. Crozier spoke more like a general than a Borders outlaw. At the threat of impending danger, his men grew sharper witted, their spines stiffer, their minds more military. By the end of the conference Crozier's Keep was on a footing for war.

It was a sombre dinner that night. Crozier's men supped in near silence, and Mother Crozier offered a plain-song of sighs from her stool by the fire. The food, however, was as tempting as ever, testimony to a creative talent beneath the scowls. Louise smothered a smile as Hob licked his fingers and pushed back his dish, almost before the others had lifted a spoon. Not until his men had melted into the night to start their tasks did Crozier turn his attention to her.

He looked first at Gabriel. 'You are recovering, I believe?' he asked.

'Indeed I am,' said the courtier, with something like a grateful smile. 'Thanks to Wat's knowledge and skill. He would be invaluable in an Edinburgh hospice. Never more so than in these times.'

'He has enough to do here,' said Crozier, shortly.

He looked at Louise, her sleeve brushing the courtier's as she wiped her dish clean with bread. Crozier leant forward and poured a ruby wine into her cleared bowl, and a generous splash into Gabriel's tankard, which he drained off at once.

He addressed Louise, but as if to acknowledge the bond between the pair, he included Gabriel in his glance. 'We cannot know, of course, if Benoit was taken to Durham. My best advice to you would be to go home now, and leave well alone. However, little though I know you, I suspect you will ignore that, and go your own way. Which would be dangerous. What I propose, therefore, is that tomorrow I set out, with one of my men, to Durham, and scout around there, as I did in Berwick. If your brother is indeed a prisoner, I will be back with the news in a week or so. At that time, we can plot how to rescue him. In the meantime, if a way can be found, I can smuggle a letter in to him, for good cheer's sake.'

Louise began to protest, but he silenced her. 'This is no act of idle courtesy, in case that's what's worrying you. As in Berwick, I hope to be able to learn more about what Surrey and Dacre are plotting for the Borders from the garrison there.' He sipped his wine, as he waited for Louise's answer.

She raised her bowl and drank deep, staining her lips red. 'I cannot allow you to do this for me and my family,' she said, at last. The words seemed to pain her, but she pressed on. 'You took risk enough in Berwick, but the ride to Durham, and the city itself, are too much to ask from a stranger. This is something I must do alone.'

The courtier took her hand. 'Not alone,' he said quietly.

'I am grateful to you, good sir,' she said. 'You are kindness itself.' She took a deep breath. 'Well then, you and I shall make our way there. We can travel swiftly, and should we find him there, we can bring him comfort, if only in knowing he is not forgotten. To tell truth' – she lifted her eyes, and held Crozier's gaze – 'to tell truth, I doubt there is a single thing on God's earth any of us can do if he is under guard in the castle's cells. But for the peace of my soul, and I hope for his, we can try to see each other one last time.' A sob rose in her chest, and she lowered her head. Gabriel put a hand on her back, and eventually she grew calm.

Crozier spoke roughly. 'Your plan makes no sense, ma'am. You do not know these parts, or the road to England, and without a guide you would fall into the enemy's hands within an hour of these gates. For many years now, none of us has been able to travel in England without a pass.' A look of disgust crossed his face. 'That was another of King James's petty devices to crush the Borders.

'However, while I can forge passes that may prove useful if you are challenged, I cannot tell you the paths through the hills. Since the battle, the patrols on the border and on the highways will be doubled, or worse. Only the wild tracks will be safe. Unless you agree to let me be your guide, I will not allow you to leave this place.'

Gabriel drew a deep breath.

'I can, and I will lock you both up until you see sense,' Crozier continued.

The courtier leapt to his feet. 'Scoundrel!' he cried. 'You cannot keep us prisoner. I remind you it is a capital offence to assault, far less imprison, the king's men. Already you have committed both crimes, and could swing for them.'

Crozier waved the flagon of wine at him, before pouring himself another draught. 'Do take your seat, sir. My intention is not to threaten you, but to help. Such agitation is unnecessary. Your recent beating no doubt clouds your judgement.'

Gabriel began a heated reply, but Louise put her hand on his arm. With a glower, and a fiddling with his sleeves, he sat, and leaned back in his chair. Only the trickling of wine into their cups broke the silence.

After a long drink, Crozier spoke. 'Here is a plan, the best I can think of. We leave tomorrow afternoon, and proceed beyond the border only after dusk. There will be a moon, cloud permitting, to light our way. Even without it, we can make steady progress. By my calculation, it will take three hard nights on the road to reach the city. Once there, you and I, sir, will gain entry to the castle, to inquire, in our finest English accents, what has become of a close and dear relative of yours we believe to have been wrongly imprisoned after the battle. That he is from Spain but learnt our language from a Scot is his only sin, we will say. Otherwise, his heart is as English as roast beef.'

'That is surely a deadly plan,' said Louise.

'Ma'am, every step of our way will be perilous. If any of us gets back in our same skin, I will be astonished.'

'We must do it, dear one,' said Gabriel. 'I am willing. More than willing.'

'But your head is still bleeding,' said Louise. 'How will you fare?'

'I will be fit to ride, never you fear. Nothing would prevent me coming with you. And as you rightly said yesterday, you cannot afford to wait. Your brother may be suffering torments far greater than my bruised skull.'

'One other thing,' said Crozier, interrupting. He stared

at Louise, not unkindly. 'It will be necessary for you to return to your matronly guise. It might be useful, if we are stopped, to be travelling with an aged woman. We can say you are my aunt.' He looked across the kitchen. 'My mother will help. She has cowls and cloaks of a sort to make you drab as a washerwoman. Hair dye too, I believe, which could turn you white overnight. Made from pigeon stoor, I am told.'

He ignored a noise from the fireside.

Louise put a hand to her net cowl, through which her auburn hair glowed in the firelight. 'Dye?'

The Borderer looked at her, a strange light in his eyes. She wondered if he was laughing at her. 'You are right,' he said. 'Ashes will be sufficient.'

CHAPTER FIFTEEN

8 October 1513

At the gatehouse the Earl of Surrey and his men dismounted. Their spurs clinked, as did their belts, weighted with swords and daggers. Lord Dacre's guard knew Surrey well and stood aside with a salute. 'Fiendish day,' the old soldier said to him, leading his horse through the archway. The guard nodded, dislodging a runnel of rain from his helmet that splashed onto his boots.

The horses picked their way up the track beneath the trees, snorting and shaking their sodden manes. Morpeth Castle rose out of the murk, black as soot in the downpour. It was barely midday, but the sky was so dark it might have been dusk. A stone causeway led through the mud, and as the riders approached, a burning brazier beckoned from the castle gates.

Leaving his men to stable the horses, the earl strode across the courtyard. Dacre met him at the door, his boots red with Northumberland mud. The march warden's unkempt appearance was at odds with the castle's splendour, where there was no sign, thought the earl, of the poverty its owner persistently complained of. Indeed,

Morpeth was so lavishly appointed, it might have been a royal palace.

Dacre's greeting was brusque, but his regard for this venerable campaigner was plain. Had he heard nothing more than his reputation, he would have treated him with respect, but having seen him in the field, transforming tired and demoralised troops into fearless fighters, he held him in awe. Surrey, he believed, was a man of his own kind.

The night after the battle, the two had shared quarters in the village of Branxton. Unsure of their losses – Surrey initially feared English casualties might be severe, Dacre cared not so long as they had won – neither had even attempted to sleep. It was just as well. Every hour the earl's lieutenants brought fresh news, the number of deaths mounting for the Scots with each report, and a miraculously low toll confirmed on their side. As the picture of the final outcome emerged, the companions drank long into that cheerless dawn, reliving events by the embers of a hearth, while the hovel's owner, an elderly priest, whiffled and snored under his cloak as if the day had been like any other. Surrey envied him his stolid nerves; Dacre scarcely noted his existence.

The march warden was later hailed as the saviour of the day, his cavalry holding the English line against the Scottish onslaught and turning the tide of the battle. Surrey's own son, Thomas Howard, was also commended for leading the vanguard, but everyone knew it was the earl who had made victory possible, and that the laurels were his. Henry, it was said, would reward him well when he returned from France.

But reward in this life did not matter to the earl. In the

weeks that followed Flodden he had barely eaten, and slept less. Pride in his army and relief in winning vied with revulsion for war, and what it required of him, and his men. Nearly a month later he felt as tired as if the battle had just ended.

The march warden noted his wan complexion and gaunt cheeks, but with the unseeing eye of a man who had never encountered illness or doubt, he assumed these were symptoms of senility, not conscience.

'Come,' he said, ushering the soldier ahead of him into the castle's hammer beam hall, where dogs prowled the walls and servants bustled with ale and meat.

At a table near the fire sat Thomas Ruthall, Bishop of Durham, already at his dinner. He inclined his head at the earl's arrival, but did not rise. His cheeks bulged, as did his eyes, and his skin was mottled purple. A fur was draped around his shoulders, as if he were an old man afraid of a chill. Surrey stared. In the space of a few weeks the king's secretary had aged like a barrel left outside in winter. They made a matching pair.

'Your lordship, be seated,' said Dacre, dragging out a chair shaped like a throne. The earl took his place, and found a beaker of ale placed before him by invisible hands. He pushed it aside, so too the food. There were more urgent matters, as his expression suggested when Dacre pulled a dish towards himself, and began to eat.

From across the table, the bishop cast a bloodshot glare on the earl. 'I'm ruined,' he said, his voice awash with sorrow. 'Done for. Destroyed!' He swept a jewelled hand around the hall, with its carved panels and silverware, its portraits and hangings. 'My Lord Thomas has all this, but my home, my sanctuary is gone. Razed to the ground. Reduced to rubble.' Tears overwhelmed him, and he buried his face in his hands, fur heaving around his shoulders as if it were still alive.

'Ruthall exaggerates, as ever,' said Dacre, his face stony. 'He has many homes at his disposal. Yet one has sympathy. He talks of his pride and joy, his castle at Norham, which the Scots levelled.' The march warden caught the earl's cold glance, and explained. 'Your lordship, Ruthall is still in shock. He has only recently seen the devastation they wrought there.'

The bishop emerged from his hands. 'It was impregnable, or so I was assured. And they flattened it, like a child's toy, or a beetle, crushed underfoot.' His eyes narrowed and he jabbed a finger at the earl. 'And not one of them hurt in the attack. My men slain or maimed, and James's brigands unscathed. The town a smouldering ruin, and the army, those vandals, untouched.'

He gathered the fur close around his throat. 'I will never recover from this. It will put me in my grave.' His voice thinned to a hiss. 'But every night I get down on my knees and give thanks to the Almighty that he brought his vengeance down on that rabble. I only wish I too had seen James's body, cut up and faceless as it was. He will have enjoyed meeting his maker in that condition, I am sure.' A mirthless smile fattened his cheeks.

'No,' said Dacre quietly, 'you would not have wanted to see that. I wish to God I had not.'

'Yet it served a useful purpose, did it not?' said Surrey bracingly. 'Since you identified the body, you can help refute the rumours which have James escaping and regrouping his men in secret. Some say he's plotting in a Highland glen. Others that he's in France, where his kindred spirits hold out hope he can still come to their aid.'

The bishop scoffed. 'French fools – pathetic, puny, and anything but a friend to James. What I've seen of them, they have fewer morals than the infidels. I almost pity the Scots. I hear James had offered them the shirt off his back and they gave him nothing but empty promises. Could not even reach him in time for battle. Pah!' He made as if to spit, but at a glance from the earl swallowed his bile.

The march warden took a draught of ale, and wiped his mouth with the back of his hand. 'In the end we outwitted him, but James was a noble man. Treacherous maybe, but a worthy adversary. I am sorry he is dead.'

The bishop whickered. 'Some soldier you! If I had got my hands on James after what he did to Norham, I would have laughed at the sight of him begging for mercy, even as I choked the life out of him.'

Dacre looked at him with dislike. 'He did not beg, I am told, even at the very end. But shame on you, a man of God and a soldier for Christ, for your lack of heart.'

The bishop began to splutter a riposte and was rising to his feet when Surrey thumped the table.

'Gentlemen, please! This is no time to squabble. We are here for a purpose, and I suggest we address it now.'

His voice doused the bishop's fury. Grumbling, he sat down and began to tear a wing of chicken apart as if it had wronged him.

Dacre spoke. 'You're right. We must finish what we began at Flodden.'

'His Royal Highness depends upon us,' said the bishop

thickly. 'He was gratified at the massacre of the Scots, but it is not enough. Not nearly enough. In his absence, as his secretary and counsellor, I speak for him, and for the privy council, and I urge – nay, demand – that the Scottish border is crushed beyond recovery. Nothing will make Henry sleep sounder than if he knows the root of his troubles has been stamped out. James has proved to be a venomous enemy, but even though Flodden has closed that chapter, the border remains a snakepit. Until it has been brought to heel, none in England is safe.'

The earl watched as Dacre's eyes brightened. The march warden cracked his knuckles, staring into space, as if he were already coming face to face with the Borderers who had dared to defy him. The call to arms was the sweetest song to this man, who lived by the sword and was at his most contented, the earl had heard, when patrolling his marches and dealing out the sort of justice possible this far from the crown's heartlands.

Dacre laid a conciliatory hand on the bishop's sleeve. 'You can put your faith in me, Ruthall,' he said. 'I know this border and its troublemakers better than they know themselves.' Picking his bone clean, the bishop did not reply, but his hands grew steadier, and his colour slowly began to fade.

'What report from the widowed queen?' Surrey asked the march warden.

'Nothing yet,' he replied, 'it is likely too soon to hope for a reply, but I am told that before even she received our offer, Margaret was saying that until Henry made reparation for killing her husband, she would do nothing to help our cause. An alliance with us was repugnant to her.' He sighed.

'That was perhaps only to be expected, so soon after her bereavement. We might still dare hope that she will come out of her gloom and see sense in time. All Hallows' Eve, when we told her we would be obliged to take action, draws close . . . '

'No,' said Surrey, the word falling like a stone. 'She is a woman, weakened by grief and without a counsellor worthy of the name to advise her. Be assured, Dacre, she will not see the necessity of joining forces with us to tame the border. From this moment we must assume we proceed alone. Forget the terms agreed, and act on our own behalf. And do so at once.'

The bishop nodded vigorously. 'Far better to have nothing to do with her,' he said, his mouth full of pigeon. 'Henry says she is a wildcat, feral and vicious.'

After a moment's rumination, Dacre nodded. 'Very well,' he said. 'So we are all agreed who we first turn our attention to?'

Surrey raised an eyebrow. 'I assume you refer to the men who manhandled your messenger?'

'Indeed,' he replied, 'the Croziers. A poxy clan from Teviotdale, of no influence since I dealt with the chief some years back. But they are impertinent, and have grown audacious while our backs have been turned. I fear rebellion is brewing in that quarter. With your assent, gentlemen, I will set my men upon them as an example of what to expect when you meddle with me. With us, I should say.'

'It sounds,' said Surrey, 'as if you will enjoy the chance to take your own private revenge. And who could blame you?'

Dacre shook his head. 'My lord, I will leave that to my

lieutenants. I will be far more useful raising the west march against the Scots from my castle at Naworth. I will launch an attack on Liddesdale shortly after the killing of Crozier and his clan. That way, fire and death will spread through the Borders from both ends, and meet in the middle.'

'A joyous conflagration, my son,' said the bishop, licking his fingers as if they were the enemies' bones.

'While you deal thus with the middle and the west marches,' said the earl, 'I will handle the east, to ensure it does not rise to support our foe. The merest whisper of this campaign could ruin everything. Surprise is essential. When we strike, the Croziers must be beyond hope of help.'

He took a first sip of his ale and stretched out his legs, cheered at the prospect of action and a respite from his brooding thoughts.

The bishop lifted his tankard. 'To the Croziers. May we trap them like fish in a net.'

'Mice in a butterchurn,' said Surrey, raising his ale.

'Lice, more like,' said Dacre, tipping his drink towards them with a smile as sweet as honey.

CHAPTER SIXTEEN

9 October 1513

It was a subdued party that left Crozier's Keep the following afternoon. Louise's head was floury with riddled ash beneath its linen cap, though in the gathering cold of autumn she was glad of the padded jerkin beneath her dress. It was borrowed from Tom, the slimmest of the family, and when he saw it on her, falling below her knees and trebling her girth, he smiled. 'You look like a bairn playing dressing-up.'

'This is no game, lad,' said his brother, but he too lingered on the sight of Louise, transformed once more into a stout old biddie more likely to be found stirring suet pudding than creeping under darkness into enemy country with a dagger in her boots.

In the stables, Hob was sulking. He did not want to be left behind. 'I should be with the mistress,' he had said that morning, when Crozier explained their plans. 'She might need me. I dinnae trust that fancy chiel.'

Crozier had no time to humour the boy. 'You would only give her something else to worry about,' he said. 'She'll get on better knowing you are safe here. And I will watch out for the courtier. I have my eye on him, never fear.' Hob drew his sleeve across his nose, and ran into the yard, hiding his tears.

At midday, when the horses were saddled, the boy threw his arms around Louise, and buried his head in her cloak. 'Dinnae forget tae come back for me, promise?'

She hugged him, and laid her cheek on his head, straw dust tickling her nose. 'I will never forget to come back for you, I give you my word, however long it takes. But I need you to look after Hans and the vixen. Crozier says I'm to ride one of his horses.'

She lifted her head to look at him. 'I trust no-one with old Hans but you, and once I have news of my brother I will be back for you all. Look after Hans and the vixen well. The vixen especially. She will need to sleep with you.'

She felt a pang. Despite his air of independence, he was still only a child. 'Will you mind very much staying behind?'

'Naw,' said the boy, with a rich sniff. 'I like it here fine, with the animals and a', but I will like it better once ye're back again.' His eyes narrowed. 'But will ye be bringing yon courtier when ye return?'

Louise blushed. 'I couldn't say, Hob. Why – would you like me to?'

'I'm no fashed,' he lied, and ran back into the stables, where he hid in the hayloft until they had left.

While Mother Crozier and Louise were packing the saddlebags with food, the Borderer took Gabriel on one side. His mistrust of this man had grown on acquaintance, and it was for fear of what he might do, even more than a wish to help Louise, that he was prepared to risk the

242

journey to Durham. He suspected that if he let the king's man out of his sight, he would conspire with Dacre to destroy him and all his kind. When it came to the Borders, the ties of that class of man were far thicker than those of patriotism, and he had seen in Torrance's eyes his loathing of Crozier, and his men.

Unused to dissembling, the Borderer spoke quietly: 'I owe you an apology.' The courtier could never know what it cost him to utter those words, treacherous though they were. Crozier swallowed, and continued: 'I was churlish last night, and uncivil. I'm sorry. From that first night on the moors, I've treated you roughly. No wonder you don't trust me. But what lies ahead of us these next few days will be tough. We need to pull together.' He put out his hand: 'For the sake of Mistress Brenier, we should settle our differences and try to get on. At least for now.'

Gabriel hesitated. He looked at the Borderer, his harsh face, and uncouth dress. He was little better than a brigand, but out in these wild parts, under such circumstances, a truce might be more useful than to be at each other's throats. He inclined his head: 'You are right. I am willing to be friends. Besides,' he added, 'my own behaviour has not been as good as it might. Not all the blame is yours.'

They shook hands, the woodsman's calloused palm gripping fingers so slender, pale and soft they might have been carved from wax.

For the first few hours they rode in daylight, following a trail due south, and crossing the border under cover of woodland after the sun had set. They moved swiftly and with little noise beyond the clink of bridle and spur. Louise's sturdy pony cantered close on the tail of the Borderer's mare, Gabriel bringing up the rear on his stallion. As the light faded, and the land quietened, their pace slowed and the courtier found himself looking over his shoulder. It was dusk when he heard a snapping of twigs that confirmed his suspicions. 'We are being followed,' he said in a harsh whisper, and pulled up. He and Crozier drew their swords, and in the deepening gloom they watched the path. Leaves rustled, there was a quivering of bushes and the vixen trotted into sight. With a bark, she scampered to Louise's side and pawed at her boots.

'She can't come with us,' said Crozier. 'It's well over a hundred miles to Durham, and we'll be riding too hard for a dog her size, even if she weren't injured.'

'She will learn as much if we simply ride on. She will tire, and fall behind,' said Gabriel, who had not yet forgiven her for biting him.

Louise rubbed the vixen's ears. They were right. There was no place for her on this journey. Yet seeing her she realised how much she wanted her company.

'I'm vexed I didn't think to have her tied up until we were long gone,' she said. 'But now she is here, I don't know how to make her go back. She's stubborn. She will run herself dead, rather than give up.'

There was silence, as the men considered the animal. Gabriel's face hardened but before he could speak Crozier dismounted. He bent to pat the mongrel. 'You are trouble,' he said, 'as if we needed more.' The vixen sat back on her haunches and looked into his eyes, tongue lolling.

With a shake of his head, he picked her up. 'We'd better take her with us,' he said. 'What else can we do now? She can ride pillion tonight.' He looked up at Louise. 'You and

I can take turns carrying her when she tires. But let me be very clear: you must make sure she does not bark or whine, or put our lives in danger. Otherwise we will have no choice but to leave her behind. D'you understand?'

Louise nodded, reaching out for the dog, who settled on the pommel between the reins and stared over the pony's head, as if her role was lookout. Gabriel shook his head. Nothing good could come of bringing a menagerie.

On they rode. As night settled around them, they slowed to a walk. The horses were uneasy, snorting if a startled bird flapped from its roost or a fox crossed their path. The riders kept them on a short rein and spoke to them gently, as if they were children afraid of the dark.

The woodlands stretched mile after mile. There was a dreamlike monotony about their plodding passage, trees so densely packed they were like battalions awaiting inspection, each trunk identical to the last. Louise started to feel drowsy, and only the thought of what might happen if she fell asleep and let the reins fall kept her alert.

In a while the trees began to thin, and Crozier halted at the edge of the woods. A brackish plain stretched before them, lit by a watery moon. 'We're onto the moors here,' he said. 'It's going to get harder now, and there's a steep climb ahead. Fortunately, there's little chance of meeting anyone out here. Keep close behind me and don't leave the path. There are sheer drops in places.'

'Where exactly are we?' Gabriel asked.

'We're heading towards the Kielder pass. Beyond that is Redesdale and the road to Otterburn. When we've got over the pass, we can take cover, and get some food and rest. So far, we're making good time.'

They set off, the horses following each other dutifully, nose to tail. The wind whistled across the marsh grasses, its pitch deepening as they rode down into the valley, before rising, step upon step, up the side of a hill whose dark bulk loomed over them like a raised fist. As they picked their way up the slope, Louise's pony stumbled, sending pebbles tumbling over the edge of the path. She heard them clatter onto distant rock. Were the pony to lose its footing, he and his rider would fall like stone, to be broken a hundred feet below. She gripped the reins and turned her face towards the steep bank, rather than the cavernous air that breathed too close on her shoulder.

Eventually they reached the valley head, where Crozier reined in. He pointed backwards, over the road they had just taken. By moonlight the rugged bowl they had climbed out of looked fierce and wide as a hungry mouth. 'That's known as the Witches' Clutch,' he said. 'There's more than a few have lost their way there, and gone over the edge. Some say that when the witches are out in force, the hills close in on their victims, and crush them to death. That's why their bones are never found, just dust on the valley floor.'

'That's no more than an old wife's tale, surely,' said Louise.

'Peasant superstition,' said Gabriel with a laugh, 'never you fear.'

'Superstition it may be,' said Crozier, 'but strange things happen out here that folk find hard to explain. I'm not saying I believe the witches have anything to do with it. But there's something uncanny about these parts. I wouldn't want to live hereabouts, that's for sure.'

They spurred their horses into a canter along the broad ridge path. Picked out against the moonlit sky, they were too conspicuous for Crozier's liking. It might be the middle of the night, but the sooner they were out of sight, the safer he would feel.

But already they had been spotted. In a thatched stone hovel on the hillside, a shepherd's widow first heard and then saw them. She watched the riders pass before picking up her skein of wool. She spat into the fire. 'Let them that wants to stay hidden be found, and them that wants to be found be hidden from all but the true.' She shaped an effigy from a hank of wool and cast it onto the embers. 'Go after them, little one.' The wool crinkled, kinked, and slowly curled, to die in a flicker of flame.

*   *   *

Louise's bones felt as if they had been shaken out of their sockets, and rearranged in an order God had never intended. She worried how her pony was faring, yet his pace never faltered, and after that stumble, he had been sure-footed as a goat. Borders horses, it seemed, were as hardy as their owners.

The night had no end. So long as the sky was dark, and the moon high, Crozier kept them on the trail. Only when a thin line of pale blue appeared on the horizon, and the first blackbirds greeted the day, did he let them rest. A second night's riding followed, as tiring as the first, and by the time Crozier called a brief halt Louise was dizzy from peering into the dark, her legs unsteady as she dismounted. While the horses drank from a stream, the Borderer stood apart, looking into the thinning sky. They were still some miles from the hideout he had planned to reach. Gabriel drew Louise to one side, and shared bread and ale with her, talking in a low voice.

At length, Crozier spoke. 'We've passed far beyond Redesdale. This next stage will be the most dangerous. There is a place near the Packman's Ford where we can lie up till night, but it's a good few miles from here. We risk being seen, but there's nothing we can do about that. If you are ready for it, we must start now, and ride as fast as the track allows. With luck, we will be there before full light.'

They came down off the hills without encountering anyone, covering the ground so swiftly that only the keenest observer could have given their description. As they reached the ford, and the straggling settlement beside it, they slowed to a walk. Louise pulled her cap low, and Crozier and Gabriel kept their heads down beneath their leather brims. A man with a cartload of winter feed was crossing the ford ahead of them. They waited on the bank. Only the horses' foaming flanks gave a hint of their impatience.

The man's wheel caught on the crooked stone causeway, and however much his mule pulled, it could not be dislodged. He cursed loudly and threw down his whip, his roars bringing a boy running from the village. But the lad was puny, no match for the cart, and before he could reach the ford, Crozier dismounted, and approached. 'Let me help you, my friend,' he said. The farmer grunted, and got off his cart. Together they wrenched the wheel free. With a lurch, the mule dragged the cart across the ford, and started off up the street, his owner chasing to catch up. Not once had he looked at Crozier or his companions.

The three crossed without a word and passed through

the village at a sedate trot, as if going no further than to market. Once they were out of sight of the cottages, Crozier turned off the road, and into the hills. Some miles later he dismounted, and led his horse sharply uphill to a spindly copse of birches. Hidden by the trees, in the side of the hill was a mossy crack, barely wide enough to allow a horse to enter. Beyond was a high-roofed cave, cold, bare, but dry. 'A rustlers' hideout,' said Crozier, in answer to their unspoken question. His voice was loud and unfamiliar in the enclosed space. 'It was a place my grandfather used. He brought me here a few times. God knows how he found it, but it saved his skin on more than one occasion.'

After unsaddling and feeding the horses, they spread their bedrolls on the hard earth floor. Gabriel and Crozier took it in turns to stand watch. Louise lay, with the vixen at her side, and despite the lack of pillow or rug, was asleep in a moment. For the next few hours she gave no sign of life, other than a flicker of eyelids, as if she were still peering through the dark for shapes she hoped not to see.

When she woke, the cave was in darkness. A flint was struck at her side, and in its light Gabriel loomed over her, with a flask of ale and a slice of cheese. 'Take these,' he whispered, his hand squeezing her shoulder. 'We will be setting off shortly.' She got up stiffly, a palm to her back. She sensed a new mood. Crozier was tense, and Gabriel too. 'What is it?' she asked.

'Voices,' said Gabriel. 'Crozier has heard men on the hill. They have torches. Could be they're looking for us.'

She joined them at the cave mouth. Their horses were saddled and ready, hooves scuffing the dust. Beyond the birches torchlights bobbed on the lower slopes of the hill. The group stiffened at the sound of baying hounds. 'Are they loose?' asked Louise, her heart skipping. Crozier nodded. 'They've let them off, to search. Most likely they are only hunting. Problem is, they might pick up our scent.'

At their heels the vixen began a low growl. The horses tossed their heads. Peering into the dusk, the three scarcely breathed. Gradually, as the torches moved off across the valley, the yelping grew fainter.

'We must leave now,' said Crozier, 'before they return. They're heading south, the way I had hoped to go, so we'll have to take a different path, but we cannot stay here any longer.'

He scooped up the vixen. 'She can ride with me until we're beyond the reach of the hounds.'

They crept out, leading their horses downhill to the trail. There was still light enough to be seen, and with a hunt at large, they felt uncomfortably exposed. Quietly but quickly, they turned east. The hills here were high but flat-topped, and for many miles Louise could see the hunters' lights, dancing across the land they had left. Only when they were beyond sight did she give her full mind to the ride ahead.

As before, the night stretched on forever. In the rising wind, the moon's light was fitful, veiled by scudding clouds that blotted out the stars. Progress was slow, Crozier less sure of his road than before, and the horses spooked by the memory of the hounds. Yet by dawn they were far on their way to Durham. The landscape was changing, from broad hill plains to a rougher, rockier warren of small hills and vales. On a few occasions they rode through a settle-ment, setting dogs barking as they passed. The vixen, under Crozier's firm hand, did no more than growl in reply.

This deep into enemy territory the Borderer took no risks. As soon as the night lightened to grey he found cover, heading off the trail and into a pinewood that even in daylight would be secretive and dim. Their horses' hooves were muffled by drifts of ancient brown pine-needles, and with this as a mattress, their bedrolls felt like eiderdown. With the trees swaying above them, hushing their thoughts, they slept.

When they woke it was late afternoon, and there was time to kill before they could set out. Sharing their food, they talked, as if they were ordinary folk taking a break between chores.

'How much further?' asked Louise.

'I reckon we are only a few hours' ride from the city,' Crozier replied, biting deep into one of his mother's pies. He spoke through his mouthful: 'We should be in place sometime after midnight.'

Gabriel nodded, wiping crumbs from his mouth with his handkerchief, and swallowing before he spoke. 'A fine cook, your mother, may I say. Nothing could be more welcome after these long days than provender like this. No wonder you Borderers can stay on the road for so long without tiring. She is a marvel.'

Louise looked up at him, grateful at the effort he was making with a man he did not trust. In their pride and quick tempers, and above all in their courage, these two were more alike than they would care to know. The courtier, however, with his fine accent and clothes, his flashing ring and golden hair, was like a creature from a higher plain, somewhere between the earth and heaven. Crozier, meanwhile, might have been a woodcutter or herdsman, so well did he blend into the trees and hills in his weathered leather jerkin and leggings. Louise lowered her eyes, but not before the Borderer had caught her admiring glance, and the unguarded warmth with which Gabriel returned it.

When they had eaten, Crozier laid out his plans. They would find a secure place in the hills outside the city, leaving Louise hidden while he and Gabriel made their way there in daytime to scout out around the castle.

'I think not,' said Gabriel, cutting him short.

Crozier looked at him in surprise.

'I go alone,' Gabriel explained. 'You will only hinder me.'

Crozier was incredulous. 'How so? You cannot possibly do this on your own. It would be madness. This expedition is folly enough without you running such risks.'

'I go alone or not at all,' said the courtier, his voice as harsh as if he were issuing a command to recalcitrant troops. A startled pigeon rose from a pine, flapping its way through the trees.

Louise was almost as alarmed. 'Sir,' she began, touching the courtier's cloak.

'No.' Gabriel ignored her, but spoke more quietly. 'It surprises me, Crozier, that you would be so heedless. I cannot, and I will not allow Louise to be stranded out here without protection. Better that we leave empty-handed than that she is put in such danger.'

Crozier began to speak, but Gabriel raised his hand.

'Sir, if you insist, then go to the castle yourself. I, however, shall remain here with Louise.'

Crozier was terse. 'You know very well I cannot pass myself off as a courtier, not in this garb – not in any.

You have the manner of one born to command the lower orders. That's the only chance we have of getting past the guard.'

Gabriel shrugged. 'It is your choice,' he said. 'I will not seek out danger, but I need hardly tell you, nor do I run from it.'

Nobody spoke. Gabriel stared at the Borderer, who was frowning. The pines swayed above them. A squirrel dislodged a cone, and it fell with a splash of leaves. Finally, Crozier spoke.

'Very well,' he said. 'I will keep guard here with Mistress Brenier. But I warn you. If you run into any trouble, you are on your own. We will wait till dusk, but no longer.'

'Perfectly understood,' said Gabriel.

'How will you explain travelling alone?' said Crozier. 'Will that not raise suspicion?'

'I see no problems with that.' Gabriel smiled. 'Of all the questions I dread, that is the least troublesome.'

Crozier nodded, reluctant still, but unable, or unwilling to argue. His manner became brisk, as much like one born to command as the courtier, though without the flourishes of accent, dress or style. 'So then,' he said, 'if you can gain access to the cells, that would be an unexpected stroke of luck. But as I said before, you'll need to pass yourself off as an Englishman. Your strange tongue would otherwise have you put in irons.'

Gabriel put down his pie, tilted his hat to the back of his head, and turned from soft-spoken Irish Scot into a boastful Yorkshireman. 'Happen I can deal wi' the likes o' that, y'oul fool,' he said, his brogue so thick they stared in astonishment. 'From the Dales, I ahm, and reet proud o' it,' he added. He bowed modestly at their amazement. 'The English court sends us ambassadors from all parts,' he explained. 'I can make a good fist of a Wiltshire gentleman too, but you wouldn't understand a word of that.'

Louise dug into the breast of her jerkin, and pulled out a folded paper, creased and splattered with ink. 'I'm no great hand,' she apologised. 'This is a note for Benoit. It says very little, beyond sending him love from me and my mother, and promising to do whatever is within our powers to make things more comfortable for him. There was nothing else I could think to say that would not offer false hope, or put you in danger if this note were intercepted.' She handed the letter to Gabriel, and bent her head. 'I wanted to say we would help him escape, but how can we do that?'

Gabriel looked grim as he put the letter in his shirt. He had not visited Durham before, but he had heard of its castle. Beyond the Tower of London, he doubted there was a stronger or more heavily guarded fortress.

'It'll be difficult for you,' said Crozier. 'The city will be on high alert for trouble from the north. I am told they have sent additional troops there from Surrey's headquarters in Pontefract. Any stranger will be viewed with suspicion.'

'I anticipate trouble,' said the courtier. 'I'd be a fool not to. But my hope is to bluff my way into the castle, and to see, if not the prisoners themselves, then the record of their names. They will, surely, keep a roll of who they hold, and the charges against them. If that were possible, and assuming always that Benoit is actually in their keep, we will at least know what his situation is.'

Louise grasped his hand. 'You are too, too good, to do this for my family.' Her eyes sparkled with tears. 'I can never repay you. Either of you,' she added, looking at Crozier, who was picking stones from the soles of his boots. He did not meet her glance. She put her hand on his arm, and he looked up, his eyes a tarn of border grey. He stood, and her hand fell.

'I don't envy you looking for a record book,' he said to Gabriel.

'Why – can you not read?'

Crozier ignored the jibe. 'In times like these,' he replied, 'with the number of prisoners they will be holding, it'd be a miracle if a scribe was called in to help. My guess is the cattle market will keep a closer account than the castle guards.'

'You may be right,' said Gabriel. 'I can only pray not.'

As the last of the daylight faded, they packed their saddlebags. Crozier left to refill their flasks from a stream at the foot of the hill. As soon as he was gone, Gabriel took Louise in his arms. 'I've been wanting to do this for days,' he murmured. He held her for a long time, before pulling away and looking anxiously down at her. 'You must be brave,' he said. 'Even more brave than you have already shown yourself. Tomorrow I may bring bad news of Benoit, or no news at all. This is the last throw of the dice. If he is not here, our options run out.'

'I know,' she said. 'And I promise to be strong.' She raised her face to him, and it would have taken a man of stone not to meet her lips. Gabriel was many things, but passionless was not one of them. He pulled her roughly to him, and kissed her long and hard, until she thought her back would break from his hold.

When he released her, he kept an arm around her and pulled the ring from his finger. 'You must have this,' he said. 'If I should not come back safely tomorrow, then it is yours, in memory of me – of us.'

Louise stared at an emerald the size of a robin's egg, embedded in a heavy gold claw. 'I cannot . . . ' she began.

Gabriel kissed the top of her head. 'My sweet, you must. It was my father's. He gave it me on his death, as his own father had done. The emerald is an emblem of my country, but it is also the colour of my father's eyes. I think of him every time I look on it, and I wish you to remember me also, should I die.

'But,' he continued brightly, 'I do not intend that to happen. I plan to come back, and to marry you. This ring is my pledge.'

'Marry me?' she asked. 'Marry?' She took a step back. 'I am flattered, my lord, deeply. And yet . . . ' She looked at him, troubled though she was not sure why. 'We scarcely know each other. And I thought we said nothing could be settled between us yet . . . '

Gabriel placed a finger on her lips. 'I spoke like a fool,' he said. 'How could I not want you for ever? We are made for each other.' He kissed her again, his tongue deep in her mouth, and a hand undoing her jerkin and finding the thin bodice beneath.

After their first kiss, Louise had day-dreamed of such a moment. But now he was pressing against her she felt panic. His grip was becoming too tight, squeezing the breath from her. As his hands moved over her, pulling up her skirts, he gave a moan, and his knee pushed her legs apart.

With a wrench she pulled herself out of his hold. She stared at him, too shaken to speak.

'You're right, my love,' he said, stepping back. 'This is

not the place. Not the time. What are we thinking? Any minute now our chaperone will be back. But soon now, sweet little one, very soon . . . ' His face was flushed, and he looked on her with an expression she could not read, or did not want to.

Her voice trembled. 'I will take your ring,' she said, 'and keep it safe. But be very clear, I will give it back to you the moment you return. I cannot think of marrying right now. Not you. Not anyone.' She could not meet his eye, but Gabriel seemed unaware of the shadow that had passed between them.

Turning from him, she slipped the jewel into her chemise, where it pressed hard against her heart. At that moment, Crozier returned. She did not think he had noticed her adjusting her clothes or blinking away her tears.

*   *   *

After days in the wilds with only the sound of birdsong, the noise of Durham city was like a hammer on Gabriel's skull. He put a hand to his bruised forehead to steady himself, then marched on with an expression of disgust at the squalor around him. Tall and imposing though he was, with his riding cloak and sword, and his broad-brimmed hat, he had to stand aside for the urchins and street sellers who barrelled their way along the cobbled streets as if they would rather trample over him than deviate from their path by a single step. Their cries made his head ache, as did the bells of beggars, hirpling from door to door, and the stench from the tanneries, no less pungent here than it had been on the bedraggled outskirts.

Gabriel led his horse up towards the centre, taking care

not to step in the gutters, where liquid filth bubbled and swam. The city was a warren built on a hill as steep as a belfry, and the streets snaked this way and that, as if in playful mood. None led him where he expected, and many disappeared into shadowed alleyways he preferred to avoid, even at this innocent time of day.

At the city's crown stood the cathedral, soaringly massive against the sky. For all its plain beauty, it cast an admonitory eye over the streets below, a severity echoed by the castle which was not only as plain but forbidding. It stared down on its citizens as if hoping to catch them in crime, but Gabriel headed straight for it. He brushed past the ale-sellers and flower girls whose booths ringed the castle mound, and was soon at its gates. Rapping on the sentry's grille with his whip, he demanded to see the governor. There was no trace of doubt in his manner. 'Tell your master he has a visitor from the court. I must see him this instant. It is the Viscount Rutland.'

'He ain't here,' said the sentry. 'Gone north with the bishop.'

'Well, his deputy then,' said Gabriel, feeling sweat prickling on his neck. 'Just fetch whoever is in charge, will you?'

'That'll be Constable Ridley,' said the sentry. He disappeared, and a few minutes later the side-gate was unbolted, creaking as if it had not been opened in years.

The governor's office reeked of sweat. Under a clammy brow, the constable looked warily at his guest, but offered him a tumbler of wine, which Gabriel downed in the time it took his host to remove his helmet, and settle behind a desk that all but filled his chamber.

'What brings you so far north, my lord?' he asked. 'I thought there was business enough at court to keep you and your kind close to the crownhead in these desperate times?'

Gabriel gave a cold smile. 'With Henry in France, and affairs settled in Scotland, it matters not where the court finds itself. Anyway, that is none of your concern. But what must and does concern you is one of your prisoners. I have been sent by the lord lieutenant to find him.'

The constable was stung by his tone. 'That a fact?' he said, with a look that was turning swiftly from surly to suspicious. 'It's not so many days since Surrey was last here, and he said nothing about this matter.'

'How could he, since it has only just come to light? Events are moving swiftly, dear fellow, on all our borders. Let me explain.'

Gabriel bent forward and lowered his voice, obliging the constable to lean across his desk if he wanted to catch his words. The viscount talked as if he was rolling damsons around his mouth, so elegantly English he might have been the king's brother.

'We believe you might be holding the man in part responsible for the king's present troubles in France and in the north. A spy in other words, who has been passing information to both enemy sides.'

The constable frowned. 'We have taken many prisoners here since Flodden, both Scots and French. I have no note of their names, and in their condition it's hard to tell one face from another. Where they're going, it hardly matters.' He swallowed. 'Who is this man, and how will you recognise him?'

'His name is Benoit Brenier, and I know him well. His

complexion is so poor, I could find him blindfold, but I trust that won't be necessary.'

'And if he is here, as you suspect, what next? I cannot release him unless you bring orders from the king or his lieutenant.'

'There would be no need to release him,' said Gabriel, 'but I do have authority from Surrey to interrogate this prisoner and handle him as I see fit. The lord lieutenant has been called urgently to London, otherwise he would have seen to the matter himself.'

He handed the constable a parchment stamped with Surrey's seal. 'One would only need to spend an hour in conversation with the suspect, nothing more.' He met the soldier's eyes. 'I am sure you understand me perfectly. We need information. And names. We may be obliged to find ways to persuade the prisoner to offer these up. In that enquiry, I feel sure you would be an able assistant.'

The constable scanned the letter. It was simply worded, and the signature was Surrey's, or very like, as was the seal. He sensed something was awry, but if the viscount's request was legitimate, he would lose his post for refusing it. And there could be no harm, he reasoned, in showing this man the cells. At the very least he would enjoy seeing his lordship pale at the scenes below.

With a grunt he rose from his chair, lifted an iron ring dripping with keys and led Gabriel into the passage. Summoning a guard to accompany them, he unlocked the first of many doors that led to the dungeons.

*   *   *

On the hill, behind a bluff of rock and gorse, Louise and

Crozier hid. Durham stretched out far below. From this distance its streets and houses looked orderly and neat as a game of counters on a board.

As the day progressed, a pall of smoke thickened over the rooftops, but the smell of burning firewood only made them colder. To help pass the time, they eked out their day's ration of food, but they spoke very little. Voices carried far in these hills, and Louise was busy with her own thoughts. Crozier too, it seemed.

From their post, they watched farmers and pedlars making their way to town. A party of monks filed by, so close they could smell beer and onions on the air. Flattened on the ground, and praying the men did not turn and see the horses tethered among the willows, they waited for a cry of discovery, but none came. Thereafter, they took turns watching for intruders over the rocks, taking care not to show more than the top of their heads.

As the day slipped away, Louise grew anxious. Crozier was leaning against a tree, his brim low over his eyes. The vixen lay by him, head on paws. Louise crept to his side. 'What do we do if he doesn't come back by dark?' she whispered.

'We leave.'

'Abandon him? He might need our help. How can you even think of it?'

Crozier sat up, and pushed back his hat. 'Look, lassie, how many search parties do you intend to lead? First your brother, which I understand, and now this silver-tongued lord, which is harder to fathom.' He raised his hand to cut short her protests. 'If he does not return, he has either run into trouble, and there's nothing either of us can do about that. Or he is delayed. If that's the case, he will know to head north on his own. But we can't sit out here overnight, it would be deadly dangerous. It's unsafe enough as it is.'

He could see she was not convinced. 'Listen, lass, Torrance knew the risks when he agreed to do this.'

'I know,' she said, 'but I don't think I did.'

Crozier sighed. 'I can see you have an affection for him, and he for you. That's plain to anyone. But you are here for your brother's sake, and if you can't get news of him tonight, you must make your way home. There's nothing more you can do for Benoit out here, and with each day in these parts you put your own life in peril. If we must set off without Torrance, once we reach the border I can set you on the road to Edinburgh with one of my men, but I must then get back to my people. I've already been away too long.'

She looked miserable, and he put a hand briefly on her arm. 'But it's early to be thinking like this. We have another few hours before we must leave. He may well be back before then.'

There was a rustle of grass behind them, and they turned, expecting to see the courtier. Before they could take in what was happening, an arm caught Louise around the waist, and she was dragged to the ground, with a knife at her neck and a hand over her mouth. A soldier stood with his boot on Crozier's chest and his sword pricking his throat. The vixen was barking like a banshee, darting in to bite the soldiers, retreating to a safe distance when they swung their blades at her, where she continued to yap.

'Will you look at this, then!' cried the one holding Louise, who was the older and fatter. 'A cosy little party for two. Mind if we join ye?'

The soldier standing over Crozier snickered. He moved his blade across the Borderer's throat, as if tracing the gash he planned to inflict. 'I wonder what youse are doing out here, so secret like,' he said. 'Nothing good, I reckon. But ain't she a bit old and lardy for the likes of you?'

Crozier looked to Louise, whose eyes were frantic above her captor's hand. Imperceptibly he shook his head, but it was too late. In that instant she had bitten the hand so hard she reached the bone. The soldier squealed and released her, doubling up over his injury. Louise scrambled to her knees, but before she could run, he reached out his bloodied hand and caught her ankle, pulling her back towards him. He twisted her arms behind her back, and spoke over her shoulder into her ear. 'Nasty little thing, you are. You need a lesson in manners, don't you?'

Pinioning her with his knee, he began to unbuckle his belt. His friend laughed again. 'You're gonnae enjoy this,' he said to Crozier, 'and come to think of it, so am I. It's my turn next.' He pressed the sword tip deeper, and a trickle of blood ran into Crozier's shirt. The Borderer's breathing quickened and his hand inched towards his hilt. Seeing this, the soldier stamped on his chest, knocking the breath out of him. 'Don't even think of trying to move,' he said. 'I wis a butcher's boy one time, and I can do things with flesh that wid make ye regret it.'

Beside herself with fury, the vixen bobbed and barked, nipping the older soldier's heels as he fumbled under his jerkin. Cursing the dog, he jabbed his sword at her, then loosened his britches and hoisted up Louise's skirts. She kicked and squirmed, but he was too strong for her. Rage and humiliation washed over her, scalding as boiling water as she waited for what must follow. But as the soldier rolled onto her he gave an eerie whistling sigh, and she felt his full weight slump down, heavy and dead as a sack of meal. The younger soldier gave a surprised holler, then a shriek. At the same time there was a gurgle and a hiss at her ear and a spurt of pumping blood hit the grass by her head.

She was screaming when Gabriel dragged her clear of her attacker, whose throat he had slit. By the time she was on her feet, and ripping off her blood-soaked cap, Crozier too was free, kicking his assailant's body aside and wiping his sword on the grass. The dead man's stomach gaped.

'More coming up the hill,' cried Gabriel. 'Get out of here!'

Blinded by panic, half-crazed by the smell of blood on her face and hands, Louise ran for the horses. Crozier pitched her and the vixen into the saddle, and gathering her reins, leapt onto his mare and tugged her pony into a gallop at his side. They blundered their way through the wood, branches whipping their faces. When they reached the hill-top Crozier handed Louise her reins and they turned, panting, to catch the gleam of pikes as soldiers milled around their hiding place. Hooves pounded the earth close by, and Gabriel rode into sight, crouched low over his horse's neck.

'Get a move on!' he shouted. 'There's mounted soldiers close behind!'

What followed was the terrified flight of the hunted animal, whose pursuers never tire. Fast though their horses could gallop, they did not know these parts, and at every hill and turn the hoofbeats that once were faint, grew louder. With two murdered comrades to avenge, and the knowledge that they were dealing with no ordinary criminals, the soldiers were not going to give up.

Even Crozier began to flag. Wheeling to a halt, he held up his hand. In the darkness, they listened. The rumble of hooves down the track told them the soldiers were a mile or less behind. 'We can't throw them off,' he said. 'We have to hide and let them pass.'

'Here? Where can we hide?' Louise's voice was shrill.

'I don't know yet, but somewhere close. When I dismount, follow me quickly.'

A few miles later, he leapt off his mare and led them down a steep embankment into a wooded gully where a stream tumbled off the hills. 'For God's sake keep the dog quiet,' he hissed, and Louise put her hand over the vixen's snout.

They had barely hidden themselves when the soldiers could be heard approaching. Louise felt light-headed as they got close. A jingling posse of twenty or more, they rode past, black against black. As they drew level, Gabriel's stallion raised its head and whinnied. The courtier quickly calmed it, but Louise shuddered. If the soldiers found them, they were as good as dead. She could only hope it would be swift.

The stallion went unheard. It was their only stroke of luck that miserable day. Weary, and frightened, Louise said a silent prayer of thanks to the Blessed Virgin, and soon there was only the sound of rushing water in the night. For the moment, the soldiers were gone.

'Well done, sir,' said Gabriel. 'That was a clever move.'

'Maybe,' said Crozier, 'but now we must find our way back, without running into them. We have no choice but to ride on tonight, and through the day. It'll be hazardous.'

Gabriel took Louise's arm in the dark. 'Take heart. We are safe now. And I have news of your brother. He is alive.'

'Alive? Alive? Oh sweet Jesus, I can't believe it . . . ' She dissolved into tears, and Gabriel held her until she was quiet. 'I'm sorry,' she said, pulling herself from his hold. 'It's just . . . I had almost given up hope.'

'Naturally,' said Gabriel. 'How could you not.'

'Was he there? Did you speak with him?'

The conversation that followed would stay with Louise for the rest of her life, as an encounter with pure horror. The courtier's voice was eerie, hushed and close as it was in the darkness, but it was his words that chilled her. As he spoke, he took her hand, as if to charge her with courage. By her side, Crozier stood, silent and solid.

'There is something you need to know,' he said. 'Your brother was indeed a prisoner at the castle. Few Scots soldiers were brought there, other than those who would fetch a good ransom. Benoit was easy to remember because he made quite a nuisance of himself. The constable did not know his name, but after I made him realise how important this matter was, and made it worth his while to search his memory, he did eventually recall that a man picked up at Flodden had hammered on the cell door day and night demanding to be released.

'When nothing would shut him up, the governor asked what he meant by it. He said he had a right to be set free, and if anyone doubted it, they should speak to the lieutenant of the north, Lord Surrey, who knew him, and the services he had rendered the country, very well.'

'Knew him well?' A barn owl glided low over their heads, a glimmer of white against the dark, and Louise found herself following its ghostly flight as if to deflect the words that kept falling, a slow drip of poison.

'He made such a fuss, the governor eventually summoned Surrey. I spoke to Benoit's cell mates, such as could still talk.' Gabriel hesitated. The memory of the dungeons was raw, and he felt queasy as he revisited the scene. He swallowed. 'One old Highlander told me that Surrey arrived late one night, and after a brief parlay through the bars, had Benoit removed from the dungeon. He swears he heard a bag of coins being put into your brother's hand as the door closed behind him.'

Louise was perplexed. 'What does all this mean?'

'It may not be as bad as it sounds,' said Gabriel. Louise pulled her hand from his, and folded her arms. She would not cry. The vixen pressed against her legs, as if to comfort her.

'What does it mean?' she repeated.

'I admit it looks suspicious,' he replied. 'On the face of it, it would appear he has committed treason. We have first-hand evidence that he has been in the English commander's pay. There is nothing I can think that he would have been able to offer but information. After all, thanks to your sister, and his work at the shipyards, he was close to the court – '

Louise gasped, but Gabriel pressed on. 'Is it possible he also passed news from the French ambassador to Surrey? It seems conceivable, since he too is French.'

'So you believe he is a spy,' said Louise in a voice so hard none of them recognised it. 'Well, you could not be more wrong. Benoit is the most loyal man I have ever known. To pass secrets to the English would be to betray both his countries. He is a Frenchman, yes, but Scotland is his home. He loves it. You call yourself my friend, and yet you doubt my brother, on the basis of nothing but hearsay.'

'Dearest . . . ' Gabriel reached for her, but she stepped back.

'If what you say is true, there will be a good explanation for it. I will not believe him a traitor. Nothing will convince me of that. I am grateful to you for the trouble you have gone to, but if you want to believe the worst of him, I will have nothing more to do with you.' At this, a cry escaped her and she buried her face in her pony's mane, muffling her sobs.

Gabriel sighed. He moved towards her, but Crozier stopped him. 'Leave her be,' he said. 'She's in shock. She's had a desperate day. No doubt she'll come around.'

They moved away and stood silently, listening to the wood around them, though it could not mask the sound of her tears. Some time passed before she could face them again. Patting the vixen, she wiped her eyes and joined them. 'Forgive me,' she said, though it was unclear to whom. 'I'm not entirely myself. If I can only wash the blood off my face, I will be better.'

Crouched on the stream's bank, she splashed icy water over her face and hair. When eventually the stickiness and stench of the soldier's blood was gone, she rose. She ached in every bone, but she knew the cause was fear rather than fever. The soldier's assault had left her trembling, but that was as nothing to what she had learnt about her brother. If such damning evidence could be brought against him, he would not only die, but publicly, and most cruelly. 'We should be off then,' she said, clenching her teeth to stop their chattering.

Gabriel touched her arm. 'Louise, your brother may already be safely back in Scotland. It's likely that as . . . as an associate in some way of Surrey, he will have a safe conduct, and can travel by day. We must make for Leith, and hope to find him there. He will be able to explain everything when we see him.'

'No doubt you're right,' she replied, stonily. 'So let's make a start.' She picked up the vixen, and tucked her under her arm.

Crozier approached her. 'Ma'am,' he said, 'there's a long ride ahead, and you will be cold. Take this.' Without waiting for a reply, he draped his riding cloak around her, the old, soft leather blanketing her from the night air. She pulled the hood over her head, and smelled pinewood, the scent of Crozier's Keep. 'Thank you,' she said, but he was gone, leading the mare out of the wood and onto the trail.

CHAPTER SEVENTEEN

14 October 1513

They rode through that night alert to the slightest noise in case it brought the enemy. Often they halted to listen closely to the wind, before moving on. Sensing their fear, the horses were skittish, and only when morning broke did they and their mounts grow calmer. Under the Borderer's command, they travelled long into the day, stopping briefly to water and feed the horses, and eat the dwindling remains of their supplies. Crozier kept them to the hill-tops and forests, where few would be about. Heedless of their route, Louise was white-faced and silent. As they rode, she went over the information Gabriel had learned, as if by revisiting it from every angle she might find an answer, a clue they had overlooked.

Perhaps Surrey had given Benoit money to pass a message back to Patrick Paniter and the Scottish court? She could think of no other explanation for that sinister transaction. And yet it did not explain why Benoit was already known to the English commander. That knowledge lodged like a fishbone in her throat. Had he, like her father, lived a double life?

Her head ached. As they headed north, a gruelling, sleepless slog across hills and marshes, she passed from fury and fear to exquisite pain. Not since the news of her father's and sister's deaths had she felt like this. It was as if her heart, battered by too much emotion, had gone cold in her chest. She felt numb, while at the same time hurting as if mortally wounded.

No direction she turned brought comfort. Benoit must be innocent, but who else would believe that? He would never be given a fair hearing. In this climate, the country needed a scapegoat, and who better than a swarthy foreigner to bear the burden of guilt for a battle lost, and the nation's future with it?

The pony's hooves drummed beneath her: Benoit was as good as dead. Better he had fallen at Flodden. The words knitted themselves into the hoofbeats, and she pushed back her hood, to let the wind clear her head of the wicked refrain.

They were two days on the road before the country began to change. Yellow, grass-blown hills stretched to a blue horizon, where the Cheviots melted into the border. If anything had the power to cheer Louise, it was the sight of ragged, nimble sheep on the crags, whose pinched northern faces were as familiar and welcome as a dear friend's. She patted her pony's neck. Only a few miles more and they would be back in Scotland.

Under a stand of pines they pulled up to rest, knowing there was as much danger in the final few miles as on the long road they'd already taken. Mud-spattered and weary, the Edinburgh pair were in a very different mood from the day they had set out. Then they had left with anxiety tempered by hope. Now, they were not only disheartened, but filled with dread.

As he unsaddled his horse, Gabriel shot an uneasy glance at Louise. For once she met his eye. 'I'm sorry,' she said. 'It's not your fault, any of this.' He beckoned her, and after a moment's hesitation she walked into his embrace. 'I'm sorry too,' he said, whispering into her hair, 'I've been too urgent with you. I will do better.' He kissed her gently, and let her go. 'We will sort things out, never fear.' Unfurling their bedrolls they slept side by side on the heathery turf. Gabriel reached out for her hand, but Louise appeared already asleep, her arms tightly wrapped around herself. Crozier kept lookout. When the watch changed, he stretched out at a distance from the girl. He did not want to see her disappointment when she woke and found him and not her courtier at her side.

Near the border they picked up a well-trodden drover's road. Though the day was fading, they passed a pair of herring wives returning with empty creels, and a herdsman whipping his cattle into line with a stick. The riders doffed their hats, but did not speak, nor were they questioned. Everyone was intent on getting off the hills before night. Not until they could see the river Tweed did they see signs of trouble. Along the riverbanks soldiers were patrolling. Their shouts were faint, at this distance, and in the purple haze of an autumn dusk they looked harmless, almost comical, boys at play with outsized toys. Gabriel looked at Crozier. 'What now?'

'We head westwards,' he replied. 'It's a bit out of your way, but the safest road. We'll be near Yetholm shortly, and there's good cover as we come off the hills there. There may be guards posted, but I doubt many. If we're seen, we should be able to outride them.'

Some time later, they crept off the English hills and climbed into the oak-lined cleuchs of the Scottish Border-lands. Crozier smelled home in the bitter grasses and the peaty fires of the valley hamlets and for the first time since they had left Durham, his spirits lightened.

It was not long before he drew to a halt. 'This is where I leave you,' he said. 'Down there, by the village, is the road to Kelso, and Edinburgh beyond. It's not a difficult journey. If you are tired, of course, you can come back to the keep for a night's rest.'

Louise shook her head. 'I cannot,' she said. 'I must get to Leith as quickly as I can. We will sleep rough, if we sleep at all. But please tell Hob I will be back for him as soon as things are sorted at home. I hope that won't be long.'

Gabriel made a courtly salute. 'I pray we meet again,' he said. The Borderer wheeled his horse, speaking over his shoulder. 'I wish you well with your brother, ma'am. If there is anything I can do, just get a message to me. Other-wise I will see you again when you come back for the boy and your horse. We will give you a warmer welcome than on your first visit, I promise.'

'Thank you. Thank you for everything,' she said, but he was gone, giving his horse its head for the homeward stretch. Knowing its stable was near, Louise's pony tried to follow, but she reined him in. The vixen too ran after him, barking, but when her mistress called, she turned back, her tail low as she padded beside her.

Once through the village, they moved faster, riding abreast. 'We must rest the horses at some point,' said

Gabriel, 'but I would like to get onto the Edinburgh road before then. Can you manage a little longer?'

'Of course,' said Louise. 'I would happily ride all night.' She was uneasy at being alone with him. At the sight of Crozier heading into the night she had felt an urge to call out and join him. After what she had been through, Crozier's Keep felt like a haven, dark and decayed though it was. With a rush of understanding, she realised that wherever Crozier went, she would feel safe.

The sudden revelation made her shiver. It made no sense. He was rough and dangerous, an expert killer, as she had seen, and not to be trusted. Nor had he shown any sign of interest in her, despite his many kindnesses. Gabriel meanwhile had been braver in a single day than most men would be in their lifetime, and there could be no doubt he had acted out of love for her. Talking his way into Durham Castle was an act of heroism that might have cost his life, and by rescuing her from the soldiers, he had not only saved Louise but Crozier too. She was grateful, and humbled by her debt to him. And yet the more he talked of love, the less she felt it. She hoped she was not turning into a prude, who quailed at the prospect of lying with a man. Yet how else to explain the revulsion she had felt at the sour taste of his tongue, and his greedy, grasping hands?

She sighed. Marguerite had said there were acts of love one grew to enjoy in time. Maybe that was all there was to it. She would have to become accustomed to being handled as if her body was not her own to command while her lover was taking his pleasure. Whistling the vixen to heel, she pulled Crozier's cloak closer against the cold and bent her head into the wind. They had a long way still to travel.

It was close to midnight when they reined in. The night was clear and the moon bright, yet they heard rather than saw the danger ahead. Senses sharpened from their days on the road, they caught the sounds of men on the move. 'Listen!' said Louise, as the rattling tread of a band of riders reached them. An iron-wheeled cart creaked, its mules slow footed. Heavily mounted horses trotted, snorting at the dark, but it was hard to guess how many.

The forest funnelled the noise, bringing it closer. Irritated at the delay, they led their horses into the trees, and waited for trouble to pass. Gabriel was beginning to chafe at the number of occasions he had been obliged to hide, to keep his sword sheathed, or his tongue guarded. He had taken no pleasure in killing the soldier, yet it was a welcome reminder that he was still a soldier himself, and a finer one than most. Holding the advancing soldiers at bay while Crozier and Louise made their escape counted, he reckoned, as one of the most courageous acts of his life. That he had done so without using his sword was little short of miraculous. Adopting the hauteur of a man above doubt he had made them believe he was a scout from the castle who had that minute discovered the warm, wet corpses of his compatriots. As they crowded around the bodies, the patrol had not even noticed him leading his horse away.

He reached for Louise's hand. With her at his side, there was nothing he could not achieve. Louise let her hand rest in his, and in this he read not the guilt that filled her with regret and shame, but love. He was soon to discover his mistake.

The minutes passed, but the road remained empty. The

sounds had diminished, but there was an occasional whinny, a grumbling voice. 'We can't go on down this road now,' whispered Louise.

'But nor can we go back,' said Gabriel. 'Sounds like they're setting up camp. We can skirt them by finding a higher trail through the forest.'

Louise shook her head. 'I don't like this. We need to know who they are.' She lashed her pony to a tree. 'I'm going to find out.' Smothering a sigh, Gabriel followed. They crept through the forest, light-footed as dancers. In the bustle of unpacking, the soldiers did not hear their approach. Moving from tree to tree they drew closer, until they were near enough to snatch a plate of broth from the cook who was ladling from a cauldron, heedless of the eyes at his back.

To Louise it looked like a small army, bristling with pikes, guns and bows. Their commander stood at the centre of the clearing, directing the men as they queued for food. 'Four hours' slumber, gentlemen,' he shouted. 'If we set off in the early hours, we will be through Coldstream by cock's crow, and in Teviotdale at first light.' He put his hands on his hips, though there was little space for them among the scabbards and belts and bugle. 'We will have the advantage of surprise, but do not underestimate these people. Even the women and weans are venomous as vipers, and will slit your gizzards open as soon as look at you.'

He raised his voice.

'At the risk of repeating myself until you're bored witless, give no quarter. Kill, or be killed. With these filthy tribes, there's no other way. And to cheer you on this dreary night, I am authorised to tell you that the warden of the marches himself has offered a reward to all who play their part well. So bear that in mind as these louts charge at you. Each flea-bitten head is worth a purse of gold.'

The men raised a throaty cheer, and the commander left them to settle down. He made his way to the cook's station, where he was handed a bowl of stew, drinking it in a few gulps as if it were beer. 'I don't like being out in these parts one little bit,' he said, running his tongue around his mouth, collecting morsels that had strayed into his beard. The cook grunted, and wiped down the dirty plates. 'Don't know what it is,' he continued, 'but I feel there's eyes on me behind every rock and tree. They're savages out here, untouched by charity or God.' He tossed his bowl into the cook's tub. 'Well, Dacre will have his revenge tomorrow all right, and very satisfying it will be.' He slapped the cook on the back. 'Make sure and stay near the wagon when we start rampaging. And sharpen your kitchen knives. You might just need them.' The cook gave another grunt, though to Louise's ear it was more like a whimper.

Gabriel tugged at her cloak, and signalled her to follow him back into the forest. Neither spoke until they had reached their horses.

'We'll have to take the top road, and circle around them,' Gabriel whispered, untying the stallion. 'A damned nuisance, but there's nothing for it.'

'What do you mean? Those are Dacre's men. Didn't you hear him?' Louise stared at him in disbelief. Under moonlight Gabriel's face was bleached, his hair drained from gold to silver. 'They are heading for Crozier and his people,' she said, as if he were dim-witted and needed the situation decoded. 'Crozier told me their plan was not to make a move till All Hallows' Eve, yet here they are. They want revenge, and nobody's going to care about promises or the law, if it's only Border folk that are murdered.'

Gabriel said nothing, and she caught his sleeve. 'My Lord, we must get to Crozier's Keep! We must go immediately, to warn them! We can give them time to prepare, to escape.'

He covered her hand with his own, pale eyes gleaming. 'No, Louise. We must get to Leith. Your brother's plight is more urgent, more important. We need to find him, and help him. He must have a chance to put the truth to Patrick Paniter, if he's to have any hope of surviving. He may even need to hide. Don't you see what danger he is in now that the news is out about the bribe he has taken?'

She pulled her hand away. 'There is nothing we can do for Benoit in the next day that will help anything. He might not even be in Leith, and then how would we feel, if we'd left Crozier and Hob and Wat to be killed?'

Gabriel shook his head. 'This is folly, my sweet. You can do nothing to help. Crozier and his gang are cunning enough to know what's heading their way. Why else did he rush off as he did? I wager his castle is already on full guard.'

Her eyes were bright with fury. 'Don't you care if they die? You saved Crozier's life the other day, if you remember. Is it worthless to you now?'

'It meant nothing to me then,' he replied, stung. 'By saving you I merely distracted the other soldier and gave Crozier the chance to run him through. It was you alone I thought of. It has always been you.'

He moved towards her, but she took a step back.

'And spare a thought for your poor mother,' he continued. 'She will be fretting herself ill, waiting to hear if I have found you. I set out to bring you back to her, and I intend to do just that.'

Louise's eyes narrowed. 'Nobody cared much about our family when Marguerite died,' she said. 'I wonder why suddenly all this concern? What is my mother's misery to you? Tell me truly why you came after me, and why you risked your life in Durham for a man – and a girl – you barely know?'

'For love,' he said. 'How often must I tell you?' But his expression was the opposite of love. Hot words rose to her lips, but it was not the need to whisper that held them back. The forest pressed in around her, and a cold sweat crawled down her back. 'I must go,' she said abruptly, 'whatever you think.' She untied the pony and, forcing herself to walk slowly, made for the path.

'Louise.' Gabriel spoke quietly, but the command was clear. She continued, quickening her pace, though the forest clawed at her.

'Come back, or you will regret it!'

On she walked. She had stepped out onto the path, into the open air, when the undergrowth crackled, and he was upon her, grabbing her arm, and wrenching her around to face him. She screamed, and raised her fists to defend herself. Catching her by the wrists, he pulled her to him, looked into her eyes and kissed her, crushing her mouth as if he would print his lips on hers forever. She tasted blood, and tears. Then, with a cry, he threw her from him, sending her reeling across the path.

'That is love, my pretty,' he hissed. 'It hurts. It bleeds – as your unhappy sister learned. It is not the tame thing you women like to imagine. It is as violent as hate.' He picked his hat from the dust, and brushed it down. His expression was unearthly in the elvish light. 'But I will always love you, Louise, with a passion you will never understand. That much is the truth, I swear to God.'

With these words, uttered more like a confession than a declaration, he strode off. She was alone, shivering in the starlight, the sound of Gabriel and his horse growing fainter as they climbed into the forest.

*   *   *

Turned towards home, the pony made its way west, needing barely a touch on the reins as it cantered across the moorlands and onto the road for the Croziers' stronghold. When at last the scented pinewoods closed in above them, Louise spurred the pony into a last burst of speed. She was crouched low over its mane when a black figure stepped out onto the path. The pony reared, and she screamed, fighting to keep her seat. When the animal had calmed, she found the shadowy figure of Tom at her side.

'Saints alive!' she cried. 'You nearly scared the horse to death.'

'Sorry,' he said, 'but I'm on lookout, with orders to stop anyone who passes.' He put a hand on the pony's nose. He had known her since she was a foal, and she nuzzled his palm as if he had been no more frightening than a fly. 'Adam said you were back off to Edinburgh. What's going on?'

'Dacre's men.' She took a deep breath: 'They'll be here by daylight.' Tom looked at her, suddenly stilled. After a second, he cupped his hands over his mouth and whistled like an owl. Moments later more men appeared on the trail. The news was passed on, and they melted back into the trees. With Tom riding pillion, Louise made for the keep. By the time they got there, the place was bright with torches, and the courtyard busy as a fair. Tom slipped from the pony, and hurried off.

Crozier met Louise in the yard, and as she dismounted, took the reins from her. He looked at her gravely, before leading the pony down a makeshift ramp into the great hall, where its companions were already stalled.

'Where did you meet them?' he asked, as the pony slithered down the planks.

'East of Coldstream. About three hours from here.'

'And what's happened to his lordship – he surely didn't leave you to ride here alone?'

'He's gone,' said Louise.

'Gone?'

'Forever,' she said, turning aside. 'He's on his way to Leith. I was a fool.'

'You're not alone in that,' he said grimly, and put a fleeting hand on her shoulder, as a brother would.

In the hall Crozier's men swarmed, arming themselves and those villagers who had joined them for the fray. Crozier turned to Louise. 'You can take refuge in the armoury. It's the safest room in the house. Only if they overwhelm us will they reach it. And I don't plan on that happening.'

'I don't want to be safe,' she replied. 'I want to help. I won't see this place or your people destroyed.'

He looked grim. 'You are quite certain about this?'

She nodded, and he held her eyes, as if seeing her clearly for the first time. 'I won't forget this,' he said. 'But if you are going to help, you need a weapon.' From a rail on the wall he took a narrow iron pipe, a culverin which she first mistook for a club. 'Old Wat here will show you how to load it. It works much like a peashooter, but it's deadly. Station yourself on the battlements, where you can get a clear shot. But you must take care. I will not have you hurt. You need a helmet and a tabard.'

'For me and all!' piped a voice. 'Cos I'm coming wi' ye!' and Hob threw himself at her, wrapping his arms around her cloak as if he could anchor her to the spot for the rest of her life. She had time only to kiss his head when she found Mother Crozier at her side, beckoning her to the kitchen. 'You'll be famished,' she said. 'You must eat afore the fight. It won't be cooked, but it'll be filling.' It was the first time Louise had seen her face soften into something like a smile.

*   *   *

Dacre's men entered the pinewoods as daylight was beginning to finger the trees. They rode with an air of authority, unafraid of the shadows that closed in on the path. Only those with second sight would know they were coming, and at this hour none but forest creatures would be abroad.

At the first glimpse of the keep, rising skywards through the morning mist as if to speak with the eagles, the commander called a halt. The woods were quiet, not yet woken. Nothing stirred. He stroked his beard and listened, the frosted damp settling on his lip. Satisfied that they were not expected, he gathered his lieutenants to issue his orders. Dismounting, they assembled at the front of the troops, but their leader had barely started to speak when the air darkened, and hummed. Startled, they looked up, covering their faces with their hands, but it was too late. Arrows flew into their midst like a swarm of hornets, quivering as they found their target in breast and eye, throat and back.

Even if he'd been a praying man, Murdo Montgomery could not have asked for a finer prize than to have the leaders caught together in a circle neat as a bull's-eye. From their eyries, he and his archers had picked off half of them with their first fusillade, though the commander escaped by ducking beneath falling bodies while he fumbled for his horn and blared the signal for the army's archers and billsmen to be loosed.

As English arrows found them, Borderers tumbled out of the trees at the feet of men whose billhooks were waiting. But while too many were lost this way, Crozier's ambushers were the more skilled, and by the time the air had cleared enough for Dacre's fighters to scan the tree-tops, Crozier's men had flown, to await the soldiers when they reached the keep.

All but leaderless, save for the commander whose voice was drowned out by the uproar, the troops stampeded their way to the castle. There they were brought up short by a sea of felled pines that lay between them and the castle's outer walls. They could get closer only on foot. A fluster of abandoned horses added to the disorder, and before those few men who kept a calm head could trample their way over the trunks and branches, the first assault from the castle rained down on them, sending their already panicked steeds fleeing into the trees, and scything the front ranks of the army with a hail of arrows, gunshot and cannon fire.

On the battlements, Crozier's men were busy. Wat had explained to Louise how to ram shot into her gun and train her sights on her target, but there was no room for her at the walls, where men crowded every inch. Her only use was to reload the serpentines for Wat and his cronies. The fuses sizzled, the guns screamed, and soon the air was thick with smoke. At her side Hob was hopping with excitement and passing her the cannonballs as if they were bannocks for the oven, and not the harbinger of some poor fellow's death.

In the initial flurry, it seemed the enemy had been repelled. Dozens lay dead or maimed around the keep's walls, their comrades stumbling over them to reach the fight. Stunned by the fury of the Borderers' defence, the soldiers' response was sluggish and weak. But just as it seemed they might be on the point of slinking away they regrouped. There was a few minutes' silence as they conferred, and then came a surge upon the walls with a roar that made Louise's stomach somersault. As a volley of arrows began to bring down the men on the battlements, grappling irons found their hold on the walls, and in a matter of minutes Dacre's men were dropping into the keep's outer yard, swords in hand, and knives between their teeth.

Crozier's marksmen found them, but though many fell, they kept coming, crawling over the walls and scuttling across the yard for cover like ants whose nest has been disturbed. 'Useless guns can't reach 'em at this angle,' roared Wat, as he abandoned his cannon and grabbed a hand-held culverin, leaning dangerously far over the wall to take his shot. Louise and Hob took charge of his serpentine, but what had been exhilarating a minute before was now slow and, Louise feared, useless, their aim soaring high above the soldiers on the edge of the wood, and landing deep in the trees.

As the frenzy increased, and the noise with it, an ominous beat began to sound. It could be felt as well as heard beneath the quickening tempo of the fight, the gathering fear on the ramparts. Doomful as a funeral bell, Dacre's men were battering at the inner gates: slow, steady, patient. Were they to give, things would get a great deal worse.

It was then Louise heard a splintering of wood and a cheer that set the rooks in uproar. The cheers became a chant, and a minute later the gates cracked, groaned, and gave way. Dacre's men were now at the very door of the keep. Should they breach that, the fight would be lost. Crozier's voice could be heard, shouting instructions. If she had looked over the walls, she would have seen him, striding among his men, a fierce figure in full fighting gear, his voice sharp as the sword in his hand. But she had no time to look. The fight continued from the battlements, but there were gaps now on the walls, where the enemy had found its mark.

The injured sprawled behind the parapet. 'This is hopeless,' she said to Hob, wiping sweat from her face. 'We're wasting our time with this wretched gun. Stay here, while I fetch water and bindings for these men. And keep your head down.' Even as she spoke, arrows whined over the walls, spearing the stonework above their heads before falling with a clatter.

She ran down the stairs, a corkscrew of twists and turns that brought her, at last, to the keep's well by the kitchens.

From the yard she heard the cries of fighting men, and the rasp of swords. In the great hall, the horses shifted and snorted in the sooty light.

At the kitchen table Mother Crozier was ripping sheets into strips, and bathing them in a solution of water and moss. Without a word, she handed an armful to Louise, along with a gutting knife, and a pail of water. 'I have my own dagger,' Louise stammered, 'that's all I need if I have to defend myself.'

'It's for the men, lassie. To dig out the shot and arrowheads.' She made a sickening stirring gesture. 'And once you've dealt with the ones on the tower, get down here and you can help out with the others as they're brought in.' Louise nodded. 'Of course.' She left, and then turned. 'Where's Crozier?'

'Out there,' replied his mother with a nod to the yard, 'at the gates.' She caught Louise's stricken look. 'He has his faults, that lad, but he's a fine one with a sword. It's possible we might never see him again, but if that's the case, we're all lost.' She returned to her task, and Louise hurried back to the stairs, wondering if her heart would burst with fear even before the soldiers reached her.

Yet by the time she reached the battlements, she was calm. It was as if desperation had worn itself out, leaving a quietened mind and steady hands, which was as well, given the delicate business that lay ahead. With Hob's help, she dragged the wounded to shelter. Most required no more than a bandage, but a few needed the knife, which they endured by clenching their teeth and telling her to get on with it. 'Do yer worst, hen.'

Sweat dripped into their eyes, and their fists were

clenched so tightly they turned white, but they uttered no murmur. 'Well done, sir,' said Louise as they let her dig, shovel and twist until the shot or lead-tip was removed. Behind her, Hob passed around a flask of aqua vitae. Some took only a swig, before crawling to their feet and picking up their bows and guns. For the next hour, a willpower and stamina as ancient as the hills they stood on kept them at their posts, as did regular refreshment from Hob's magical flask.

The most grievously hurt, however, were beyond Louise's help, and for these men she could do no more than raise water to their lips, and bathe their faces. She watched Hob for any sign that this was too much to bear, but he continued as if the sight of blood and death meant nothing more personal to him beyond another task to be dealt with. She tapped his helmet, and smiled. 'You're a natural nurse, boy. Your father would be proud of you.'

'Learnt among his horses, didn't I?' he said, 'and they're a lot harder to handle than these chiels.'

What neither cared to think about was the battle below. The noise had quietened, but far from receding the fight had taken on a new and more deadly quality, as Crozier and his men faced their opponents hand to hand. Locked together in pairs, they danced and dodged around the yard, swords saying what words never could.

Murdo, Tom and their followers defended the shattered gates, which to many of Dacre's men were to prove the mouth of hell itself. The Borderers were pitiless, and their savage skills made an end of all but the doughtiest of the march warden's servants. But those that did get through the breach were more than a match for the last line of the keep's defence, and Crozier knew it. He and his finest fighters kept their backs to the keep and took on each new assailant as if he was their first. Standing at the door was a guard of three, under the charge of Old Crozier. When men fell, they were hustled and dragged into the keep, where they came under Mother Crozier's and Louise's care.

The morning drew on. Swords clashed as duels sparked into life across the yard and at the gates. The glitter of blades was soon doused in blood. As Crozier despatched soldier after soldier, he sickened of the smell of flesh. Worse, though, was the thought that he and his cousins were only a few yards short of losing the keep. Dacre's men were thinning, but the danger remained acute. It would take only a few to storm the keep for their final sentence to be passed.

Images of his mother and grandfather, of Tom, Hob and Louise flashed through his mind as he sidestepped a lunge before taking advantage of the soldier's momentum to bury his blade in his heart. As his tiredness grew, so did his ferocity. His sword learnt economy, jettisoning the courtly flourishes of the French fencer he had learned from, and concentrating purely on results.

The few that got beyond the gates faced him with the heady mixture of fear and elation that only a trained warrior can understand. As mettle met mettle, what was at first a professional exercise became a private conflict between equals, in which a lifetime's store of technique, experience and daring were the virtues by which one lived or died. Respect for the calibre of the foe left no room for enmity, only regret, when they came in for the kill.

So it was that, as the sun rose high above the tower,

Crozier came face to face with the commander. 'The spider at the heart of his web, eh?' said the Englishman, as he parried Crozier's opening move. Retreating beyond his reach, the commander gripped his sword in two hands, and swung for him with a force that showed he had kept himself out of the fight these past few hours.

With the part of his mind that was free to roam Crozier calculated that if the soldiers' leader was now at his door, the fight was almost at an end. Who would triumph was not yet decided. Around the yard, unwary English were falling prey to arrows and shot from above as they ran from the gate with swords drawn, but the wisest hugged the walls, where they were assailable by nothing but sword, and made the Borderers come to them.

Bodies sprawled across the cobbles, treacherous hazards for men blinded by sweat or blood. Hard-pressed and distracted, they could not spare a glance over their shoulder, and the results were grim. Crozier's cousin Andrew fell with a cry as his enemy lured him off-balance, but he could do nothing for him while he fought off the commander. He merely noted, from the corner of his eye, the young man's final seconds, before the soldier's blade severed his throat. True Borderer that Andrew was, he did not scream, nor did he let the English fighter win all. As the sword finished him, his own blade found the soldier's groin. The pair breathed their last in a clumsy embrace that, when they were later found, looked almost brotherly.

As the commander and Crozier fought, the world contracted to the shifting square in which they duelled. The Englishman was broader but less nimble than Crozier. He had enjoyed more sleep and food this past week, but nothing depended on his victory beyond his own life. Crozier, meanwhile, was fighting for the people and place he loved. The cobbles were slick with blood, and they slithered across the yard, matching the other for every slice and thrust.

'You fight more like a gentleman than a knave,' panted the commander, when Crozier had allowed him to retrieve his sword, after plucking it from his hand by a movement that was as elegant as it was lethal. The Borderer kept silent. He would not waste words or breath on a man who wanted to destroy him, but it had been useful to learn that the commander was all but winded. The next few minutes would be decisive.

Cries came from the battlements and the stable yard, and he cast a quick glance over his shoulder. What he saw threw him momentarily off guard. A cloud of smoke, brightened by flames, was billowing from the stables, and beginning to lick up the tower walls.

In that second's distraction the commander saw his chance. He lunged, getting under the Borderer's defence, and though Crozier scrambled out of his reach and deflected the blade's full force, it caught him across his chest, ripping through his tabard, and slicing into his breast. A shard of frozen heat seared him, and he staggered. He could hear a distant rumble, whether of hooves or voices he could not tell. It grew louder, and more pressing, until he realised it was in his head, and he was close to fainting. The gathering clouds of smoke were no thicker than his dimming sight. He fought on, willing himself to stay up-right. 'You made a big mistake just there, didn't you, good sir,' said the Englishman, sounding almost regretful. 'I am grateful for that, obviously, but it will be the last mistake you ever make.'

His love of talking was his undoing. He was grinning, trying to catch Crozier's eye to drive home his advantage, when the Borderer's sword found its way into his gullet. Their eyes met at that moment, and the score was settled. Gasping, the commander toppled, clutching his throat. Before he drew his last breath his blood was running between the cobbles as if seeking to find a way out of the yard.

Crozier stumbled to the wall, where he slumped. There was a hand under his arm, and Tom half dragged, half carried him into the keep. The door clanged behind him, and the gloom spun around his head in a sparkle of pinpricks, then without warning turned black.

CHAPTER EIGHTEEN

16 October 1513

Woodsmoke was rising from the village inn when Gabriel rode off the hills and down the steep, mossy street. Daybreak was some hours off, but he could go no further without rest, and his horse was stumbling with fatigue.

The innkeeper, clutching a candle, was dishevelled in grimy apron and cap, but at the sight of a customer his sour expression lifted. Calling the stable boy to take the stallion round the back, he ushered Gabriel into a dank, beery cavern, where the new-laid fire was not yet lit. He struck a flint as he sat his guest, and by the time a pint of ale and a plate of cold mutton was placed in front of him, the flames were merry, even if the room would never be.

'Goin far?' the innkeeper inquired, hands clasped behind his back as if anticipating a protracted reply during which he'd have no use for them.

'Edinburgh,' said Gabriel. He swallowed a greasy mouthful, and took a long draught of ale, as if to wash away the taste. 'I'll need another horse. I will pay your boy to bring mine to the city in a day, once he's rested. And I must have a room, for a few hours' sleep. Make sure the bed is aired and the linen fresh.' He slapped a coin onto the table and lowered his head to eat, signalling an end to the conversation.

His host was undismayed. The finer the dress, the worse the manners, was his experience, and in this, the first settlement at the edge of the Lammermuir hills, or the last, depending on your viewpoint, he got all kinds of visitors. Few of them were men he'd wish to know better.

'Right away,' he said, touching his cap, and heading for the back quarters where his wife would not appreciate being woken and asked to run the warming pan over their best bed and pick cat hairs from its pillow.

Neither sheets nor room was clean, but Gabriel was so tired he barely noticed. Clambering fully clothed into bed he snuffed the candle and was asleep before its glowing eye had faded. No bad dreams, no thoughts at all disturbed his repose, and when he woke to bright light beyond the shutters, he was smiling.

On the road again, his mood matched the sunlit day. He would be in Leith before nightfall and Madame Brenier would tell him where he could find her son, willingly or not. He reflected on the satisfaction it would give him to come face to face once more with the young man who had caused him so much trouble.

The thought of Benoit swiftly brought him to his sister, and for a moment Gabriel's spirits faltered. He was not so self-deluded as to think he could easily repair the damage he had done. Whatever her girlish faults, Louise was no fool. She had seen more of his character last night than he had shown anyone he'd ever loved, and it was possible he had frightened her off for good. Women scared easily, he had learned. It was an endearing trait so long as they could be won around, but tiresome when this took effort. Louise, however, was worth all the skills he could muster, and once this business over Benoit had been settled, he intended to devote himself to regaining her trust. He had no doubt he could do it, and spent the rest of the morning savouring the ways in which he would woo her back.

Gabriel had never considered Edinburgh his home, but the pleasure he felt when he caught his first glimpse of the smoky, grimy jumble of houses, set against the turquoise firth, surprised him. He crouched over his horse's neck and dug in his spurs, his cape billowing like a main sail as he galloped the last few miles to the widow's house.

Vincent opened the door. Whipping off his cap and bowing low, he led the courtier to the kitchen, where Madame Brenier was dressing a chicken.

She clapped an oily hand to her mouth when she saw him. Vincent pulled up a stool, and she sank onto it, wiping her hands on a cloth. 'Well, my lord,' she said, 'tell me. Je suis preparée.'

'Madame, there is some news that will cheer you,' Gabriel said, dragging up another stool to sit beside her. He took her hand, and rubbed the blood back into it. 'Your daughter is well, that much is certain. You need have no fear on that score. I saw her only a few hours ago, and she will be returning shortly. For the moment, she is with friends, who will give her an escort home.'

Madame crossed herself in thanks, but her eyes were wide and anxious. 'And Benoit?' she asked, dry-mouthed. 'Do you have any word?'

Gabriel looked across at Vincent, whose attention was fixed on a shoe he was brushing. Madame Brenier caught the courtier's meaning, and shook her head. 'He is family. Anything you have to say, he can hear. Better he does.'

Gabriel sighed. 'Madame Brenier,' he said, 'I have reason to believe your son may still be alive.'

Madame shrieked, hands flying to her face. 'Oh Lord!' she cried, 'Vincent, did you hear? He is alive! Lordy, Lordy, this is the happiest day of my life!'

'Aye,' said her tenant, but seeing the look on the courtier's face his expression remained tense. Madame was out of her seat, but before she could say another word, Gabriel silenced her. 'Alive, yes, good lady, but perhaps not for much longer.'

'Je ne comprends pas,' she said. 'First good news, now it is bad. Explain, please, if you will.' She sat, and folded her hands in her lap. Her lips were white.

Gabriel described the scene in the English prison, where Benoit had been heard demanding an audience with Surrey; how, once he had spoken to him, he had been released, and paid.

Madame Brenier frowned. 'But he is alive,' she said, as if that were all that mattered. 'He survived the battle and he will be coming home. Coming home, soon.' She turned to Vincent, her smile childlike and uncertain.

'Aye, mistress, so it seems,' he said, but he gripped the shoe as if he were throttling it, and his eyes stayed on their guest.

'I know it is painful, a dreadful thing to contemplate, Madame,' Gabriel said softly, 'but it is possible your son is a spy.'

The word sizzled on the kitchen air, as if someone had spat on the fire.

'Un espion? Benoit?'

'He has been passing information to the English, it would seem. The very fact he has not come home, when he is plainly uninjured, tells its own story. Were he innocent, he would be with you now.'

Madame Brenier rose. She opened the shutters and stared out onto the night, as if she could find comfort in its sheltering dark. There was silence, until eventually she spoke. 'If that is so, then it is all my fault. Mine alone.'

Gabriel drew in a sharp breath. 'How can that be? Spying against one's country is a capital offence. I cannot imagine you persuaded him into this wicked act. Please tell me you did not, Madame, otherwise you are as liable to swing for it as he.'

'Swing?' The word jolted the widow back to her senses, and she faced the courtier, her head high. 'My son is to be hanged? Well, if that is the case, I go to the scaffold with him, and gladly. Because he will have acted only because of the things I said to him. Harsh things, but true. I, toute seule, must have driven him to it.'

Gabriel looked to Vincent, who had dropped his shoe and was gaping.

'Whit are ye sayin, woman?'

Madame looked at him, and her eyes filled with tears. It was Vincent she addressed. Gabriel was of no more importance at that moment than the firedogs.

'Remember the night when he came back from the Borders, happy as a skylark? I'd never seen my boy smile so wide. Tu te souviens de celui, oui?'

Vincent nodded.

'He sat at this table, and he said how much business he was getting, and how the woodsmen over the border could teach the Scots a thing or two, and they had the finest oaks and beeches this side of France?' She looked into the fire, twisting her hands.

'I knew it was not the work that was making him so happy, though it was good for his purse. Marguerite looked at me, I looked at her, and we both knew. It was love. Il était fou d'amour, a man besotted. And we' – falling tears made a dark brooch on her bosom – 'we were joyful, because there was not a better, kinder man in the country, and he would make some woman a very good husband.' She swallowed, and her voice tightened. 'If she were good enough for him.'

She passed a hand over her eyes, and her voice grew softer. 'The girl he had found was from over the border. English. He met her here, though, right here!' She pointed to the street outside. 'Her father was a silversmith, and they'd come up, two or three times a year, with their packs, to sell from the quayside. Pretty stuff, I'm told. They made enough in a week to last them months.

'But it was when Benoit was on his trips through the Borderlands that he got to know her. He sought her out, he told me. Took him a while to find her too. She was living in a village near Jeddart – Belscreek, Bellscleugh, something like that. She was sixteen, and, to my thinking, she saw a good thing in Benoit. Well,' – she sighed, as if she could not blame the girl – 'what young woman wouldn't?

'Alors. He told us he had asked her to marry him, and she was willing. We were raising our drinks, d'you recall,

Vincent? A fine bordeaux, brought up from the cellar to welcome him home. Marguerite blooming, close to her time, Louise chirping away like a canary, and then he told us. Casually, as if it was nothing.' She stopped.

'Told you what?' asked Gabriel.

'That the girl was one of the Elliot clan,' she said, without turning to him.

Vincent nodded. 'Ah remember it fine, mistress. Ye dropped yer goblet, and it spilled a' ower the place.'

'Elliots,' repeated the widow, sensing Gabriel's confusion. 'Worst enemies of my husband's family. Wretched people, les enfants du diable.'

Dimly Gabriel remembered. Years back, the Elliots had ambushed one of the Bartons' ships off the Holy Isle, murdered all on board and stolen its cargo. The Bartons had more than avenged the original crime as they swept down on the Elliots' fortress and lands, and the villages around. Ever since, a state of warfare existed between them, waged at sea, or on land, whenever chance allowed.

Gabriel nodded slowly as the story became clear.

The widow looked at him. 'Enfin, vous comprenez, Monsieur le Viscomte? If he had married her, he would have had to leave the country, and she hers. It was a marriage not possible. A sad fact, but not a tragedy, so long as no-one at the shipyard ever knew they'd been friends. Otherwise he'd have lost his job, or worse.

'I told him, mon fils, I said, there are plenty of young women out there for you. Hundreds who will snap you up. You say she is the only one for you, but be patient. You will see.'

She shook her head. 'You can imagine the scene, j'en

suis sûre. Mine was not the only drink untouched that dinner. And from that night, he was a different boy.'

Vincent's expression confirmed this, as he recalled those miserable months.

'A few weeks later,' the widow continued, 'Marguerite was taken from us. So, we lost her and we lost our old Benoit too. He never whistled like before, and did he talk? Pah, not a word. He had left his tongue in the Borders.

'But now I begin to understand.' Her voice thickened with fresh tears. 'He was all the while thinking how to make his escape. He would need money. Money to make me and Louise secure before he left us, and money to run off with this girl of his. How would he make that sort of sum, in his line of work? Impossible, bien sûr. But he was always a clever one, mon petit. He must 'ave seen his chance, with the court always at the shipyard, and the talk loud and loose.'

She faced Gabriel, her eyes glittering. 'Do you see now? It was your beloved king that made my boy loathe the very sight of the court. Moi, I was more pragmatic, but I too could not look on the bonny king without a knife twisting in my heart. He could smile, and dress in velvet, while Marguerite was turning to dust in her grave.'

The widow stood before Gabriel, magnificent in her pride, as if willing him to break her spirit, to condemn her own son. She gave a bitter laugh at his stare.

'Can we really blame the boy if he took against the crown, and all this grande folie, these family feuds that last for generations? What is war, but our own squabbles on a grand scale? And who is to say what is the right side, and what party deserves to win? English, Scottish, French, they're all as wicked and wrong as each other. They can all be damned. They can all burn in hell. I have had enough, je vous dis. Assez! Assez!'

Sobbing, she hid her face in her apron. Vincent laid a tentative hand on her back. 'Calm yerself, sweetie,' he said, close to tears himself, 'dinnae take on sae sair.' But she cried as if the world had ended. And who was to say that in this household, this country, it had not.

*   *   *

Curfew was approaching when Gabriel left the widow's house. The streets were empty, and the road to the castle was hushed, his horse's hooves loud on the cobbles as he rode up the high street and dismounted outside Patrick Paniter's door. Goodwife Black took her time answering, and her smile was chill as she led him into Paniter's room, where a meal for two lay half-eaten on the table. The secretary welcomed the courtier with an embrace. He smelled of soap, and Gabriel was suddenly aware of his travel-stained clothes and unscented hair.

'Forgive me,' he said, with a deprecating sweep of his hand, 'I look like a ragamuffin, and no doubt smell like one too. I hope I do not put you off your dinner?'

'No, no, my lord,' said Paniter with a laugh, 'we were finished.' With a glance he dismissed Goodwife Black, who disappeared downstairs, still hungry, and found consolation in a bottle of beer.

'Come, sit,' said Paniter. The courtier took a seat opposite him on the settle, by the fire, and the pair sat knee to knee in its warmth. Gabriel hesitated, unsure how to proceed. Paniter watched him with curiosity and affection. His absence had been sorely felt. 'You have been away on business, or so your letter said. Urgent private matters, I assume, to take you from me at such a time as this.' His voice was gentle, but he needed an answer.

'Indeed, sir,' said Gabriel, 'they were urgent in the extreme, but in no way private. They concern you, and all of us, very directly.'

Paniter motioned him to continue.

'Sir, to speak plainly, I believe I have learnt of a spy who may have helped bring about our defeat at Surrey's hands.'

Paniter said nothing, his face rigid.

'I have been on the trail of a most cunning young man, who appears to have been in the English commander's pay, and passing information directly to him. For how long, I cannot say, but at the very least since the army left for the muster.'

'Who?' From the harshness of the word, no-one could have guessed Patrick Paniter's heart was beginning to beat as it had not done since he had left the battlefield. As the courtier described his hunt for Benoit, the secretary ate every crumb of the story as if he were a starving man. If there had been a spy, passing on their decisions, and in-decision, then the rout of the army, the failure of the guns, the sheer bloody horror of that day might not be wholly his fault. The guilt that had been suffocating him might not be all his. He took a deep breath, and as his lungs filled his back straightened.

'We must find this cur,' he said, with a voice like sharpened steel, 'and bring him to justice. The country must be told about him, and his crime. And, my dear lad, everyone will be told the part you have played in bringing him to the gibbet, as I have every confidence you will.'

Gabriel bowed his head. 'My role is of no importance,' he said. 'All that matters is finding him.'

He explained how he had convinced Madame Brenier that if Paniter could speak to her son before anyone else, he would have a better chance of winning a morsel of mercy, which no court would offer. 'I told her that he might be able to claim madness, a spell of lunacy, following his sister's death. At the very least, it might render his form of execution less terrible.'

Paniter nodded, but charity was the last thing on his mind. 'Do you need men to accompany you? He will be dangerous, you know.'

Gabriel shook his head. 'I will travel more swiftly and secretly alone. And I can more than handle myself with a man like that, never you fear. He may be good with a carpenter's tools, but he is a stranger to swords.'

Paniter smiled. 'Bring him to me, then,' he said, rising, and kissing the courtier on each cheek. 'When you deliver him, we will deal with him immediately, and as he deserves.'

There was more colour in Paniter's face as he bid the courtier goodbye than if he had downed a quart of claret. When Goodwife Black returned to clear the dishes, he caught her by the waist and whirled her round the room, singing snatches of half-remembered tavern songs as he went. She shrieked, then giggled, then relaxed into his hold. Cheek to cheek they shuffled in quickening, tightening circles until, panting, they toppled onto the bed where they set about a more satisfying dance whose music they knew note by note.

When the secretary woke, as always in the very heart of the night, he was not lathered in sweat. His pulse was steady, his heartbeat slow. The dreaded faces that hovered under the canopy seemed tonight to be in retreat, dissolving in a fog that muffled their words. He almost laughed at the sight of old Bishop Elphinstone, who had warned against war with England, as he struggled against the mist, his lips moving, his meaning lost. 'Maybe you were no more right than I,' whispered Paniter. 'Old as you are, your wisdom was that of a coward, the fear of daring all on the spin of a coin. I am not young, nor am I wise, but perhaps our fate lay outwith our hands.' A roar of insults from the rest of the council who had thought Elphinstone a dotard and a fool chased the old man out of the room. Paniter was warmed by the feeling, rare these days, of not being alone.

One by one, as was their nightly habit, his tormentors paraded above him. But where before they had been more vivid than in life, each now was faint, and it took only a puff of breath to send them spinning into oblivion. The king alone refused to be dismissed. He looked down on his secretary, his jewels bright in the hour before dawn, his eyes glinting as keenly. 'My mother was right,' he said, 'nothing achieved by violence can endure.'

Paniter had heard this too often. 'Your Majesty,' he said silently, 'we have been over this and over this. Calling Henry to order was a sensible move. He needed his wings clipped, his ambitions curtailed.'

The argument the pair had had, long into their first night camped on Flodden hill, was now repeated, word perfect in Paniter's memory, rehearsed as it had been each weary night since he arrived back in the city. At the time, though, bent over the card table in the king's wind-blown tent, Paniter had scarcely listened to the king, whose tender conscience would always prick him in times of stress. For a man of warm and strong opinions, he could be vexatiously indecisive, procrastinating and deliberating when it was clear there was only one path to take. Paniter saw God and the long dead queen behind these episodes, pulling the king's strings like those puppet masters he had seen at James's wedding feast, making a wooden toy dance as if alive, its mouth opening and closing with the flick of invisible fingers behind the tiny stage.

Irritated at his dithering, Paniter was perhaps rougher than he would have been. When James repeated, for the hundredth time, his mother's dying words, and his promise to abide by them, the secretary waved them away as if swatting a bluebottle. He did not hide his exasperation. 'Your mother, God rest her soul, did not mean you could never go to war. What king could make that promise?

'No, sir, it was your father she was talking about. She was cautioning you not to live as harshly, or heedlessly, as he had done, for fear of coming to an ugly end as he did, losing not just his life, but his family. I cannot believe she would ever have asked you to turn the other cheek in the face of a threat such as Henry, who breathes down the neck of our country.' Paniter stretched his legs out, and yawned. 'Nor,' he added, 'would she have expected you not to press your claim to his throne for fear that some blood might be shed in the process. She was not a faint-hearted woman, as you well know.'

James sighed, drank his wine, and poured a fresh goblet. He sat back in his rickety chair and pinched the bridge of his nose. He was tired. They had had a long, hard, and successful few weeks since leaving Edinburgh. The army was much reduced in size and vigour, but their carts were full of booty from the fortresses and towns they had taken. First Norham, then Etal and Ford castles had fallen into their hands as easily as ripened pears. Long-standing scores had been settled, and now James was sated. He was not in the mood for war. He was beginning to believe that by stepping onto English soil, by rattling his pikes and swords and marching his men this way and that, he had fulfilled his obligations to King Louis, without irrevocably provoking Henry's wrath. His objective, he told himself, had been to alarm Henry sufficiently into sending an army north, thereby diminishing the troops available to him, and distracting him, momentarily at least, from his French assault.

It seemed to an incredulous Paniter that despite taking up position on Flodden hill, despite his years of elaborate planning and fighting talk, the king was hoping soon to ride home without a cannon being fired, or a sword unsheathed against the upstart English king's army. The man was wavering, of that there was no doubt, and he could not bear the thought. His fatigue fled, and he leant forward, speaking urgently, for this might be his last chance.

'Your Majesty, we are in danger of forgetting how big is the board on which we stand, and what an important part your pieces play. You, my liege, are one of the finest kings in Europe, if not indeed in Christendom, and to retreat now, to allow yourself to be checkmated, would be to admit to the world that Scotland is a provincial outpost, a mere pawn in the grand game, which can be pushed this way and that at the whim of your allies.

'I believe, no, I know for certain, you are far greater than that. Henry has deluded dreams of winning the French crown. Well, let him dream. He is a braggart and a fool.

But you, Your Highness, might one day take his throne and add it to yours. Everyone knows this. So tomorrow, if you give the order to tiptoe back to Scotland, you diminish your own hopes of a glorious future, and snatch wealth and renown from your people.'

'But, Paddy, I will have spared our country a battle we need not have.' James's brown eyes held his, reproachful at his lack of understanding. 'That, surely, stands for something. I will have walked the tightrope between the French lion and the English bull, and got off it without falling, alive and fit to continue the fight.'

'None of us would ever go to war without sound reason, Your Majesty, and as you know I am a man of books and letters, not of war. But you must consider whether having negotiated so delicately and cleverly with both sides up to now, you do yourself and your country justice by creeping away?'

'Tiptoeing, creeping – you use language fitted to a coward, sir, and that is one thing you know I am not.' James's eyes flashed. 'There is wisdom in retreating when more is to be gained by quitting the field, and I am surprised you do not acknowledge that.'

'Certainly, Your Majesty. But I am convinced that in this instance you stand to win far more by taking on the enemy, than in postponing your confrontation to another day. Consider the facts.'

Paniter counted them off on his fingers. 'One: Henry is out of the country. Two: Lord Surrey is old and weak. Three: His army is hurrying north in this foul weather. Four: Our army is likely stronger than his, and even if that proves not the case, our weapons more modern by far. Five . . . '

James waved a hand to hush him. 'I know all this, Paddy. We have rehearsed it a thousand times.' He fell silent, staring into his wine. 'I am not sure what is for the best. You are my closest advisor, yet even now I am not convinced you do not talk from vanity and ambition rather than commonsense.'

Paniter began to speak, but the king motioned him to be silent.

'Enough for tonight, sir. I must think, and I must pray. My mind is uneasy. Leave me, please, and send in my priest. You and I, we will speak again tomorrow, in full council.'

James's face shimmered above Paniter, growing fainter as the scene began to fade. His king's sweet face, his warm, tender eyes held his, as so often since the battle. It was one of the last conversations they had had alone, one of the last undisturbed hours in a friendship that stretched back twenty years, in which angry words had been far rarer than in a happy marriage, their faith in each other as strong, Paniter believed, as that between any man and his wife. And yet as the end approached, his king had not trusted him. The fact was like gall, scorching his lips. Because of course the king had been right.

'Forgive me,' he whispered. 'Forgive me.' He fingered his rosary. 'Confiteor Deo omnipotenti, beatae Mariae Semper Virgini . . . ' The bedchamber lay in darkness, but when at last the first birds woke and the dunghill cockerel crowed, Paniter was still mouthing penitence, staring wide-eyed and unseeing at the breaking day. 'Mea culpa, mea maxima culpa . . . ' The beads clicked between his fingers like a scolding tongue.

CHAPTER NINETEEN

16 October 1513

Hands were fussing about him, clipping away his jerkin, baring his skin to the cold keep air. He tried to push them away. The keep was in danger, the commander's men were circling, closing in on him, and he had no sword, no knife, and now no shirt. He sat up, swung his legs off the bed and reached for his scabbard, but the buzzing in his ears surged, and the darkness pressed in on him, hot and thick as burning pitch. He fell back, unconscious, running with sweat.

The hands again, gentle but persistent. A cold, damp cloth was pressed to his ribs. He clenched his teeth, and a low voice shushed him as his chest was swaddled in bandages. He smelled heathland and forest floor, but could not know that moss and cobwebs were bound around his cut, as if he were a witch's pie, ready for the oven.

He was warm now, the oven door invitingly wide. He heard the crackle of its flames, and he turned his head this way and that, roaring with fear for those inside the burning tower, hearing the snap and snarl of fire around their bones . . .

The hands again, this time on his brow. A woman's voice, soft, soothing. And a kiss, cool on his eyelids. The flames retreated. The buzzing was stilled. He took the hand in his, and clasped it tight to his aching chest. He slept.

*   *   *

When he woke, the room was silent. Fresh pine logs burned in the grate. A tallow lamp flickered on the wall, casting sooty shadows up to the rafters and darkening the window to midnight blue. At his side Louise was slumped in a chair, wrapped in a blanket. On the foot of the bed the vixen was curled. When she saw Crozier open his eyes, she thumped her tail before burying her nose in her paws, and going back to sleep.

He lay for a long hour, watching firelight dance on the beams. He felt bruised but weightless, as if his body had been drained of everything but breath. There was so strong a sense of peace in the room it was as if a storm had passed, and everything stilled in its wake.

After a time the door creaked, and Wat's face appeared. Seeing his master awake and calm, he was pulled up short. He was about to speak, when Crozier nodded towards Louise. With a finger to his lips Wat retreated. Once in the corridor, he covered his eyes, fighting back emotion. Crozier's fever had passed. It took Wat a minute to compose himself, before making for Mother Crozier's room, to pass on the news, which licked around the keep faster than its winter draughts.

Cold air from the passageway reached Louise, and she woke, pulling the blanket tighter around her shoulders. When she found Crozier's eyes on her, her mouth opened in silent surprise. He smiled, but she did not smile back. She was shaking her head, a hand flattened on her breast, and he saw she was crying. The tears quickened, but all he could do to stop them was reach out. Pushing off her blanket, she sat beside him on the bed and put her hand in his.

'You are awake,' she said, stupid with relief.

'Of course,' he said. 'Why wouldn't I be?'

She gave a watery laugh, looking at his face as if she had never thought to see it again, though it had been in front of her for days. He tried to pull her close, but his arms were not his own. 'Come here, damn it,' he said, and with a deep sigh she laid her head on his shoulder, and wrapped her arms around him.

They slept like that for a while, and when they woke again, in the fireside light, their eyes met, and then their lips. They kissed as if this was a conversation that was picked up from a moment before, unspoken questions answered, doubts laid to rest. Crozier's arm was stronger now, and he held her tight. Lazily, slowly, he kissed her hair, her eyelashes, her forehead, as if he was discovering her by touch rather than sight.

Louise lay close against him on the narrow bed. His eyes closed, he took her hand, pressed it to his heart, and was asleep again, breathing soft and deep.

There would be no more sleep for Louise that night. Crozier's recovery was so unlikely it felt more like a miracle than anything she and Wat had brought about. As delirium had taken hold, she thought she had lost him. He had thrashed, the fever mounting and his colour high as a farrier's fire. He babbled nonsense, furious words giving way to shouting, and it took two men to hold him down as he tried to fight his way out of bed. Murdo and Mother Crozier, Hob and the other men, had hovered outside the door, wringing their hands while Wat and Louise bathed the patient with cold cloths and dabbed water on his lips, trying to douse the fire that consumed him.

He could not be left for a minute, and they took it in turns to sit with him. It had seemed hopeless. Louise had lost count of the hours, and barely knew if it was night or day, though later Hob would tell her it was five nights since Crozier had been carried unconscious into the keep. His fever had blazed for three.

After he had carried his brother into the keep, Tom had led the final charge. Dacre's men were driven from the courtyard and the forest with a fury that was not only murderous but mad. It would have given the young man some satisfaction to know that stories of his and his clan's courage and skill spread through the English border swift as the plague. Within a few weeks, Crozier's Keep was considered Satan's own seat, its men in the devil's pay. Nothing else could explain their ravening swords and un-quenchable anger. That a word as short as Dacre could rouse such wrath was beyond most people's compre-hension. The supernatural was far more credible.

With the fever passed, Crozier began quickly to recover. His nurses could at last sleep in their own beds, though Wat and Louise would sometimes bump into each other in the passage in the middle of the night, on their way to make sure their patient was safe.

In the early morning and at dusk, Louise would change Crozier's dressing. The infection had cleared, and the wound was knitting well. It would leave an angry scar the width of his chest, but already he was regaining strength, his body shrugging off its savaging. As she cleaned the cut and rebound it, she did not rush, enjoying the touch of him under her fingers, the sight of his slim, firm body. She did not dare meet his eye as she did this. Since that first night they had not kissed again, nor spoken of it, and she wondered if it had been delirium that had prompted him. Crozier seemed not even to recall it, and though he spoke to her warmly, he did not refer to what had passed. Had she seen the way he looked at her as she dressed him, however, she would have had no doubt about his feelings.

While she had been closeted in the sick room, the keep had been busy as a hive. Dacre's men had left the outhouses smouldering, the yards and forest a scene of devastation. The horses had been returned to their stables, where the fire had done little damage, but the great hall was still a hospice for the injured. The dead had been buried beyond the walls in the clan's graveyard, their resting places marked with rough pine crosses.

Tom had led the clear-up, and taken charge of the keep. New gates had been made and heaved into place, and masons were repairing the ramparts. He was in a frenzy, moving so fast his spurs struck sparks on the cobblestones, shouting orders and overseeing work late into the night, all the while unable to contemplate the fact that his brother might die.

When he heard that Crozier was going to live, he shook Wat's hand so hard the man thought he would never hold a sword again. Without a word Tom then fled into the forest where he cried like a child and gave thanks to a god he had previously never troubled, and rarely would speak to again. His temper would never be quiet or calm, but from that day he was less of a boy, and more of his brother's equal as a man who understood what the world held in store for him and his kind.

A week after the attack, order at the keep had resumed. Mother Crozier grumbled in the kitchen as she made broths for her invalid son. Murdo and the men spent the days cleaning, sharpening and restocking their armoury, and the nights talking of revenge. The last of the wounded had limped back to their own beds, the hall had been swept, and the lingering smell of fire-blackened stone was the only reminder of how near disaster had come.

'I must think of leaving,' Louise said to Wat one morning, as they stood at the keep's walls, enjoying the last of the autumn sun.

'I reckoned you were set on staying,' he said slyly. 'Mother Crozier seems to think so, and though she's crabbit, she's rarely wrong.'

Louise said nothing, but stared into the forest where russet leaves were fiery in the morning light. Their colour was defiant in the face of approaching snow, whose breath was on the air. The next high wind would sweep them away, and the trees would soon be bare. She would have liked to see the woods in winter, but by that time she would be long gone. The thought of the road to Edinburgh, where her troubles awaited, was unwelcome.

She wandered into the forest, to the edge of the crags, where the land fell away steeply. Leaning against a towering beech, broad and smooth as a rocking chair, she gazed across the valley, its lonely beauty chasing all thoughts from her mind but how much she would miss this place.

It was here that Crozier found her. He was pale, but his step was firm, and he was dressed for work.

'Wat told me you'd gone traipsing,' he said. 'You must be needing fresh air, after being shut up for so long.' She nodded, and smiled.

They stood, in silence, looking across the sea of trees that stretched down the valley and out of sight. 'To think I nearly lost all this,' said Crozier, after a long while. He kicked at a drift of leaves, for the pleasure of the sound. 'You know, there was a time when I wished I'd never been born here. It felt like a prison. If I'd not been the elder son, I'd have left the first chance I got. Now, I would die to protect it.'

'You nearly did,' Louise said, keeping her eyes on the horizon.

He hesitated. She was standing stiffly, hands at her side. He reached out, and touched her shoulder. 'It was your voice that saved me,' he said, moving close. 'I knew I was dying. It was like falling off a cliff, into an inferno. And then I felt your hands, heard your voice. I can never thank you enough for that. Even if I'd gone, I'd have had the comfort of knowing you were with me at the end.'

Louise stifled a cry, and covered her face.

'What?' Crozier turned her gently to him, but she could not look at him.

'My love, what is it?'

'I thought . . . I was so afraid I had lost you,' she sobbed, so quietly he barely caught the words. 'That you would die before I could tell you what I felt for you, and how much I owed you.'

'You owe me?' At the fierceness of his words she looked

up, and saw in his eyes a blaze of passion that took her breath.

He pulled her to him and kissed her, so long and sweet her head began to spin. Heat ran through her as if a fire had been lit, and only Crozier's arms, locked around her, kept her on her feet.

When finally they could speak she gave a shaky laugh. 'So you do remember that night?' she asked, clutching his jerkin.

'I have thought of nothing else since – or before,' he said, pulling her down to sit next to him against the tree.

She laced her fingers in his. 'You are a hard man to read. You give away nothing. I've hardly ever seen you smile,' she said.

He frowned. 'For a long time I've felt I was smiling every time I looked at you.'

'I never noticed.'

'Well, you can hardly blame me. You were in love with another man, or so I believed.'

She turned her face away. 'No, I was not. I just imagined – and only for a short while – that I might be. I was childish, an utter fool. I didn't know what love was. To think I might have let you go.'

He pressed her hand to his heart. 'But you did not, thank God.' Then abruptly, as if to learn the worst at once, he asked, 'And now, where do things stand between you and him?'

Louise picked at the leaves by her skirt. 'He knew some time ago that my feelings had changed. Before we had even reached Durham I'd made that clear. And he no doubt could guess what you meant to me, when I left him to warn you. Though I only knew it myself that night.'

Crozier put his arm around her, and she put her head on his shoulder where it fitted as if he had been shaped for that purpose alone. 'Saved all our lives, you did,' he said. 'If they'd caught us without notice, we'd have been dead.'

As the morning passed overhead, they sat without talking. Crozier laid his cheek against her hair, breathing in the perfume that had been in his dreams, waking and sleeping, since the day of the fight.

Looking down, he found her asleep. He nudged her. 'Wake up, birdie.' She moved drowsily and nestled closer. Her hand was on his chest, small and white. He caught it to his lips.

'Could you bring yourself to live here? It won't be easy. The life is hard, and so are we.'

Suddenly awake, she looked up at him, into the face that had once seemed so harsh. The lines of fever and pain were receding, but its lean, wolfish look would never fade. Nor, she knew, would her love of him. She kissed him softly and deeply, breaking off only to whisper, 'Yes, oh yes.'

*   *   *

Father Walsh made his way to Crozier's Keep, his horse plodding up the frostbitten trail. The dead he had buried here so recently were now under earth as hard as stone. Beneath the grey midday sky the valley was steely cold, and the keep more forbidding than ever. Purple clouds were gathering. If the snows came, he might have to stay the night, but if Mother Crozier was in a hospitable mood, and her kitchen oven well-fired, that would be no hardship.

Louise and Crozier were married before the great hall's

fire, with the clan at their side. The hall had been trans-
formed into a festive bower of pine branches and berries,
with ribbons strung over the fireplace, fresh rushes on the
floor, and logs enough to burn till Candlemas roaring in
the grate.

Louise wore a green velvet gown, a trimmed and
tightened hand me down from Mother Crozier. Around
her shoulders was a fur cape, Crozier's first gift to her,
brought that morning by the village trapper. Her hair was
caught up in a golden net, but its lustre was as nothing to
the brightness of her eyes. Crozier's boots had been
polished, and for the occasion he had worn his grandfather's jewelled sword hilt, which glinted in the firelight.

During the service, Hob stood behind them, clutching a
narrow gold ring set with pearls. When the wedding mass
had been said, and the vows exchanged, he handed it over,
blushing as if he were the bride whose finger it was slipped
onto.

The Croziers ate and drank long into the small hours. It
was many years since the keep had enjoyed a party, and the
clan did not intend to waste this opportunity. Even Mother
Crozier was seen to laugh. Roasted chicken, braised duck
and rabbit stew, with chestnuts, leeks and honeyed parsnips,
were washed down with mead, and ale, and the richest
claret Crozier could find in the cellars. A brandy syllabub
shivered on the table, but went untouched until the priest's
eye fell on it. While feet tapped to the hornpipes, and the
clan kicked up the rushes as they whirled their wives and
wenches around the hall, Hob fell asleep under the table
and slept till morning, the vixen curled under his arm.

When at midnight the party gathered in the courtyard

to raise a toast under the stars, the season's first snow was falling. Louise and Crozier lifted their faces to the night, and felt the cold kiss of flakes on their cheeks. They reached for each other's hands, and stared into the flurrying sky long after the others had retreated inside.

As the night gathered pace the couple left, noticed by none. Before they had reached the staircase the pipes and singing were muffled. When the door to Crozier's rooms was closed, the only sound was the crackling fire.

By its ruby light, Crozier undressed his wife. As he unbuttoned her dress and raised it over her head, her hair fell out of its net, tumbling around her shoulders and down her back as if to cover her. Soon her chemise lay on the floor, a pool of white that mirrored her skin. She stood before him smiling and shy, but not about her nakedness. She reached out her hands, and drew him to her. His heart was beating so hard she could feel it through his shirt as if it were her own. Which, in many ways, it now was.

CHAPTER TWENTY

25 October 1513

In a boarding house on the road to Leith, Gabriel leant over his table. There was no need for secrecy, and tonight his candle burned by his hand as he wrote.

'Dearest mother, star of my soul,

'I am returned safe from the battle, as I promised. Soon I will join you, and I hope to bring with me a woman I am most eager for you to meet, who will be a good daughter to you, and a fine wife for me.

'Before then, I have business to conduct which will take me out of the capital for some days. As soon as that is seen to, I and my beloved will be at your door, to bring you back to Edinburgh with us where at last we can live like a proper family. Pray tell Mamie to pack your winter clothes for the journey.

'I am desperate keen to see you once more, but until then, I remain your only and most loving son.'

He sanded and sealed the paper, for the morning's courier.

Shortly after the letter had been dispatched, Gabriel too rode out of the city. He had been there a week, awaiting the return of his horse from the innkeeper's stable. When the stallion arrived, it was plain he needed more rest. The courtier could not afford to hire another horse, and besides, this creature not only anticipated his every wish but could gallop as fast as the incoming tide. The delay was galling but unavoidable and, he reasoned, if Benoit had taken refuge in the Borders with his lover, as Madame Brenier had suggested, then it was not likely he would be going anywhere soon. Gabriel amused himself with the thought of the young Frenchman playing house with his girl, unaware that while he dallied, retribution was closing its net around him.

A north wind drove the courtier out of town and across the Lothian plains. Pressing his hat low over his eyes, he cursed the wintry air and prayed he would reach Benoit sooner than the snow.

Mile by mile, the road south passed in a canter of muck and grass. Heartily sick of this route, which he felt he could ride blindfold, the courtier vowed that once he had brought Benoit back to the capital to face justice, he would never pass this way again. In the meantime, he must suffer long hours in the saddle, and longer nights in whatever hostelries he could find. His saddlebags were stuffed with food and spirits, but he expected no comfort on this journey. The only certainty was that he would not be stopping at the flea-ridden Lammermuir inn. Even the thought of the place made him want to scratch.

Over the days that followed, Gabriel was wind-blown, rain sodden, and chilled. In the few short weeks since he had set out to find Louise, the Borders had been trans-formed. Chestnut brown and bonfire yellow had been replaced with sere green and grey, as if the land had been scraped clean of paint and redrawn in charcoal. The going was muddy and slow, and it took twice as long to cover the ground as before. His impatience mounted, stoking itself like a fire beneath turf, growing hotter for lack of a vent.

As he rode, he thought of his mother. Soon she would be a respectable lady, given the honour and place she had always deserved. He tried to picture her pleasure in her new life in Edinburgh, but his thoughts kept wheeling back, as if to show him who was master. More vivid than the road beneath his feet, the Home appeared before him, timbers buckling beneath a crooked slate roof as it stared out across the river while Glasgow milled past its gates, unaware of who lived here, and in what condition.

When as a boy Gabriel had first knocked on the door, Mr Henderson had opened it no more than a sliver, as if afraid of fresh air. Gabriel squeezed through, and kept close to Henderson's slippered heels as they passed through unlit corridors, behind whose doors he heard mutterings and cries, and smelled the sickly sourness of women whose bodies were as unruly as their minds.

'They're not all mad when they come here, laddie,' said the keeper, shuffling ahead, 'though most often they end up that way. But your pretty mother, ken, she was a lunatic frae the start, God bless her soul.'

His mother's room was small, the window too high for her to see anything but a handkerchief of sky. She would sit sewing all day at her table, stitch after stitch on the same blessed sheet, until it was as solid as armour. Her sister Mamie spent part of each day with her, but even as a child it had been apparent to Gabriel that his mother kept her own company, that of the people in her head.

He was told she had not always been this way. Before she met the baron, she had been a beauty with a quick wit, whose conversation kept admirers enthralled. But when she caught the eye of the Scottish lord, she was like a linnet that is netted and caged. After a period of cheerful trilling, she drooped, her feathers fell out, and after she had battered fruitlessly against the bars, she lost her mind.

The baron was a married man, but in her infatuation Valerie had not cared. They met in Bristol, where he had shipping interests. His wealthy wife was in Glasgow, so far off as to be unimaginable, and they had a fine year together, his lordship parading his mistress around the town and its parties without a thought for propriety. Valerie was the daughter of a yeoman farmer from the west country. Years later, she would tell her wide-eyed son tales of smugglers and wreckers from her homeland, of the day the king came riding through their village in an ermine cape and threw her a coin. 'He knew I was special,' she would murmur, patting her own cheek and preening before his long-gone eyes.

The idyll with her lord ended when she found herself with child. She was delighted, envisaging a happy family home. The baron was appalled. First he abandoned her, then he returned and flung himself at her feet, pouring out his apologies into her lap. She must know he loved her, and only her, but he could not leave his wife. She could have the child, and he would provide for it, but nobody must know it was his.

Already Valerie's senses were weakening under the strain. If it had not been for her sister, she might have become one of Bristol's desperate women, found wandering the quayside taverns in search of a farthing, however hard earned. Mamie, however, was her father's child, square of shape, and indomitable. She made a deal with the baron, and obliged him to sign his name to it. Valerie, she promised, would never trouble him so long as he found her a house in his home city, and made her a settlement that would keep her in comfort for the rest of her days. There would need to be enough money for three, since Mamie would also be coming north.

The baron understood at once the threat implied by her insistence on living on his doorstep. At any time she might demand more money. Yet reluctantly he agreed. The house was bought, and a servant installed. By the time Valerie arrived in Glasgow, in hysterics after a journey that had threatened to dislodge her baby a month before its time, her sister had furnished the house, and made a home. Had Gabriel's mother kept her wits, theirs might not have been so bad a situation. But the ordeal of a long labour and difficult birth was too much for her enfeebled mind, and while Mamie did her best to keep her sister in her care, it was soon clear that the young woman was mad.

The baron never visited, though his estate was only a few miles out of the city. Mamie would have preferred never again to meet the man who had destroyed her sister, but when Gabriel was old enough to learn to read, she hired a mule, found the estate, and in the tapestried hall, which was as far as she was allowed, she importuned his lordship for school fees. Horrified at her arrival, and fearing any minute the appearance of his wife, the baron agreed to her conditions and hustled her out of the door, muttering that any further such encounters would result in him cutting them off entirely.

But he kept his word, and Gabriel was sent to the Glasgow Grammar School, where he mimicked the refined accents of the pupils, and then to the city's university, where he adopted the mannerisms of the highest-born around him. To his aunt's distress he lost all trace of the family's Wiltshire burr, but what he did not lose was his love of his mother's country. As soon as he could talk, Gabriel considered himself an Englishman, and was encouraged to do so.

Valerie and her sister spoke ceaselessly of their childhood home, its people and their habits. They liked nothing about Glasgow, or Scotland. The place was noisy, dirty, the Scots uncouth. Jamie III, his aunt told him, was a tyrant, with fewer brains than his valet. When James IV was crowned, she denounced the boy king as a mere tool of the most vicious court on God's earth. That the baron sat in parliament added an edge to the sisters' loathing. 'Dimwits, the lot of them,' they said, stitching as if their needles were winkling out these gentlemen's eyes. 'If we'd more money, we'd be back off to Bristol,' sighed Mamie. 'There's no finer or more honest country than ours, and why we ever left it I do not know.'

Brought up by his aunt, with weekly visits to his mother, Gabriel immersed himself in the history of what he considered his true homeland. By the time he was at university, his love of the south was a source of private pleasure. His sweet-tempered face concealed growing contempt for the rough and backward nation around him.

Such fervour might have remained nothing more dangerous than a pastime had the baron not died when and as he did. During the Michaelmas term, a letter from him arrived for Gabriel. The delivery boy handed it over with care, for it was wrapped around a small parcel, which fell to the floor when the ribbon was untied.

The baron wrote that he was failing fast, and wanted to make amends. He enclosed a letter of recommendation for Gabriel to the Scottish court, where he would find a position, though he begged him never to reveal his relationship with his father. It was clear the man knew nothing of his son, for whom the shame of his birth was a stain on his honour. It was a secret he would reveal to no-one, and it was on that day that the Irish viscount began to take shape in his mind.

The parcel, the baron informed him, contained an emerald ring he had received from his own father and worn since that day. The pale band it had left on his finger would remind him hourly, until his death, of the able son he had fathered.

When he died, the baron continued, a final consignment of money for Gabriel's mother would be delivered, but after that he could do no more for her, or any of them. He trusted Gabriel would soon find an honourable occupation and provide for her as she deserved. After some pious maunderings, in which the ailing man showed more concern for his immortal soul than for the welfare of his hidden family, his lordship signed himself off, and out of this world.

Gabriel's tutor could teach him nothing that day. The lad stared out of the window, twisting the enormous ring on his finger. He had no intention of using the baron's letter to further himself. He could make his way alone. The professor, assuming the boy had fallen for some wench, dismissed him with a weary flick of the hand, but the passion that consumed the young man was far more fierce than that.

*   *   *

An arrow of early sunlight speared the bed-chamber. In the darkest corner, where Crozier's boots stood to attention, there was a glint of light. Louise bent, and found Gabriel's emerald ring, kicked out of sight and long since forgotten. It sat in her hand, heavy as guilt, bringing with it unfinished business, and the promise of trouble. Rubbing the dust from it, she took it to the window, where its gleam brightened.

Some time later, when Crozier found her with it, her face was sombre. He took the ring from her, twisting it in the light, where it flashed as if with temper.

'The courtier's finery,' he said. 'How come you have it?'

Louise sighed. 'He gave it me for safekeeping before he went into Durham castle, in case he ran into trouble. In the panic afterwards, I forgot about it.' She did not mention that Gabriel had tried to use it as a token to seal their betrothal, but Crozier guessed it brought unwelcome memories. 'I found it on the floor,' she continued. 'It's probably worth more than everything we possess. I will have to give it to him when I go to Edinburgh. He was very attached to it.'

Crozier smiled. 'He'll be half the lord he is without it.'

Louise could not imagine the Borderer wearing such a thing. There was a self-importance about the jewel that did not fit into these surroundings. Crozier's authority and power came from strength of mind and body, not pomp.

They placed the ring in a box, but Louise could not forget it. It was like a never-sleeping eye – Gabriel's eye – watching everything they did, and she could not wait to be rid of it.

Since Crozier's recovery, her thoughts had returned to her brother, and she knew she must very soon visit her mother and find out if there was any news of Benoit. She did not like to contemplate what she would do if there had been no word from him.

Louise and Crozier had been married a week. There were knowing nudges and smiles behind their backs as they went about the keep, wrapped in a dreamy world of their own. 'They'll be returned to earth soon enough,' said Mother Crozier with unusual forbearance, when Tom complained that they had eyes for no-one but each other. 'Let them have this time. God knows, they've earned it.'

One afternoon, Louise sat down to write to her mother and tell her of her marriage, but as she began to scratch out the words, it was not her husband's face that filled her mind, but Gabriel's. She put down the pen. A sense of cold calm came over her. She took the ring out of its box and thought back to the night Gabriel had found her and Hob in the wood. 'I've been riding since dawn,' he had said.

At the time, she had been too relieved at the sight of a welcome face to question why a man barely known to her family would have left at an ungodly hour to find her as a favour to a woman he was no more than civil with. Setting off to track her down and at such speed was no act of honour or kindness. Nor of lust. Even his obvious interest in her did not explain his headlong pursuit. Knowing him as she did, he was not the sort of man to be swept away by desire.

But one thing she now recognised: it had been pursuit. She stared at the ring. For the duration of their journey, from when he had crept up on them in the terrifying dark until he flung her across the forest path and rode off into the night, Gabriel had kept as close to her as if he had been wrapped around her finger, the sort of ring that slowly bites into the flesh. As she recalled his eagerness to help her find Benoit, his behaviour took on a sickening meaning. Could it be he had been using her simply to reach her brother for his own purposes?

Her hand closed over the ring, gripping it so tightly it hurt. If that were so, then he must have private business with Benoit. That would certainly explain his insistence on going into Durham castle on his own. His ferocity as he turned down Crozier's assistance had startled her even then, when she had had no suspicion over his motives. Now, it looked like dreadful proof of an alliance.

Slowly, the truth took shape. If he and Benoit were secretly in partnership, then they must both be spies. There was no other explanation. The thought made the room turn dim and for a long time she sat, wide-eyed but seeing nothing. First her father, then her brother, and now Gabriel too. She had been surrounded by lies, all her life. Slowly, the half-written letter grew wet with tears, the words trickling off the paper as if they knew they were not wanted. Only the thought of her husband, whose face finally came between her and her grief, gave her strength. Wiping her eyes, she screwed up the ruined letter. She would write it tomorrow.

It was a subdued dinner that night. Crozier put his arm around his wife, and asked if she was feeling unwell. Louise shook her head. The horror of her brother's treachery was too raw to speak of now. She would tell him, but not until later, when they were alone.

But her suspicions were to be forced from her sooner than that. Dinner was eaten, and the table cleared, when Murdo birled into the keep, forgetting to remove his spurs, and earning a sharp rebuke from Mother Crozier as he scraped over the flagstones. 'I ken, I ken,' he said testily, 'but this is urgent.'

'What news?' asked Crozier, who was seated by the fire, a hand on Louise's shoulder as she stirred the logs.

'An odd thing,' said Murdo, looking troubled. 'I don't know if it's something or nothing, but it doesn't smell right.'

Murdo's conversation was like a panner's sieve; much silt had to be sifted to reach a nugget of gold. 'My mate Todd in the village, the blacksmith, was out checking his snares this morning. Up beyond Whitberry Law, ken, where there's a good field for hares and the like.'

Crozier waited with rare patience.

'He says he saw your golden-haired visitor, the courtier, riding down the road Hawick way.'

Husband and wife sat up. 'Gabriel?' asked Louise. 'Here?'

'Uhuh. He swears to it. Says he would never forget the man's yellow hair, but more than that, he recognised his horse, which he shod for him while he was here, if you recall. There's no beasts as fine as that in these parts, as you know.'

Louise shivered as if an icy hand had reached out of the forest and touched her. Crozier's voice was sharp. 'What could have brought him back?'

Murdo shrugged. 'I never trusted the man, that's for sure. I couldnae fathom him while he wis here, so it's no likely I can read his mind now.'

The Borderer looked at Louise. 'When he left you, it was to continue the search for Benoit, that's what you said, isn't it?'

She nodded, her eyes filling with tears.

'Well,' he continued, 'he's obviously learned something to bring him back here. Yet not to the keep. I know you parted from him on bad terms, but we are scarcely enemies. He too wants to find your brother . . . '

Louise gave a sob. 'I know,' she said, 'And I think he is a spy.'

'Who?' said Crozier, startled. 'Gabriel?'

'Yes,' she replied, 'but Benoit too, just as we feared. I think they've been working together.' The words came out as a wail, and she hid her face in her hands. Crozier pulled her to him. 'Come on, now,' he said. 'Steady yourself.' He pressed his cheek to her hair, holding her tight. After a minute her crying ceased, and she looked up. 'I'm sorry,' she said, to the family, 'but Benoit is the best, the kindest brother in the world. The thought that he could have done this . . . ' She brushed away fresh tears, took a slow breath, and told them what she suspected.

The clan already knew the story of Benoit's alleged treachery, for she had hidden nothing from them. At that time she had assured them her brother was not a traitor, but it was soon apparent that they did not care either way. Treason, Old Crozier had informed her, was in the eye of the beholder. 'The day the royals treat us like citizens rather than vermin is the day we will fight for them,' he said. 'Until then, they are as unwelcome here as foreigners. More so, indeed. Whatever your brother's done, we don't care. If he's anything like you, lass, he can't be all bad.'

But tonight, Louise could not agree. If Benoit had indeed betrayed his country, it was the worst deed he could have done, and there was no hiding how she felt.

There was silence when she had finished. When at last Crozier spoke, he sounded grave. 'It's bad, but it may not be as terrible as you think.

'If your supposition is correct – and it does make sense of the way Gabriel has behaved – then he must have reason to believe Benoit is in this neighbourhood. The question is, why. Or, rather, where.'

He spoke slowly, thinking aloud. 'But if he were on official business, to capture a traitor, would he not have come with a posse of soldiers from Edinburgh?' He rubbed a hand over his beard. 'That he has come alone gives us some hope.'

He looked at Louise. 'Don't you see? It might be that your brother is not a criminal, but that Gabriel wants to make people think he is, and thereby cover his own tracks. That it is Gabriel, and he alone, who is the spy.'

His expression was grim. 'But if that is the case, he won't want Benoit to be taken prisoner alive.'

Louise looked perplexed, and he took her hands between his. 'The way I see it, there are two possibilities. Either Benoit is indeed acting with Gabriel as you have suggested. Or Gabriel has some compelling reason to make him the scapegoat. Whatever the truth, the viscount can lead us to him. Because from what we've just heard, and everything that's gone before, he is out hunting for him.'

The colour left Louise's face.

'That being the case,' Crozier continued, 'then it would seem your brother is known to be still alive. That there's real information to suggest that, I mean, unlike the yarn Gabriel span us after he'd been in Durham castle, which I suspect was nothing but lies. If so, that is good news. Very good news. But if it's true, then it means we must find Benoit first. Otherwise, unless he and Gabriel are associates, he could be in desperate danger. And even if they are spies, the pair of them, I am certain Gabriel intends him harm.'

He chafed Louise's cold fingers. 'Think, my love. Why would Gabriel be looking for Benoit this far from Flodden? What might your mother have told him? Who does he know that lives in these parts?'

'Ella,' said Louise slowly, to herself. 'I can't believe I had not thought of her. I am a fool. How could it never have occurred to me?' She raised her head, and her voice. 'Long before the battle – before even my sister's death – Benoit fell in love. My mother forbade the relationship, because the girl was one of the Elliot clan, who our family is at war with.'

'Her name?'

'Eleanor Aylewood. Ella. She lived in a village near Jeddart. Benoit never spoke to me about her once Maman made him promise to give her up. I assumed he had obeyed her – it would have caused a family break-up if he had not. But of course, he didn't give her up, did he?' She looked at Crozier, her eyes alight with tears. 'And that's where he has been, all this time, isn't it?'

'It might just be,' he said, giving her hands a squeeze before standing up. 'But if Gabriel is on his trail, he is already well ahead of us. We must set out first thing tomorrow. We should pack now, for the road.' He looked to Tom. 'You and I will go.' Tom nodded, and also stood.

Louise put a hand on Crozier's arm. 'What about me?'

'It's too dangerous for you.'

'I see,' she said. 'You and Tom will knock on Ella's door and tell her you are Benoit's friends. And my brother, who's been in hiding for weeks now, and has never heard of you, will jump up and come back to your castle, just because you ask him to? How's he to know you're not in league with Gabriel, or – if he too is a spy – the government?'

'You could write him a note?'

'But you might be a kidnapper, and have forced me to write it at knifepoint.' Louise's eyes glittered.

Crozier looked at his brother, who bit back a smile. Mother Crozier nodded, as did his uncle.

He sighed, shaking his head. 'I cannot put you in such danger.'

'You cannot stop me.' They looked at each other, a hard, searching stare in which more was said than if they had spoken.

The Borderer sighed. 'Very well. Join us if you insist. But I am not happy about this.'

'Nor am I,' she retorted, 'what with you not long out of your sick bed. I can find my brother alone, if I must. I didn't marry you to gain a personal guard.'

'You are a besom,' he said, with a bark of laughter. 'God knows, you set my head spinning at times. But come what may, between the three of us – one of us a weakling, one of us a woman – we will manage.'

Louise put her hand in his. 'We must.'

*   *   *

Unaware he had been observed, Gabriel spent that night in a roadside inn where the alewife's daughter chased away the chill of his winter bed and gave him an appetite for breakfast. In the morning, he continued on his drear road. Other than the previous night's entertainment, he had had little luck on this journey. He would happily have set light to the Borders and seen it all consumed, English soil as well as Scots. He loathed the place. Its mud clung to his boots, its grit scratched his eyes. He had ridden countless miles, back and forth like a piece on a chessboard, yet he was no closer to finding Benoit and his mistress.

He was beginning to wonder if Madame Brenier had deliberately misled him. In the bleak heathland village of Bellscleugh, where the hovels as well as its people were gnarled by perpetual gales, nobody had heard of a silver-smith called Elliot. He was lucky if a door was answered to his knock, and when he had posed his question, it was shut almost before the words 'never heard o' him,' or 'cannae help ye' were uttered. Some didn't bother to speak, before dropping the latch or sending their dog out to chase him off.

In the end, he had to resort to measures he despised. On his way out of the village, he rode past an old shepherd, corralling a flock of goats whose ragged coats matched that of their herder. Gabriel dismounted and had the man by the throat before he could scream. 'There used to be a silversmith lived around here,' he hissed, shoving the shepherd against a tree. 'People tell me they've never heard of him. Elliot is his name. Somehow I don't believe them. He has a lovely daughter, girl called Ella. The kind of wench a man like you has dreams about. Does that ring any bells?'

He tightened his hold. Terrified, the shepherd nodded, but the courtier's grip choked him too tight for words. Gabriel relaxed his collar, but kept him pinned against the tree. 'As I thought,' he said. 'So go on then, speak, man.'

The shepherd swallowed. 'Moved, he did, some time back, took all the family.'

'Where?'

'Along the border, I was telt. To the Elliots' lands, near Hermitage.'

Gabriel examined the man through narrowed eyes. Was he lying? There was no knowing. He took out his knife, and the shepherd's eyes widened in fear. 'That's God's own truth, I swear. They went tae Hermitage, cos a' their ain folk is aroon there. Said he could tell trouble wis comin.'

Gabriel kept the knife pressed to his chin a moment longer before he sheathed it and let him go. He was far down the road on his stallion, no more than a black speck on the hill, before the shepherd was steady enough to walk. His goats bleated, their bells tinkling as they nudged him onwards, back to their shed. He patted their heads and thanked the Virgin Mary for his narrow escape. There'd been no Elliots in this village since he was a lad, although there had been a silversmith, some time back. But why would he have told him that? It was none of his business.

CHAPTER TWENTY-ONE

3 November 1513

The Bellscleugh shepherd would never know the good turn he had done for Louise and her family that day. Because the old man rarely spoke, the villagers thought he was simple, but if anyone had heard how easily he had diverted the courtier from his path, when he had been within an hour of his quarry, they would have regarded him with new respect. The look in Gabriel's eye would have been enough to scare the wits out of most of them. To have come up with a story that sent him haring across the country was little short of genius.

While the shepherd was slurping his soup that afternoon, Gabriel was riding across the hillside, through the hamlet of Old Jeddart and past a lonely cottage half-hidden by trees, whose lights he ignored as he thundered down the track.

It was late morning the following day when Louise, Crozier and Tom reached the hamlet. They had ridden hard since daybreak, and their horses' flanks steamed as they entered the woebegone moorland place.

'The house is beside an old chapel,' said Louise, as they looked around at a straggle of cottages and byres. 'Benoit

336

said he wanted to marry there, only a step away from Ella's door.' They rode down the silent street. There were no villagers about, though chimney smoke told them they were being watched. Crows flew overhead, as if curious, their cawing like an alert.

They had ridden beyond the hamlet before the chapel could be seen. A mossy grey building with a Norman arch over the door, it stood on the edge of a wood in a necklace of crooked headstones. Some way into the trees there was a low thatched cottage, woodsmoke swirling around its roof in the icy air.

Louise was trembling. As they tied up their horses, Crozier took her gloved hand in his. Their boots crunched on the hoary grass. He knocked at the door. The place had been quiet before, but now the silence thickened. He knocked again, and there was a scuffle from inside, no louder than a rat running across a board. The threesome did not see an eye peering at them through the shutters, but they could feel it.

Louise stepped back from the door. 'Benoit?' she called. 'It's Louise. Are you there, Benoit? Please open the door.'

A bolt was drawn, a key turned, and the door was flung open. A strapping young woman faced them, so heavy with child she filled the door frame. Louise and she stared at each other. Neither smiled. 'Is my brother with you?' Louise asked at last, when it seemed the girl had no intention of speaking. She did not reply, but stepped aside, to let them in. At the sight of Crozier's and Tom's swords, she put a hand on her belly.

In a box-bed by the fire, propped against a bank of pillows, was Benoit. When Louise stepped into the room, his expression froze. It was as if he could not believe what he saw. Louise hesitated, shocked at the change in him. His face was wasted, his complexion yellow, and he was thin as a child. She took a nervous step forward. 'I never thought I would see you again,' she whispered, tears spilling down her cheeks. 'Everyone thought you were dead! Almost everyone else did die. Almost everyone.'

She hurried over to him, hands outstretched, and her brother reached out to grasp them. They hugged, rocking with emotion, bathing each other with their tears. After a minute, they laughed, and sat apart, holding hands. Benoit's face was pale with sweat.

'He canna take much excitement,' said Ella, standing by the bed, as if to warn Louise away from him. 'He's healed now, or almost, but he gets exhausted awful quick.'

'I'm fine, Ella, dinnae fuss,' said Benoit. He looked at Louise. 'Ella saved my life. Without her care, I'd be long deid.'

Ella stood awkwardly by, but there was colour on her cheeks. Louise caught her by the hands. 'I don't know what to say. I can hardly begin to thank you, or tell you how much I, my family, owe you.' She hugged the girl, her arms barely reaching around her, since Ella was twice her size, in height as well as girth. The girl flinched, then slowly put a hand on Louise's back, and returned her embrace.

'I love him, is all,' she said quietly.

'Thank God for that,' Louise replied. 'And when is your child due?'

'End of next month,' Ella said, sinking onto the bed beside Benoit, 'though it's been kicking up a storm, so it may be sooner.'

'We are married, Louise,' said Benoit quickly. 'When it looked like I wouldnae make it, the priest came. It wisnae the wedding I'd planned, not what you'd want for your girl . . . '

'It was beautiful,' said Ella. 'I'll never forget a minute of that day.' When she looked at Benoit, her wan face was lit with something like beauty. 'I think it was knowing you were a husband, with obligations, that brought you through. You knew you couldn't wriggle out of it now.' She smiled at him, and brushed his hair off his forehead.

Crozier scuffed his boots. 'I'm sorry,' he said. 'There's much news to catch up on, I know, but now is not the time.'

'Who are you?' asked Benoit, seeming only now to notice him.

'He is Adam Crozier, my husband,' said Louise. 'But we've no time to go into all that now. We've got to get you out of here, at once.'

She pulled up a chair. 'Listen, Benoit. I know you've had dealings with Patrick Paniter's man, Gabriel Torrance. That maybe you've been in league with him . . . '

In the face of Benoit's expression, she faltered.

Benoit sat forward, his face darkening. 'Jesus Christ, Louise, it was Torrance who tried to kill me, and very nearly did it too, the bastard.'

She shook her head, puzzled. 'I don't understand. I thought you'd been wounded in battle.'

'It is a long and fearful story,' said Ella. 'I will bring food while he tells it.'

Reluctantly, Crozier agreed. As the party picked clean a platter of oatcakes and cheese, Benoit recounted the night he had almost perished. It was a couple of days before the battle, he said, staring over their heads as he relived it, as if his memories were painted on the rafters. He did not see relief spreading over his sister's face, as his innocence became clear – relief mingled with shame, for having ever doubted him.

'Me and Ella,' he began, 'we'd agreed tae meet. Her family knew nothing about us, then. The month before, she'd told me she was pregnant. We arranged to run away and marry in secret, at the next full moon, but then the king called the muster, and I had tae fight. So we were forced to postpone our plans.

'It was risky, because her family would soon start to see her condition. I was frightened how they would react, if they found out afore we'd got married.' He chewed his lip, a gesture Louise had forgotten, it was so long since she'd seen him.

'Well, we knew the battle was soon coming, so I wanted to see her before it.' He caught his wife's eye. 'I could not believe it when she came to meet me with her father. She'd told him, or her mother had guessed, I forget which now.' He passed a hand over his face.

'Anyway, everything was fine, and there was no need for a moonlight elopement. Her family had been furious, like ours, but they're sensible folk, and they realised it was too late for that. They didnae want to lose their daughter for- ever, so they got over it. If only our mother had thought the same way,' he added, bitterly.

'Go on,' said Louise gently, sensing Crozier's impatience.

'Well, we said our goodbyes, and I left her. I had a long walk ahead of me. I was ploughing across the fields, soaking wet, when I heard a horse coming up on me. Morning was just breaking, and I wasn't far from the camp. I looked over my shoulder, and even at a distance I recognised the rider. It was the hair. His hood couldnae hide it. I was about to step out of his way, when I realised there was something wrong about this.'

As he recalled that moment, Benoit plucked at his shirt, his fingers as agitated as his thoughts.

'I could never abide that man,' he confessed, 'puffed up with importance, as he seemed. But that wisnae what made me suspicious. A few times before, in camp, I'd come on him acting strange. If he wisnae stuck to the side of Master Paniter like a leech, then he wis all alone, a solitary creature.

'Fair enough. Many an honest citizen prefers his own company to the blethering of a crowd. But once, it was late at night, and I wis watering the horse. I was leading her back up the hill when there he wis, crouched behind the king's tent. At first I thought he had taken ill, and wis about to be sick. But when I stood for a bit and watched, he did not move. Not until I approached and called out did he get up. Very grand he wis. Asked what I wis doing near the king's quarters.

'I wis canny enough no to ask him the same. But I could hear voices from the tent, even from where I was standing. He had been listening to them, that much wis clear to me.'

He sighed, straightened his shirt and continued. His shoulders sagged with fatigue.

'I kept an eye on him, after that, and on a few occasions I saw him loitering near the king's tent, or Master Paniter's, when he had no business to be there. Doing nothing, like, just acting ordinary. But to my mind, he was skulking.

'I suppose I thought he was nothing more than a schemer, the kind of man who collects secrets and gossip, and uses them to his advantage. But when I saw him charging like a demon out of the dark on his horse, I knew something was wrong. I couldnae stop masel.'

Benoit had stepped into the horse's path, raising his arms. The black stallion reared, and by the time Gabriel had reined him in, the carpenter was at his side, a hand on his hilt. He watched the courtier's expression flicker between light and shade, like a hillside under scudding clouds. It was as if he was considering and discarding one lie after another, and finally decided not to waste his breath. Benoit's suspicions were plain to read, and even if he managed to allay them, they would very likely flare again, at a more inconvenient time. This must be settled now.

Cursing, the courtier slipped off his horse, and loosed his sword. 'You wretched little man,' he said, circling around Benoit, his blade pointing at his chest. 'What are you doing, Master Brenier, creeping around the countryside at this hour? Been wenching, have you? Had your fill?' He laughed, and jabbed at Benoit's jacket, making the young man leap back. 'Is that the only thing your family can ever think about? What a pathetic lot you all are.' His lips curled in a sneer as he advanced. 'I promise you, my friend, this will end as badly for you as it did for your sister.'

With a roar of fury, Benoit lunged. He was a clumsy swordsman but strong, and the weight of his attack took Gabriel by surprise. As their blades met, the courtier reeled, wet earth gripping his boots like quicksand. His face tightened as he found his footing and regained control. Inch by inch he edged Benoit out of the field and into the copse at his back. It was a deadly dance, every step fought for in a clash of steel. Sweat was running into the carpenter's eyes, and his strokes grew wild. When he found himself cornered against a tree, he knew the end had come.

A shimmer of satisfaction passed over the courtier's face as he moved in for the finish. As his sword found the carpenter's stomach, Benoit saw Ella's face swim before his eyes. With a cry, as much of anguish as anger, he twisted his blade under Gabriel's guard and, with the last of his strength, plunged forward. He felt his blade slice through leather. Then the sky turned blacker than night, and he remembered nothing more, beyond the kick of a boot as the courtier turned him over, to watch his blood spilling out onto the leaves.

'It was a young trapper that found me,' said Benoit, voice trembling. 'He put me on a dray, and dragged me to the village healer. When I came to, I told them tae fetch Ella. I thought I was dead meat, but she thought otherwise. Her father put me ontae a mule to bring me here. That journey was hellish. Dying seemed the easier option, but she wasnae having any of it. And I woke up again, here in this bed. I havenae moved since.'

'Where are your parents?' Tom asked Ella.

'They're out at the All Hallows' markets. It would normally be me goes with father, but I couldnae go anywhere like this. And anyway, there was no way I would leave Ben.'

Crozier was at the window, squinting at the sky. 'We'd better get going, if we're to avoid the weather heading this way.'

Now it was Benoit's turn not to understand. As Louise

explained that Gabriel knew he was alive, and was trying to find him, he shuddered. 'I will have my revenge on him one day, but it will have to wait until I am fit enough tae face him. Until then, we will gladly come.'

'We can discuss revenge once you're safely at the keep,' said Louise. Ella began to pack a bag. She was shaking. A shawl, and then a nightshirt fell from her hand. 'Let me help,' said Louise, and the girl looked at her gratefully.

But before the bags were ready, the cottage went dark, as if the lamps had been snuffed. The sky had turned grey, and when they opened the door, snow was falling, thick and steady. Already the path was hidden. As they watched, the snow began to spin, and in seconds it had become a spitting, savage whirlwind of white, driving under the eaves as if to find them.

Crozier slammed the door. 'Jesus and Mary,' he muttered, brushing the flakes from his beard. His face was anxious, and Louise's heart contracted. He spoke to Tom. 'Let's get the horses out of sight round the back.'

'There's a barn,' said Benoit. 'They will be fine and warm in there.'

Crozier nodded curtly, and disappeared with his brother into the snow. From the window Louise watched them, mere shadows in the blizzard's maw. If Gabriel were to steal up on the cottage in this, they would not know he was here until his hand was at the door, his face at the window.

*   *   *

Gabriel Torrance was a man with many regrets. He could not remember a time when he had not wished his life was different, that other people had made wiser decisions, or given him a better deal. Rarely had he found fault with his own behaviour, but in one matter he knew he had been careless, and for this aberration he could not forgive himself.

Back in that accursed wood, as he kicked Benoit's body over to make sure he was dead, he had heard someone approaching through the trees. It would have been simple to drive his knife through the carpenter's throat before leaving, to make sure the job was done. Perhaps it was because Benoit was sliced open like a gutted fish, or perhaps because he too was wounded and not thinking clearly, but for whatever reason, he had not finished the task. Instead, he got onto his horse and galloped off before the intruder could catch sight of him.

Late the same day Gabriel returned to the wood with a shovel, expecting to find a corpse. He was met instead by a cold pool of black blood, and a scraping track through the leaves, as if Benoit had risen like Lazarus, and dragged himself to safety. He sank to his knees, uttering a howl so furious, it was heard in the village below. They took it as an omen. The battle's almost upon us, they whispered, gathering their children and barring their doors.

Though Benoit's wounds had looked mortal, Gabriel reflected, no good Samaritan would have carried him from the woods if he had been dead. The man must have had enough life left in him to leave on his own feet, or with help. The danger he now posed to the courtier was as life-threatening as any sword's blow. Until Benoit was despatched, Gabriel would be a haunted man, never sure when his deeds would catch up with him. The worst of it was, he had no-one to blame but himself.

The road to Liddesdale passed through land so barren it felt as if even God had abandoned it. He had never seen a place so pitiless. Heathland stretched to the horizon on every side, and the hills were treeless and scarred. A knifing wind made Gabriel's eyes sting, and the day was growing still colder, the sky bruised and threatening. Dusk was falling when Hermitage castle appeared below him, a gaunt fortress cupped in a valley's palm. He urged his horse on with a weary kick.

Though the castle looked like a prison for the worst kind of offenders, he was given a warm welcome. The owner, Patrick Hepburn, had died at Flodden, and mourning flags draped the hallway. Hepburn had been an ally of James, and his people were close associates of Patrick Paniter. They knew of Gabriel, and without hesitation they offered him a good dinner, and a soft bed. What they could not do, however, was tell him of anyone in the neighbourhood who matched the silversmith's description. He went to bed perplexed, but not yet beaten, and his optimism proved well founded. The next morning, over breakfast, he learnt what he needed.

'Elliot was the name, you say?' asked Hepburn's uncle, Archibald, refilling his guest's tankard with beer and proffering oatcakes and honey to follow the mutton stew he had just devoured.

Gabriel nodded, too busy eating to speak.

His host fiddled with the ears of his hound, whose head rested on his lap. 'Thing is, it's a large family, with many branches. Makes we Hepburns look like monks, the number of houses they've spawned.' He cackled. 'Mind you, I've known monks who've fathered a dynasty or two.'

Gabriel kept his eye on his plate, and continued to chew.

'They go by different names, is what I mean,' continued Hepburn, unnerved by his guest's silence. 'Some Elliots are known as Redheugh, some call themselves Ellworthy. There was even a Dalliot around here, once, who was more Elliot than the clan chief. Wouldn't hear a word against them without settling the score at knife point.' He laughed. 'They're a fiery breed, safest kept out in these empty hills where there's not so many folk to quarrel with.'

Gabriel finished his meal, and sat back. 'Go on,' he said, cleaning his fingernails with a toothpick.

'Well, now I think of it, there was a man once – about my father's age – who spent his life in the hills with his hammer, mining and chiselling for tin, and such like. I seem to recall he was a smith of some sort. May have been silver, for all I know.'

Gabriel sat forward. 'His name?'

'Now, there you have me.' Hepburn furrowed his brow. He stared at the timbered roof, and down at his dog, as if searching for a piece of his memory mislaid years earlier. He shook his head. 'I'm damned if I can remember.'

Gabriel's eyes gleamed, but before he could speak, Hepburn slapped his hand on the table. 'Of course! It was Aylewood. How could I forget? His son won the archery tournament five years in a row.' He laughed. 'We hated that boy like poison. He was a good enough lad, as I recall, but something of a loner. We always thought he cheated, but we could never prove it.'

'So he might be the silversmith I'm looking for?'

'Mmm?' replied Hepburn, lost in the past. 'Oh, no. Not him.' He shifted uneasily under the baleful eye of his guest, whose temper he was beginning to find irksome. 'No, the poor man died some years back, drowned in a spate while he was fishing for pearls. No, it's most likely his brother you're looking for. Edward, I think his name was. Hopeless with a bow and arrow, but fingers nimble as a spider's legs. Used to make nets and lace for the ladies' headdresses. I suppose he might have gone into silverwork.'

Gabriel's smile fooled neither of them. 'And if you dig deep into your memory, sir, might you recall where this man lived?'

'Jeddart,' said Hepburn, his eyes narrowing, and his voice cold. 'I don't know what you want with him, but if I were you, I'd set out now. It's a long ride across the moors. And you'd better watch out for the bogs. They're more treacherous than the Armstrongs or the Taylors, and believe me, that's saying something.' He stood, and held out his hand in farewell with a smile as practised and false as the courtier's.

By the time the snow came, Gabriel had crossed the highest moorland. Had it arrived earlier he would have been in trouble, for even in full daylight the way across the heath was difficult, the path meandering into swampy marsh, or snaking into gullies, when it had seemed to promise firm, flat land. Several times he had been obliged to retrace the path, and find another.

Yet even though he was off the hill-top when the blizzard began, Gabriel was unnerved. The snow flew at him as if it held a grudge, and his world was reduced to a tunnel of relentless driving white. His horse snorted and stamped, before settling into a stoical trudge, his forehead and mane quickly caked in snow.

The remaining miles to Jeddart were a torment, the stallion stumbling and slithering in the deepening drifts, the courtier's face and hands numb from cold, and pain throbbing in his arm. Had he spied a hovel where he could have taken shelter, he would have battered down its door, but he could see barely a hand's reach in front of his nose, and any houses he passed were hidden, for all they might be only a few yards away. Once he caught the smell of welcoming woodsmoke. He stopped, sniffing the air. The cottage was so close he could almost hear the crackling of the fire, but he dared not leave the path. Fixing his thoughts on reaching the town before nightfall, he rode on.

He arrived in Jeddart late that evening. As he descended from the woodlands to the streets, he could not see much of the place, though the lamp-lit abbey soared above him as he passed. The torch over its gateway picked out a cowed, whitened figure more ice than blood, the only one abroad at this hour.

It took The Lion's finest claret and roasted fowl and a seat by its roaring fire to thaw the chill in the courtier's bones, and even then he went to bed shivering. By the next morning he was snuffling with a head cold, and sneezing so loudly he sent the cat flying out of the taproom as if a bulldog was at its heels.

From his bedroom window he looked out across the blanketed town. Benoit, he sensed, was very close. He smiled. He could afford to wait another day. Nobody would travel in this weather. Meanwhile he would make some enquiries.

The snow fell all that day, and the next. Gabriel nursed his cold with hot honeyed wine, and sat by the taproom fire. The town was hushed, going about its business as if silenced by a gag. He made only one foray, and returned with the expression of one whose troubles have been lifted. The serving maid assumed he had been to confession, and smiled to think of his shriven soul.

The woman he had been visiting was not smiling. She lay unconscious on her earthen floor, her bottles and jars smashed into pieces around her, their contents soaking her skirts.

The healer had not expected any customers in such weather. Like a true gentleman, her visitor had stamped the snow off his boots before stepping into the hovel, where he swept off his hat. With interest he surveyed the herbs hanging from the rafters, the jars that lined the walls. As he did so she eyed his riding boots, his lined cape, the fur stole around her throat. She had never served anyone so grand.

'Is it something for yerself, sir?' she asked, hobbling to her shelves. 'Something for yer sore throat, perhaps?'

'No,' he said, 'nothing like that. I'm trying to find some-one I believe you may have treated.'

She raised her eyebrows. 'Aye?'

'A young man, stabbed in the stomach by some scoundrel who pounced on him on the highway. A sturdy-looking lad with a poor, pocked skin.'

The old woman's eyes were glassy. 'I've had no patient of that kind, son,' she said, her hands shaking as she plucked at her shawl. 'I dinnae deal wi' anything serious these days. It's mostly snivels and rashes.'

Gabriel advanced on her, so close she could smell the wine on his breath. 'I hear otherwise, my good woman. The finest of her kind, they told me. Nothing she won't turn her hand to. To listen to your admirers, you have powers enough to raise the dead.'

He took her by the wrist. 'So I will ask you one more time. Have you had a man like that in your care of late?'

She was trembling so violently Gabriel could almost hear her joints rattling, but she looked him in the eye and shook her head. His hand moved to her throat. Under his fingers her swallowing gullet felt like a sparrow squeezed in a fist. She was gobbling for air, her eyes turning bloodshot when finally she nodded.

He let her go, and she bent over, struggling for breath. When she could speak, she was hoarse. 'He wis at Aylewood's house by the chapel, on the road outae Old Jeddart. I dinnae ken if he'll still be there, though, it wis some weeks back.' She held out her hands, warding Gabriel off, but he had her by the arms. She whimpered. 'Tell no-one I have been here, or else I'll be back,' he said, before flinging her across the room, where she landed with a snap of bones.

CHAPTER TWENTY-TWO

5 November 1513

Snow rose around the silversmith's cottage, a frozen noose that held them fast. For two days Louise watched it tumble, as if the sky was a bottomless sack emptied over their heads. Her fingers twitched with anxiety. Crozier and Tom took turns keeping watch. Benoit offered to take his share, but did not take offence when they refused, and Louise sensed his relief. 'You must rest,' said Tom, 'ahead of the ride. We two don't need much sleep anyway.' His brother gave a rough laugh, recalling the times – some of them recent – when Tom could not be dragged from his bed by anything less than the threat of a skelping.

These drawn-out hours of perpetual twilight gave Louise time with her brother, in which they chattered, without drawing breath, as they always had. Benoit was astonished at how grown-up his little sister had become. For her part, she found him greatly changed too, less sure, but more settled. His eyes followed Ella wherever she went, and when she was close he was calmer. Despite the trouble their dangerous alliance had caused, he had chosen well. Shy as she was, Ella had a spirit to match his.

Yet the joy of finding her brother was tempered by fear of what lay ahead. Louise pictured Gabriel making his remorseless way towards them, plodding black-cloaked on his black horse through the falling snow, the very eye of the storm.

On their second night in the cottage, when Crozier and she lay blanketed on the floor by the fire, and Tom kept watch by the shutters, she could not sleep for thinking what kind of man she had been duped by. She had not for a moment questioned the courtier's affection, or his lightning fast courtship. For a lord of his standing, she now realised, a girl like her could at best have hoped to be his mistress. Had that been what he was offering all along? She clenched her fists. What else could it have been?

Worse than Gabriel's calculated deceit was her own vanity, which had led to her being tricked into a liaison that might, like her sister's, have ruined her life. Had she not come to her senses in time, she would not now be with Crozier. The thought that she might have thrown away his love made her eyes smart. She held tight to his hand, as if he were a shield behind which she could take cover from these hard facts, but she knew that there was no-one to whom she was answerable except herself. Yet when her sleeping husband put his arm around her and pulled her closer, she was comforted. He was no fool, even if he had married one. Eventually, she slept.

When she woke, Crozier and Tom were conferring at the door. They turned as she lifted her head, and Crozier's face lightened at the sight of her sleepy eyes, the wayward curls that made her look as if a gale had passed through her hair.

Day had barely broken, but Louise could tell that the snow had stopped. 'Can we leave now?' she asked. Crozier nodded. 'Soon as it's light.'

'I'll feed the horses and bring them round,' said Tom, letting a blast of icy air into the cottage as he left. The chill woke them fully, but by the time Ella and Benoit were dressed, and they had eaten a morsel of bread and dripping, and packed food for the trip, the sun was up.

In their bustle and relief to be setting out, none thought to listen for trouble. Tom tied his and Crozier's horses to the post by the door, and went back to the barn for Louise's pony. While he was gone, the horses lifted their heads, ears pricked.

It was shortly after that Crozier asked, 'What's taking Tom so long?' Just then, the horses began to shuffle. Crozier's mare threw back her head and neighed, a full-throated whinny. When an answering whicker came from the woods, everyone in the cottage froze. Louise felt as if a hand had reached into her chest and squeezed her heart. She could not breathe. In that moment's silence, they heard a soft step outside the shuttered window. As Crozier leapt to the door and slammed the bar into place, the latch was raised. It clicked, uselessly, and a shoulder was pressed against the wood with a sullen creak.

'Benoit Brenier!' cried Gabriel, thumping against the door as if he could batter it off its hinges. 'Open up! I know you're in there. You and the silversmith, by the looks of it.'

Nobody spoke. Crozier motioned them away from the door and they crept to the rear of the room where they stood in a huddle, eyeing the latch as if the devil himself were behind it.

'Come on now, Master Brenier,' called Gabriel, 'We need to talk, you and I. The business we started in the woods must be finished. Let's make a deal, and be done with all this. Then we can go our separate ways.'

Brenier seemed about to reply when Crozier put a finger to his lips and shook his head.

After another pounding, things went quiet. They followed the sounds as Gabriel moved around beneath the trees, a prowler who did not care if he was heard. The horses were restless, and at first it seemed as if he were calming them, his voice low and gentle. Then he gave a shout, slapped a rump, and there was neighing and the slushy canter of hooves disappearing into the woods.

Gabriel's footsteps crunched around the cottage. Its only windows were at the front, so there was no knowing what he was doing, though they could guess. The scuffle of his heavy tread, his grunts and groans, lasted for what seemed like an age. There was a dragging, and a rustling. Crozier looked up at the rafters, his face grimmer than Louise had ever seen it. Then came the noise they had dreaded, the rasp, rasp, rasp of a tinderbox, followed soon after by the smell of smoke.

Ella gave a moan, and sank onto the floor. Benoit gripped her hand, and rubbed it. 'The thatch will be wet,' he said, 'it may not take light.'

But Gabriel knew what he was doing. He had lit tapers in the straw beneath the eaves, where it was dry, and in a matter of minutes, runnels of flame had burrowed deep into the roof, which would shortly turn into a frying pan.

'Will you come out now, laddie?' he called wearily from the front of the cottage. 'If you don't want to save yourself, think about your family. Burned alive is not a good way to go, or so the martyrs' faces tell us.'

Crozier crouched beside Ella and Benoit. 'This place will soon go up like a torch. It doesn't sound as if he knows that Louise and I are here, though God knows what he's done with Tom.' At the thought of his brother hurt, his hands turned into fists.

He looked from one to the other. 'If you go outside, you might be able to distract him long enough for me and Louise to slip out. I can then attack from behind. It's not a good plan, but it's our only option. Unless you can think of something better?'

But they could not. Hand in hand they rose, and stood by the door. 'I am coming out,' cried Benoit. 'My wife is with me. Let her go, and you can have me.'

'That's the spirit,' called Gabriel. 'I knew you'd see sense.'

Crozier lifted the bar, and opened the door. He and Louise flattened themselves against the wall. They heard Benoit and Ella walking over snow, away from the cottage.

Already the room was growing warm. Smoke was curling from the rafters, but until Gabriel's back was turned, they dare not leave. Louise put her hand in Crozier's. He opened the shutters an inch, and watched, unmoving. Then he gave her a quick hug. 'Right,' he said, 'let's get on with it.'

They crept out into the snow. Gabriel stood side on to the billowing smoke. If he caught a movement in the corner of his eye as the pair slipped out, he thought it was only a flicker of flames as they crept over the roof fast as tomcats, and leapt into the air with a whoosh that cast an orange glow over the snow, and shadowed their faces in crimson.

The courtier stared at Ella, as she clung to her husband.

'This your fancy piece, is it, Master Brenier?' he said, casting his eyes over her, from boots to cap, lingering on the bulge beneath her cape. 'Have you perchance bitten off more than you intended?'

'Your quarrel is with me, fils de putain,' Benoit replied, his voice stronger than seemed possible for one so whey-faced.

'Indeed,' said Gabriel. 'Don't I know it.'

There was a crack and a groan as timbers began to shift under the flames. Gabriel pointed his sword at Benoit, and directed him away from his wife. 'On your knees,' he said, as if suddenly tired of conversation.

Crozier crept up behind him, sword outstretched. His footsteps went unheard in the crackling flames. Not until his blade was pressed between Gabriel's shoulders did the courtier know he was there. Crozier spoke loudly, over the blaze. 'Don't move or the sword will go through your heart. It would give me great pleasure to send it home.'

For a second time, Benoit was privy to the passage of emotions across the courtier's face. Fury was uppermost, but this was swiftly overlain by cunning. An oily smile spread over his features. He raised his hands above his head, and turned, slowly, to face the Borderer.

'Drop your sword,' barked Crozier. Gabriel did so, and Benoit quickly retrieved it. Only when Gabriel saw Louise did his face register something honest. The flicker of distress was fleeting, however, rapidly concealed behind a smile that made Louise feel queasy. It was the very smile she had fallen for, a lifetime earlier. Only now could she see that it did not reach his eyes, which glowed green and cold as an emerald in the fire-lit morning.

'My sweetness,' he said, 'I have missed you.'

'Quiet,' growled Crozier.

'Oh I will be, sir, I will, once I have had my say. But surely you can't deny me the chance to say a last farewell to the woman I love? And who – dare I boast of it – loves me? We were to be wed, you know.'

'That is a lie!' cried Louise, drawing closer. 'I never once said I loved you. I never promised to marry you. I was just a stupid, needy little girl.'

'But so soft and delicious, my sweet,' he said, raising his eyes as if to savour the memory. 'And, if I may say so, without lowering the tone too far, so terribly, delightfully generous.'

'Ohhh!' With a cry Louise hurled something at him. It struck his face, and he winced. When he looked down, the emerald ring was bedded in the snow at his feet.

'You return it?' He sounded shocked, his mocking tone fled.

'It was never mine,' she said. 'I told you I would not keep it.'

Gabriel met Louise's eye. 'I remember, but I did not believe you meant it. I wanted you as my wife. How could you not want to marry me, when I loved you so well?'

'Your manner was not of love, sir, but of p . . . p . . . possession,' she stammered. 'I would have been another trophy, like your ridiculous ring.'

He looked perplexed. 'But what is wrong with that? I would have been proud to have you as my wife and show you to the world. You are more beautiful than any jewel. I wanted to have you, as mine.' He paused. 'It is not too late, even now.'

Louise turned away, sickened. Crozier's lips thinned.

'You've said enough,' he snarled. 'From now on, keep your mouth shut.'

'But what about the ring?' the courtier asked, his hands still aloft.

'Pick it up,' said the Borderer, which he was forever to recall as the most stupid thing he had ever said in his life.

The courtier bent, but as his fingers closed on the ring, he lunged headfirst for Louise, catching her around the waist in a tackle that threw them both to the ground. Before Crozier could react, he had a knife at her throat. She had not had time to scream.

'Idiots, the lot of you,' he sneered, clasping her to his chest. With the knife point pressed to her neck, he slowly got to his feet. 'And now, I have what I want. She'll come with me, won't you, my sweetness, and we won't bother anyone ever again. We'll be out of the country before any-one hears a word of what's happened here today.' He looked at Benoit, who was trembling. 'That's my deal to you, Master Brenier. I will take your sister in return for sparing your skin. The love of my life for yours. It's only fair.'

Gabriel was backing slowly to the woods, where his horse was tethered. His face was white with exhaustion, yet lit with an exalted expression that made Crozier feel ill. He was helpless. This man would not think twice about slitting Louise's throat. He dared not attack, not yet. He caught Louise's eye, with a look that told her he would not let her come to harm. She nodded imperceptibly, eyes bright with terror as Gabriel dragged her slowly into the trees.

Step by step they retreated. They were half-hidden in shadow when a figure appeared from behind the trees. It was Tom. With a roar, he brought down his cudgel on the courtier's arm. As the knife dropped from his hand, Tom yelled at Louise to run, before smashing his fist into the courtier's face, and launching himself upon him.

But there was no fight left in Gabriel. His arm was broken, his nose bloodied. Worst of all, he was humiliated. That ruffians such as these should bring him down, and for Louise to witness it, was mortifying. He closed his eyes, to block out the sight, and as he did so, a wave of tiredness hit him so powerfully it was as if he had been punched a second time.

'What's he muttering?' asked Benoit, as they bound his hands and feet.

'Sleep,' said Tom, puzzled. 'I'm quite sure he said "Let me sleep".'

'Where he's going it'll be eternal night,' said Crozier grimly, tying the last knot. He dragged Gabriel to his feet. When the courtier refused to open his eyes, he slapped his face. 'Wake up! There's a long walk ahead of you.'

The courtier blinked at him. There was a blankness in his eyes that was more frightening than any expression he had yet shown. From a distance, Louise and Ella watched. 'I think he has lost his mind,' said Louise quietly. 'I had not seen it before, but look at him. He is perfectly mad.' The courtier caught her horrified gaze, but he might have been looking into empty air. She was invisible to him now.

There was a shout from deeper in the woods, and Benoit limped into view, leading the Borderers' horses. 'They hadn't gone far,' he said. 'Thank God they were hungry.'

It was a sombre party that filed out of the woods and onto the Jeddart road. Behind them the fire was smouldering, the cottage sinking lower into the earth as if burying itself. Tom and Louise led the procession, followed by Crozier on the courtier's stallion. Lashed to the saddle by a leading rope, with loose shackles around his ankles, Gabriel shuffled through the snow. His eyes were fixed on the white road ahead, where the hoof prints from his earlier journey were a reminder of the freedom he had lost. Ella sat on Crozier's mare, which was no doubt grateful for the dolorous pace.

The sergeant of Jedburgh gaol could not believe the prize that was handed to him. 'Tell me all that again, like,' he said to Crozier, taking off his steel hat and rubbing a hand over his head, as if this would make everything clear.

By the time the man understood who his prisoner was, daylight had faded. While Crozier was detained by the sergeant's never-ending questions, Tom found them cheap beds for the night, and Benoit wrote to Paniter, to tell him the traitor was caught. It was a difficult letter to compose, but not as difficult as it was for Paniter to read.

It was several days later when the travel-stained document was put into his hand by one of the sergeant's men. 'I have been told to wait for your answer,' said the messenger, cuffing a drip from his nose. He could smell a rich broth, and hoped the secretary would offer him a meal after his miserably cold ride. But Paniter was too excited to notice the man's hunger. Expecting news from Gabriel, he eagerly broke the seal. When he saw the signature he was not dismayed, anticipating a confession of sorts. Then, as the message unfolded, he was filled with disbelief, followed by molten rage, and finally the bitterest guilt.

With an imperious hand, Paniter dismissed the

messenger, who was obliged to sit in the unheated hallway, so full of whistling winds and fluting draughts it was like a minstrel's gallery. Alone, the secretary dropped his head in his hands. At first he had wondered if this was yet another of Benoit's tricks, deflecting blame onto the courtier when it was he who was the criminal. If that were the case, he had been mighty clever, outwitting and overpowering the viscount, and handing him over to the law. Yet if Benoit had had Gabriel in his power, why had he not simply killed him, and fled?

That troubling detail made him pause. He sat up and read the letter again. Calm enough now to make the words stand still under his eye, he saw there were too many witnesses to the Frenchman's story to dismiss it as a lie. Truly it seemed as if his protégé, the young man he had taken under his wing, was the viper who had tried to bring down the king and his country.

He cast the letter aside and closed his eyes. Would his torments never end? But whereas a month ago he would have retreated to his bed and pulled the covers over his head, he was stronger now. Summoning the messenger, he wrote a swift note to the Jedburgh sergeant, advising him that he would shortly be sending a guard to bring the prisoner back to Edinburgh. He pressed a meagre coin into the messenger's hand, and directed him to an inn on the high street, where they would feed him well.

When the man left, still sniffing, Paniter buttoned his tunic, tied a cloak around his neck, and made for the castle. There he gave orders for a guard of twelve to be assembled the following morning, and a cell to be prepared for the spy, and the interrogation he would face. 'Special implements required?' the castle governor asked, inspecting his nails. 'No,' the secretary replied. 'I can make him talk.'

Yet when he came face to face with the spy, he had little appetite for questions. After an hour with him, Paniter had had enough. His guilt was not in question, and pressing him for details would reveal nothing he wished to know, and perhaps more than he would want to.

Paniter had endured many unpleasant encounters in his career. None compared with Flodden, but on his death bed, many years later, he would rank the time he spent with Gabriel Torrance in his cell second only to that horror. The grimy, pale young man who stared back at him from his chains was unrecognisable. He had lost none of his hauteur, but the face that Paniter had once thought handsome was overlain with a malevolence that took his breath.

'I treated you like a son,' Paniter said, with a note of peevishness, as if the courtier had been guilty of bad manners, rather than a heinous crime. The secretary stood before the prisoner, who squatted against the wall, his arm in a filthy sling. Yet it was as if Gabriel loomed above him, so overbearing was his presence. Paniter's pulse raced as the green eyes swept over him.

'You were kind to me, I grant,' said Gabriel, giving no sign of discomfort at being pinioned in leg-irons. 'But there are many rotten fathers in this world. Feeling fatherly does not in itself make you a parent, or give you any hold over me.'

Paniter searched his face. 'Gabriel, Gabriel my lad, is it really possible you were passing secrets to the English all the time I knew you?'

'Oh yes,' he replied. 'It was I who was the spy. With

my little eye. I saw everything, and I did not like much of it at all.'

'Do you have accomplices? Are you part of a wider plot? Give me names, and I can lighten your sentence. One alone will suffice.'

Gabriel shook his head. 'I worked by myself. Why would I want associates? My aim was simple, to bring victory for England, and shame for Scotland. I could do that single-handed.'

In his agitation, Paniter paced from wall to door. Outside the guard watched through the grille.

'Were you being blackmailed? There must have been a reason why you turned against the country. I need to understand, boy. You make no sense to me at all. You had everything. You had a future, yet you have behaved worse than a cut-throat.'

A flash of spirit put colour into Gabriel's face. 'I am an Englishman, sir. That is all you need to know.'

'Not Irish as you said? Not the son of a viscount?'

'Not Irish, and not Scottish. I am indeed a nobleman's son, but I was born an Englishman, and everything I have ever done, from the moment I could first speak, was for my homeland. For my family.'

Paniter rubbed his face. 'Laddie, you make no sense. You are as thirled to Scotland as I. You were educated here, brought up here – why would you want to destroy this country?'

'I have told you. My allegiance is and always will be to the English king. There is nothing more to say.'

Paniter sighed. 'Yet you fought at Flodden. What if the English had killed you there, or you had cut them down?'

Gabriel spat, the first and only coarse gesture the secretary ever saw him make.

'Of course I did not fight. How could I harm a hair of my countrymen's heads? No, you old fool. While you and your gang were running around demented, I was well away from there. Only an idiot would have been blind to what quarter the wind was blowing.'

'And your arm, the wound – was that all a pretence too?' Paniter's voice was low.

Gabriel gave a thin smile. 'Sadly not. That was the work of Master Brenier, the only noble stroke in an otherwise woeful demonstration of swordsmanship. I probably did the Scottish army a favour keeping him from the battle-field.'

The back of Paniter's hand cracked across his face, knocking his head against the wall. His ring caught his eye, and blood began to ooze down his cheek where it dripped, unheeded, onto his shirt. Gabriel continued to smile.

'I could throttle you this instant, and no questions would be asked,' Paniter hissed, rubbing his knuckles. 'You would not be the first man I have killed bare-handed. But I wouldn't sully myself.' His lip curled. 'You are a disgrace to the race of Adam and Eve. Even England deserves better than the likes of you. If King Henry ever met you, he would be disgusted to think you were in his service.'

Gabriel paled, but he said nothing.

Paniter clasped his hands before him, as if to keep them from flying again at the courtier. He trembled with rage. 'Only you will ever know why you have acted as you have. I no longer care. If you had shown one good reason, I would have asked for clemency on your behalf. As it is, I will cast you to the court, and the gallows, without a word. Yours will not be an easy death, young man. May God have mercy on your pitiful soul. If indeed you have one.'

'And on yours,' the courtier whispered as Paniter summoned the guard to open the door. 'And on yours,' he repeated, louder. The secretary glanced over his shoulder. The knowing smile with which Gabriel met his eye, and the sting of those words, would be with Paniter until he died.

CHAPTER TWENTY-THREE

21 December 1513

The spy's execution was set for the shortest day of the year. This was Paniter's decision. The darkest time, he told the privy council, was a fitting date for ridding the country of such a man. Gabriel Torrance's body would still be growing cold as the year began to turn and with it, one could pray, the fortunes of the nation. Nobody would be sad to see the solstice pass, to watch new hope born with each lengthening minute of light.

Unvisited but not forgotten, Gabriel sat in his cell. When the prisoner was brought before the high court, Patrick Paniter looked at him as if he were a stranger, though a tic jumped in his cheek. There was to be no trial. After all, the man had confessed, without the least persuasion. But for the record, and so none could accuse the infant king's court of foul play, various procedures had to be observed. The first of these was a written testimony from Benoit Brenier, which the judge read out, raising his eyebrows at every oddity of grammar or expression.

'Do ye have anything to add tae that?' the judge asked Gabriel when he had finished, peering at him as if he were a specimen in a physician's jar. The courtier shook his head, and primped his sleeve. The rest of the day passed in a tedium of legal detail and ritual as privy councillors and court clerks trotted to and fro with scraps of paper, muttering to each other, scribbling amendments, and enjoying the solemn fuss of it all. Throughout, Gabriel stared out of the window at the gunmetal sky, his face impassive.

At last the session was brought to a close. With a rustle of cloaks, the high court rose. 'I hereby pronounce ye, Gabriel, Viscount Torrance of Blaneford and Mountjoy – or so you style yourself – guilty of treason,' intoned the judge. 'This being the most awful of crimes on this country's statutes, far exceeding murder in its vileness, ye will be taken on a date still to be appointed, to the place of execution. There ye will be hanged till ye are near death, then taken down and quartered. Only at this point will your heid be cut off and your agony put to an end. Thereafter your various pairts will be displayed around the city walls as a warning to any who might be tempted to follow in your wicked ways. There the said pairts will hang until a year henceforth, when your family will be allowed to bury ye in unconsecrated ground.'

Above the court chamber, a bell tolled. Those gathered in the courtyard below bowed their heads, listening to the verdict. The bell rang on, not stopping until the thirteenth strike. The crowd murmured with satisfaction. It was the worst of penalties, and it was just.

Gabriel had one task to complete before he was ready to leave this life. He pulled a sheet of paper towards him across the damp cell floor, but before he had lifted his pen his eyes filled with tears and, putting his head on his knees, he sobbed as if his heart would break. These were the only tears he had shed since he was a child, and had realised that his mother did not recognise him from one day's visit to the next. 'Who's this sweet little poppet?' she would ask, fingering his curls, not seeing in their sunny profusion the mirror of her own.

Drying his eyes, he lifted his head. The guard leered at him through the grille, but Gabriel did not see him. These days the only people he noticed appeared in his dreams, or in the faded hours around dusk. They would hold lively conversations, amusing the courtier so that his laughter would bring his jailers to the bars, wondering who was with him.

'Beloved Mother, star of my soul,' he began, the writing slow and messy and painful. 'It is as I feared. I must go ahead of you into the next world. My plans have come to nothing, and my hopes for our home together must wait.

'If you hear terrible things about me, I entreat you not to believe them. If Mamie speaks cruelly or meanly of me, tell her that to the end I have been true, honest and loyal to you and to her, and to our fine family name. I have done nothing to besmirch its honour. Quite the opposite. Your next letter may be from the king of England, thanking you for your son's part in his glory. If he should not write, I advise you to contact him, though I have not his direction. He will want to reward you handsomely.

'I am well, I am not afraid, and I pray the same is true of you. While I am gone, the good Lord will take care of you. And when we meet again, all will be well with us, all manner of things will be well.

'Do not forget me, mother.

'Your only, and most loving son, Gabriel'

The guard sniffed when he took the letter, holding it between thumb and finger as if it would contaminate him. Gabriel leaned back against the wall and nursed his aching arm. There was no more now for him to do but count the days to eternity.

*　　*　　*

On the morning of Gabriel's execution, Patrick Paniter rose early. He washed in water so cold it made the blood course around his body. Goodwife Black helped him into his shirt and hose, and buckled his boots. She too would watch the execution, though from the street. Before breakfast she left the secretary to spend an hour with his bible, as was his habit these mornings.

It was mild for the time of year, as if the gods wanted a good turnout for the traitor's death. The remnants of the city's nobility had gathered, dressed in their brightest colours. Ordinary citizens came out in cloaks and caps of red and yellow and blue, and those who had no fine clothes carried ribbons to wave. There were to be no mourning weeds. This criminal's death was a cause for celebration.

The gibbet stood at the mercat cross on the high street, where four streets spilled into a cramped square, frowned down upon by stern, crooked houses. As they caught their first sight of the scaffold, people quietened, like mice under a hawk's shadow. Soon, however, their chatter resumed, and by the time the hour was close, and Paniter arrived to take his seat, the babble was like bedlam.

Picking up his trailing cloak, Paniter climbed onto a rickety stage close to the gibbet, set with benches for courtiers and dignatories. From here they would have a clear view of proceedings. He sat with the privy councillors, and they talked of everything but what was shortly to unfold. He heard of the young king's painful teething and he learned that the queen's finest horse had been surpassing itself, though for decency's sake it was ridden only at private races. It was too soon after Flodden for public games.

At ten minutes to noon, a guard of pikemen marched through the crowd, and stood to attention at the foot of the scaffold. Their blades caught the sun, sending arrows of light flashing across the square. Drummers began a low, rattling roll, and gradually, row by row, the people fell silent. The drums beat on.

The slow marching of boots could be heard, coming down the street from the castle. People craned to see as a column of soldiers appeared, a horse dragging a dray in their midst. Strapped to the dray, like a hog trussed for the spit, lay Gabriel, his hair gleaming greasy and gold in the noonday sun. He was dressed in a shirt, hose and riding boots, the linen grimed, the boots stained. Paniter was shocked at the gauntness of his face. This man had betrayed him, his friend and mentor, as well as the country, yet he could not be unmoved by his suffering. He braced himself for what was to come.

There was a fanfare of trumpets as the horse halted, and the soldiers untied the prisoner and dragged him to the gibbet. When they set him on his feet, his hands cuffed behind him, Gabriel looked up at the swinging noose, then out across the marketplace, packed from wall to wall with onlookers. A few jeers came from the crowd, but they were quickly hushed.

The executioner led him up the steps, and turned him to face his audience. The hangman placed the noose around his neck and tightened it, like a valet adjusting his master's collar. Gabriel was offered no blindfold, and he stared, head held high, beyond the audience's heads to the comfortless sky. His lips moved, though whether with fear or in prayer was impossible to tell.

The drumbeat quickened. A seagull flew overhead, raucously mewling as if mimicking the mockers. Paniter could no longer look at the spy, whose legs were shaking. He stared instead at the pikemen, who held their weapons at the ready, perhaps fearing this miserable roped man would break free and fly over their heads.

The seagull passed, the drums stopped, and after a never-ending minute, when nobody and nothing moved, the hangman pushed the prisoner off the steps, and Gabriel sank, kicking, into the air.

At the sight, Paniter felt he too was falling. He uttered a cry that was lost in the crowd's bloodthirsty screams. The sky whitened before his eyes, and the world contracted and shrank to the size of a coin. He dug his nails into his palms as he fought a tide of giddiness but while he kept his seat, he could do nothing to prevent the images and smells that engulfed him.

As the guards' pikes flashed, and the crowd bayed, and Gabriel twisted and jerked like an old hound strung up by its master, Paniter saw and heard nothing of it all. The present scene was hidden by a mist, out of which worse apparitions loomed.

*   *   *

From the top of Branxton Hill, the English army looked wary. Their cannons were light, and the soldiers' spears were short. They would need to be hand to hand with their foe to do any damage.

On the lower hill, across the valley, Surrey's men were planted, unmoving. After a gruelling race to switch hills, the Scots had hauled their guns into place, their horses were safely tethered back at camp, and each commander was standing, grim-faced, at the head of his men. All was set for the fight.

The afternoon was dank with drizzle. James stood at Paniter's side, a hand on the largest serpentine as he surveyed the enemy. His nose was purplish with cold, his face bright with excitement, and beneath his helmet his long hair whipped as if to encourage the flags his standard bearers had raised. He smiled at the sight of the Scottish troops, whose pikes soared like a harbour filled with masts.

The king's eyes were sparkling. He kissed Paniter loudly on both cheeks, and slapped his back. 'What a night we will have when this is over!' he cried. He made the sign of the cross, kissed the crucifix around his neck and raising his lance to the heavens roared, 'For God and King and Country!'

At its cue the bugles blared, there was a cheer that could be heard far out at sea, and the guns on both sides roared. Heedless of the shots flying into their midst, the Scottish flanks moved down the hill. As they seethed forward, like a wave beginning its deadly roll far from shore, the air went black. A hail of arrows from both sides blotted the light, and for a second Paniter thought it was his own senses that were failing, and he were about to swoon. Useless against the Scots' jerkins and bonnets, the arrows fell like kindling, crunched underfoot as Home and Huntly's men swept on.

It was the silence that startled Paniter. After the first cries of attack, the Scots moved as if by stealth. The English were chanting, jibbing their billhooks, hurling obscenities as they awaited the order to advance, but the surly quiet of the Scottish soldiers was more intimidating than screams, and Paniter watched the English bravado falter, and their shouting fade in the face of this ominous calm.

Borthwick was at his elbow, his helmet pushed far back on his head. He had regained his composure after his humiliation the day before, and was acting as if it were he, and not Paniter, who was in charge of the guns. Indeed, it seemed to Paniter that he treated him with a hint of contempt. But that could not be so. Nerves must be making him fanciful.

After their opening salute, the gunners were biding their time as they had been instructed. Cannons of such size and weight would win the day, but should not be fired until the troops were well advanced. So Borthwick's men crouched at the ready, one to each hungry mouth.

That wait was an agony, the gunners' nerves strung so tight that taking no action was worse than being in the frontline, or so they thought. For Paniter, watching the first wall of soldiers flatten the English, while they did not light a single fuse, felt criminal. But when Paniter looked to the king, he bade them wait. 'Not yet,' he mouthed, patting his hands in the air to urge restraint.

The first engagement was dreamlike in its simplicity and success. Levelling their pikes at the short English billhooks, Home and Huntly's men scythed the enemy flanks like weeds. Barely a Scottish bone was broken in that fiendish attack. As they wheeled off the field, to the roars of their comrades, the centre of the army began to move, with James at its head.

The colours and finery of the Scottish side were a taunt to the drab, brown Englishmen, a sign of the confidence with which the north faced the south. As the soldiers unfurled, line by line, they moved down the hill like an avalanche, slow to start, then gathering speed. On the far hill, the English readied themselves. Paniter sent up a prayer and fingered the rosary beads at his waist. Finally, the guns could be fired.

Not a day had passed since that afternoon when Paniter had not relived those terrible opening minutes when the artillery was in his charge. Screaming at the gunners to light the tapers, he watched the first volleys with elation, his spirits flying high as the cannon balls. The thundering kick of the fuse-lit guns brought a moment's exaltation, as if this smoking hill-top were the very foundry of war, and these soldered warriors the arbiters of victory or defeat.

And so it proved. When the first curtains of smoke cleared and the enemy's hill could be seen, the truth was plain. They were vastly overshooting. The howls of the English as they flattened themselves beneath the artillery's whistling flight soon gave way to cheers as the fist-sized balls flew far beyond the field. It was then that Paniter first thought he would collapse. In the hours that followed, the dizziness came upon him in waves, so that the spinning behind his eyes was as much a part of the mayhem, in his memory, as the turmoil around him.

While the cannonballs were sailing wide, word spread

through the ranks. Montrose was dead. Shortly after, it was Crawford. Then Argyll. Then Erroll. At that point Paniter's heart took up residence in his throat. From the crest of the hill, surrounded by his graveyard of iron, he looked down on a sea of reddening steel and falling bodies. While he stood, transfixed at the scene, Borthwick repositioned the smallest culverins further back on the hill. He passed out hand-held guns to those prepared to follow the troops down the valley, though he might as well have sent them to the executioner's block. The time it took to reload and fire made them a childishly easy target, and none was ever to return.

Billowing smoke, rain and arrows turned day into dusk, but the darkening of Paniter's mind was blacker still. At the hill's foot a once douce little burn was a torrent, swollen by weeks of rain. The blood drained from the secretary's face as he watched his countrymen reach the valley bed, where they staggered and squirmed, sinking up to their knees in molten mud as if it were wrapping them in chains. The charging ranks behind piled into them, tumbling under each other's feet. Those who fell pulled themselves caked and sopping out of the glaur, like wraiths rising from the grave. As word passed back, men wrenched off their boots and moved down the hill in their stockinged feet. The Highlanders went barefoot.

It was in the valley's bed that the battle was most fierce. Fighting at close quarters, the Scottish pikes proved useless. A well-aimed chop from an English bill and they were gone, leaving the Scots to take to the sword, which was no match against the billhook. As soldiers plunged into the quagmire, where they struggled like flies in resin, they were picked off one by one. The place became a charnel, strewn with bodies, many dead, some crawling feebly like insects trodden underfoot, injured beyond repair. To Paniter it was a vision of hell, arms raised against blows, teeth bared in pain, limbs and necks severed. All it needed were horned devils with tridents for the allegory to be complete.

He squinted into the rain for a sight of the king, and eventually found him. Clambering beyond the worst ruck James had made his advance upon the English hill, bringing down men on every side, first with his lance then, when this was snapped by a billsman, with his two-handed sword. Where he fought, only the tattered lion rampant was visible, carried by a pageboy who risked death with every step, since it took both hands to carry the flag.

By this banner, stealing steadily closer to the English centre, Paniter gauged the king's progress. Even though he had a loyal knot of men around him, what he was doing was madness. For every inch he gained, another inch was filling at his back with those intent on cutting off his retreat. Paniter could see no way out for him, save slaying the entire hillside, or killing Lord Surrey, who was still some distance off, surrounded by a posse of prize fighters.

Fear and fury rose in the secretary's throat, and he turned aside, to spit out his bile. He looked up, wiping his lips, to find Borthwick by him again. Time slowed to a crawl, and the noise of the field grew faint as the master gunner pressed a pike into Paniter's hand, and gestured down the valley. An odd smile played on his lips. Obedient as a pupil, the secretary took the pike, balanced it before him, like a knight of old, and made off down the hill. He slipped on sodden grass and skittered over spread-eagled men, but in his mind the way was clear before him, a tight-rope that led straight to his king. He needed only a steady foot and a steely nerve to reach him.

No more at first than looming shadows in the mist, vicious packs of soldiers emerged in full colour when Paniter got close. As soon as he had passed, they melted out of sight, once more shrouded. English shouts thickened the air, the boom of the deadly English cannonade louder still, but there was eerily little sound from the Scots. They put all their energy into their blows, shrieking only when begging for mercy, which they neither gave, nor were given.

Blocking out the roars, Paniter crept across the western side of the hill, crossing the stream where the ground was least churned. Even so his boots grew heavy as if bathed in lead. He was clambering up onto the English hill, using his pike as a staff, when a face glowered down at him out of the rain, a barrelling red-cheeked soldier whose hooked bill was pointed at his chest. Paniter spitted the man like a boar. It was almost as hard pulling the spear out of him as it had been sucking his boots out of the mud.

Across the field the battle raged, a devilish dance daubed in crimson. On this lower slope, where the carnage was worst, the smell of butchered flesh and spilled guts was enough to dement a man. If a cow going to slaughter can go mad with fear at the smell of blood, why not a soldier? Paniter's feet slipped on the remains of men and his nose filled with their stench. He passed a hand over his face, then fixed his eyes high on the English hill, where the king's flag still fluttered. He pressed on.

To either side, men fell back before his pike. One who tried to bring him down by the legs breathed his last when the secretary stamped in his face. On he went, sliding, crawling, scrabbling, hands and knees more useful than feet for covering the ground when it was a sheer rink of bloodied grass.

Men laboured all around him, and he could have joined any of a hundred fights. But he had no time. His vision narrowed as if it were a spy-glass, with room for no-one but his king, and finally he found him. A huddle of Englishmen parted and there was James, spinning a flashing arc of steel around him as his sword sliced the head from a man with silver hair, which rolled off down the hill like a bobbin of wool.

Paniter was less than ten feet from him, but between them was a wall of English. They circled the king like wolves, all but slavering in anticipation of what was to come. There was an ugly gash on James's cheek, and his jacket was ripped, wet with liquid thicker than rain. He leaned for a moment on his sword, and drew a rasping breath. As he did so, the wolves prepared to leap. An archer's bow was bent, a bill was bounced in a hand, a dagger unsheathed.

Paniter tried to shout, but his tongue would not work. It was like a dream, where no warning can be uttered, when arms and legs and voice are paralysed, and one can only watch. Before his horrified stare the arrow was released, the bill swung, the dagger plunged.

The earth stood silent as Paniter saw his king stumble. He was on his knees, helmet knocked off, blood pouring over his face. Paniter caught a look of bewilderment and disbelief as James observed a thickening pool of blood gathering under his hands. He tried to rise, and it was pitiful to watch as he staggered, arms out to fend off his attackers, blindly feeling for his fallen sword. Those leaden, life-long seconds, when the lost king looked around for help, knowing there was none, were for Paniter worse than his own death. As the pause lengthened, and his head throbbed, it felt as if he was the one about to perish, that it was his life that would soon be ash, his hopes ground to dust.

It was a mercy when Surrey's bodyguard brushed his way past the soldiers. Without ceremony, he kicked the king onto his back where he lay, turning his bloodied head from side to side as if to make sense of this toppled world and his place in it. The bodyguard placed a boot on his chest. Ignoring the eyes that looked up at him, the cries of the pageboy and Paniter's scream, he brought down his axe.

*   *   *

Paniter found himself far from the valley, splashing water from the burn on his face. Here it ran clear and innocent. Somewhere over the hill the battle continued. At this distance, the noise of it bellied on the wind, surges of sound filling the air, before a sheet of quiet dropped over it all. Stooping like an old man, Paniter drank from his cupped hand, and stumbled upstream, his back to Flodden. The clash of the conflict receded.

A moment after the king was killed, when Paniter stood rooted, staring at the body of his dearest friend, a hand had grabbed his arm. He flinched, expecting a blow, but it was young Alexander, though few would have recognised him. Mud-spattered, blood-stained, he was staggering, one arm hanging at his side. He shoved Paniter towards the fight that had broken out around the king's last assailants, where the remnant of the royal retinue was bellowing with murderous grief, their swords speaking for their loss. The secretary looked at Alexander, and saw the end that awaited not just his pupil but himself. With a shake of his head he hurled down his pike, brushed past him, and broke into a downhill run, away from the field, and an otherwise certain fate.

As he fled, Paniter's mind was empty. He had acted on instinct. He had had no choice but to escape, hide, survive. But the sound of his king's dying scream would be with him forever, as if punishment for the part he played in bringing the country to battle. And Alexander's look, as he turned and ran from him, would in time burn even deeper into his soul.

Thus, as on the mercat cross gallows Gabriel was cut down, empty faced, and tied to a board, where his limbs were severed as if he were a surgeon's toy, the secretary was blind to him. Instead, he put his hands to his nose and smelled war. They looked clean, but in his mind they were black with the death of thousands.

When he ran from the battle, his fingernails were rimed with blood, his hose soaked in it, yet there was not a scratch upon himself. The image of the king's dying moments was all he could see, as he stumbled for the cover of woods, and the bleak road back to Scotland. James's dead eyes rose before him that day and for weeks to come, turning every scene scarlet, rendering everything foul.

From his seat by the gibbet, shoulder to shoulder with the queen's courtiers, he shrank from them and himself. He could no longer deny it. He had abandoned the field and left his men to die. He had fled. He who had urged war, had proved himself a coward, unable even to avenge his king. And now he understood Borthwick, and his sleekit glances. He had guessed what the secretary was made of. When he handed him the pike, it was a challenge, and Paniter had lost, and everything with it.

As Gabriel uttered a last, shuddering cry, his lifeless body found peace at last. Paniter kept his eyes screwed shut. He could not bear the sight of any more blood. The agitated crowd milled closer to glimpse the mutilated corpse. When the hangman held the golden head up on a pike, the cheering and stamping made the mercat cross shake. The privy council applauded, whistling and hollering in delight as the spy's dismembered limbs were carted off to decorate the city gates.

The spectacle over, the crowd quickly dispersed, but Paniter remained in his seat. The privy councillors brushed past him, eager for their dinner. Only when the square had emptied and it was quiet did the secretary look up. The cobbles by the gibbet were wet with blood, yet a stab of envy pierced him. Gabriel's torment was over, but he would never be at peace, not in this life, or any other.

Slowly, Paniter picked his way across the square. In his black cloak and black-feathered hat, he was the only one that day who had been dressed for mourning. Whether this was for the spy or himself, or for his sad, sorry country, nobody, not even he, would ever know.

AFTER FLODDEN

Rosemary Goring was born in Dunbar, and took a degree in history at St Andrews University, winning a prize for Scottish History in her final year. She began a career in publishing in the role of in-house editor for *Chambers Biographical Dictionary* and has since edited and written for many reference books.

She was Literary Editor of *Scotland on Sunday* for several years before taking up the position of Literary Editor and columnist at the *Herald* and *Sunday Herald*. In 2007 her book *Scotland the Autobiography: 2,000 Years of Scottish History by Those Who Saw It Happen* was published to great acclaim by Viking. *After Flodden* is her first novel.